M000272949

By Elle E. Ire

STORM FRONTS
Threadbare

Published by DSP Publications
www.dsppublications.com

ELLE E.
IRE

THREADBARE

DSP PUBLICATIONS

Published by

DSP PUBLICATIONS

5032 Capital Circle SW, Suite 2, PMB# 279, Tallahassee, FL 32305-7886 USA
www.dsppublications.com

Trade Paperback ISBN: 978-1-64405-365-2
Digital ISBN: 978-1-64405-364-5
Library of Congress Control Number: 2019932543
Trade Paperback published August 2019
v. 1.0

Printed in the United States of America

This paper meets the requirements of
ANSI/NISO Z39.48-1992 (Permanence of Paper).

To my amazing, talented, understanding, supportive spouse—being married to another published author certainly keeps life interesting, but I know when you encourage me, when you remind me I can do this, when you share your sympathy, you really GET IT. This one was a long time coming. Thanks for your confidence in Vick's story and in me every step of the way. I love you beyond words, and for a writer, that's saying a lot.

Author's Note

SPECIAL THANKS go to Jennifer Lindman, without whom the character of Vick wouldn't have been created. Though Vick went through a lot of changes before this final version, Jen is responsible for helping me give her initial life.

Thanks to my writing group, both current and former members, especially author Jan Eldredge and Amy Paulshock for reading early drafts, Mark Chick for his fight choreography expertise, and Ann Meier and Gary and Evergreen Lee for help with queries and blurbs. Thank you also to author Vivi Barnes for beta reading and giving positive feedback when I needed it to keep trying, and author Gini Koch for all her encouragement along the way. Also thanks go to all my friends and family who kept me sane throughout this long, crazy process.

Extra special thanks to my agent, Naomi Davis, who believed in this book from the get-go and dauntlessly stuck with it until it found its home. She is the best adviser, negotiator, and cheerleader a writer could ever hope for. Also much gratitude to publisher Lynn West, my editors Rose, Yv, and Brian (any mistakes left are mine, all mine), my cover artist Nathalie Gray who captured my internal vision of Vick so accurately I wondered if she had invaded my dreams, and all the other wonderful people at DSP Publications.

Last but not least, one more thanks to my family for their support, especially author and Nebula Award finalist Jose Pablo Iriarte for being my first, middle, and last reader always. Without him, I would have given up a long time ago.

ELLE E. IRE

THREADBARE

CHAPTER 1
VICK
NOT QUITE UP TO SPECS

I AM a machine.

"VC1, your objective is on the top floor, rear bedroom, moving toward the kitchen. Rest of the place scans as empty."

"Acknowledged." I study the high-rise across the street, my artificial ocular lenses filtering out the sunlight and zooming in on the penthouse twelve stories up. A short shadow passes behind white curtains. My gaze shifts to the gray, nondescript hovervan parked beside me. In the rear, behind reinforced steel, my teammate Alex is hitting the location with everything from x-rays to infrared and heat sensors.

Our enemies have no backup we're aware of, but it doesn't hurt to be observant.

I switch focus to Lyle, the driver, then Kelly in the passenger seat. Lyle stares straight ahead, attention on the traffic.

Kelly tosses me a smile, all bright sunshine beneath blonde waves. My emotion suppressors keep my own expression unreadable.

Except to her.

Kelly's my handler. My counterbalance. My... companion. My frie—

I can't process any further. But somewhere, deep down where I can't touch it, I want there to be more.

More what, I don't know.

Midday traffic rushes by in both directions—a four-lane downtown road carrying a mixture of traditional wheeled vehicles and the more modern hovercrafts. As a relatively recent colonization, Paradise doesn't have all the latest tech.

But we do.

Shoppers and businessmen bustle past. My olfactory sensors detect too much perfume and cologne, can identify individual brand names if I request the info. I pick up and record snippets of conversation, sort and discard them. The implants will bring anything mission relevant to my immediate attention, but none of the passersby are aware of what's going on across the street.

None of them thinks anything of the woman in the long black trench coat, either. I'm leaning against the wall between the doctors' offices and a real estate agency. No one notices me.

"Vick." Kelly's voice comes through the pickups embedded in my ear canals.

She's the only one who calls me that, even in private. I get grudgingly named in the public arena, but on the comm, to everyone else, I'm VC1.

A model number.

"The twelve-year-old kidnap *victim* is probably getting a snack. He's hungry, Vick. He's alone and scared." She's painting a picture, humanizing him. Sometimes I'm as bad with others as Alex and Lyle are toward me. "You're going to get him out." A pause as we make eye contact through the bulletproof glass.

"Right," I mutter subvocally.

Even without the touch of pleading in her voice, failure is not an option. I carry out the mission until I succeed or until something damages me beyond my capability to continue.

Kelly says there's an abort protocol that she can initiate if necessary. We've never had to try it, and given how the implants and I interact, I doubt it would work.

"Team Two says the Rodwells have arrived at the restaurant," Alex reports in a rich baritone with a touch of Earth-island accent.

The kidnappers, a husband and wife team of pros, are out to lunch at a café off the building's lobby. Probably carrying a remote trigger to kill the kid in their condo if they suspect a rescue attempt or if he tries to escape. They're known for that sort of thing. Offworlders with plenty of toys of their own and a dozen hideouts like this one scattered across the settled worlds. Team Two will observe and report, but not approach. The risk is too great.

Which means I have maybe forty-five minutes to get in and extract the subject.

No. *Rescue* the *child.* Right.

"Heading in." My tone comes out flat, without affectation. I push off from the wall, ignoring the way the rough bricks scrape my palms.

"Try to be subtle this time," Lyle says, shooting me a quick glare out the windshield. "No big booms. We can't afford to tip them off."

Subtlety isn't my strong suit, but I don't appreciate the reminder. Two years of successful mission completions speak for themselves.

I turn my gaze on him. He looks away.

I have that effect on people.

The corner of my lip twitches just a little. Every once in a while an emotion sneaks through, even with the suppressors active.

I'm standing on the median, boots sinking into carefully cultivated sod, when Kelly scolds me. "That wasn't very nice." Without turning around, I know she's smiling. She doesn't like Lyle's attitude any better than I do.

My lips twitch a little further.

Thunder rumbles from the east, and a sudden gust of wind whips my long hair out behind me. Back at base, it would be tied in a neat bun or at least a ponytail, but today I'm passing for civilian as much as someone like me can. I tap into the local weather services while I finish crossing the street.

Instead of meteorological data, my internal display flashes me an image of cats and dogs falling from the sky.

This is what happens when you mix artificial intelligence with the real thing. Okay, not exactly. I don't have an AI in my head, but the sophisticated equipment replacing 63 percent of my brain is advanced enough that it has almost developed a mind of its own.

It definitely has a sense of humor and a flair for metaphor.

Cute.

The house pets vanish with a final bark and meow.

The first drops hit as I push my way through glass doors into the lobby, and I shake the moisture from my coat and hair. Beneath the trench coat, metal clinks softly against metal, satisfying and too soft for anyone around me to pick up.

The opulent space is mostly empty—two old ladies sitting on leather couches, a pair of teenagers talking beside some potted plants. Marble and glass in blacks, whites, and grays. Standard high-end furnishings.

"May I help you?" Reception desk, on my left, portly male security guard behind it, expression unconcerned. "Nasty weather." A flash of lightning punctuates his pleasantries.

Terraforming a world sadly doesn't control the timing of its thunderstorms.

My implants reduce the emotion suppressors, and I attempt a smile. Kelly assures me it looks natural, but it always feels like my face is cracking. "I'm here to see…." My receptors do a quick scan of the listing behind him—the building houses a combination of residences and offices. If we'd had more time, we could have set this up better, but the Rodwells have switched locations twice already, and we only tracked them here yesterday.

"Doctor Angela Swarzhand," I finish faster than the guard can pick up the hesitation. "I'm a new patient."

The guard smiles, and I wonder if they're friends. "That's lovely. Just lovely. Congratulations."

"Um, thanks." I'm sure I've missed something, but I have no idea what.

He consults the computer screen built into the surface of his desk, then points at a bank of elevators across the black-marble-floored lobby. "Seventh floor."

"Great. Where are the stairs?" I already know where they are, but I shouldn't, so I ask.

The guard frowns, forehead wrinkling in concern. "Stairs? Shouldn't someone in your condition be taking the elevator?"

"My condition?"

"Vick." Kelly's warning tone tries to draw my attention, but I need to concentrate.

"Not now," I subvocalize. If this guy has figured out who, or rather *what* I am, things are going to get messy and unsubtle fast. My hand slips beneath my coat, fingers curling around the grip of the semiautomatic in its shoulder holster.

"You're pregnant." The giggle in Kelly's voice registers while I stare stupidly at the guard.

"I'm what?" Sooner or later this guy is bound to notice the miniscule motions of my lips, even speaking subvocally.

Alex replaces Kelly on the comm. "Dr. Swarzhand is an obstetrician. She specializes in high-risk pregnancies. The guard thinks you're pregnant. Be pregnant. And fragile."

Oh for fuck's sake.

I blink a couple of times, feigning additional confusion. "My condition! Right." I block out the sound of my entire team laughing their asses off. "I'm still not used to the idea. Just a few weeks along." I don't want to take the damn elevator. Elevators are death traps. Tiny boxes with one way in and one way out. Thunder rumbles outside. If the power fails, I'll be trapped. My heart rate picks up. The implants initiate a release of serotonin to compensate, and the emotion suppressors clamp down. Or try to.

In my ears, one-third of the laughter stops. "It'll be okay, Vick." Kelly, soft and soothing.

Of course she knows. She always knows.

"Just take it up to the seventh floor and walk the rest of the way. It's only for a few seconds, a minute at most. It won't get stuck. I promise."

"Thanks," I say aloud to the guard and turn on my heel, trying to stroll and not stomp. "You can't promise that," I mutter under my breath.

"It'll be okay," she says again, and I'm in the waiting lift, the doors closing with an ominous *thunk* behind me.

The ride is jerky, a mechanical affair rather than the more modern antigrav models. I grit my teeth, resisting the urge to talk to my team. Alex and Lyle wouldn't see the need to comfort a machine, anyway.

Figures the one memory I retain from my fully human days is the memory of my death, and the one emotion my implants fail to suppress every time is the absolute terror of that death.

When the chime announces my arrival on seven and the doors open, I'm a sweating, hyperventilating mess. I stagger from the moving coffin, colliding with the closest wall and using it to keep myself upright.

There's no one in the hallway, or someone would be calling for an ambulance by now.

"Breathe, Vick, breathe," Kelly whispers.

I suck in a shaky breath, then another. My vision clears. My heart rate slows. "I've got it."

"I know. But count to ten, anyway."

Despite the need to hurry, I do it. If I'm not in complete control, I can make mistakes. If I make mistakes, the mission is at risk. I might fail.

A door on the right opens and a very pregnant woman emerges, belly protruding so far she can't possibly see her feet. She takes one look at me and frowns.

"Morning sickness," I explain, grimacing at the thought on multiple levels. Even if I wanted kids for some insane reason, I wouldn't be allowed to have them. Machines don't get permission to procreate.

The pregnant lady offers a sympathetic smile and disappears into the elevator. At the end of the hall, the floor-to-ceiling windows offer a view of sheeting rain and flashing lightning, and I shudder as the metal doors close behind her. I head for the stairwell—the nice, safe, stable, I'm-totally-in-control-of-what-happens stairwell.

"Walk me through it," I tell Alex. I pass the landing for the eleventh floor, heading for the twelfth.

"The penthouse takes up the entire top level," his voice comes back. "Figures. No one to hear the kid call for help. Stairwell opens into the kitchen. Elevator would have let you off in a short hallway leading to the front door."

Which is probably a booby-trapped kill chute. No thanks.

"Security on the stairwell door?"

A pause. "Yep. Plenty of it too. Jamming and inserting a playback loop in the cameras now. Sensors outside the door at ankle height, both right and left. Not positive what they trigger. Could be a simple alarm. Could be something else."

Could be something destructive goes unsaid. I might have issues with my emotions, but that doesn't make me suicidal. At least not anymore. Besides, with the kid walking around loose in the penthouse apartment, all the doors have to have some kind of aggressive security on them. Otherwise he would have escaped by now.

"Whatever it is, I won't know unless you trip it," Alex adds.

Oh, very helpful. I'm earning my pay today.

My internal display flashes an image of me in ballet shoes, en pointe, pink tutu and all.

Keeping me on my toes. Right. Funny. I didn't ask for your input.

The display winks out.

I take eight more steps, round the turn for the last flight to the top floor, and stop. My hand twitches toward the compact grenade on my belt, but that would be overkill. No big booms. Right. Give me the overt rather than the covert any day. But I don't get to choose.

I verify the sensor locations, right where Alex said they'd be. He's right. No indication of what they're connected to.

And time's running out.

If it's an alarm, it could signal the Rodwells at the restaurant. If they have a hidden bomb and a trigger switch....

"Wiring on the door?" I weigh the odds against the ticking clock. They don't want to kill their victim if there's any chance they can make money off him. If I were fully human, if the implants weren't suppressing my emotions, I wouldn't be able to make a decision. Life-or-death shouldn't be about playing the odds.

"None."

"Composition?" Some beeps in the background answer my request.

A longer pause. "Apartment doors in that building were purchased from Door Depot, lower-end models despite the high rents. Just over one inch thick. Wood. Medium hardness."

"The door at the bottom of the stairwell was metal."

"But the one on the top floor isn't. It's considered a 'back door' to the apartment. It's wood like the front entries." Alex's info shifts the odds—odds placed on a child's survival. I try not to think too hard on what I've become. It shouldn't matter to me, but— The suppressors clamp down on the distraction.

"Give me a five-second jam on those sensors," I tell him and count on him to do it. Damn, I hate these last-minute piecemeal plans, but we didn't have much time to throw this together.

"Vick, what are you—?"

Before Kelly can finish voicing her concerns, I'm charging up the last of the stairs, past the sensors, and slamming shoulder-first into the penthouse door. Wood cracks and splinters, shards flying in all directions, catching in my hair and driving through the material of my jacket.

Medium hardness or not, it hurts. I'm sprawled on the rust-colored kitchen tiles, bits of door and frame scattered around me, blood seeping from a couple of cuts on my hands and cheek. The implants unleash a stream of platelets from my bone marrow and they rush to clot the wounds.

I raise my head and meet the wide eyes of my objective. The kid's mouth hangs open, a half-eaten sandwich on the floor by his feet. I'm vaguely aware of Kelly demanding to know if I'm okay.

Her concern touches me in a way I can't quite identify, but it's... good.

"Ow," I mutter, rising to my knees, then my feet. "Fuck." I might heal fast, but I feel pain.

The kid slides from his chair and backs to the farthest corner of the room, trapped against the gray-and-black-speckled marble counter. "D-don't hurt me," he stammers.

I roll my eyes. "Are you an idiot?"

"Oh, nice going, Vick."

I ignore Kelly and open my trench coat, revealing an array of weapons—blades and guns. "If I wanted to hurt you...."

His eyes fly wider, and he pales.

A sigh over the comm. "For God's sake, Vick, try, will you?"

My shoulder hurts like a sonofabitch. I try rotating my left arm and wince at the reduced range of motion. Probably dislocated. I'm in no mood to make nicey nice.

"You're not the police." Oh good, the kid can use logic.

"The police wouldn't be able to find you with a map and a locator beacon."

My implants toss me a quick flash of the boy buried in a haystack and a bunch of uniformed men digging through it, tossing handfuls left and right.

"I'm with a private problem-solving company, and I'm here to take you home," I continue. "Will you come with me?" I pull a syringe filled with clear liquid from one of the coat's many pockets. "Or am I gonna have to drug and carry you?" That will suck, especially with the shoulder injury, but I can do it.

Another sigh from Kelly.

I'm not kid-friendly. Go figure.

My vision blurs. We're out of chat time. A glance over my shoulder reveals pale blue haze filling the space just inside the back door, pouring through a vent in the ceiling. A cloud of it rolls into the kitchen, so it's been flowing for a while. "Alex, I need a chemical analysis," I call to my tech guru. I remove a tiny metal ball from a belt pouch and roll it into the blue gas. Several ports on it snap open, extending sampler rods and transmitting the findings to my partners in the hovervan.

A pause. "It's hadrazine gas. Your entry must have triggered the release. Move faster, VC1."

Hadrazine's some fast and powerful shit. A couple of deep breaths and we'll be out cold, and not painlessly, either. We'll feel like we're suffocating first. If I get out of this alive, my next goal is to take down the Rodwells.

"Report coming in from Team Two." Alex again. "You must have tripped an alarm somewhere. Rodwells leaving the restaurant, not bothering to pay. They're headed for your location."

A grin curls my lips. Looks like I might get my wish.

I know I'm not supposed to *want* to kill anyone. I know Kelly can pick up that urge and will have words for me later. But sometimes… sometimes people just need killing. But not before I achieve my primary objective.

I'm in motion before I finish the thought, grabbing the kid by the arm and hauling him into the penthouse's living room. Couches and chairs match the ones in the lobby. "Tell Team Two not to engage," I snap, not bothering to lower my voice anymore. The boy stares at me but says nothing. "They may still have a detonator switch for this place." And Team Two is Team Two for a reason. They're our backup. The second string. And more likely to miss a double kill shot.

"You're scaring the boy," Kelly says in my ear.

I'm surprised she can read him at this distance. Usually that skill is limited to her interactions with me.

"Jealousy?" she asks. "What for?"

Or maybe she's just guessing. Where the hell did that come from, anyway? I turn up the emotion suppressors. Things between me and Kelly have been a little wonky lately. I've had some strange responses to things she's said or done. I don't need the distraction now.

"Never mind," I mutter. "Alex, front door. What am I dealing with?"

"No danger I can read. Nothing's active. Doesn't mean there isn't some passive stuff."

"There's a bomb."

I stare down at the boy by my side. "You sure?"

He nods, shaggy blond hair hanging in his face. I release him for a second to brush it out of his eyes and crouch in front of him. He's short for his age. Thin too. Lightweight. Good in case I end up having to carry him. "Any chance they were bluffing?"

The kid shrugs.

"The café manager stopped them in the lobby, demanding payment," Alex cuts in. "Doesn't look like they want to make a scene, so you've got maybe five minutes, VC1. Six if they have to wait for the elevator."

Maybe less if the gas flows too quickly.

Right.

I approach the door, studying the frame for the obvious and finding nothing. Doesn't mean there isn't anything embedded.

There. A pinprick hole drilled into the molding on the right side of the frame. Inside would be a pliable explosive and a miniature detonator triggered by contact or remote. Given the right tools and time, I could disarm such a device. I have the tools in a pouch on my belt. I don't have the time.

"Um, excuse me?" The boy points toward the kitchen. Blue mist curls across the threshold and over the first few feet of beige living room carpet.

I race toward a wall of heavy maroon curtains, shoving a couch aside and throwing the window treatments wide. Lightning flashes outside the floor-to-ceiling windows, illuminating the skyscraper across the street and the twelve-story drop to the pavement below.

Oh, fuck me now.

"Lyle, I need that hovervan as high as you can get it. Bring it up along the east side of the building. Beneath the living room windows."

"Oooh. A challenge." He's not being sarcastic. Lyle's the best damn pilot and driver in the Fighting Storm.

Too bad he's an ass.

The van's engines rev over the comm, and the repulsorlifts engage with a whine.

"Vick, what are you thinking?" Kelly's voice trembles when she's worried, and she rushes over her words. I can barely understand her.

"I'm thinking my paranoia is about to pay off."

I wear a thin inflatable vest beneath my clothes when we do anything near water. I carry a pocket breather when we work in space stations, regardless of the safety measures in place. I'm always prepared for every conceivable obstacle, including some my teammates never see coming.

So I wear a lightweight harness under my clothes when I'm in any building over three stories tall.

Alex teases me about it. Lyle's too spooked by me to laugh in my face, but I know he does it behind my back. Kelly counsels that I can't live my second life in fear.

Sorry. I died once. I'm in no hurry to repeat the experience.

Using my brain implants, I trigger an adrenaline burst. The hormone races through my bloodstream. I'll pay for this later with an energy crash, but for now, I'm supercharged and ready to take on my next challenge.

The hadrazine gas is flowing closer. I shove the kid toward the far corner of the room, away from both the kitchen and the damage I'm about to do.

For safety reasons, high-rise windows, especially really large floor-to-ceiling ones, can rarely be opened. Hefting the closest heavy wood chair, I slam it into the windows with as much force as I can gather. My shoulder screams in pain, and I hear Kelly's answering cry over my comm. With her shields down, she feels what I feel. They're always down during missions. I hate hurting her, but I have no choice. I need her input to function, and I need the window broken.

The first hit splinters the tempered glass, sending a spiderweb of cracks shooting to the corners of the rectangular pane. Not good enough.

I pull my 9mm from a thigh holster and fire four shots. Cracks widen. Chips fall, along with several large shards. There's a breach now. I need to widen it. I grab the chair and swing a second time, and the glass and chair shatter, pieces of both flying outward and disappearing into the raging storm.

Wind and rain whip into the living room. Curtains flap like flags in a hurricane, buffeting me away from the edge and keeping me from tumbling after the furniture. I'm soaked in seconds. When I take a step, the carpet squishes beneath my boots.

"VC1, I think the Rodwells made Team Two in the lobby…. Shit. I'm reading a signal transmission, trying to block it…. Fuck, I've got an active signature on the bomb…. It's got a countdown, two minutes. Get the hell out of there!"

Alex's report sends my pulse rate ratcheting upward. Other than not being here in the first place, no paranoid preparation can counter a blast of the magnitude I'm expecting.

Judging from the positioning of the explosives, anyone in the apartment will be toast.

I take off my coat and toss it into the swirling blue gas, regretting the loss of the equipment in the pockets but knowing I can't make my next move with it on. The wind is drawing the haze right toward the windows, right toward me. I grab gloves from a pocket and yank them on. I unsnap a compartment on my harness and pull out a retractable grappling hook attached to several hundred coiled feet of ultrastrong, ultrathin wire.

Once I've given myself some slack in the cord, I scan the room. The gaudy architecture includes some decorative pillars. A press of a button drives the grappler into the marble, and I wrap the cord several times around the column and tug hard. I'm not worried about the wire. It can bear more than five hundred pounds of weight. I'm not so sure about the apartment construction, given the flimsy back door.

The cord holds. I reel out more line, extending my free hand to the kid. "Come on!"

He stares at me, then the window, then shakes his head. "You're crazy. No way!" He shouts to be heard over the rain and thunder.

My internal display flashes my implants' favorite metaphor—a thick cable made up of five metal cords wrapped tightly around each other. Over the last two years, I've come to understand they represent my sanity, and since Kelly's arrival, they've remained solid. Until now.

One of them is fraying, a few strands floating around the whole in wisps.

Great. Just great.

The image fades.

"Die in flames or jump with me. Take your pick." The clock ticks down in my head. If the boy won't come, I'm not sure I'll have time to cross the room and grab him, but my programming will force me to try.

He comes.

I take one last second to slam myself against the pillar, forcing my dislocated shoulder into the socket. Kelly screams in my ear, but I've clamped my own jaw shut, gritting my teeth for my next move.

One arm slides around the boy's narrow waist. I grip the cord in the protective glove.

"Five seconds," Alex says.

I run toward the gaping hole and open air, clutching the kid to me. He wraps his arms around my torso and buries his face in my side.

"Four."

"Oh my God," Kelly whispers.

"Three."

Lyle and the hovervan better be where I need them. The cord might support our weight, but it won't get me close enough to the ground for a safe free-fall drop.

"Two."

The sole of my boot hits the edge and my muscles coil to launch me as far from the window as I can. There's a second of extreme panic, long enough for regrets but too late to stop momentum, and then we're airborne. Emotion suppressors ramp up to full power, and the terror fades.

My last thought as gravity takes hold is of Kelly. My suppressors have some effect on her empathic sense, but extremely strong feelings and emotions like pain and panic reach her every time.

If she can't get her shields up fast, this will tear her apart.

CHAPTER 2
KELLY
MEETING OF THE MINDS

Two and a half years earlier....

VICK CORREN *was broken.*

Oh, Kelly, what have you gotten yourself into?

Recyclers filtered and processed the air I breathed, and if I looked up and up, I could make out the sheen of the main protective dome and the glitter of stars beyond. There on the landing platform at Girard Moon Base, I stood awkwardly with the other passengers disembarking the shuttle from Earth. We were both outside and not—within the dome but outside the colony's prefabricated buildings.

Graduation was only a month behind me, and already I was a long, long way from the Academy for Special Abilities.

The gravity here was artificially increased as well; the hum of generators created a constant vibration I would have to adjust to. Irritating but manageable if I—

"Kelly LaSalle? I'm Lyle Walters, here to escort you to the Storm's Girard headquarters."

I jumped. Damn, no one should have been able to get that close without me sensing them. *Not the best first impression you're giving, Kelly.* I smoothed an imaginary wrinkle from my cream-colored business skirt, then tightened the hairband around my ponytail—anything to cover my unprofessional startle.

Stepping away from the ramp, I nodded to the soldier. "How long were you waiting there?" How long was he watching me gawk like a tourist?

"Caught the empath by surprise, huh?"

Teasing. He's teasing you, Kelly. Don't stress about it. Except I wanted this job, or at least thought I did.

I scanned him from head to boots, a long scan considering he towered over me. Red hair, brown eyes, a sprinkling of freckles. Good build—a given for fighters. No visible weapons. His tan uniform shirt bore a patch embroidered with his last name. He was older than me, probably somewhere in his mid to late twenties. I forced a smile and shook the offered hand.

"You ready for this?" He took my bag and started across the shuttle platform. I fell into step behind him.

The Fighting Storm, a mercenary military organization, had a "test subject" (I hated the term) who had suffered severe brain damage. Despite implementation of regulating devices, their *patient* was no longer able to express and absorb her emotions in a reasonable, rational manner.

If I met the Storm's requirements, they wanted to train me to be part of some kind of team, pair me with this individual on missions, and have me provide ongoing emotional support to enable her to function in the field. Their science research team assured me that if they found the right empathic match, their patient would be capable of continuing to work as a soldier.

Specific details were withheld due to them being classified, but I had absolutely no doubt this person needed the services of a good empath.

"I don't even know what 'this' is, exactly," I admitted. I had to yell to be heard over shuttle engines, air processors, and ground vehicles carrying luggage to the terminal ahead. "Your bosses offered me a brief description, an interview, and a first-class ticket. It sounded… interesting."

I could have taken a cushier, planetside job in one of the hospitals' psychiatric wards, gone into school or marriage counseling, or joined my mother working for the One World government, helping different cultures understand one another better, promoting world peace. But I wanted something different.

Walters snorted and kept walking while I hurried to keep pace. "Yeah, interesting is one word for it. Impossible might be a better one. We've had four empaths out before you. All of them older, one with prior military experience. No one can handle VC1. Sooner or later, they'll have to shut the project down."

I didn't like the way he said that. "What's a VC1?" Could he possibly have meant the patient? And what did he mean, "shut it down"?

"You'll see." At my frown he added, "I'm not authorized to give details."

I resisted the urge to roll my eyes.

We proceeded into the terminal, passing through an airlock, its hydraulic hiss loud but comforting to an Earther like me. When I commented on it, Walters explained the structures like the terminal were there first, so every building had airlocks instead of doors and we'd go through a lot of them. The domes (one main one and a series of smaller ones connected by airlocks and enclosed walkways) came later. So truly interior locks remained fixed in their open positions while the exterior ones continued to operate normally.

The crowd of travelers thinned the farther into the structure we went. The few people in this area all wore the Fighting Storm uniforms and moved with purpose, though some pairs laughed and exchanged conversation as they walked.

Perimeter hallways displayed holos of recruitment posters—smiling uniformed men and women beckoning the eager and naive youth to join up, see the universe, have adventures beyond their imaginations.

With my empathic sense, I touched a few of the soldiers we passed, picking up boredom, along with high levels of barely restrained aggression. There was guilt too, and stress, and a smattering of depression, and I wondered what battles these soldiers had fought, won, and lost.

Maybe this wasn't such a great idea.

Sooner or later, they'll have to shut the project down.

Something about that statement and the way in which Walters delivered it sent chills crawling up my spine. If the Fighting Storm shut down the project, what happened to the patient? If the patient *was* the project, what did shutting it down mean, exactly?

More hallways and we arrived at a door where a grim-faced woman in the same brown uniform as all the other members of the Storm I'd seen checked my identification. She scanned my fingerprints and retinas and presumably compared them to the ones on file at the Academy. The woman meant business, a holstered pistol visible at her side. She carried the first weapon I'd seen on any of the Fighting Storm's personnel, and I assumed I was about to enter a secure area. When she waved us along, I let out a breath.

We took an elevator to another floor, where wall and furnishing colors changed from utilitarian gray to medical white, and I began to associate paint choices with departments: gray for public areas, visitor spaces, white for medical, and I assumed other colors for other services.

We stepped off the lift, and we were halfway to a curved desk and a white-coated receptionist when the pain wave hit.

It doubled me over, drilling like a laser through my brain, tightening all the muscles in my body, then turning them to jelly under the onslaught. My knees hit the floor. My vision went red.

Shouting came from all around me, but it rose and fell in my ears, the blood pounding too hard for clear hearing. I wanted to scream, but I couldn't take in enough air, and all I managed was a wheezing gasp and a groan.

I felt Walters's hand on my shoulder and jerked away from the contact, unable to take increased emotional input from him along with the pain I suffered. I squeezed my eyes shut, but tears leaked from beneath the lids. A door hissed open, and for an instant the agony swelled to even greater heights. Flashes went off behind my eyelids, and I feared I might pass out. The door closed, providing a slight buffer.

Empathic pain. Red vision. Red meant pain. It was how my empathic sense translated emotions and feelings into something I could understand—through colors. My Academy instructors called it synesthetic perception. For a moment, the red blinded me.

I'd spent years building and strengthening my mental walls against the emotions and feelings of others until my instructors compared my protective capabilities to three-foot-thick slabs of metal—the strongest they'd seen in nine years of graduating students.

This pierced them as if they were tissue paper.

Heavy footsteps rapidly approached, and something thin and sharp jabbed my neck. A few torturous moments later, a heavy fog descended, enveloping my brain, and the pain receded to a manageable level.

They knew. They knew to expect my collapse. They were ready for it. What the hell?

I straightened on my knees, blinking my teary vision at the gray-haired man in a lab coat crouched in front of me, the receptionist to my right, and Walters on my left. Glow panels overhead reflected off the white tile floor, too bright. Walters shook his head. The woman's lips were tight and her eyes wide. The doctor—Dr. Whitehouse by the name badge clipped to his front pocket—smiled?

"Congratulations," he said. "That's the strongest reaction we've seen so far. We didn't want to compromise the test by warning you."

Not an apology and definitely not good enough. I was still incapable of speech, so I glared instead. It didn't faze him.

Okay, I wasn't much of a glarer.

With the torture dimmed, I could analyze the source, and I realized it wasn't just pain but a combination of various emotions so powerful that they manifested themselves as one tremendous ongoing agony. Pain, yes, but also fear, confusion, depression, anger, and overwhelming frustration. Red, purple, gray, so many colors they melded to black and I couldn't separate them. Someone suffered horribly, and with a sinking feeling in my stomach, I had a pretty good idea who.

I struggled to my feet, using Walters's shoulder for support. My limbs trembled with the effort, but I started walking, pushing past the doctor, who was a little slower to rise. I reached the door behind the desk, and no one stopped me. It slid aside with a soft hiss at my approach, and I stood in a corridor.

The smell hit me first. Everywhere inside the base, the recycled air had a slightly stale scent. One could only do so much with arboretums and scrubbers. But here…. Here the air carried overtones of fear, sweat, and death.

A long window taking up most of the right-hand wall, probably one-way glass, looked in on a patient room. The rolling tray table and nightstand had been demolished, the bed, metal and heavy, overturned on its side, and the remains of a lamp shattered across the tile floor. Thick wrist and ankle restraint straps dangled from the bed frame, ragged and useless.

The sole occupant lay on the floor in the farthest corner. I wasn't surprised to find a woman. Her emotions, violent or not, felt feminine in nature. She faced away from the observation window and door, so I couldn't see her face, but long black hair hung down her back, in stark contrast to her torn white pajamas. The doctors had shaved one patch on her head, showing red, angry scars on the scalp. The rest of the hair twisted into a matted mess, the rips in the pajama fabric exposing wide swaths of skin covered in scratches and shallow cuts. From fingernails. I guessed her own.

The doctor arrived beside me, but I couldn't tear my gaze from the woman in the corner. She slept, her back rising and falling in slow, even motions, though every few seconds she jerked violently. Even in sleep, her emotions roared, blocking out everything else, including the man on my left. I'd have given anything to be fully telepathic right then, to have been able to reach and comfort her. But no true telepaths existed, at least none we'd discovered yet.

Right there, right then, there was only me.

"What's her name?" I whispered.

"VC1."

I looked at him. "What's. Her. *Name?*" It came out as a growl, and he took a step back.

He studied me for a moment and nodded once like he'd come to some decision. Then he stared through the window, focusing on the patient as if seeing her for the first time. "Victoria Corren," he said, his mouth twisting downward as if he'd tasted a sour fruit. "She preferred 'Vick.'"

Preferred. Not prefers. Like postsurgery she'd become a nonperson to them.

Dr. Whitehouse hated his patient. Or she disgusted him. Or something. I couldn't filter his emotions over the screaming of Vick's, but I didn't need empathic skills to read his expression. "What happened to her?"

"That's classified." At my huff of impatience he added, "Unless we decide to give you the job."

Oh, they'd offer me the position if Whitehouse had anything to say about it. He may not have liked me, but he was too excited about my reaction in the outer room.

"Why me?"

He nodded. Now I asked the right question. "You're a 91 percent empathic brainwave match, the closest we've found, and the most likely candidate to reach her."

That explained a lot. In my studies and internships at hospitals, my mentors exposed me to plenty of suffering people. Nothing hit me the way she did. Granted, she suffered more than most, but a brainwave match-up like that would have provided a direct link between her emotions and my senses and doubled or tripled the effect. And if there were physical contact....

I shuddered. Even without much for comparison, working with Vick Corren would undoubtedly present the challenge of a lifetime.

Raising my hand, I brushed my fingertips across the observation window, darkening the glass to opaque, blocking her from my view.

Whitehouse took a breath. "The Fighting Storm needs her." A grudging admission. "She was the best damn soldier we'd ever trained, and the organization's spent a lot of money to test this experimental equipment to repair the damage, but it's not enough. We need her. We need the technology to work. And she needs you."

I USED a stylus to sign a trial contract with the Fighting Storm and passed that datapad back to Dr. Whitehouse. He exchanged it for a second one displaying Vick's file. We sat across from each other at a square table in his spacious office, coffee in the warmer on a nearby counter, personnel schedules scrolling on a wall monitor, fake potted plants for ambiance.

More color coding. Beige walls for office spaces. Code for "lack of imagination."

For the next month, the doctors and trainers would test and evaluate me, see how I worked with my patient, see what progress she made, and take it from there.

I pored over the file, noting the rows of Xs where information had been deleted—the "classified" parts, Whitehouse informed me. I pieced together the gist of her horror story.

Enlistment at eighteen. Superior rankings in martial arts, expert marksman, highly intelligent, remarkably stable psychological profile, fast-tracked for team leadership positions, 94 percent mission success rate.

It was easy to see why the Storm wanted to keep her.

Then the accident—mechanical failure combined with careless error. I read the words on the screen, the only sounds the bubbling of the coffee and the ever-present hum of the gravity generators. They wrote it in clinical language, but I was the creative sort, and my imagination filled in the gruesome details. During a timed training exercise, an airlock refused to release. Three soldiers inside, one of them Vick. They didn't give the others' names, likely to preserve their privacy. Air depleted. One soldier panicked and opened fire on the mechanism. Ricocheting bullets ripped Vick's skull apart and killed the other two instantly. I closed my eyes and breathed, trying to clear the image from my mind.

"If he'd waited patiently for help, they all would have lost consciousness, but they wouldn't have died," Whitehouse said. "And there were other mistakes made." I picked up his bitterness, more than the accident explained. A tinge of deep orange registered when I read him. I chalked it up to his profession and his failure to save them all, even if trying would have been futile.

"Vick didn't panic." With her background, it was an easy assumption to make.

"No," Whitehouse said, confirming it.

Impressive.

She was brain-dead when they retrieved her body from the airlock, but the medical staff felt they had enough tissue left to work with using implant technology developed by the research department. Vick had one highly experimental chance of survival, the equipment barely past the initial testing stages. No family on record meant no one to ask for permission.

I paused. "Who signed off on the experimentation?" *Whom should I be blaming for Vick's torment?*

"The Great and Powerful Oz."

"Pardon?"

"We're a Wizard of Oz operation. You know, 'Pay no attention to the man behind the curtain' and all that. Nobody knows who Oz is. There are dozens of front men and mouthpieces between us and him. For security reasons."

Made sense. I hadn't read *Wizard of Oz* since I was eight, but I got it, and I could see where the owner of a mercenary organization would have lots of enemies.

"I sit on the board that makes most of the day-to-day decisions, but we didn't make that one."

Dr. Whitehouse, professional buck passer.

I dug for the feelings beneath his response. If it had been up to him, I don't think he would have saved her at all. I got animosity, not mercy or pity, not concern or nervousness about using potentially unsafe technology. Part of him wanted to let Vick die, but Oz overruled him.

Oz signed off.

And Vick Corren became VC1.

I returned to her file. She'd lost most of twenty-five years of memory (*God, she's only three years older than me*) and all ability to express her emotions like a "normal" human being. The technology was supposed to make her into some sort of super soldier. Among other enhancements, it suppressed her feelings so all focus went toward her job. Except it didn't work quite the way the researchers planned. Feelings built and built within her until she lashed out at anyone and anything within range. By the time they figured out the cause, they'd driven her half mad. Drugs failed. They slowed her down, made her unusable in the field. The implants could dampen her emotions temporarily, but they couldn't permanently erase them. Sooner or later, she needed an outlet.

In the last couple of weeks, they'd taken to keeping her constantly sedated. My hands clenched on the datapad.

No one here knew exactly what Vick felt. They hadn't had the services of a reliable empath. Even among the talented, empathic skills were rare. And they didn't have time to get much from the few other applicants before they washed out.

But I knew. I knew how much she hurt. The drugs Whitehouse gave me were wearing off, and her pain bled through my shields, manifesting in a massive migraine.

The last section of her file showed my brainwave patterns obtained from Academy records, and Vick's, superimposed on top of each other. Whitehouse was right. They matched almost perfectly. A one in a million shot. We didn't think the same thoughts, but we thought in the same way. Truly amazing, considering our different occupations. I rubbed my temples and pushed the datapad away.

"Let me talk to her."

"She doesn't talk."

"She can't?" That would make my job a lot harder.

"The implant technicians assure me she can. But she doesn't."

Given how they treated her, I didn't blame her one bit. "Let me try."

He reached for a call button embedded in the table's surface. "I'll arrange to reduce the sedative gas."

I covered his hand with my own, ignoring the upward surge of his emotional input at the contact. "Turn it all the way off."

Whitehouse shot me a look like I'd lost my mind. "She'll tear you to pieces. We have to feed her through a slot." He leaned forward, eyes cold and hard. "She's trained to kill in a hundred different ways. We're not sure which skills she's retained and which she's forgotten. We won't know until we can communicate with her. But she clearly possesses some of them."

I remembered her demolished room and furnishings and swallowed hard.

My chair squeaked when I shoved it back and stood. "She needs to *express* her emotions in a healthy way. Her brain has forgotten how. At a guess I'd say she's using your implant technology to avoid feeling anything, but a person can't bury emotions forever. They're coming out, and not the way you want them to. Dulling her brain makes things worse and will impede my efforts to reach her." I paused at his expression. "You've been sedating her a lot, haven't you? And I don't just mean mildly."

"VC1—"

"Vick."

"Excuse me?" He wasn't used to being interrupted. Irritation boiled beneath his calm exterior.

"Vick," I said, softening my tone. "It's her name. A human one. Surely she has a right to the use of her own name. If you want her to act human, you'll need to treat her humanely."

Immediate resistance. I doubted he'd ever think of Vick as more than a test subject, a project.

"That's what the Storm wants, right?" I asked, trying a different approach.

Reluctant capitulation. Okay. Pleasing the organization was important to him. To do that he needed me. And Vick. At least I knew which angle to play there.

"Very well, Vick, then." He spit the name like venom.

Working with this man was not going to be easy.

Whitehouse fetched a mug from a cabinet and filled it from the coffee dispenser. The aroma called to me, but I didn't want any distractions right then. "Yes, we've routinely sedated the sub—*patient,*" he said, returning to my original question, "in order to perform tests without risk of injury to her or ourselves."

"Idiots." I couldn't help it. It just slipped out. My stomach muscles clenched while his anger seethed. He went completely rigid as his practiced professional gaze settled on me.

Oh, they must really have needed me. Otherwise I'd have been fired by then. "Have you ever had a nightmare, a really really bad one?"

The doctor hmmphed. "Of course. Who hasn't?"

I paced the length of the office. Expensive wood desk, comfortable leather chair. "Have you ever had one you had to fight to wake up from?"

He had. I knew he had, and they'd traumatized him. His emotional response was painful and… personal. Much more powerful than I expected. I could only guess about treating a team of mercenaries. He worked to save soldiers. Soldiers died. A lot.

"Make your point."

I traced my fingers along his very clean desktop, then crossed to the opposite wall to admire a framed Earth holo. Mountains and a river, the water flowing incessantly. It was very soothing. I fought down a twinge of homesickness and focused. "Sedating someone like Vick is like trapping her in the worst nightmare you can imagine. Only she can't wake herself up, no matter how hard she tries. No matter how much she knows it's just a dream." I drew on Academy lectures and an internship I completed with their affiliated hospital. Nonempathic physicians rarely possessed the experience to know how to handle that sort of impairment, so they needed a specialist like me. "The drugs hold her under. Multiply your darkest nightmare times a hundred. That's what sedation is for her."

I saw his realization like rays of light in a dark room, and yet the mixed emotional response surprised me. He was chagrined, but I sensed pleasure. Pleasure at her suffering. And he hated himself for that.

Dr. Whitehouse had something personal against Vick Corren. And I had to save her from it, whatever it was.

"You want me to make progress." I knew he did. His pride in the Fighting Storm was beacon-clear. "Don't sedate her, not unless her life depends on it. Restrain her if you have to, but leave her conscious. Now," I said, stopping my wanderings to stand beside him, "let's wake her up."

I DIDN'T think my headache could get any worse, but when Vick regained full consciousness, I realized I was wrong. I fought to keep my eyes open and place one foot in front of the other. Every sound screamed, every light glared, and my vision narrowed to a tunnel before me.

"You should have let us put her in binders before we woke her," Whitehouse said from my right.

"I don't want her seeing me as the enemy."

"She already does."

We stopped outside the one-way glass.

"You signed a waiver as part of your contract," Whitehouse reminded me.

In other words, once I stepped inside Vick's space, I was on my own. Nice.

Vick paced the room, darting furtive glances at the mirror. She knew we watched, or suspected it strongly. Her face bore as many scratches as her arms and back, along with bruises and swellings. I saw signs of attractiveness beneath: rich brown eyes—though her file said these were manufactured to replace the ones damaged from the inside out by bullets—sharp, well-defined cheekbones. But the injuries would take weeks to heal. A wave of despair rolled off her, adding to the pounding in my head.

Earlier I only had eyes for Vick. Now I studied the walls, noting the indentations and sporadic streaks of blood.

I pressed my palms against the glass, half an effort to remain upright, half in response to my urgency to get in there. If I thought it would speed things up, I would have broken the barrier to reach her and begin easing her pain and mine.

"How many times has she tried to kill herself?"

Dr. Whitehouse blinked, then settled himself. "Three. The implants prevent her from doing fatal damage."

Even awake she had no real control over her life.

I walked to the room's entry. Whitehouse reached over my shoulder and pressed his palm against the lock. Within the door, gears whirred and grated. It slid open, and I was amazed at its thickness—three inches of steel.

They did not want her getting out.

I was three steps in and the door sealed behind me with a *hiss-thud.* Vick retreated to the far side, shoulders hunched, muscles tense, a drape of hair hiding her expression. In the swirling miasma of her emotions, I had no clue what reigned first and foremost.

Four steps into the room. Five.

I never made it to six.

She charged me headfirst, knocking me flat on my back and forcing the air from my lungs. Bits of broken furniture gouged my skin. My skull hit the tile. I had no breath to scream, and my struggling had no effect; she was too strong. I tried to say something reassuring, anything to calm her down, but I couldn't speak.

There was no sense of urgency, no panic from outside the room. No help would come.

Hands wrapped around my throat, skin-to-skin contact. Every sensation I got from her multiplied tenfold, like we shared a single body.

Vick froze.

Her eyes flew wide as mine closed.

Training and instinct took over, replacing my panic. I opened a conduit between my emotions and hers, letting her feel my fear, my sympathy, my desire to help. It was hard, almost impossible, because the communication had run both ways, and the force of her trauma nearly knocked me unconscious.

I was a pathway, an escape route, a lifeline. And with our brainwave patterns so close, the path ran clearer than any I'd formed before.

All the tension fled her. She released my neck. Her forehead sagged to rest on mine. Warm tears bathed my cheeks. She trembled, wracked by sobs. My arms went around her, and I tugged her gently downward. Her head tucked under my chin.

Beneath the more aggressive emotions, some of the weaker ones peeked through: gratitude and humiliation.

"There's nothing to be ashamed of," I managed, though I was still winded. I stroked her hair as a mother would a child's. Disappointment joined embarrassment—disappointment in herself. She had let someone down, and she hated herself for it. "Let it go. Let it all go."

Indignation rose up—she was a soldier after all—but it carried no force. "I don't cry," she informed me, voice hoarse and raw. I wondered if that came from screaming or disuse. She didn't raise her head. I didn't think she could.

I couldn't imagine more telling first words.

"You do with me."

"Who the fuck *are* you?" The last of her defenses shattered like a physical wall collapsing.

"A friend."

We stayed there, lying like that, for a very long time.

CHAPTER 3
VICK
ROLE REVERSAL

Two and a half years later....

I AM an idiot.

Jumping out of a twelfth-floor window may very well be the dumbest thing I've ever done. Having lost twenty-five years of memories, it's an unfair assessment, but I'd still lay good odds.

Rappelling line or no, the frantic leap makes it free fall. There's no time for a leisurely descent. My stomach feels like it's in my mouth, but it's not like I had a choice with a bomb about to explode right above me.

We drop like lead weights into stormy darkness ripped by flashes of light. Rain and small hail pelt my face, and I pull the boy as tightly against me as I can manage with one arm. I think he's whimpering, but it's hard to tell. I wouldn't blame him.

Without the emotion suppressors, I'd be screaming my ass off. As things stand, I look down, calmly calculating my speed (too fast) and the distance to the roof of the hovervan (too close) rising to meet us. We're right on target.

A sudden gust tosses us sideways, whirling dizzily on the twisting line that zings through my grip and cuts into my glove. Gorge rises in my throat while my implants attempt to reestablish visual tracking.

We spin, out of control, and the side of the building looms. I wrench myself around to take the brunt of our impact, and we slam into the brick wall. My implants register bruising, but I remain functional. There's a four-inch metal bar replacing a segment of my spine, courtesy of an encounter with a damaged shuttle engine a year and a half back. It would take much greater force to do any real damage there. At least we didn't strike a window. The glass would've torn us to shreds.

A tremendous explosion blasts from above, spewing more glass, mortar, and—is that a chair?—a variety of other furniture to rain upon us. I jerk and twist on the line, my grip glove slipping farther with so much moisture and motion, then kick off the wall. A few more feet down and my boots impact metal with a resounding clang. We're standing atop the van, about seven stories up.

Most hovervans can't rise that high. The legal limit is twenty feet. But we get all the bells and whistles on our toys.

"You aboard? Or was that a lamp?" Alex calls.

"So much for no big booms," Lyle grumbles.

Alex and Lyle. Not Kelly. I can't hear her—my rock, my support, my constant adviser. If she's not talking, something is very wrong, and even with the suppressors, it scares the hell out of me.

"We're aboa—shit!" My boots slide on the wet metal roof as wind buffets the van. Three scrunches of my toes activate the magnetic clamps in the soles, and I yank the boy beside me down into a crouch for better balance.

He looks up at me, and I'm startled by his grin. "That was wild!"

Huh. "See me for a job when you're older," I shout over the howling gale. "Lyle, keep us steady. Alex, let us in."

"You forget who you're talking to," Lyle says. Then under his breath, "...taking orders from a walking computer."

He can bitch all he wants. I'm team leader on this mission.

The sliding door opens. I lower the kid, and Alex grabs and pulls him in. I swing myself inside and seal us shut.

The interior is chaos—equipment scattered about by the buffeting winds, electronics flickering wildly, but my eyes go straight to Kelly, zooming in on her. She's huddled in the middle of the converted cargo space, pale and trembling under the yellow dome light, back pressed against the metal wall beside Alex's high-tech gear.

Emotion shock. I've seen it before, but this is bad. Very, very bad.

"We're in. Set us down," I tell Lyle. "As gently as possible." I never look away from Kelly.

"Nah, I thought I'd crash us. Figured you'd think that would be fun."

"Shut up, Lyle."

He shoots me a startled glance over his shoulder.

I approach her, swaying from side to side as I fight to maintain my balance, and crouch in front of my partner. Alex draws the kid to the pair of seats farther back in the van and shifts so he's between the boy and us. With the idling engine providing steady background noise, if I keep my voice low, they shouldn't be able to hear me from there.

"Hey." I draw a lock of her long blonde hair out of her face. She stares at nothing with wide, vacant eyes, her chest heaving with desperate gasps for breath. I'm not sure she can see or hear me.

I remind myself one more time (too late as usual) that Kelly is *not* military, no matter how much training the Fighting Storm gives her. She's medical support, breakable, and I've broken her.

"Kelly," I try again. "Kel. Hey. I'm here. I'm safe." I tap her face lightly with my fingertips, then yank my hand away when she recoils and an electric jolt runs up my arm. "That was… different."

Stupid, Vick. Stupid. Physical contact makes it worse, and she's still wrapped up in my emotions, all the emotions I would have felt from the elevator to the stairwell to my swan dive. I should know better. This isn't the first time I've overloaded her with one of my crazy stunts, but it's definitely the worst. I've never gotten feedback like that shock from her before.

I drop my hand to one of my pants pockets and the hypo-press I always keep for her—drugs to calm her when I shoot up her nerves. But they can't be administered unless she's at least a little bit responsive. Otherwise they could plunge her more deeply into her comatose state.

I'm going to have to do this with words. I suck at words.

"Put your shields up, Kel," I whisper. "I'm okay. I don't need you right now."

Something inside me twists, and I swallow bile. My internal display shows an image of a seesaw, me on one side, Kelly on the other, the board perfectly balanced.

That's not helpful.

The image fades.

I'm lying to her and the implants know it. I need Kelly. I always need her. Maybe not right this second, though there's a disturbing trembling in the hand I used to touch her—a precursor to the meltdowns that follow my missions. If she doesn't get it together, I'll revert to how I was after the surgery.

But I've got more reasons for doing this than protecting my sanity. I can't quite isolate them….

The flooring vibrates beneath my boots, the tires unfolding from the base of the van, and we settle to the street with a soft *clank*.

Everyone watches me, the van's interior silent except for Kelly's panting.

A soldier who can't control her feelings trying to bring an empath out of emotion shock. We're so screwed.

"Won't she just come out of it on her own? She always has before," Alex says, his quiet voice like thunder echoing in the metal van.

"Too much. It was too much. She could go into a coma. Or die. So stop interfering in what I'm fucking trying to do." *Not helping, Vick.* I quit ranting. I need to be calm for her to be calm. I take a long, slow breath.

What should I say to drag her back? One thing I know. I shouldn't lie.

"Okay, I'm full of shit." Unable to look her in the eye, I stand and pace, two feet left, two feet right. "I do need you." The tremors pick up in intensity. This is going to get bad. My jaw tightens. My throat closes. Kelly once told me I could always cry with her, but I can't do that here in front of Alex, Lyle, and the kid. I won't.

I stop pacing and stare down at the top of her head. Somehow I choke out words. "I can't show you how I feel." I can't explain what she means to me, how much I depend on her, how important she is. Not with the suppressors working overtime to keep me from freaking out. I should turn them off. Kelly would want me to, now that I'm out of immediate danger. We've worked on that a lot. They're a crutch. But I can't handle what I'm feeling without their cushion. Besides, shutting them down would expose her to more of my anxiety and stress. I want to break something, and my hands clench and unclench at my sides.

Words try to form, pushing their way through my constricted throat… words that might, somehow, convey the insane chaos of feelings clamped down beneath the tech. The thought dies before it's born. I force out the only four I can shape into something coherent: "I'm human with you."

Her rapid panting slows, then stops. Her head comes up, a few inches at a time. Kelly smiles. Strained as it is, it still doubles the light in the van. "You're always human," she says, attempting to rise to her feet and swaying into the wall. I grab her by the arm, steadying her until she finds her balance. She doesn't pull away but instead leans in close. "I'd hug you if I didn't think I'd totally embarrass you."

I glance around the van, stiffening at the sight of three fascinated sets of male eyes watching our every move, with Lyle leaning around his driver's seat to get a better view. "Good call," I tell her. "Shields up?"

She nods. "I'm fine. You're not."

She's not, either. Her eyes are haunted, her skin still pale, but she takes one of my hands in both of hers. Even her firm grip can't steady the shakes in mine. She tugs me toward the pair of seats positioned in front of the rear doors, shooing Alex and the boy forward.

The kid's not doing as well as before. He looks shaken and tired. We shouldn't be worrying about me. We should be getting him home.

"Go find something to do," Kelly says to Alex. "If no one's figured out we're the source of all this commotion, tell Lyle to maintain position for a few more minutes."

Alex consults one of the built-in wall screens on his way up front. "We're drawing some attention," he says. "Not a lot of folks out in the storm, but the ones who were saw us go up and then land. Plenty of people coming out now to watch VC1's fireworks show."

Hey, I didn't set the damn bomb.

A glance over Alex's shoulder shows one view of the street, one of the building with flames shooting from most of the windows on the top floor. As if to accentuate the destruction, several more bits of debris patter the hovervan's metal roof.

The kid continues to the front passenger seat. Alex has an earbud in now. "Emergency crews heading in. The Rodwells have engaged Team Two in the lobby. Shots fired. I hope they can handle it. Local law's moving in too. Not coming after us at the moment, but they have us boxed in with their vehicles close enough it's not safe for us to lift."

"I'd rather not move, anyway," Kelly says. "I'm not at my best. I'll need to concentrate. That means no jostling me around."

"I can hold out 'til the port," I offer. With our shuttle, and privacy.

"No, you can't. You're too close to a breakdown."

She would know. Kelly can detect subtleties in my emotional shifts and physical status even I'm not aware of with all my internal technology. If she says I'm in that much trouble, I have to believe her.

She waits until Alex responds to her pointed look, abandoning his gear and going forward with the others. He crams himself in between Lyle and the kid. Then Kelly settles me in one rear chair and takes the other, shifting it on its floor tracks so her body blocks mine from view. Placing both palms on the sides of my face, she says, "Let it go."

I want to. God, I want to. My emotions push and shove at me from the inside, bottled up and ready to explode. But I hang on a little longer. "You sure?" It's such a delicate balance, my emotions, Kelly's tolerances, my implants. We've postulated over the past two years that denying my release could either send me back into the psychotic state where she first found me... or turn me over completely to the control of the implants, effectively making me the machine I sometimes appear to be. I can't think of a worse fate, but.... "You looked pretty ragged a minute ago." Something in me always wants to protect her, even more than I want to protect myself.

Kelly's smile is soft. "You're made to jump out of windows. This is what I'm made for. Let it go."

No, I'm not made to do the insane stunt I just pulled, and she's still paying the price for it. Guilt gnawing at me, I give in. I close my eyes and latch on to the channel she opens. The trembling picks up. I could so easily break down and destroy her again, but I've gotten better at this over two and a half years, and I hold it together, easing the suppressors off little by little, letting my feelings out in a trickle rather than a flood, knowing no matter what she says, she can't take it all at once. Pain, fear, anger, absolute panic. It all goes.

In exchange, I get the gift of reading her. Calm, peace, weariness, fear for me. It's all there, wrapped up in caring and compassion that staggers me every single time. She's learned, too, over the years, and some of her more private emotions she keeps hidden. I resent that a little. I can hide nothing from her. But I understand.

By the time Lyle interrupts us, I'm exhausted. So is she. We're only halfway through, but I can breathe again.

"Hey, guys," Lyle calls from the driver's seat, "I hate to break up the warm fuzzies, but we have company."

Tired beyond words, I pull from Kelly's grasp to study two monitors flickering to life on my right. A man and woman have emerged from the lobby of my favorite skyscraper—the Rodwells. Shit.

"Team Two, report," I call over my internal comm. "Team Two, respond now!"

Static, then silence fills my ears.

The couple scans the street until they settle on our van. The man carries a semiautomatic pistol in a casual grip. Despite graying hair and a bit of a paunch, I doubt he's lost any skill with that weapon. The woman has a gun in a holster on her thigh. She's younger, more attractive, with long auburn hair and sharp eyes.

We've cost them their victim, their ransom, and their hideaway. The Rodwells want more payback.

Good.

"Vick, don't. I'm not up to much more."

Neither am I, but I'm not telling Kelly that. Besides, I'm sure she already knows. I'm drawing my pistol and crossing the van, headed for the side doors, before she can grab me.

"It's not part of our mission," she says.

We're contracted by the kid's parents. They paid to get their boy back. Killing the kidnappers would cost extra. A lot extra. They didn't spring for it. I don't care.

"Consider it pro bono." Gas me, bomb me, force me out a twelve-story window, you've got this coming.

"It's not your personal vendetta," Kelly pleads.

Fine. "Alex, give us the rundown." We know the mission. HQ doesn't usually include details unless they're pertinent, but Alex can look them up. "How many kidnappings have the Rodwells committed?"

He leaves the front and slides into his spot by the comps. "Forty-seven."

Holy shit. I hear the awe in his voice too.

"And how many were returned alive when the demands were met?" I pause with my hand on the door handle, waiting for his response.

He sucks in a breath. "None."

Exactly.

"There's more," Alex continues, swallowing hard. He's got some images on his screen. I can't make them out from where I stand, but he's struggling with whatever he sees. "The victims, they've been beaten, tortured. No clean kills. Profiling report says the Rodwells enjoy it. It's not just about the money."

Damn, I hate dealing with psychopaths.

"Three previous attempts to stop them, by three other mercenary companies, have failed," he finishes.

I shoot a quick glance at Kelly, then make a chopping motion, telling Alex to close the pictures down. She doesn't need to see the Rodwells' handiwork. His screen goes black.

"You're going to regret this!" One last plea from Kelly. She means the nightmares. I have lots of nightmares. The worst ones follow a killing.

"That's what I've got you for." More guilt tightens my fist on the handle. I don't want to take Kelly for granted, but the Rodwells can't be allowed to continue. I slide the van door open and drop to the street. My knees buckle a bit on impact. I'm that tired. The adrenaline surge that carried me through the rescue is taking its toll. All that energy has to come from somewhere. In minutes, it will drain my reserves dry.

So I better make this fast.

I hesitate just for a moment to be sure my implants won't override me. They can. Thirty-seven percent free will doesn't always win out.

My internal display shows a thumbs-up symbol. Guess the technology didn't like being forced out a window, either.

I blink the image away and take stock. People race away from the building. Emergency personnel pour from siren-blaring fire trucks and police cars. Lots of bystanders crisscrossing my line of sight to my targets.

We're far enough away, across the street and down half a block, with plenty of innocent citizens between us, that the kidnappers see no need to take cover. They're making straight for the van, and me.

This time, my smile is genuine.

Implant technology has a lot of downsides. Computer-enhanced aim isn't one of them.

I'm told I was an expert sharpshooter and quick on the draw before the accident. Now....

I raise my pistol, arm steady as granite. I calculate the movements of the bystanders, the approach of the Rodwells. Hell, the implants even factor in the dying wind from the scary-ass storm.

Mrs. Rodwell raises her weapon, pointing it not at me, but at the driver's side of the windshield. Our glass is bulletproof, but a few of the high-tech rounds can pierce it, and the Rodwells can afford them.

"Shit," Lyle mutters through the receiver embedded in my ear canal.

The first bullet I fire hits Mrs. Rodwell between the eyes. It's cold and precise, and even without my suppressors on full, I feel nothing.

No, I'm not always human. Not by a long shot.

Then again, neither was Mrs. Rodwell.

My ocular enhancements zoom in on the husband. Shock wars with hatred in his expression. He's targeting me, and innocent people aren't going to stop him from firing either. My arm comes up, then falls to my side, dead weight. The pistol drops from my grip. The world spins, my vision flickers, and I'm on my knees, a volley of bullets passing over my head.

People scream and run for cover, but I'm immobile, drained, the half release of my emotions and the physical exertions taking their toll. Lifting my head requires more energy than I can spare, but I do it. Rodwell's pounding toward me, shoving everyone out of his way. Old ladies fleeing the destruction are pushed into concrete walls. He knocks some kids exiting a store to the asphalt.

A screech of tires, a rev of a motor, and a crash of metal on metal drown out the panic. Next thing I know, one of the cop cars has been bumped aside, and the van is between me and Rodwell, bullets ricocheting off the steel.

A couple pierce the metal exterior. That shouldn't happen, and I damn well hope no one was in the way of those bullets. How the hell—?

The door facing me slams open, and Alex and Kelly each grab an arm. They haul me up, Alex doing most of the work, his big muscles straining. Kelly's trembling, tears streaming down her cheeks.

Death. Right. Even though I felt nothing, she would have felt Mrs. Rodwell's death in all its gruesome glory.

With our brainwave match, if her own shields are down, she reads me all the time. Granted, only the most intense emotions make it through the suppressors to her. With strangers, she usually has to be right next to them or in physical contact. Not this time.

My legs don't function, and they have to drag me into the vehicle. Kelly and I collapse in a heap on the flooring, Alex abandoning us to take control of his surveillance systems. Fuck embarrassment. I pull my sobbing partner against my chest, but I'm too weak to hold her and my arm falls limp.

I may have come a long way in dealing with my emotions and my releases, but today was too much for my damaged brain.

God, I hate it when I'm stupid.

"Alex, send everything we've got on Rodwell to the local law. Don't let him get away," I manage before the exhaustion wins and I lose consciousness.

CHAPTER 4
KELLY
SELECTIVE MEMORY

Two years and five months earlier....

VICK CORREN was resilient.

Blue designated the base's fitness and training facilities—blue walls, blue seats, blue mats.

I stood to the side of the practice mats, too exhilarated to remain seated on the benches lining them while Vick went through her stretches and martial arts forms, then faced off against one of the lifelike practice fighting drones. She possessed grace and agility, a perfect build and balance. I envied her. With my considerably larger breasts and shorter height, I would have toppled over trying to emulate the moves she made. Watching a well-trained fighter spar was like attending a performance of the Grand Ballet. Only with a lot of bruises. And grunting. And expletives.

Vick's training was my training. While she rebuilt her body strength and awakened muscle memory, I learned when to put up my shields. I had to do it quickly. Without my walls firmly in place, I felt every hit she took. Secondhand hurt less than first, but my ribs ached as she absorbed a kick to hers. Couldn't get my protection up in time. Didn't see it coming. Needed to predict her opponent's moves and her reactions better. Having the gravity in the gym set higher than Earth normal didn't help. By the end of a workout session, we both collapsed physically and mentally.

No matter what I did, some of the strongest emotions and feelings would bleed through, at least a little, due to our brainwave compatibility. Pain, frustration, reds and grays—I was more familiar with those than I ever wanted to be.

Vick finished up her routine and dropped onto the mats, one tired wave beckoning me over to join her. Emotions boiled within her. She'd need to purge them through me soon.

"They can't send me into the field when I have to discharge every hour. I'm useless." Vick's voice distracted me every time I heard it. It rarely had inflection, though I was picking up more tone changes than when we first met. She relied less heavily on the emotion suppressors—a good sign her brain was adjusting to the damage and the new equipment. I'd set a goal to get her to stop using them altogether when she relaxed. She used them as a crutch, a shield against pain. She would never regain emotional control if she depended on the suppressors all the time.

"It's like someone who's broken an arm or a leg," I told her. We sat cross-legged on the practice mats, facing each other. I was in uniform. She wore loose workout clothes that clung to her with sweat. "As physical therapy progresses, the damaged limb gets stronger. The exercises become easier. You'll develop endurance. You won't have to stop so much. You won't be useless for long," I assured her, patting her hand. She pulled away, but not too quickly.

Internally, I sighed. I tread upon new ground, unexplored territory for me. Maybe for anyone. I certainly never encountered such an extreme case in any of my textbooks at the Academy. They described plenty of examples of emotional impairment, but with the technological additions complicating matters, I was an empathic pioneer. Sometimes I wondered if befriending her, getting so close, made things better or worse.

"I'll never fully heal." She was upset. I didn't need to be an empath to read that.

"No, you won't." I couldn't lie to her. Well, I *could*. She didn't know me well enough to tell the difference. But I wouldn't. The accident damaged Vick's brain beyond healing. That was a fact, but not the end of her world. "You'll learn to compensate. You'll get better at releasing your emotions through me without wearing me out in one blast. You'll express them in a more normal way once you're not bottling them up. It all works together." God, I hoped I said the right things. I hoped she'd prove me right.

She nodded, but she wasn't convinced. Nothing would do that except time.

Vick stood and gave me a hand up. We both wobbled on our feet and shared a weak laugh. Vick's chuckle was forced, a deliberate attempt to copy a natural reaction, but she had to start somewhere. We headed for the gym's airlock, connecting the public exercise facility to the corridor that would access the Fighting Storm's dome and areas.

Vick hesitated. She did it every time we went through a lock. Up until then, I'd had so many other issues of hers to deal with that I'd avoided that one. But I thought it was time. I tapped her feelings. The suppressors ran on low, so I could pick up things without opening a full link. Her emotions mixed and swirled. Not claustrophobia, not that kind of fear; fear of the lock itself, I thought. I couldn't be sure, not without a deeper probe.

Vick died in an airlock. However, with so many of the damn things all over the base, she should have been used to them by now.

She wasn't supposed to be capable of remembering her death.

The existence of the fear indicated that at the very least bits and pieces came back to her. Which shouldn't have happened, according to Dr. Whitehouse. The bullets took those memories. Gone was gone.

But blocked was a different story. Blocks had a bad habit of failing.

And they were illegal.

"Vick?" I studied her response. A quick catch of her breath. A frown. A tensing of the shoulders.

"Let's go." She slammed a palm against the locking mechanism and the door cycled open. Stepping over the threshold took concentrated effort. She had to close her eyes and force the motion.

As always, inside the lock, things intensified. She sweated and shook and tried to hide both by wiping her palms on her pant legs and tucking her hands in her pockets. I wished I could make the mechanisms cycle faster for her. I placed a hand on her shoulder, but she moved out of reach. No more coddling. Okay. I got that. But this was my job. We stepped out the other side of the lock.

Up until now I'd never questioned her inexplicable reactions to the locks. This was as good a time as any. We started down the hall. "How much do you remember about the accident?" I asked it as casually as I could manage.

More tension. She wanted to shut me out but knew she couldn't afford to do that. Several soldiers passed us in the corridors. Then she responded, "Nothing."

"That's not true."

She stopped and faced me. A pair of white-coated doctors skirted around us. We blocked half the hall, but she didn't care. "It's not a lie. I can't lie to you. You'd know." Vick paused. "Right?"

I grinned. "If you're looking for me to admit a weakness, I won't. No, you can't lie to me. You believe you remember nothing. But it's still not true. You know what happened." It wasn't a question.

She nodded. "I've read the official report."

With all its classified blacked-out bits. I gestured in the direction we came from. "Those reactions at every airlock, they're not from reading an account on a datapad. Those are visceral." I lowered my voice even though we were alone. "You have nightmares about it, don't you?" I'd felt this same fear from her, deep in the station's "night." It woke me sometimes, shivering from nonexistent cold.

A tentative nod, then a shake of her head. "It's impossible. They told me those memories were lost. All my long-term memories are lost."

And there was that disturbing question again. Lost or blocked? I didn't want to believe I worked for a dishonest organization, but all the long-term memories.... Vick knew her name, knew how to fire a gun, how to fight. Specific things, as if carefully chosen.

She knew everything the Fighting Storm needed her to know.

"We'll talk more about this tonight."

When I took off at a brisk clip, I picked up her confusion and sense of abandonment, but I couldn't deal with that then. She'd made enough progress that I could leave her alone for an hour or so without problems. There was someone I had to chat with.

I arrived minutes later in Dr. Whitehouse's office. He was in a meeting with some sales rep from a pharmaceutical company, but I took priority, or rather Vick did. Same difference. The salesman went and I stayed.

"This couldn't wait?" He gestured at a dark leather chair in front of his desk. Now that I'd worked there awhile and had a basis for comparison, I knew this was a cushy office for Girard Moon Base: fake paneling hiding the metal walls, tan carpet, wood and leather furnishings.

I skipped the chair and leaned on his desk, both palms flat on the smooth surface. No clutter there. No knickknacks. He lived for the mercenary organization.

"I want to know why Vick has the specific memories she has. I'm not a doctor, but it seems to me she should have a little of this and a little of that. A few childhood moments, a bit of her teen years, a romance, graduation. Instead she's got the Storm and all its training—everything she needs to do her job and nothing else."

Whitehouse reclined in his chair. His gaze never left me. "That's because the Storm put her back together. We absorbed the cost of the technology. We got to choose. And to be honest, if Oz hadn't taken a special interest in her, she isn't the one I would have chosen for this experiment. She was good. Very good. But not that good. Still, we do what the boss says."

I blinked at the admission and mentally kicked myself for not arranging to record this conversation. "She's not a slave. She doesn't belong to you." I wondered how much memory was truly lost, if any. And how much they just took under the pretense of her accident.

"Actually, she does." He opened a narrow drawer and removed a datapad. After tapping in a few commands, he shoved it toward me. I stared at the legalese for several moments. "Vick's contract. Note the death clause."

I scanned for it. Since it was in capital letters, I found it without effort. I read aloud, "In the event of death, the party's body shall be donated to the scientific research division of the Fighting Storm." I placed the pad on the desk carefully. Otherwise I would have smashed it in my anger. "Vick's not dead."

"Yes, she is. Look," Whitehouse said before I could interrupt, "I humor your need to call her Vick and treat her like a human being. We need her functional. You've made her functional. But VC1 is no longer Vick Corren. She stopped being that when we declared her brain-dead. At that moment, by law, she became ours."

And he believed he was in the right. Legally, the moon's system might have supported him. Certainty poured off him in almost tangible waves. I wanted to smack them back into his smartass head.

"Did you choose to have her remember dying?" I snapped.

He stiffened. I surprised him. Well, that was something.

"She has nothing to cushion that moment, nothing but rules, regulations, and cold skill sets. No family, no love, no warmth. Dammit, could you make my job any harder?" I thought of my own parents back on Earth, living out their retirement in the North Carolina mountains. In five more months, once I'd earned leave, I'd visit them. It was a long time to wait, but I pictured them and knew they missed me. I received regular communications from them. Vick had none of that. Not even a memory.

Maybe I'd take her with me when I went home.

Whitehouse sat up straight. "She's not supposed to remember the accident. We put in blocks—"

"You put in blocks for a lot of things, didn't you? She didn't lose all her long-term memory. You made that happen. It violates all the ethics codes."

"Not for a corpse. VC1 is the perfect soldier, or she will be when you've finished fixing her. There will be no memories to distract her from her duties. The implants will suppress her emotions and you'll help her discard them, so she won't have those complications—complications that can cost the lives of her comrades."

I threw my hands in the air and paced the office carpet. "They're not complications! They're human feelings." Feelings that should have made her a better soldier, not a worse one. And yet, from the Storm's perspective, soldiers who could feel were a liability. They wanted automatons—killing machines that had the agility of human beings but wouldn't balk at orders. "No matter how well you think you've blocked memory and emotion, the strongest ones *will* come through. Her *death* comes through. The emotions you tried so hard to stop end up growing and building and she needs me to release them. This experiment of yours is one screw-up after another."

"This experiment of ours gave her life and the potential to surpass all the company's expectations."

But was it worth it? If I quit, they'd terminate the project. I didn't know if that meant a second death for Vick or life in an institution, but either way, I wouldn't cause it. No. I needed to carry on, play their game. And maybe somewhere along the way, I could break down some of the barriers they'd put up, restore the blocked memories. Given enough time, I knew I could make her *feel* again and understand and properly act upon what she felt.

"You don't know what really happened in that accident," Whitehouse said, interrupting my plans. I got the distinct impression he'd guessed the path of my thoughts and didn't like that path one bit. "Here." He picked up the pad and accessed a vid record. He typed in a complex security code. "Let me show you."

My hand took the datapad, but my brain shouted to put it down. Whitehouse was too confident, too comfortable, his emotions registering in greens and blues. Whatever he wanted me to see, he expected to convince me of his righteousness, of the righteousness of the entire research and medical department of the Fighting Storm. Lowering myself into the seat opposite him, I waited for instructions.

"VC1 has never seen this, knows nothing of its existence," he said before I started the visual recording rolling. "It is the unanimous decision of the board that she never will. Her implants have... evolved... to the point where they could hack into our main database if she wanted them to, if she knew there was something to look for." He leaned forward, his cold eyes boring into mine. "You recall your contractual obligation never to disclose classified information, correct?"

I did, but I shook my head. "Show me or don't show me. You hired me to look after her mental health. That's also part of my contractual obligation." And if I wouldn't keep it a secret from her, what then? Would they block my memories too? I suppressed a shiver and wished I'd read my contract a little more carefully.

Whitehouse nodded too quickly, and the shiver made it past my resistance. I rubbed both arms, pretending the cold office affected my delicate senses. All the soldiers there saw me as frail and weak. Not that they were wrong. Whitehouse smirked and tapped on his embedded desk screen, turning on the office heaters. The extra warmth didn't help.

The date in the corner of the playback read about six months prior to then. The time was 1404, military-style. Midafternoon to civilians. I hit Play. The speakers crackled with static, but the picture showed sharp and clear, focused on three Fighting Storm soldiers entering an airlock I guessed was somewhere on Girard Moon Base. The camera hung within the lock itself, showing them stepping inside and the first door cycling closed behind them.

"It's a covert ops timed training scenario," Whitehouse said. "That means no communication with their observers at any time. They aren't told specifics, only that they must move from point A to point B in a certain number of minutes while overcoming unknown obstacles."

I studied the three figures on the screen. The two men I didn't recognize, but I couldn't mistake Vick's dark hair and the way she carried herself. And yet when she faced the camera, the resemblance ended. Her eyes burned; her lips turned downward in a scowl. That was Vick Corren expressing her emotions without help. I couldn't read feelings off a vidfilm, but a blind person could see her rage.

"And what the fuck were you two doing, Devin?" She stomped to the control pad on the far side of the lock and punched in a code, her back to the other two soldiers.

"I told you. Studying," Devin replied. His blond hair and blue eyes gave a contrasting innocence to his big, brick-wall build, but he looked nervous in the face of Vick's fury. I didn't blame him. I'd been on the receiving end of that anger. *"We've got a weapons' exam tomorrow. She's the fastest at disassembling the K12s. Faster than you."*

"Bullshit. On both counts." Vick whirled on him, ignoring (or more likely missing) the keypad's telltale light flashing a steady red.

The third soldier pointed and mumbled something, but they couldn't hear him over their own argument and neither could I.

"Vick and Devin were lovers," Whitehouse muttered.

I paused the playback and stared at him. Something about that revelation bothered me, mixing with my shock and sorrow that her lover clearly would be a fatal victim of that accident, but I couldn't quite put my finger on it. Sometimes I got so involved in everyone else's emotions, it became hard to pinpoint my own.

"Vick just made what she has no idea was a fatal mistake." He rubbed a hand over his face, hiding his eyes from me, and slowly I became aware of his emotions fading from my senses, just a little at a time, his mental walls coming down as the story unfolded before us. "The Storm doesn't forbid in-house romances, but we do monitor them. In addition to other goals, this scenario was meant to test if Vick and Devin's relationship would distract them from their jobs. We didn't know about the argument until we'd set them in motion. I doubt it would have mattered, but we didn't know." More emotional absence, replaced by a cold emptiness like fire snuffed out by ice. Every word said as if it were matter-of-fact.

I shifted to study him from the corner of my eye. Emotional blocking wasn't impossible for untrained individuals. Sometimes it occurred as a natural defense mechanism, and that's what I suspected was happening here. Whatever Whitehouse should have been feeling, his psyche didn't think he could handle it, so it blocked him off from himself.

Of course, the side result was that it blocked me from reading him just as effectively, and without express permission, I couldn't probe deeper.

The vidfilm resumed playing.

"You were studying," Vick sneered. *"Really? In bed? Studying what, anatomy? Or maybe K12 is your new pet name for it."*

"The code she pushed into the door lock was an older one, an incorrect one," Whitehouse closed-captioned for me. "She should have been able to get that right in her sleep, but she wasn't concentrating." He'd dropped into a monotone. No inflection. No emotion.

In that moment, he reminded me of my Vick.

"How the hell would you know where we were?" Devin said.

"Heat sensors don't just work in the field." Vick was smug. *"And you two were giving off a lot of heat."* She folded her arms across her chest, her slung rifle hanging at her side.

"You were fucking spying on us? Jealous, paranoid bitch."

"It's not paranoia if it's true."

A low alarm sounded, just audible over the shouting. *"Um, guys...."* The third soldier would clearly have preferred to have been anywhere but trapped in an airlock with the quarreling couple.

Vick noticed the red lights on the control pad at last and cursed under her breath. She returned to it and tapped the code in a second time—the same code. The wrong code. Upset about her lover's affair, she must have forgotten. She tried again, a different sequence, but with no greater success.

"Fuck. Stephen, what day is it?" she asked the third soldier.

"Tuesday." His eyes darted around the airlock like it had a life of its own.

"He's claustrophobic," Whitehouse confirmed. "Another goal of the test—to probe the extent of the phobia, see how it might affect him in the field. We knew about it, but it was categorized as a mild case. We figured on some nerves, maybe a botched code entry like Vick's. But they weren't supposed to be in the lock this long." Now a touch of emotion broke through. Sadness and regret. Guilt... and anger. But none of it more than a hint that only a very strong empath could have picked up, the very tip of the iceberg.

Something here felt very wrong.

Having read the report, I was nervous and saddened by what I knew would occur, but I hadn't actually seen it. Whitehouse had. He should feel residual pain for those lost, but it should have faded over time and repetitive viewings. That wasn't his stoic demeanor's fault. That was the way human emotions and memories worked. And none of this explained what had to be an emotional cataclysm occurring beneath his psyche's façade—a cataclysm that *should no longer be there.*

I hesitated, then gave in to the pull of my empathic sense. Despite my dislike for that man, I reached out and took his hand in my own. He allowed it for all of five seconds, then drew away without a word. But it confirmed what I'd suspected. He felt more than he was showing, and the whirlwind of emotions lay clamped down beneath a natural block so strong I had never before seen its like and could not penetrate it to identify the range or the cause.

"That was the Tuesday code. I'm sure of it." Vick searched out the camera and glared into the lens. *"Okay, I screwed up twice. You gonna keep us in here all day? This isn't supposed to happen...."*

The alarm blared so loudly it almost drowned out her words, and there was a hiss of escaping air. A red strobe mounted on the airlock wall flashed on and off, casting their faces in an eerie, intermittent bloody glow. Stephen's chest rose and fell with near-hyperventilation, his hands clawing at the sleeves of his uniform as if trying to contain his own fear.

"She's right," Whitehouse whispered.

"What went wrong?" Tears ran down my cheeks. No idea when they started. No idea when they'd stop.

"A security feature. By inputting the wrong sequence twice, she locked out the system. That was as designed. What wasn't intended to happen was the override lock failure that triggered the defensive response, cycling the lock, emptying the air as it would in the event of an enemy attack. The opposing forces would be trapped inside and suffocate."

Instead it had trapped them.

"It should have simply released them when she got the code right, subtracted points from her test score, and sent them on to the next portion of the scenario. We saw them on the monitors immediately, but they weren't carrying comms, and there was no way to contact them. Right now…. Right now!" Whitehouse stabbed a finger at the screen. "There's a maintenance team outside, working on the malfunction. Minutes. They only needed to wait a few minutes." He trailed off and glared at the playback as if the force of his stare alone could turn back time.

I watched him, his brief outburst snuffed out almost instantaneously.

On the screen, Stephen's panic peaked. He unslung his rifle and aimed it at the locking mechanism.

"Hey, Stephen, calm the fuck down!" Vick shouted.

Whitehouse drew in a ragged breath. He'd seen this before. It was no surprise to him. *So why is he reacting so strongly?*

I watched Vick make a desperate grab for the rifle. The weapon fired. The bullets ricocheted. Devin and Stephen were hit and fell, but the latter's finger still squeezed the trigger. Vick caught Devin. She screamed, eyes wide with shock, shaking her head in denial. The gun continued to fire.

Two bullets pierced Vick's skull. I expected blood and brain matter, but there was little gore. I remembered things Vick had taught me over the past weeks, about the ammunition they used, how it entered the body and fragmented, tearing apart the internal organs.

I let the datapad clatter to the desktop and barely managed to shove my seat away and reach the garbage can before I vomited. By the time I regained control of my stomach and wiped my mouth on my sleeve, the playback had stopped.

"You see?" Dr. Whitehouse said as my shaky legs returned me to my chair. "Without her jealousy, none of them would have died. Emotions!" He pointed a finger at my chest. "Emotions killed them all."

He believed that. And I supposed it was partly true. *I* believed Vick should never know the contents of that video. She carried enough guilt around to start a religion, and I hadn't even begun to identify all the sources yet. With trembling fingers, I reached out and slid the datapad across the desk. "I won't tell her."

No matter what Whitehouse thought, the accident wasn't Vick's fault, not alone. Devin cheated and the lock glitched, both of which contributed to the disaster. The Storm never should have sent Stephen into such a situation in the first place, not with a documented phobia.

But Stephen died and Vick survived, leaving someone to blame. As I probed the depth of Whitehouse's determination, I knew he wouldn't forgive her or anyone else for what he considered to be damning emotions.

Ever.

CHAPTER 5
VICK
CONTROL FACTORS

Two years and five months later....

I AM a royal bitch.

Dreams are my enemies.

I'm drifting through Girard Moon Base, but some piece of my subconscious places me first in a bunk on one of the Fighting Storm's shuttlecraft, heading back from the kidnap rescue mission, and then in bed in my quarters.

I float along the passageway, soldiers and a few white-coated medical personnel going about their own business around me, taking no notice. The edges of my vision blur and shift. Sounds echo in my ears: conversations, air ventilation systems, feet on metal flooring—except my own, which make no noise at all.

A door on my right opens, and a soldier stands inside, his back to me. He's tall, well-built, familiar and yet not. When he turns to face me, I'm certain I should know him, should recognize the two bullet holes in his chest and the blue tinge to his lips.

Devin. My implants supply the name I've forgotten. The name of a man who died with me in that godforsaken airlock.

The dead should be remembered. I hate that I forget.

Devin opens his mouth to speak, but I'm already in motion, leaving the room, leaving him behind. I'm not sure where I'm headed, but a sense of dread builds in my chest, constricting my lungs and tightening the muscles in my shoulders.

A knowing shiver runs through my bones.

A sign on the pressure door ahead confirms my fears—the morgue. I press my palm against the locking panel. It shouldn't open at my touch; I'm not authorized. But it does.

The interior of the metal-walled room is frigid, becoming colder still when I look down and realize I'm naked. This should embarrass me, but no one's around. I'm alone with the dead in their storage drawers, and the corpses won't care.

My feet move of their own volition, carrying me to an unmarked drawer. My hand reaches to activate the mechanism, which will slide the unit open and reveal the contents.

So it's business as usual, then. I've had this dream before, usually with one of my dead enemies in the box. Guilt taking its toll. Lucky me, my implants let me analyze even while I'm asleep. In some of the rarer variations, Dr. Whitehouse lies inside, or a faceless figure my dream-self recognizes as Oz, owner of the Fighting Storm.

In the most disturbing version, the box is empty and I climb inside and seal myself in, the seals *clunking* into place, the air hissing out like a depressurizing airlock. I suffocate in darkness, slowly, until I wake up in my quarters, gasping.

The drawer opens before I press the activator, and I've got a new contender for the worst of my nightmares.

Kelly lies in the featureless metal interior.

She's naked like I am, her thick blonde hair lying in waves long enough to cover her bare breasts, and I wonder why I'd picture her this way.

This is a dream. Anything goes. It's not real.

I search the impassive face, watch her chest for the rise and fall— but she's motionless, her skin ashen. When I touch her hand, she's ice-cold.

Her eyes open, bright blue amidst the gray of her pallor. She raises her arms, holding them out to me, reaching.

Then I'm in the box beside her. As is the way of dreams, I have no idea how I got there. I just am. We're skin to skin, my warmth against her ice—an odd reversal. There's no fear, no revulsion. I know I should feel something. It's pressing at me, scratching and growling, but whatever it is, it's buried too deep.

Kelly's arms wrap around me, holding me in place as the drawer slides closed. In the dark, the air grows thinner. The cold creeps beneath my flesh, piercing to my bones. In the last seconds, I struggle, fighting to escape her death grip, kicking at the base of the drawer so hard the clanging echoes and resounds. She releases me, but it's too late. The container is locked from the outside, and I'm so weak I can't break it open.

"I'm sorry," she whispers. "So sorry."

"Not your fault," I tell her. "I climbed in on my own."

"You never had a choice."

My heart stutters, then stops.

DISORIENTATION WARS with terror. I gasp and sit straight up in my bed, the sheets dampened by sweat and tangled around me like creeping vines. With a half shriek, I struggle free, kicking them to the floor. Bed. Chair. Desk. Utilitarian furnishings. The constant hum of the gravity generators and the hiss of recycled air. My gaze falls on the ficus plant, healthy and green in its pot by the nightstand—a gift from Kelly, one she stops by to water once a week or it would be dead.

I'm in my quarters on Girard Moon Base. My acrobatics with the twelve-story leap, coupled with the adrenaline crash, had me unconscious for hours—the entire travel-time between Nascent and the base. Not unusual after a taxing mission, but annoying. It used to give the medical department fits. They're used to my emotion-suppressing shutdowns now, and they no longer check me into their facility for observation every time my team drags my ass home. Instead, they just put me to bed, counting on my implants to alert them in an emergency. But that doesn't change the fact that I've missed half a standard day.

That's not what's got all the alarm bells ringing in my head, though. It isn't the dream, either, although that's fresh and plenty disturbing all by itself.

I'm killing Kelly? She's killing me? We're killing each other? Fucked-up, bizarre shit. I could spend hours trying to make sense of it.

I'm struck by an image of the last time I saw her—pale, shaking, and sobbing—and I have to swallow against a sudden lump in my throat. I put her through a hell of a lot in the past day and a half. I'm using her up, and I hate myself for it.

I take a deep breath, let it out. Dreams are what they are. If my subconscious, or more likely my implants, are sending me a message, it will come clear on its own, eventually.

I have bigger problems than nightmares. Across from my bed, the red light is flashing on my comm system, and I know it's not anyone congratulating me on a job well done.

I operated outside the specifications of my orders. I put my team and the kid I rescued in unnecessary danger to do so. I nearly got my head shot off. And I only took down one of the damn kidnappers.

Stress and anxiety swell, making my stomach churn. It's not Kelly calling, either. She always uses my personal comm, the one embedded in my skull. Honestly, I'm surprised she isn't calling to check on me, especially after the nightmare. Means she's still as wiped out as I am. Worry for her adds to my stress.

I killed someone in front of her. She had to have felt that. It's not the first time. When I'm thinking clearly, I try to avoid it.

I wasn't thinking.

My internal display flashes an image of me beating myself over the head with a stick, like some character from a Punch and Judy puppet show. It fades with my sigh.

Every muscle complains when I swing my legs over the side of my bed. Somewhere along the line, my shoulder and bruised ribs got treated, but that doesn't mean I don't hurt. I'm in sleeping shorts and a white cotton T-shirt. I really hope Kelly did the honors. I don't want to think about Alex leering at me. At least I don't have to worry it was Lyle; he avoids touching me whenever possible.

My uniform is folded neatly on the bedside chair. Kelly, then. Don't know where my weapons ended up, but I'm betting she locked them in the steel box at the end of my bed, probably holding them by the tips of her fingers like dead rats while she did so.

The image prompts a grin, which fades when I flex my legs and arms. The parts that aren't bruised are scratched and scraped. The dread and despair take a firmer hold, building into pressure I haven't felt in years. Twenty-seven is too old for this shit.

I shamble across the room and access the message on my desk datapad. It's text, not audio. On the plus side, I don't get to hear the disappointment. On the negative end, official texts get stored in my permanent records.

This one's official and marked "Urgent."

It's also not from Whitehouse. My stomach drops out from under me when I read the sending address—Storm Center. The great and powerful Oz himself.

Oh, I'm so fucked.

CHAPTER 6
KELLY
HOMECOMING

Two years earlier....

VICK CORREN was unwelcome.

"You really need to go openly armed?" I glared at Vick's pistol as we settled into our seats on the shuttlecraft to Earth. The grip clattered against the armrest, drawing further attention. She had a couple of boot knives tucked away as well. The Storm fully licensed her to carry, but this was a vacation. Across the aisle, a civilian woman clutched her baby to her breast, stood, and moved to a different row far in the rear.

"Have you watched the newsnets lately?" Vick stowed her duffel under the seat in front of her. It contained all she brought for our week of leave. Even after six months with the Fighting Storm and three successful mission excursions, I hadn't learned to travel as light. My two suitcases were stored in the baggage compartment.

Then again, it might have had something to do with how intensely security scrutinized her carry-on and how much explaining she had to give for each and every item in it before they allowed her to board. Me, they let pass without comment. Vick? Her nonhuman Girard Base status as property earned her an interrogation that almost made us miss our flight. That, and the weapons she carried as a member of the Storm. I took a deep breath and let my indignation on her behalf go, even when I saw similarly armed mercs proceeding to other flights unaccosted. For Vick, this was part of her life. She barely seemed to notice the imbalance of respect afforded to her.

I cast another appraising glance at her from the corner of my eye. For our trip, I'd opted for casual, comfortable travel wear—jeans and a light sweater. Vick was in uniform. Besides that and her workout gear,

I didn't think she owned other clothing. My mind wandered to what shopping with Vick might have entailed, and I discarded the idea. Some poor, overenthusiastic saleswoman would have ended up shot.

Vick sank lower into the cushions, her weariness palpable, a blue-gray haze to my senses. Despite how far she'd come emotionally and physically, we both needed this vacation.

I needed to go home.

"What *about* the news?" I asked, finally responding to her question. No, I hadn't kept up with Earther current events. Between working with Vick and my own training, I hadn't had time. I wondered how she'd managed, but then, she could access newsnets in her head.

"Terrorism." One word to sum up a million fears.

I ignored the auto-message playing at the front of the cabin, giving the standard lecture about flight safety, and waited for her to elaborate.

"You *are* out of the loop, aren't you? Half the Storm's been deployed to help defend one high-threat target or another. Eco-terrorists are on a rampage, protesting about atmospheric irradiation. Five shuttleports blown in five different countries in five weeks. All the usual shit but more of it." As if to punctuate her words, the shuttle's engines roared to life. The "remain in your seat" lights went live, and the restraints across my shoulders and lap tightened to hold me in place.

I smiled at her usual paranoia. "And you think Asheville, North Carolina, is the next major urban target?" My parents lived in one of the most beautiful—and rural—places left on the homeworld. Rolling mountains, unpolluted due to their heights, and isolated. It was home to some of the wealthiest people on Earth.

That thought sent my mind in another direction. I wondered how Vick would react when she figured out my parents fit right in among the North Carolina well-to-do. I needed her to like my parents and them to like her.

Vick shifted to face me, not easy in the restraints. Her expression was dead serious. "I think eco-terrorists want to protect what they consider to be one of the last clean air zones, yeah. I think attacking a shuttleport in a high-profile area where politicians and celebrities live would also gain them some much-wanted media attention for their cause. And the US hasn't been hit yet." She settled back, her point made.

"Way to ruin a holiday," I muttered.

Her hand fell on my arm. "Sorry. It's how I'm programmed. I'm probably wrong."

I flinched at her mechanical terminology. "You know I hate it when you use words like that. You'd think some of what I've been saying would have rubbed off by now."

She parroted back at me, "'Vick, you're a human being, no matter how much of your brain is mechanical,'" then softened the mockery with a rare smile. "You've taught me a lot." Her grip on my arm tightened for a moment. She released me without another word.

We spent the hours of the flight lost in private thoughts. I stared out the viewport on my left, the yellowish haze blurring the outlines of continents and oceans. Once upon a time, I was told, Earth shone in vibrant blues and greens. Not any longer. But summer in North Carolina produced flowers and morning fog and violent but amazing storms. Mom and Dad had arranged vacation time to match mine, and we'd all be together.

All of us.

When we were on final approach, I cast a surreptitious glance at Vick, wishing for the thousandth time I could read her mind. She had left her suppressors off more and more, facing the difficulties with her emotions, not hiding behind the technology that made everything worse in the long run, but it cost her. Half the time she didn't understand what she felt or how to deal with it. Her bravery made me proud. Right then I sensed traces of pleasure, but anxiety and tension and a touch of depression almost buried them, and I wondered what bothered her.

"I'm intruding," she said, half to herself.

So that was it. "You're sharing."

My voice startled her. Maybe she wasn't aware she'd said that out loud. "What?"

"Sharing. My family. You can't remember yours"—and the Storm had no record of them—"so you're sharing mine. I've told them all about you." Well, as much as regulations allowed. The Storm classified a lot of what made Vick, well, Vick. "They can't wait to meet you." Also a half truth. Dad never changed, but Mom's communications had been… odd… of late. Asking lots of personal questions. How many hours a day did I spend working with my partner? How well did I like working with her? Was Vick's care entirely my responsibility or were other doctors and empaths involved? I wasn't sure how to take those.

I'd told Vick a lot about them, too, with the exception of their financial status, which could have been a little embarrassing. I thought to fill in her gaps with my own family's details.

Psychic abilities often ran in families. Dad was a microtelekinetic doing freelance work for a number of technology corporations. He manipulated delicate components inside computer systems when they malfunctioned, eliminating the need to disassemble the equipment. He never gave me problems.

Mom provided lots of challenge. She was an empath, though not nearly as strong as I was. In my teenage years, I discovered I could put up walls against her prying. It probably saved our relationship.

She worked for the One World government. She led a team of empaths who mediated representatives of the member countries. Given Vick's statement about terrorist activity, her getting time off surprised me. I'd have thought she'd have been needed in talks between the eco-terrorists and the world's leaders, but what my mom wanted, she usually received.

She expected me to follow her into a nice, safe field, like politics. It was one of the few things she wanted that she didn't get.

"Everything will be fine," I assured Vick.

If I could only reassure myself. The more I thought about the strange messages from Mom, the more worried I became. Maybe she didn't care for my choice of professions, but she'd never directly expressed her displeasure, and yet I couldn't interpret her interrogating questions about my work environment in any other way....

We touched down without a bump, taxied into a hangar, disembarked, and headed for baggage claim. Only one terminal, one bag claim area.

Asheville had a relatively small port compared to those in the major cities—seven ports total in the US. We wouldn't have even rated one there if not for the large number of retired and currently employed government officials living in the area.

I wove through the arriving and departing crowds of summer travelers, my nerves putting my observation skills on alert despite myself. Vick wasn't alone in wearing a weapon. The port terminal swarmed with police and military personnel. Even a few civilians bore arms—pistols in thigh holsters and rifles slung over shoulders.

Half of Asheville seemed as paranoid as Vick.

We found an escalator and boarded, passing under a red, white, and blue banner as we descended to the lower level.

"Twenty Fabulous Years Serving the Asheville Area!" the banner proclaimed.

A knot of tension tightened the muscles in my neck. "What month? What day was this shuttleport opened?" I asked Vick, standing silent at my side.

Her mechanical eyes went unfocused as she searched her implants for the relevant information—one of the few ways I was frequently reminded that there'd been more damage in her accident than just to her brain. Anyone who didn't know her wouldn't notice. "July 17, twenty years ago," she said.

That week marked the shuttleport's anniversary. Which made it an even likelier target for terrorism. Vick followed my gaze to the banner, and her lips tightened.

"You knew?" I asked.

"Yeah. Didn't wanna say anything else to upset you."

She worried about *my* feelings? Now there was a switch. I opened my mouth to point out her very human response, but the sound of my name being shouted over the noisy crowd stole my teachable moment.

Mom stood at the escalator's base, waving both hands over her head like we'd never have spotted her in her bright red rain jacket. A couple of elderly women winced at the noise when she shouted again. I grabbed Vick's hand and pulled her past the old ladies, using the escalator like steps to reach my mother faster and prevent her from screaming a third time.

"Mom!" I said, embracing her and drawing her out of the line of foot traffic. Vick trailed behind and hovered, observing our reunion.

"You've lost weight," Mom said, holding me away from her. "Got some muscle, though." Her fingers poked my biceps.

Her observation pleased me. She always kept herself in great shape. I was about to comment on the Fighting Storm's exercise training when she glanced over my shoulder, noticing Vick for the first time. And frowned.

It was there and gone in an instant, that fleeting expression of displeasure replaced by a smile that didn't quite reach her eyes. I prayed Vick missed it, but judging by the sudden plummeting of her mood, she saw it just fine.

"And you must be Vick Corren. I hope you had a nice flight. I've heard much about you." Polite words but no warmth. She had her diplomat expression on: practiced, composed, and controlled. "Well, come on, then, you two," my mother said, heading for the closest exit. The door slid open, wind catching her white-blonde hair and swirling it around a face with wrinkles not quite hidden by tasteful makeup. "Your father's already got your bags. He'll have the car pulled up by now." She flashed another fake smile at us—at Vick. "You didn't bring anything except the duffel, right? Soldiers carry so little on vacation." Her eyes dropped to the gun at Vick's side and she frowned again, then schooled her expression.

"No, Ms. LaSalle. There's nothing else." Vick's tone was flat. She turned her suppressors on. Damn. Though I could hardly blame her. She shouldn't have had to deal with that, and I glared at my mother's departing back. When Mom passed through the doors, Vick raised her eyebrows at me.

I shook my head and shrugged. My mother's emotions were as closed to me as mine to her. I had more strength, yes, but when she figured that out in my teen years, she started thinking sexual thoughts every time I tried to read her. Nothing like receiving lusty emotions from your mom to get you to stop probing. I got them right then, and I withdrew fast, leaving me with no idea of what irked her. Empaths knew when other empaths invaded. It felt like a prickling sensation where the spinal column reached the neck.

Maybe this wasn't such a great idea.

As Mom predicted, Dad had the green monstrosity hovering at the curb while a red-faced man in a shuttleport security uniform argued with him through the driver's side window. We climbed into the back of the six-passenger vehicle. Mom hopped up front, and with a last wave to the guard, Dad pulled out.

He had his ball cap on, covering the balding spot at the back of his head that probably spread farther since I left. Then again, maybe not. It had only been a year since I saw them last. It just seemed like longer. The Yankees logo on the hat had faded. He gave me a wink in the rearview mirror. His blue eyes twinkled with good humor.

The sun shone, though gray clouds hung in the east and the pavement glistened from a recent rain. A number of patrol cars stood ready at the port exit. They checked Dad's identification before letting us through.

"So," Dad tossed back once we drove a few miles. "Kill anyone yet?" He kidded. Him, I could read. But Mom's shoulders stiffened.

I opened my mouth to answer, but Vick surprised me by speaking first. "She's support personnel, Mr. LaSalle. Kelly wouldn't hurt anyone."

"What about in self-defense?" my mother murmured, just loud enough for everyone to hear.

"That's my job," Vick said, "to protect her and the rest of our team."

I heard the edge and dropped a hand on her leg, shaking my head in warning.

"Let it go, Bea," Dad said.

Thank God for Dad.

I risked another glance at Vick, but she stared out her window, emotions locked down tight.

No one uttered another word for the rest of the drive to the house.

Chapter 7
Vick
Too Close For Comfort

Two years later….

I am a failure.

I half sit, half fall into the chair by my desk. My fingers tremble as I open the content of Oz's message—Oz, who knows everything that happens on every mission we complete, who would have received Alex and Lyle's, and likely Kelly's full reports before I ever regained consciousness. I close my eyes and take a deep breath, but it does little good.

Kelly doesn't understand my over-the-top reactions to any kind of contact from Oz, and neither do I. I suspect R&D programmed in some sort of loyalty compulsion and, as with almost everything else, got it wrong, made it too strong, something. But every time I try to discuss my suspicions with her, I'm tongue-tied, unable to form the words, which makes me believe it even more.

All I know is, I'm driven not to let him down, whoever he is. On the rare occasions I do, depression grips me and doesn't let go. And from the first few lines of the message, I see I've let him down in a big way.

"…acting outside mission parameters… endangering civilian life… endangering mental health of a team member… unnecessary risk to company equipment…."

That would be me. I'm the "company equipment." By stopping Kelly in midemotional release and charging after the Rodwells, I needlessly threw my very expensive self into the line of fire. Even though I'm assigned to do that on a regular basis, in this particular instance it wasn't part of the mission. The kid was safe. I should have called it quits at that. If the adrenaline burst hadn't caught up to me, dropping me to the pavement when it did, Rodwell's shots would have hit me. I would have died. Again. The odds are against the Fighting Storm bringing me back to life twice.

Bad enough the boss persists in calling me property. Worse that he's right, on every count he's enumerated. Only a machine would hurt Kelly the way I did without even a second thought.

I skim the rest of the message, the acknowledgment that I'd at least completed the rescue successfully. The boy returned to his very influential and very grateful parents.

Patrick Rodwell escaped the scene.

All that risk and damage, all these reprimands, and I didn't even take out both of the murderous kidnappers. If I'd succeeded, I'd probably be getting accolades, but having failed, it gets labeled as a reckless act on my part. Between the message and the dream, it's too much for my emotionally handicapped self to handle.

When I glance down, my fingers are clenched on the desk's center drawer. I keep a spare 9mm pistol inside, loaded.

What should be terror is merely detached observation.

Paranoia. Paranoia has me keeping an extra gun where I can reach it quickly. No one knows I have it hidden there. That paranoia is about to get me killed.

Suicidal coward. If this is all the strength I have, I deserve to die.

No. That's not right. My self-preservation programming should be kicking in. I can die for the Storm. I can't kill myself.

Unless the implants have found a loophole.

Beads of sweat form along my brow, one trickling into the corner of my eye, stinging painfully. I disappointed the boss. I hurt my one friend. I should receive the ultimate punishment. I should die.

I don't want to die.

Kelly won't want me to die. But my death will prevent me from hurting her further.

The drawer slides open at my gentle tug. I'm aware of the contradictions in my head, the presence of some kind of malfunction. But that knowledge flickers like a faulty comp screen. My fingers wrap around the custom grip of the pistol. I fight to let go, but my fist tightens, and I'm drawing the weapon from its hiding place.

I mentally open a transmission line to Kelly, willing her to have her comm on but knowing the odds are slim. She doesn't have communications equipment embedded in her skull. My partner has to hold a physical transmitter to receive verbal messages from me.

"K-Kel," I stammer when the leave-a-message tone sounds, "I need you, Kel. I'm in trouble." I'd say more, but my mouth clamps shut against my will. Or maybe because of it. I'm never really sure anymore. The connection is cut.

If she were here, she could use my abort code. Shut me off. Whatever. We don't know how or if it will work, but it's got to be better than dying. Of course, she's not here.

I attempt a serotonin release, hoping it will calm me the fuck down. The implants don't respond to my request.

The gun is fully visible now, clutched in my hand and turning toward my face. I slip the barrel between my lips, angling it upward toward the roof of my mouth.

Oh my God.

It's not like I haven't met with failure before. It's not like I haven't considered (and discarded) the idea of suicide, either. The way I am, it's a constant companion. But something about this particularly harsh personal reprimand from the highest level has triggered this response.

My fatal error. My blue screen of death.

Where the hell is Kelly? The emotions radiating from me have to be like someone screaming in her ears, right?

Wrong. She doesn't leave her shields down when we're off duty. I suspect she never closes me off completely, but if she's worn out or asleep....

My internal display shows the cord representing my sanity. The frayed thread is about to snap.

Lovely. And a lot too late.

It breaks. My index finger pulls on the trigger. I brace for the pain of a bullet tearing through my skull. Again. In my head, I scream, pouring every ounce of emotion I can muster into the mental cry for help.

The trigger doesn't move.

My breath catches in my throat. My pulse pounds so hard, the veins in my wrist are visibly throbbing.

I stare at the unfired pistol in my hand. The safety is on.

Thank God for following weapon storage protocols.

Relief floods my body and I breathe again. An invisible barrier inside me lowers, returning control of my actions to my more rational side.

The gun drops from my numb fingers into the drawer, banging against the metal interior. Like bare feet on a morgue storage compartment. I turn the barrel away from me and shut it inside.

Too close. Too fucking close.

Or was it?

My implants record everything I do. They have to know I'd have the safety on my pistol, that I wouldn't successfully kill myself. Maybe the warning didn't come too late at all. Maybe this close call *is* the warning that even with Kelly's help, I'm slipping, and I'd better do something about it, soon. It's experimental technology with all its quirks and glitches. I wouldn't put it past the things to find this a perfectly acceptable "hint" of problems to come.

Next time, just send a damn note.

By the time the door to my quarters slides open, my emotions are locked tight, suppressors on full. Footsteps race down the short hall between the apartment's tiny living space and my bedroom. It's Kelly. She's the only one with such a light tread who has the ability to override my access codes.

She slams into my room. Too weary to turn, I glance up. In the mirror over my desk, she's pale and out of breath, wearing her pajamas, hair matted from sleep. Her eyes scan past the bed and the door to the bathroom before she locates me in the desk chair. In a second, she's at my side, hands on my shoulders, spinning the swivel seat so I face her.

"What! What happened?"

Even without empathic abilities, I can see her fear. I want... I'm not sure what I want. To hug her? To comfort her? I can't. Not with the suppressors on so high. There's another reason, too, but I'm too blocked off to go digging.

"It's over," I tell her, voice flat.

"Over? What's over? Jesus, Vick. You pulled me out of a meditation sleep. Do you have any idea how much emotional force it takes to do that? Do you?"

I don't, actually, but I can guess it would take something like, well, a suicide attempt. I say nothing. She already knows that.

Kelly swipes a hand over her eyes, then brushes her long hair back. She kneels at my feet and takes my hands in hers. Her talents push at my mind, offering herself, opening a channel, but I don't grab the lifeline. She searches my face, her brow drawn. "Let me in."

I shake my head. If I let down my defenses, despite our progress, I'll release it all at once, and judging from the dark smudges beneath her eyes, she's not ready to take that.

I won't hurt her. Not intentionally. Not again.

"Then tell me what happened. At least give me that. I haven't felt that kind of pain from you since the day we met. You scared the hell out of me."

You and me both.

When I still refuse to answer, she pulls me from my seat. "Get some clothes on," she orders. "Meet me in the hall. Keep a comm channel open between us. If it closes, if I'm not hearing you or you aren't there in five minutes, I'm coming after you." She turns to leave, presumably to get dressed herself. Her quarters are across from mine; it won't take her long.

The door closes. I open the channel with no interference. "Where are we going?" I ask, making small talk while I pull on a clean uniform.

"Out for a drink," she answers. "We both need one, and afterwards, maybe you'll talk to me."

CHAPTER 8
KELLY
HEARTS AND MINDS

Two years earlier….

VICK CORREN was complicated.

"I didn't want to say anything while we were still in the van, but…"

I glanced at Vick. In other words, what she was about to comment on she didn't want to mention in front of Mom and Dad.

"…you live in a mansion?" Vick stared at the two-story Victorian perched on a mountainside and overlooking many more. She stood halfway up the stone walk, duffel dangling at her side, my parents several paces ahead of her.

I stopped and studied the house as if looking at it through her eyes. With her enhancements, she could probably make out every minute detail. Wide, inviting porches; white curtains in the many windows; a turret that added old-style flare. Some would have described it as a mansion, though to me, it was just home.

"Psychics make a lot of money," I replied, trying to shrug it off.

"I guess so." She took a few more steps, but I caught her arm and drew her off the path.

"Come on. Guest house is out back." Most of the time I would have given a visitor the grand tour, but not Vick. She dialed down the suppressors. I didn't read curiosity from her. It was more like… fear. The house intimidated her. I found what intimidated her. Crap.

"There's more?" Her disbelief came through, a bright yellow.

"It's a good thing," I told her. "We'll have some privacy."

"Yeah." Vick cast one more look after my mother and nodded. "Any idea why she hates me so much?"

I jerked in surprise. "She doesn't—"

"Don't, Kel. Just don't. I may not be able to handle my own emotions, but I don't have to be an empath to read hers."

"Hate's too strong a word."

"Maybe." She wasn't convinced. "But I've seen friendlier looks on enemy snipers."

It was meant as a joke, but neither of us laughed, so we kept walking.

The guest house was thankfully less ostentatious—a three-room cabin Dad had built for me when I hit my troublesome adolescence and needed space from Mom. We dropped our bags in the main room, a combination living/kitchen/dining area, and I showed Vick the bedroom with its twin beds (perfect for teenager sleepovers) and the small but functional bathroom attached.

A buzzing drew us back into the living space. I answered the intercom on the wall by the front door. "Dinner's at seven," Mom announced, too cheerful.

"We'll be there." I clicked it off. The cuckoo clock over the sink in the kitchenette read five thirty.

"I'm going to grab a nap," Vick said, tossing her uniform jacket on the wooden rocking chair. "Why don't you go catch up with your folks?"

And see if you can figure out what the hell is going on went unsaid. Or, knowing Vick, it might have been something more like *See if you can figure out what I've done wrong.* She was hurt and confused and I barely held on to my anger at my mother.

I nodded and headed for the house.

MOM STOOD in the kitchen, preparing vegetables for a salad. She had a service coming in to clean twice a week, but she preferred to do the cooking herself. It had always been a hobby of hers.

She didn't waste time on preambles, but went straight for the kill shot, as Vick would have said. "Honey, you've got yourself a big problem."

My temper flared. "If you mean that I've brought a friend home, one who needs the warmth and comfort of a family, and my mother is treating her like yesterday's trash, then yes, I've got a problem. She thinks you hate her."

Mom paused the carrot slicer in midcut. "I don't hate her," she said. "I'm concerned about her. And you."

"Vick's not dangerous." I paused, rethinking that statement. "At least not to me, or you, or anyone not trying to kill her at any given moment, if that's what you're worried about." I pulled out one of the white wooden chairs and parked myself backward on it, leaning my arms on the backrest. It was a habit I'd picked up from the soldiers—a remarkably comfortable position.

"You really have no idea, do you?" Mom wagged a carrot at me. "I could sense it from the moment I saw the two of you together. You've bonded."

"Well, of course we've bonded. We're frie—" I stopped. "Wait. *Bonded*, bonded? Empathically bonded? That's a myth." A ridiculous one—that an empath could become emotionally tied to a nonempath if they shared their feelings too frequently wasn't strange, but the idea that they couldn't *undo* that tie? That they'd be forced into an intimacy neither wanted? Ludicrous.

Mom put the vegetables aside and wiped her hands on a red-checkered dishtowel. "Then how do you explain the attraction? And don't tell me I'm making that up too. Your walls are down, presumably for *her*, and I know romantic feelings when I sense them, even if I'm not as strong as you."

Romantic. No. We worked together. I was barely past being her therapist. I—

I was lying to myself.

Was I attracted to Vick? Strong, brave, loyal....

I'd sat on the sidelines, studying her grace and beauty. I'd held her as she filled me with a stunning array of emotions reaching depths most humans couldn't touch.

My mind went to the dark-haired fantasy lover I'd imagined, the one I never allowed to have a face or a name. But she was female. Every time.

Oh....

God, I'd been so blind, so focused on her emotions, I hadn't considered my own. Looking back, I thought I'd cared for her since she first poured her soul into mine. I went and stood beside my mother and stole a cucumber slice from her salad serving bowl. "Whether I have those feelings or not, it doesn't mean there's some mythical bond forcing things."

"Hah." My mother stabbed the air with her index finger, like she won a point in some imaginary sparring contest. I hated it when she did that. "You've never preferred women. Where did that come from?"

Hmm. After the failed attempt in the shuttleport, I didn't want to try to read her again. Still, I didn't detect any prejudice in expression or voice, just a forthright question. I gave a forthright answer. "I've never preferred anyone, so there's no basis for judgment." In high school, and then at the Academy, a few classmates of both sexes expressed interest in dating me. But as an empath, I could read their motivations. My gifts intrigued them. Nothing else.

All psychics knew the rumors about an empath's skills in bed. I had no intention of sleeping with someone just to satisfy his or her curiosity.

A shiver ran through me when I considered what sex with Vick might be like: our minds open to each other, sensitive to every emotional shift and physical sensation. Apparently *my* curiosity was an entirely different matter. I put my walls up, hoping Mom didn't pick up the sudden surge of excitement, but by her smirk, I knew she had. Maybe the bond existed after all. A 91 percent brainwave match between me and Vick had to have some effect.

Mom grabbed the knife off the counter, slamming it down on the head of lettuce with renewed gusto. "So you want her. A soldier. Someone who kills people for a living. And with the bond you have no choice."

So, two separate concerns.

"There's always a choice. And she's not an assassin," I muttered, but it went unheard.

"Have you felt it? Have you felt death?"

I'd felt it. So had she. Mom was there when Grandma died. It nearly killed her.

Oh. She was trying to protect me.

Vick had to kill four people in my presence on our missions so far. One was her objective. Self-defense caused the others. It hurt. A lot. But not in the same way it would have if I'd actually known them. And Vick's pain and guilt afterward hurt a lot more.

I took one step and wrapped my arms around my mother. She placed the knife carefully on the counter, turned in my embrace, and hugged me back. Her heavy sigh ruffled my hair.

"I'm okay, Mom," I told her. "I can handle this. And Vick needs me."

"But how does she feel about you?"

I analyzed the traces of softer emotions I'd felt from Vick over the past six months. Detecting them proved difficult, buried so deep under anger and pain, and even harder to isolate. There was definitely sexual frustration, though. Tons of it. The tension drove me empathically crazy on a regular basis. And as for her preferences, well, she'd dated Devin, which might not have boded well for me. I'd also heard rumors she'd had female lovers before the accident changed how she related to everyone for almost a year. "I'm not sure," I admitted.

Holding me at arms' length, Mom said, "Then it may be time you found out. Before things become more… intense… between you. Before the bond gets stronger. Any relationship you have should be your *choice*, not a byproduct of your empathy."

Before I got hurt or we slept together. Right.

She shook her head at my blush. "I'm not talking about sex. I'm talking about dependency. Legends often have a foundation in reality, Kelly, and if this one is to be believed, you won't be able to function without each other. In her profession, that could be fatal."

For which one of us?

"If she does care for you, if you choose to pursue it, you'll both have to be careful. Very careful."

She returned to her cooking. The smell of roast pork flowed from the primary oven when she opened it to check. Yeast rolls rose in the smaller oven above the first. My mouth was watering when I left the room.

Dad hovered in the hallway, just outside the kitchen entrance. He took me by the arm and pulled me into the den across the way. Then he shut the door, closing us inside, and turned to me, a solemn expression on his normally jovial face.

"For what it's worth," he said, hands on my shoulders, "I don't care where or how happiness finds you, so long as it does. Vick seems like a fine woman. A brave soldier with strong moral values. You admire and respect her, which is how things should be. Despite your mother's concerns, I know you'll be careful, and I believe Vick when she says it's her job to protect you. You're grown now, and I have faith in your ability to take care of yourself. I wish you all the best."

I wrapped my arms around him, leaning my head on his chest, the familiar smell of his aftershave and shampoo taking me back to my childhood. "Thanks, Dad. That's worth a lot."

Now, how did I broach that subject with Vick?

CHAPTER 9
VICK
QUESTIONS OF CHARACTER

Two years later....

I AM... so confused.

Kelly sits across from me in the booth, a frou-frou pink concoction on the sticky table in front of her. Half the clientele laughed at her when she ordered it. Soldiers make up the majority of the patrons at Girard Moon Base's Alpha Dog Pub, and they don't go in for fruity drinks with little umbrellas stuck in them. I wonder where the hell the bartender found that umbrella, anyway.

I'm nursing a Crater Ale, made in a local brewery where they don't use the gravity generators. Hype says the lower-g makes for better carbonation. I think it's bullshit, but it's smooth and tastes good, and given the jitters lingering in my stomach, it's a better choice than whiskey.

I can't get drunk. The implants won't allow it. They'll let me mellow out, but if I go overboard, they'll force my body to metabolize the alcohol faster. I can, however, make myself good and sick if I chug the hard stuff. A couple of benders after rough missions taught me that much. And that's the last thing I need tonight.

My internal display shows me dancing around with a lampshade on my head. I shake the image away. Kelly waits, taking intermittent sips and watching me. She knows sooner or later, I'll talk.

She's never wrong.

I swallow hard and focus on my beer, the table, the tribute pictures of fallen comrades decorating the metal walls. I search out Stephen and Devin from the file of my own accident, the one I'm only allowed to know pieces of, but as always, where the pain of their loss should be, there's only an empty pit in my stomach. I study their faces, digging and digging for a human response that won't come. Anything not to look at Kelly. "You know that image I told you about, the one with the five threads my implants like to show me?"

From the corner of my eye, I see her nod. She's familiar with my implants' quirks. It's one of many things she's had to help me with—translating the crazy metaphors and symbols.

"One of the threads snapped."

Her hands tighten around her thick glass until the knuckles go white, but her tone is calm. "What do you think that means?"

I sigh. "I think I'm losing it, Kel. Not that you haven't done a helluva job, given what you had to work with," I rush to add. I don't want her feeling responsible, blaming herself. Without her, I would have lost it long ago. "I just don't think anyone can fix me."

"Maybe if I take a hammer to your head," she growls. She rests her hand on the table, accidentally placing it in a spill of beer or... something, and shakes it off, then swipes it on her uniform trousers. "You're not a machine, Vick. And I'm not 'fixing' you. I'm helping you compensate. I'm providing an outlet. Why don't you think it's working?"

I glance around the pub's interior. It's crowded tonight. Not a lot of action happening in the solar system. Not a lot of troops deployed. Recent peace talks have gone far in ending the eco-wars on Earth.

So everyone's out and about the base, and the pub is wall-to-wall uniforms. Many are ours, but there are a few rival mercenary organizations in the mix along with official sanctioned military types. We don't do well together, and I keep one eye on the crowd. I have to raise my voice over the noisy conversation, but I don't want anyone except Kelly to hear me.

She picks up on my concerns. "Don't worry," she assures me, leaning in to be heard. "They're caught up in their own worlds. No one is listening in. Go on, Vick."

I tell her about my overblown response to the reprimand. As I recount the details, the emotions pile up inside me, one on top of another, building and building with nowhere to go. But when she reaches for my hand, I won't let her touch me. Instead, I lift my beer bottle to my lips and take a long swallow. It's empty when I put it down.

"And that's it. I'm officially insane."

"I don't think so," Kelly says. She steeples her fingers beneath her chin. "Don't get me wrong. I'm worried. Really worried. You've been pushing yourself too hard. The twelve-story jump and shooting Rodwell took their toll. And Oz is an asshole to send you that message. The mission will go in your record as successful, regardless of your indiscretions. But I believe you're right about the snapped thread being a warning. If you were truly crazy, the whole cord would be broken, not just one thread."

"Give it time," I mutter.

I don't expect her to hear that, but she does. "I intend to," she responds. "Time off. I'll put in for it first thing tomorrow. You need some, both to recover from the last job and get yourself together after what happened in your quarters just now. You must have been so scared."

Normally I'd bristle at a comment like that. Tonight, not so much. "Still am," I tell her.

Her eyebrows rise. She knows what an admission like that costs me. Fear and I are old friends, but with the exception of my release sessions with Kelly, I never show it. And I damn well never admit to it out loud.

Unless I think I'm in immediate danger.

One thing I notice. She doesn't say "suicide attempt." Neither did I when I gave my recounting. I laid out the events; she listened. We aren't using those words.

"Still, you've been in worse situations. I'm not convinced those were the only triggers." Kelly cocks her head to one side, examining me. I almost sense the tendrils of her gift trying to work past my suppressors, but it can't. If I have a major breakdown, she'll feel that, but right now she's getting next to nothing. I've left out the nightmare on purpose. It's creepy and weird and makes her out to be my enemy. I don't want to send that message. Not now. Not ever. Not to my only friend.

She's not so pale anymore. The alcohol is doing its thing and adding a healthier flush to her cheeks. Her full lips are pursed as she loses herself in thought. She's beautiful even in the drab tan uniform.

Sudden anger roils up inside me. One hand clenches on the table's edge.

"Vick?" She feels it too. It's that strong. So strong my vision tinges with red. "Breathe, Vick. Work through it."

I follow her instructions, closing my eyes and taking deep, even breaths. The rage recedes. When I can focus once more, I look at her.

"What *was* that?" she asks.

I shake my head. "No idea."

"Has it happened before?"

"No, but it hit like the depression did earlier." I wave to the bartender, holding up one finger and then pointing to my empty bottle. He nods in acknowledgment. My hand is shaking. I tuck it in my lap.

"You can't let the implants have more control over you than you do over your emotions. You know what could happen," Kelly reminds me.

I could lose what little free will I have left. Yeah, I know.

"You've got to let me help you release the emotional buildup," she continues. "If nothing else, I need to feel what you're feeling, all of it. I can't analyze the bits and pieces I'm reading."

I manage a smile. "Not until you've slept." Risks to myself be damned. "I'm not pulling you out of emotion shock again. Once was enough." My beer arrives. I mumble a thanks and lift it to my lips.

Kelly frowns. "I'm fine. Tougher than you think. Always have been. You don't have to protect me. I'm—"

"Hey, cutie!" A shadow falls over us, blocking out the shaded lamps hanging from the metal ceiling. The source places meaty palms flat on the table's surface and leans in, carrying with him odors of sweat, liquor, and cloying cologne. He's wearing an all-black uniform with red piping down the sleeves and trouser legs and a sunburst patch on one bicep—a Sunfire merc.

We don't like them.

My hand slips to my thigh where my holster and pistol should be but aren't. Not that I'm trigger-happy or anything, but having my weapon would reassure me a lot. I left it in my quarters, both out of deference to Kelly and because I didn't trust myself carrying a gun just yet. Where was my paranoia when I needed it?

"You're interrupting a private conversation," Kelly says. I can't imagine what kind of vibes he's giving off to her, but she looks ready to throw up.

"Nothing's private in here." Sunfire shoves his way onto the bench seat next to her, Kelly pressing herself as close to the wall as she can to avoid contact.

I don't want to start a fight. I'm neither armed nor up to it. But I'm not tolerating much more of this. The rage growls low and deep in my throat. I swallow hard.

"Vick, don't." Kelly's reading me loud and clear now. Her eyes plead with me to calm down.

I'm not sure I can. I take a sip of beer, concentrating on the strength of my grip so I don't shatter the bottle.

Sunfire clearly misses her warning. He sits up straight in the booth, his expression one of sudden revelation, as if he's just thought of something clever, maybe for the first time in his life. "Hey, you know what you get when you mix the Sun with the Storm?" He turns to Kelly. "Rainbows. You get fucking rainbows. How about you and me go back to my quarters and make some rainbows of our own, cutie?"

That has to be the worst pickup line I've ever heard.

It's laughable, and it breaks through my anger as I sputter my mouthful of beer. Kelly's laughing too. She tries to hide it behind her hand, but a couple of strangled chuckles work their way through, then a few more, until she has mirthful tears leaking from the corners of her eyes.

I love it when she laughs. It's too rare a thing these days, and it gives her an innocence I know I've taken away.

The Sunfire, however, is not amused. "You think I'm funny?" He grabs Kelly by the upper arm, sliding her across the bench seat until she's pressed to his side. The other hand cups the back of her head, forcing her face up toward his.

Next thing any of us knows, Kelly's free, Sunfire's grabbing his skull, my beer bottle is in pieces scattered across the floor and table, and I'm on my feet, fists clenched.

"What the fuck!" Sunfire yells. Blood mats his blond hair where I hit him.

"Get out of her way," I order, voice low. I'm all ice now, no heat. He doesn't move. The rest of the Alpha Dog has fallen silent, patrons and staff holding their collective breath to see where this leads. I draw back a fist.

Kelly's on the bench, then scrambling over the table to climb out the other side of the booth and get to me. She wraps both hands around my arm and pulls it down to my side. "It's okay, Vick. I'm here. I'm fine. It's okay." She darts a glance at some of the soldiers moving closer, all dark uniforms. All Sunfires. Our own people hang on the periphery, in no hurry to rush to our defense.

No, *my* defense. They'll do it for Kelly, if she's in real danger, but not for me. Kelly's the only one in the pub who's on my side.

"Hey, hey, let's all calm down here." One of the Sunfires, even larger than the one I'm facing, steps into my peripheral vision. On him, the uniform stretches and strains like it can barely contain his muscles. He's got a full mug of ale in one hand and uses the other to swipe through his bright red hair. "We don't need any trouble." To his buddy he mutters, "Hal, probation, remember? One more fine and you're out." The newcomer must have just arrived. He's sober—a good thing for all of us.

"She hit me with a fucking bottle!"

"He manhandled my friend," I return.

Hal blinks at first me, then Kelly, as if seeing us for the first time. I know where his mind goes before he opens his mouth. "Oooh, sorry. Didn't realize I was invading your territory."

I don't know why his mistaken observation sends rage coursing through me.

My implants show me the sanity cord. A second thread is fraying.

It's the last thing I see before I head-butt Hal and the fight is on.

CHAPTER 10
KELLY
ONE NIGHT, ONE WEEK, ONE LIFETIME

Two years earlier....

VICK CORREN was mine.

After staying a while longer to chat with Dad, I came back to an empty cabin, both twin beds still made, Vick's duffel gone.

Dammit. I should have known, but Mom had me so frazzled, I didn't register anything else. She'd said Mom hated her. She'd turned on her suppressors. She said she was going to take a nap.

Vick never took naps.

I grabbed a set of keys off the peg by the door. I'd practically lived in the guest cabin from the start of high school to graduation, and the keys had hung there since I left for the Academy. I prayed as I ran for the little storage building out back that my bike was still there, charged up, and in working order.

Vick had a good head start on me. I assumed she'd make for the shuttleport, ten miles away, but she could have gone anywhere. She was upset and in unfamiliar territory—a bad combination.

We'd worked together for months. She'd stabilized well enough to work in the field, go a day or two without an emotion purge. But emotional challenges meant more frequent needs for release. Alone, with me, she still had breakdowns. If she had one way out here....

Nerves made me fumble the keys, and it took two tries to fit the right one in the shed's lock. The slatted metal door creaked open, dumping years of dust and cobwebs on my head. I hated spiders, and I should have shrieked and flailed, wondering if the webs had owners, but I focused on the tarp in the center of the storage space and the bulky form beneath it.

I yanked the tarp off and tossed it aside, then mounted the yellow hoverbike, jammed the key into the ignition, and gave it a kick-start.

Nothing.

The power indicator on the dash glowed green. I kicked again. Still nothing.

My eyes went to a yellow flashing light. It had been years since I rode the thing. What the hell did that mean?

At a loss, I ran a hand through my hair and froze, then gave myself a mental slap. Twisting on the seat, I snagged the helmet from its hook on the rear bumper and slammed it onto my head. The visor came down to just below my eyes, plunging me into dimness.

I kicked the bike a third time. The yellow light went out. The sensors registered my safety precautions were in place and it started. The bike rose three feet off the ground and idled, engine running soft and smooth. Someone had been maintaining it in my absence.

Thanks, Dad.

I blasted down the walkway, then the drive, and turned through the gates into the street. It was dinnertime, so no traffic. Wouldn't have seen much anyway, with the house on its isolated hill, and I zoomed along at a fast clip.

The rain started again, and I was glad I didn't have a wheeled vehicle. I'd have skidded all over the place on the slick mountain roads. The visor kept the drops out of my eyes, but water dripped from my cheeks. My soaked clothes clung to me, sending chills through my body and goose bumps rising on my flesh.

God help me if she didn't head for the port.

My senses ran on high, walls down, open to everything. In one farmhouse I passed, people argued. The owners of the tourist-trap gas station emitted greed. Reds and browns made it hard to see the road. Sickness filled another home—summer flu—and I choked on a mouthful of bile, spitting it out to the side. I could have crashed, operating a vehicle like that. I broke every rule, ignoring everything the Academy had taught me, including common sense.

I flew a couple of miles and downshifted to change course, try another direction, when I felt Vick. Her emotions slammed into me before I saw her—disappointment, self-loathing, resignation. There was no time to get my walls up, and I wrenched the handlebars hard to the right, nearly flipping the bike before I regained control of both it and me.

Reducing speed, I eased forward, and she came into view, shoulders hunched against the rain, dark hair dripping down her back, her duffel thrown over one shoulder. I pulled up and turned sharp, cutting her off. The bike settled to the ground. I tossed my helmet to the side, swung off the seat, and stood in front of her, hands on my hips.

"You," I said, "are an idiot."

Vick stared at me for a long moment, expression unreadable. Then she nodded slowly. "Wouldn't be the first time." I realized with a sudden start that she turned off her suppressors. They were supposed to be off, but under the circumstances I figured she would have used them. No, she *wanted* me to find her, or at least hoped I would, if I cared enough. "Probably won't be the last," she added with a half grin.

One step, two, and then I embraced her, and the water running down my face wasn't just rain—which stopped at last, fading into a drizzly mist. She was all right. I shoved away images of her, broken and bloody—memories of when we'd first met.

"You shouldn't have left. I needed to clear a few things up with my mother. That's all." I pressed against her soaking wet uniform. Her arms closed around my shoulders.

"I've lost my family, assuming I ever had one to begin with. Didn't want to screw things between you and yours."

"You're part of my family," I told her. "When I'm away from home, you're the only family I have."

She held me away from her. "So…?"

I sensed her hesitation, her disbelief that things were resolved, her desire to come back with me.

Oh God, how did I put this?

I took a deep breath, let it out. "My mother," I began, searching for the right words, knowing the wrong ones could ruin everything. "She thinks… there's a bond between us, because of the empathic sharing, because of the brainwave match. Who knows?"

Vick nodded. That wasn't the hard part.

"She thinks I'm attracted to you because of it, that I'm being forced into it, and she's afraid you'll hurt me." The simple statement tumbled out in a rush. My face heated. I stared down at my shoes to avoid looking at her.

Vick's hands on my shoulders went still. "And are you attracted to me?" she asked, all seriousness.

"Yes," I whispered. "I am."

"Do you care why?"

"No." I was certain of that.

"Okay." She stood quiet for a long time, and I panicked that I'd misread, misjudged. The few moments I thought maybe…. Her complexity confounded readings, and with the damage, I could have been wrong. If wrong, I'd potentially destroyed our partnership, our friendship. If premature, I'd ruined any chance of things developing later. I was so caught up in my own feelings, I couldn't read hers at all.

There was nothing for it but to ask. "Vick, you have to tell me how you feel." I hated the pleading note in my tone, but I couldn't help it. All along, I'd been the one helping her. Now I needed her guidance.

Vick laughed, and it was beautiful. "You mean you don't know?"

"Pain and anger and frustration, they block out the positive emotions, the softer ones."

Vick nodded. She had so many of those harder feelings. And I was still new to all of this.

"I'm… I'm overwhelmed," I admitted.

She leaned down, tilting my head up with one hand beneath my chin. Her lips met mine, and I was lost—lost in her emotions and my emotions, and the world faded away. She shook with the effort to hold back. I picked up that she would have preferred to crush me to her, devour me whole. But instead, it was gentle, her kiss, gentler than I would have expected, and nervous and shy, words I never would have used to describe Vick. But they were all part of her, and me, and both of us, and—

A car passed, honking its horn. A couple of young guys leaned out the windows, whistling and hooting. Vick pulled away with a regretful smile.

"I can't promise I won't hurt you, you know," she said. "I'm screwed up. And you know what I do. One way or another, I'm going to cause you pain. I know I already have. All I can promise is to try not to do it too often."

I thought of my mother's warnings. But in the face of Vick's love…. It *was* love, not just physical attraction, although I detected plenty of that, too, and I suppressed a shiver of anticipation for what the night might bring. Now that I knew what to look for, the desire flared bright and clear.

"I'll take the risk." The shiver worked its way free, born of excitement and the chill of being rain-soaked on a cool mountain evening.

Vick's brow drew in concern and she tugged me toward the bike. "Let's get back to your parents' place before you turn blue." She ran a hand over the bright yellow chassis. "Never figured you for the hoverbike type, but if you were going to have one, it would be this color."

I giggled, and Vick looked like I'd just given her a precious gift. I'd have been happy to go into regular hysterics to see that expression on her face all the time. "You wanna drive?" I offered, grabbing the keys from the ignition and dangling them in front of her.

Her eyes lit up further, a real credit to their designers that they could convey so much emotion, and she snatched them from my hand before I could change my mind. I plunked my yellow helmet onto her head. The color was ridiculous on her, but she didn't seem to care. She climbed aboard, and I swung on behind her, wrapping my arms around her waist and leaning my head against her back.

"Hang tight," she said, and we hurtled over the windy roads toward the house.

She was in her element, wind whipping our faces, the bike hugging the curves. "You've done this before," I shouted to be heard over the engine.

"Maybe. Feels right. Don't remember it, though."

Muscle memory, succeeding where mental memory had failed. As the house came into sight and we pulled around to the cabin, I wondered what else her muscles remembered, and the warmth crept into my cheeks once more.

"Let me store the bike and let Mom know we'll be late for dinner. Why don't you grab a shower?"

Vick glanced down at her soaked uniform, the pant legs spattered with mud from passing wheeled vehicles. She shivered and my body responded in sympathy. A hot shower would do us both some good. "Right." She strolled inside as if nothing had occurred between us, but under the calm exterior, I sensed anticipation and fierce desire—no barriers there now. She completely opened to me. I thought, given the option, she would have dragged me inside the cabin and torn off my clothes.

I ran to the house, left Mom a quick apology note, and sneaked a few things from the linen closet. The sound of running water carried from the bathroom as I stepped inside the cabin.

Vick's desire slammed into me, burning, driving. I staggered from the force of her intense need. Shivers crawled across my back and down both legs, and I realized she stood in a cold shower, not a hot one, trying to calm herself, I suspected.

Despite a fluttering of my own nerves, I knew without question we needed to stop this from building any further. By the time Vick emerged wearing nothing but a towel, I'd moved an end table, shoved the two twin beds together, and made them up as a king.

"Shower's all yours," Vick said. She took in the new decor. "Nice work." But a tinge of trepidation hid beneath the words. She stood rigid, like she was afraid to take a step forward.

"Too fast? I didn't mean to assume, but I felt…." I looked down at the rough wood floor, unsure of what to do or say and way outside my comfort zone.

Vick blew out an aggravated breath and plopped onto the foot of the bed. Her fists clenched in the thick blankets. "No, it's good. I'm just… I'm not sure I can control…."

Oh. Now I understood. I grabbed a towel from the shelf just inside the bathroom door, spread it on the comforter so my wet clothes wouldn't soak the bed, and sat beside her. Reaching over, I took one of her hands in both of mine. "You'll be fine. We'll figure it out." I studied her for a moment, letting her emotions run through me. Arousal warred with frustration. A *lot* of frustration.

"When was the last time you, you know?" Without meaning to, my gaze fell to her lap, jerked to her chest, then away from her suddenly very amused expression.

Vick took pity on me and didn't laugh. "Not a clue," she admitted. "I'm no virgin. My medical records tell me that much. But I have no memory…."

I tamped down on my own anger. Of course Dr. Whitehouse wouldn't let her keep a memory like that. Not when he could choose something important. Like hoverbike driving.

My brain mulled it all over. It had been more than a year since her accident, and six months since I began working with her. I wasn't aware of any relationships she'd had since then. I doubted she'd have been emotionally ready for one prior to now. Hell, *we* weren't ready for one prior to now. I would never have pursued this so long as she was still technically my patient. Now I was just her partner. Any lingering ethics be damned.

And I was sure she hadn't been with anyone. I'd have known about it.

It had been over a year since Devin. But surely…?

"You've, um, taken care of things on your own, though, right?" Not really my business, but the better I understood all the frustration and its source, the better I could help her.

I'd never seen Vick blush before, and she did it spectacularly, going red from where the towel hid the tops of her breasts all the way up to her hairline. "Um, no." She fixed me with a pointed gaze. I was supposed to be getting something there. Something so obvious I would kick myself when I figured it— Oh.

Oh holy hell.

I was the reason she hadn't satisfied her sexual needs, the reason she was so overwhelmed she was practically ready to explode and had to hold herself in check.

If she'd touched herself, I would have felt it. I would have known exactly who and when and how. Yeah, that would have been awkward for both of us.

That kind of abstinence in the constant presence of someone you wanted would have been hard for anyone to deal with. For someone with her emotional issues, well, only torture could describe it. Emotion defined sex. She bottled her emotions up inside. And mixed in with all the other more painful ones, I missed that, right along with her specific feelings for me.

Not an exact science, I reminded myself. Not even close.

"We'll figure it out," I said again. "Let me get a shower, warm up. You try to relax." I pushed her backward and she scooted up on the bed to lie down on top of the blankets.

"Easy for you to say," she grumbled.

No, really, it wasn't. I wanted her too. And I needed time to wrap my head around what we were about to do. I couldn't help her if I couldn't control myself. I didn't look behind me as I headed for the bathroom. If I did, I'd have never gotten that shower.

CHAPTER 11
VICK
VENTING

Two years later….

I AM a fighter.

While Hal staggers backward, his friend shakes his head and steps out of the way, giving in to the inevitable. I place a hand on the top of Kelly's head and shove her down. "Under the table."

She grimaces at me. "Do you really have to do this?"

Judging from the angry expressions all around me and the couple of guys blocking our way to the exit, it's out of my hands now. "Don't argue. Get under the fucking table."

Kelly frowns but complies, knees landing in the puddle and glass from the beer bottle I broke. Massive arms wrap around my torso, dragging me away from her and toward the center of the pub. I could struggle, but the farther from my partner we are when we do this, the better. Uninvolved patrons scramble out of our way, knocking over chairs, a table, and more glassware.

In a few seconds, I'm standing in a circle of five Sunfires, including Hal—who bleeds profusely from a broken nose. The Storm soldiers hang off to the side, apparently taking bets. I wonder what kind of odds I'm getting. Alex and Lyle are among them. They must have just come in. Alex takes a step toward me, but Lyle holds him back. Asshole.

"Just you and me," Hal says, stepping into the center with me.

Much better.

Until Hal pulls a knife. Just because I'm not armed doesn't mean everyone else isn't. We don't normally carry company weapons on Girard Base, but personal ones are another matter. Any other night I'd have something small and concealable: a knife, a pocket stunner. Not tonight.

The bartender shouts he's called in law enforcement. I'm familiar with the Girard Base cops—good people for the most part, not as well trained as mercs but equipped to handle most situations, only they're stretched pretty thin. It'll be a while before they arrive. In the meantime, Hal takes a swipe at me.

He catches my jacket sleeve with the tip of the blade, tearing a long, jagged slice in the fabric, and I'm pissed. Replacement uniforms come out of my pay, most of which is still going toward my two-and-a-half-year-old medical bills and will be for the foreseeable future. Just one more joy of being labeled as property.

"Nice, fair fight, huh?" I can handle Hal's knife, but I shouldn't have to. A couple of Storm guys move in. They don't like the imbalance, either.

"I recognize you now. You're that VC1 thing," Hal snarls, his speech a little mushy with the broken nose.

"What of it?"

"The Storm promotes you like some kind of super soldier. I shouldn't be any trouble for you, right?" He snorts, bubbles of blood popping from both nostrils. His buddies join in the general merriment. "Load of crap. Your people want our bosses to buy into the hardware."

The Storm advertises my skills? And the tech is for sale? Unless major advances have been made, I can't imagine Whitehouse trying to sell it. Gotta be some kind of misunderstanding. But Hal's right about one thing. He shouldn't be any trouble.

"I'll have to tell them not to waste their money. A super soldier wouldn't let herself get surrounded."

I take in the circle of soldiers, members of the Storm taking up positions beside and behind the Sunfires. A smile curls the corners of my lips. "I haven't." Maybe my comrades won't defend me in a fistfight, but they won't stand by and watch me get sliced, no matter how much they dislike me.

Well, good for them.

Bleary-eyed drunk, Hal takes in the new situation, the first hint of concern working its way through the alcohol haze.

I turn inward, adjusting my suppressors to full, then jolting myself with an adrenaline boost. I'm ice-cold outside, restrained chaos within.

"Vick?" Kelly calls from beneath the table.

I spare her a quick glance.

"Try not to kill him, please?"

Right. No killing. I'll do my best. Kelly doesn't need any more stress tonight.

Hal tries bravado with his buddies. "You hear that, guys? She's not supposed to kill me." He waves the knife around for emphasis.

"Put it down," Lyle says, low and even. "Cops are coming. Don't start something bigger than you really want." Driver, yes. Pilot, absolutely. Bar brawler, definitely not. I'm probably the only one with good enough optic enhancements to see Lyle's hand shake, but the tremor is there.

Storm outnumbers Sunfire by two to one, and some of Hal's own guys are encouraging him to give up or at least put the blade away. Most of them don't want an all-out brawl either.

"Just leave it to the two of us," I say to the others. "Don't get involved unless I go down." No point in everyone getting arrested.

The rest of the pub falls silent, though there's a clinking of coins and a rustle of more paper bills between the mercenaries on both sides.

Hal closes in. I remind myself this isn't a random thug but a well-trained rival merc—not as high-priced or sought after as a member of the Fighting Storm but up there. Rumor has it they work for slavers, drug runners—anyone who can pay. Like most other mercenary organizations, I suppose, and I'm glad not to be part of one of those.

After my memory loss, I suppose they could have made me anything.

I drop into analysis mode, my implants calculating distances and trajectories. I project when Hal will reach me and how he will strike, based upon his position and posture. When the attack comes, it's another attempt to slice me, but I dance beyond his reach.

Every swing, every kick, I'm never where he expects me to be. While I dodge the knife again, he does manage to land a punch in my ribs that cracks at least one—probably the same one I bruised on my way down the building.

I suck in a painful breath, hearing Kelly's echoing cry. She's open to me. I need to get off the defensive and end this.

A second skirmish erupts on the sidelines; it was only a matter of time. A bottle sails past my head and shatters against a table. Lyle kicks

one Sunfire in the balls while Alex takes up a defensive stance in front
of Kelly.

I lash out with my foot, the arch of my military-grade reinforced
boot connecting with Hal's knee and hyperextending it. He goes down
with a pained grunt. A heavy wooden chair crashes across my back,
breaking into pieces that splinter to the floor. At the same time, Hal
rises on his good knee. My implants shoot me a warning, and instead of
shaking off the chair's blow, I let the impact throw me forward, a split
second before Hal throws his blade at my chest.

It misses me and embeds itself in a Sunfire's throat—the same one
who'd tried to stop the fight in the first place.

"Fuck!" Hal dives and grabs for his friend as he falls, both of them
crumpling in slow motion. "Diego? Don't do this, man."

The brawl screeches to an immediate halt.

I stand, panting, each breath agony through my rib cage. The
Sunfire who swung the chair hovers at my shoulder, fists clenched, but a
glance confirms he's not focused on me.

Diego's as good as dead, even if his heart is still pumping. His
chest rises and falls, his hands grasping at the blade that's severed his
carotid artery and his trachea and protrudes through the back of his
neck. Blood pools around him, mixing with alcohol, glass, and wood
shards.

"Get a doctor in here! Any of you guys medics?" Hal casts a
desperate look around the pub. He gets nothing but shaking heads in
return.

I'm glad no one's exchanging money now.

Medical staff doesn't tend to hang with the fighter-types, Kelly
being the exception only because of me. Wouldn't matter anyway. Diego
can't breathe and he's bleeding out. At this point, nothing can stop it.

Even as I think it, Diego gives one last wheezing gasp and goes still,
taking the traces of my anger with him into death. I'm numb, standing
there, and it's not just my suppressors making me so. Hal shouts and
curses. The guy beside me mutters a soft prayer.

Kelly moans.

With the immediate threat past, Alex and Lyle have moved aside,
so I have a clear view of my partner. She's crumpled beneath the
table, face buried in her hands, her whole body slumping against the
bench seat. I'm heading for her when four newcomers burst through

the set of wooden swinging doors—ambiance decor to hide the ever-present airlock.

The authorities have arrived.

"Everybody just stay where you are," the first blue-uniformed cop orders, gun drawn. I freeze halfway to Kelly.

His three companions, two men and a woman, approach and take in the scene while he covers us.

"I need to help my friend, Officer... Sanderson," I say to the female, after a quick check of her name badge. She's a tall buzz-cut blonde with defined muscles showing through a too tight shirt, though I get the sense of brains as well as brawn, as she quietly gives orders to the others over her chin mic. One of the males kneels by Diego, assessing his condition.

Sanderson casts a glance at Kelly but shakes her head. "Nobody's moving until we take statements. Besides, this guy needs help more, if you've got medical skills." Sanderson nods toward Diego.

"Some," I acknowledge, and I'd use them, too, enemy or not, if they would have helped. "He's beyond them."

Another round of curses from the knife thrower as the other officer shakes his head at Sanderson, confirming the death.

Her eyes go from the dead man to rake over my disheveled appearance. "Your work?" She lingers on my own name patch (which reads Vick Corren, not VC1) and the tear in my sleeve. "Storms and Fires never mix well."

Actually, storms put out fires, but I don't correct her.

"Seems that way," I agree, trying for amiable, though I could count on one hand the number of bar brawls I've been in over the past two years. I usually save fighting for the field. "But I didn't kill him." If I had, it would have been much quicker and cleaner.

She looks to the other patrons, those who wear neither Storm nor Fire uniforms, and gets grudging nods. "Fair enough. You're all still going in for questioning. You know the drill."

"I know it." And I'm not arguing. It won't do Kelly any good. I lean heavily on the closest upright chair, the adrenaline wearing off and my ribs aching. "But if you could have someone give her a sedative or something, when the medics finally get here? She's an empath."

Sanderson's head turns from Kelly, huddled and sobbing, to the dead body, and back again. Understanding dawns. "I'll see to it."

"Thank you."

I let her cuff me, though I ask permission to sit down until they're ready to haul us to the detention facility, and she gives it with a sympathetic smile. I suspect she's been in one or two nasty bar brawls herself.

While I wait, the medics arrive and inject Kelly with something that dulls the emotional onslaught, reducing her to a blank, hopeless stare that tears my heart out. I barely notice when they give me a painkiller and seal my broken ribs.

At no point will Kelly look at me. I'm not sure if she's in shock or what, but it hurts.

Not my fault, I want to tell her. I didn't start it, and I didn't kill him. She has to have seen that. I'm sure she was watching, even with Alex standing guard over her. But as the security team finally hauls me to my feet and leads me away behind the other Storms and Sunfires, with Hal and Diego's body on stretchers, I know she blames me.

And I blame myself.

In my internal display, the second thread snaps.

CHAPTER 12
KELLY
STORM BEFORE THE CALM

Two years earlier....

VICK CORREN was conflicted.

I emerged from the cabin's bathroom in a white fluffy towel and approached the bed where Vick lay. If anything, she looked more tense than she did when I left: jaw set, hands clenched at her sides, eyes shut, head sunk into the thick down pillows.

Nervous knots twisted my insides, but one of us had to do something. I sat beside her, my weight making a slight depression in the mattress, the bedsprings creaking in faint protest. She had to know I was there.

"Vick?" I said softly. I stroked my fingertips down her arm.

She sucked in a sharp, hissing breath, my empathic skills telling me this was pleasure, not pain, a flash of aqua tingeing my vision like a blue-green corona. My body's answering response stunned me. Goose bumps flared from my elbow to my shoulder.

"Well, that's... interesting," I murmured. Of course, I was familiar with all the empath sex stories. How intensity of intimacy with an empath doubled for both parties. And Mom and I had "the talk" which went well beyond what most mothers explained to their daughters. But reality....

It made sense, and it was why I never slept with any of the curiosity seekers. Since it was more pleasurable for both parties, a lot of empaths were promiscuous. I wanted more than great sex.

We even explored the possibilities in a clinical manner through my Empathic Relationships course. The textbooks never prepared me for this.

"You seem surprised." Vick's voice drew me from my thoughts, her eyes wide open. "You have done this before, right?"

I considered lying to her, but that would have been unfair. She couldn't lie to me. "No. When I said we'd figure this out, I literally meant *we*."

She frowned, pushing herself up on her elbows. The towel slipped, revealing her breasts, and I was drawn to them, reaching for the already erect nipples. She caught my hands in hers.

"This isn't right," Vick muttered, though I knew her heart wasn't in her words. Her grip trembled, but she plowed on. "Your first time… it should be slow and gentle. I don't think I can be either one right now."

"You won't hurt me. I trust you."

She looked away, staring at nothing in the far corner of the bedroom. "You shouldn't." Each word was a visible effort.

"Yes, I should. Trust me to help you. Trust yourself." I pulled my hands free and traced circles around first one breast, then the other, narrowing the circumference with each swirl. My breath shuddered, my own nipples straining beneath the towel as hers, if it was possible, hardened further.

She breathed hard, too, but her eyes were intent on my face. Sometimes I wondered what additional details she could discern with those enhanced eyes. "You're feeling it, even though I'm not touching you, aren't you?" she asked me.

"Yes." It came out as more of a pleasurable sigh than a word, and she smiled.

"Guess I was right not to masturbate." Vick watched me a little longer from beneath lowered lids. "I really like being able to do that to you. What happens if I *do* touch you?"

I would explode? The thought sent warmth coursing through my body, pooling between my legs. I needed to shift positions, bringing my knees up on the bed and my feet underneath me. It placed my heel right… there, putting pressure where I wanted it so much. "I d-don't know," I stammered. Coherent speech became difficult.

The smile turned wicked. "Let's find out."

She sat up further, reaching for my towel and pulling it away with a tug. Her gaze flowed from my breasts to the juncture of my thighs, and the heat of it flooded my soul.

"You're beautiful." Vick ran her fingers through my still-damp hair and chuckled at the shivers she produced. I discovered more of my own erogenous zones, and my scalp was definitely one of them.

Where my explorations were tentative and teasing, Vick chose the direct approach. I didn't know if this resulted from her nature or need, but she cupped my breasts in her firm hands, kneading them with a rhythmic massage while flicking my nipples with her thumbs.

My response was immediate, a low moan I couldn't hold back. Vick cut off the sound with a kiss, her tongue sweeping over my lips, then darting in to explore my mouth. My mind wandered, imagining her tongue elsewhere, and my hips rocked, putting more pressure where I needed it most.

The bed squeaked with the motion, and Vick laughed against my mouth, the sound vibrating through me. "You like that." It wasn't a question.

I didn't know which of the incredible sensations she meant, but I loved them all, so I nodded. A surge of desire jolted me, but it wasn't mine. It came from her.

I separated us, drawing away from her lips with reluctance, and pulled her hands from my breasts. They ached at the loss of stimulation, but I sensed her control slipping, and if she did hurt me, she'd never forgive herself. "Sorry," I said at her look of confusion. "It's fantastic. So fantastic I can't concentrate on anything else. Like your needs."

"I'm… okay, and I liked watching you lose yourself."

"You're not okay." She wasn't. My pleasure distracted her for a little while, but the frustration rebuilt at an astonishing rate and carried me with it. "I *was* losing myself. This isn't just about me."

"It's about both of us." But her argument held no force.

"It is," I agreed. "But let's see if I can make it easier for you." Because if I didn't ease all that intensity, she could lose control and hurt us both.

I lowered my lips to her nipple, wondering when my fingers left it. She'd put me in a haze of pleasure so thick I'd lost track of my actions. I swirled my tongue across the hardness, and now she was the one shifting her weight. I paused. "Let's switch places." I braced my back against the headboard. "Now, turn around," I ordered softly.

Vick raised an eyebrow, then seemed to comprehend. If she faced away, she couldn't make an easy grab for me, couldn't lose it and do things I wasn't ready for, at least not without giving me time to calm her down. She turned away from me, sitting with her knees drawn up, legs slightly apart. Her back rested against my chest, my knees pressed to her backside.

Not quite right. I spread my legs and snugged in closer, my inner thighs on either side of her hips. *Much better.*

Reaching around her, I recaptured her breasts, massaging them as she'd done with mine, picking up immediately this was something she liked. Her spine arched, driving her nipples into my palms. She threw her head back, narrowly missing a hard crack with my skull. I leaned to nibble the taut tendons of her neck, catching glimpses of her face in profile—the full, parted lips, the closed eyes. While I kept one hand alternating between her breasts, the other smoothed over her rib cage, her hard stomach, and lower.

Her skin burned like fire; her breath came in gasps. She desperately held on, but when I touched between her thighs, every muscle in her legs went rigid with the effort of restraint.

One finger slipped inside her with ease. Sensing she wanted more, I added a second. At the same moment, I fully opened the empathic channel we shared. "Let it go," I told her. "Let it all go."

Vick groaned, hips jerking in spasms as she forced me in deeper, and I felt it. I felt it all: the need, the frustration, the desire, along with every physical sensation. My nipples were teased, though no one touched them. That place inside me that wanted pressure was full, invisible fingers driving in and out with the same rhythm I used on her.

Slower, faster, harder, my fingertips curved just so within her. Her responses through our connection drove my actions, drowning us both.

My hips rocked, slamming me up against her spine, and she reached back with both hands, gripping my buttocks and dragging me closer still, increasing the wonderful, wonderful friction. My face mashed into her shoulder, my moans smothered by her skin. She cried out breathlessly as we moved in unison, bodies whispering over the blankets like spies conversing at a secret rendezvous.

The current caught me, her will taking me with her down a raging river, and I lost track of which feelings were mine and which hers, we melded so perfectly.

"This time… you're letting go with me," Vick growled, voice hoarse and raw, and I crashed over a waterfall I didn't see coming. Her body clenched around my fingers and shuddered at the same moment I launched into violent spasms of my own. It seemed to continue forever, one drop cascading into another, and then another still, until at last she released her grip and I withdrew from her, holding her loosely to me with arms gone limp.

I was too weak to move. Our breathing slowed, and we leaned against each other in stunned silence.

After several minutes, once my heart rate returned to normal, I made a tentative check of Vick's emotional state through our still-open bond. All I sensed was a profound calm, like water motionless as glass.

"Thank you," Vick whispered.

It wouldn't last, that relaxation. We both knew it. But for then, it was the most peace she'd had since the accident. I kissed her gently, a promise to be there for her whenever she needed me, however she needed me.

"I think another shower is in order," Vick told me, just a hint of suggestion in her tone, and I suspected that need was coming faster than I planned. She stood, and I let her pull me from the bed and lead me into the bathroom without resistance.

Dinner would be a late-night snack.

CHAPTER 13
VICK
DROPPING HINTS

Two years later....

I AM in trouble.

The cell in the detention facility isn't unlike my quarters' sleeping area—minus the desk, the embedded comp, and the plant—which is kind of sad, really. I lie on the narrow cot, a loose spring poking me just to the right of my spine, staring at the ceiling panels, counting the grooves between them for maybe the twelfth time.

At least it's private. After holding them an hour or so to double-check all the stories, the cops let most of the other Storms and Sunfires go. The few who'd caused actual damage to the pub paid their fines or waited until friends or their superiors showed up to make their bail.

Security isn't stupid enough to put me in with Hal. His fault or not, the rival merc would take out his rage and grief on me. He also has a cell to himself, right across the corridor.

In addition, the cells are pretty much suicide proof. Good thing. After the second thread snapped, I experienced an accompanying plummet into depression. Not as bad as the first one, and I knew what to expect, so I handled it better. Still a small part of me is glad the cot and chair are bolted to the floor, the mattress is sheetless, and I have to be escorted if I need to use the facilities.

And so I have tons of time to just think. And count ceiling panels.

I'm officially off the hook for the murder, but I was brawling, which means a fine, and I did some damage, which means another fine. As property of the Storm, I don't have unrestricted access to funds. I'm stuck here until someone in authority from the Storm comes to bail me out.

I don't expect Kelly to show up, given the state I left her in, but she's the one who arrives outside my cell.

"Kel."

"Vick."

"You okay?"

"I'm here, aren't I?"

Yeah, this is going well.

"Tell me the rest," she says.

"Um, huh?" I swing my feet off the cot and sit up to face her. She looks like death warmed over, dark circles beneath her eyes, rumpled uniform with stains on both knees and a couple of rips from glass shards. She has her arms crossed over her chest and a set to her jaw I only see when she's furious with me.

"There's no way you should have lost your shit over a half-assed comment about sexual preferences. You don't care about your sexual preference! Nobody's cared about that crap since 2020. What the hell is wrong with you?"

And she's cursing. I must really be in trouble.

I study the floor. It could use a good cleaning.

"Dammit, Vick, somebody died tonight! I felt it. The last breath, the final heartbeat. He didn't want to die. He was terrified of it. I know you didn't do it. I know." She chokes, pauses, swallows a sob. I want to comfort her, but I can't reach her. Instead I approach the bars and wait on my side. "You're hiding something from me. Maybe if you told me everything, we wouldn't have been there. You wouldn't have been involved in that fight." She paces the length of the cell twice, her movements jerky, as if all her focus is required for walking.

I glance at Hal in the other cell, head down, ignoring us both. Good, but I keep my voice lowered anyway.

"I had a nightmare," I say. "I didn't mention it because I have them all the time. You know that."

She nods.

"And I didn't want to make excuses, didn't see how a dream could possibly be relevant. But this dream... it was about you."

Kelly stops and faces me. "Go on."

"You were killing me."

Now it's her turn to stare, dumbfounded, at me. "I *what*?"

I tell her. It's rough, coming out in fits and starts. I don't understand it, can't rationalize or relate it to some experience we've had, a vidfilm I've seen, a song I've heard, a fucking trigger to explain why I'd dream my best friend would... would....

"Vick?"

I swipe at the wetness on my cheeks and wipe the hand on my pant leg so hard I burn the skin. Tears—one bit of realism the designers of my replacement eyes could have left out. I wrap the fingers of my other hand around one of the bars in a knuckle-cracking grip. Through blurred vision I meet her eyes. "What's wrong with me?" I was doing so well. I activate my suppressors, but they aren't enough. "It feels like everything has gone to hell in the last couple of days."

She purses her lips. "I'm... not sure, but I have an idea. And I don't think it just happened. I think it's been coming for a while." Her voice is small. Whatever it is, she's not happy about it. In fact, she looks downright scared.

I'm scaring *her*? I'm scaring myself.

Kelly reaches a hand through the bars, wrapping it over mine. "We'll figure this out." She's about to say more, but a shout from the end of the hall prevents it.

"LaSalle!"

Kelly cringes at the sound of her name coming from our boss's lips.

"The fine's paid. Get her out and take her home. I'd like some sleep tonight." Whitehouse, with Officer Sanderson trailing behind at a quick pace. The dear doctor wears what looks like pajama bottoms beneath his knee-length lab coat. He's theatrically stomping, but it's muffled and ridiculous in his brown leather slippers.

I access my internal clock, connected to the base system: 0300. Yeah, I'd be pissed too.

Whitehouse's gaze narrows in on our hands, entwined over the bars of my cell. Predatory is the only way I can describe his expression. My implants agree as my display pops up with an image of Whitehouse in full hunting regalia and me in bunny ears with a fluffy cotton tail. I don't like his look. I don't like it at all. Pink suffuses Kelly's cheeks. She disengages from me and steps away.

Sanderson squeezes past the doctor and waves a keycard over a reader beside the cell. The light above it turns green and the locking mechanism clicks. The bars separate in the center, leaving a small space. With a grunt, she shoves one side of them into a gap in the wall.

I step out. Sanderson gives me a small smile and a nod.

"Jumping out of windows, unauthorized shootings, and now bar brawls. What the hell got into you tonight?" Whitehouse growls. "You keep this up, we're going to take you apart and rebuild you."

At his suggestion of rebuilding, I freeze where I stand. He could do it. From what I've managed to piece together over the past two years, Whitehouse could knock me out, take what memories I have left, and make me believe anything he wants. I've trusted him not to, but how much of that trust is me and how much is the implants?

My internal display shows an image of Whitehouse with his hair sticking out in all directions, holding bubbling beakers and vials—the perfect mad scientist. Damn, my tech is active tonight. I blink it away.

"That's not funny," Kelly says. Her grip is tight on my forearm. Her words tremble with anger.

"You think I'm kidding? Seems to me VC1 needs further adjustments."

"Vick doesn't need anything except some time off."

"Hey," I interrupt, "I'm standing right here."

Kelly sends me a sympathetic look. The doctor ignores me. "Time off, my ass. She's a machine. When a machine malfunctions to the point of inconvenience—" He points to his robe and slippers. "—it needs to be repaired. Or scrapped," he adds with a scowl.

The blood drains from Kelly's complexion. I'm not doing so well myself, and I lean against the bars for support. My reaction surprises me. I'm trained to defend myself and to survive. Would I roll over and allow the Storm research and medical teams to end my life? Is that one of the parameters of my programming?

Whitehouse waves one hand in the air dismissively. "Oh please, pull yourselves together, both of you. We're not abandoning such an expensive project. Wouldn't be the first time we tweaked a few things."

A sick feeling forms in my stomach. "We're not talking about my regular checkups, are we?" Minutes ago, Kelly said she thought she might know what's wrong with me and that it's been coming for a while. I flash back on the two of us, trapped inside the morgue's storage drawer, her arms wrapped tightly around me.

"Not now, Vick," Kelly says.

"Fucking yes, now!" I grasp her by both shoulders and wrench her toward me. "Have you and Whitehouse done something? Something I didn't know about?"

I'm not a machine. That's what she's told me, promised me. But if she's altered me without my knowledge, without my permission....

She won't meet my eyes. I release her and stagger back a step. Her silence tells me all I need to know.

"Am I free to go?" I ask Sanderson, forcing the words through my constricted throat. The implants and suppressors work in tandem to calm me, flooding my system with serotonin and clamping down on my emotions to keep me functional. Otherwise I'd drop where I stand.

"You are," she tells me. "You can collect your personal belongings at the processing desk. I'll escort you."

"Thanks." I fall in beside her, leaving the others behind.

"Vick!" Kelly calls. "It's not what you think."

I don't give a fuck. I don't think or feel anything except betrayal, bone deep. It takes effort not to break into a run. I want to put as much distance as I can between me and Kelly, as fast as I am able.

The door to the detention area slides closed, and as we approach the main desk, Sanderson asks, "Are you really some kind of machine? You seem human enough to me."

The officer manning the station passes me a metal box containing my wallet, the passkey to my quarters, a handful of loose change… and a tiny gold heart.

I close trembling fingers around the charm. It must have slipped from my wallet when I emptied my pockets into the box. A reminder of my humanity, Kelly gave it to me when the Fighting Storm returned me to field duty. If the boss of our corporation is our unseen Wizard of Oz, I am the Tin Man.

I open my hand and drop the heart into the waste recycler beside the desk.

"I don't know what I am," I tell Sanderson, finally answering her question. I gather my belongings and head for home.

CHAPTER 14
KELLY
HOME FRONT

Two years earlier....

VICK CORREN was undeterred.

The days flew. I showed Vick the natural beauties I grew up with: waterfalls, forest trails, and mountain views that encompassed four states. At night, we sat around the dining room table with my parents, catching up on Earth news and telling tales of the Fighting Storm—how we rescued some archaeologists and their findings after a cave-in in an eco-war zone, and the liberation of a load of teenage slaves off an illegal trading vessel past Saturn. The deaths connected with those missions, we left out.

Mom gave in to the inevitable. She taught Vick to bake, a skill I couldn't imagine she would ever again use, but we all enjoyed the cookies and the pie. I would forever carry with me the image of my mercenary lover wearing a frilly, flour-dusted pink apron and giant oven mitts.

We spent time with Dad in his workroom, him showing us how he detected imminent equipment malfunctions before they took down entire systems.

"Don't ignore the little things," he cautioned. "Those flickers, the half-second longer to come online, the alteration of an engine's pitch by a half tone. Machines will tell you when they aren't well, and you can feel it."

Vick nodded, and I knew she wasn't thinking about comms or hoverbikes. How much did the implants tell her? She had advance warning of her meltdowns. But so far she'd been unable to verbalize a lot of how she interacted with the devices in her head. I squeezed her hand beneath the workbench in the storage shed. In that week, she was calmer than I'd ever seen her, content, relaxed, enveloped in a blue glow to my second sight. Our connection had a more profound effect than anything the textbooks had suggested.

Dr. Whitehouse told me no cure existed for the damage she suffered. But I wondered....

When it came time for us to leave, Dad piled us into the green monstrosity to drive us to the shuttleport. I knew Mom was avoiding the final goodbyes, and she wiped her cheek on her sleeve as we pulled away. Even Vick's eyes had a slight glistening to them when Dad dropped us off, but she blinked before I could tell for certain.

"Go check us in," Vick told me. "I'll drop off your luggage." She gestured to the three suitcases beside her on the curb. Mom gave us a number of treats and extra clothing to take along, so my bags had multiplied. Vick hefted the heaviest of them onto a conveyor belt like the luggage weighed nothing. She caught me admiring her and winked, then carried on with her task.

Inside, I followed bright green signs pointing to the Girard Base shuttle launch area and rode down an escalator. The armed presence had increased, with port guards patrolling side by side with local law enforcement and a few US military. I spotted a handful of mercs too, though none of the Fighting Storm. This sort of duty would have been beneath our price range. Though the official types were in greater numbers, they all seemed relaxed, stopping to chat with luggage handlers, maintenance personnel, and customer service clerks. The distant hums of arriving shuttles added a white-noise blanket over the conversation.

Travelers packed the walkways. A businessman stood directly in front of me; unintentionally, a mother carrying a baby pressed on me from behind. Infants were a pleasure to read. I drank in the simple emotions of safety, warmth, and joy, along with a healthy dose of "want" natural to all babies. When I wiggled my fingers at the little boy, he smiled at me and gurgled. Too bad adults were so much more of a strain on my talent. Regretfully, I send a little more energy to my shields to lessen the impact of the crowd's feelings.

A flash like a sun going supernova blinded me. Sound followed—a deafening roar. The walkway screeched to a sudden jerking halt. We went down like dominoes, the people behind falling forward to crush those in front. I twisted in midfall to avoid the mother and child, but the businessman landed on them, and several others hit him, leaving only the mother's new neon pink tennis shoes exposed. Someone pinned me to the floor, pressing on my chest and knocking the air from my lungs.

A wave of fiery heat passed overhead, and only the waist-high metal walls lining the walkway shielded us. An elderly woman, still standing but thrown against the right-hand wall, opened her mouth wide. Her throat distended, though the ringing in my ears stole the sound of her apparent scream. Her hair and clothing ignited, and I screamed too, kicking and shoving to get myself farther away.

The oven engulfed me, Gretel of an ancient fairy tale and the witch shrieking in triumph.

No. Not me. Her.

I pushed my mind free of the hallucination.

I stayed low, pressing my back against the right-hand walkway wall, then jerking forward as heat radiated through my thin shirt. The woman thrashed and fell mostly still, her body twitching or shuddering as she continued to burn. My hearing, unfortunately, returned.

Crashes followed the first blast, debris raining down upon us. One man made it to his feet to be sliced in half by a flying piece of a glass display case. His torso slid off his waist in slow motion, blood pouring and drenching those around him in wet red.

"And for my next trick...." A third sword drove into the box, then a fourth and a fifth, while I remained trapped inside its confines, the willing assistant in the magician's theatrical performance.

No, dammit. No. Focus, Kelly.

Another man shoved a young girl out of his way, and a collapsing pillar crushed him, though the low wall on either side protected those who kept their heads down.

I rolled into the fetal position, hands over my head, rocking and moaning.

Abrupt and shocking near-silence fell—only crackling flames, pops of electrical wires, and sobbing.

I fumbled for my comm unit, dropping it on the corpse beside me. I didn't want to touch the dead man. Sometimes final emotions lingered after death. I didn't feel anything directly from him, but if there were contact.... I forced myself to retrieve the device, putting all my energy into my walls, but my multiple shifts from the real world already told me my walls were nearly shot.

The body fed me nothing. Dead too long. Thank goodness. The comm channel grumbled with static, but I could make out a voice.

"—oly shit! Kel. Kel, pick up your comm, dammit."

"Vick." I gasped the word, clutching the unit to my ear with one hand and shoving the man off the struggling mother and child with my other. The woman helped, bringing her baby into view. The boy stared at me. He drew a breath. His mother and I sighed with relief. "Stay low," I told her.

"What!" Vick—completely panicked. I couldn't read her through my own terror, but she shouted into the comm. All around me, the dead and unconscious moved as those beneath them pushed their way free.

Zombies, clawed from their graves, displacing the dirt, eyes and mouths wide.

I shook my head, hard. My vision cleared.

Of those draped over the walkway walls' sides, dying flames burned clothing black and singed hair off. Skin ran in an oily, greasy liquid.

Oh God, the smells. I wished for more smoke to cover them. I gagged and swallowed bile. As much as I'd trained, my empathic walls weren't enough for this. Pain and terror scraped my nerves raw, my hands clenching and releasing as I willed others' emotions away from me… and failed. If I didn't get some distance between myself and the disaster soon, I'd black out.

And then there was guilt. I couldn't help anyone because I couldn't risk touching anyone, no matter how they reached out to me or screamed or cried. If I tried, I'd never make it out alive.

The glow of fires and emergency lights cast everything in eerie shades of orange. Some of the survivors pulled comm units and tried to use them. They frowned and shook the devices, shoving them back in pockets or purses. But the Storm provided mine. And Vick's, well, her internal comm was unique and nigh indestructible. I focused on the device, squeezing it in my grip. "I'm…." Not okay. Definitely not that. "I'm here," I told Vick, who argued with someone on her end.

"Are you hurt?"

"Not… physically," I told her. The mother crawled to sit next to me. She had a gash on her forehead. It dripped on the baby. She gave a soft cry and wiped it away on her sleeve.

"Fuck," Vick breathed. She knew my limits and how far something like this would push them. Break them. Some empaths never revived from mass-trauma shock. We could handle individuals. We avoided mass suffering. "How long can you hold on?"

They screamed. Screamed in my head. All of them. The dying. The injured. I pushed it out with effort.

"Not long," I told her. "It's bad in here. Really bad. I'm… losing reality." Not to mention that stuff kept falling on people and killing them. All the sanity in the universe wouldn't help me if the building collapsed.

"Where are you?"

"One level down." I scanned for signs, finding one hanging by a single clamp from a nearby pillar. "Concourse C, maybe halfway across it."

"Shit."

More arguing on her end. I heard a male voice, no, voices, in the background. Something about fires and structural integrity.

She wanted in. They weren't allowing it.

I glanced at the ceiling overhead. It slanted in places. Furnishings hung through the new gaps. Wires dangled and sparked. The support beams creaked, making me shiver with each new metallic groan. The explosion trapped us on the lower floor with two stories above us. No stairwells nearby, if any were even usable.

"You need to find an escalator and climb up. As fast as you can." Vick had dropped into full command mode. Better than panic.

"We'll try." I hesitated. "Vick, stay out there." It went against what I wanted most, to have her by my side, but I wouldn't risk her life.

"Fuck that. I'm coming for you. One way or another." She clicked off before I could argue.

Dammit. If this building came down, it would crush us all.

Some of the living came to the same conclusion. Recognizing its walls' protective potential, figures crawled along the now stationary walkway, over and around the dead and too injured to move. Some, in a daze, clutched carry-on luggage, while those more alert abandoned it in favor of haste. They shifted in my vision, fading in and out, and I wondered how much was the smoke haze and how much my tenuous grasp on the there and then. "We need to try to get upstairs," I said to the mother beside me. She blinked at me with wide eyes, pale and trembling, in shock. "Your baby," I added, taking a different approach. "We need to get him out of here."

She looked from me to him and nodded.

"I'm Kelly," I offered.

"Maggie." She tucked the blanket a little tighter around her son. "And John."

I touched his tiny cheek and it helped ground me. "Hey, John." He cried softly, sensing his mother's fear without needing empathic abilities.

More chunks and slabs of cement, along with parts of metal counters and check-in desks, fell through the ceiling, making dents in the floor outside the walkway. We crawled. It was hard with all the debris and bodies, harder for Maggie with one arm wrapped around her son. But it beat getting crushed. I paused when my comm buzzed in my fist and raised it to my ear. "Go, Vick."

"I'm locked on to your comm signal," she said.

A bitter laugh escaped me. I never knew she could do that.

"I've made it into the upper level. Probably gonna be in some trouble when we get out of here." She chuckled without humor, and I wondered what she did to gain access. I bet she beat the shit out of someone. Hopefully nobody else was dead. "Crap, this is a mess. It's gonna take me a while to reach you. There's a lot of debris I've got to work around." Crying and screaming carried from the background. Her aural equipment fed the sound to her brain, the implants, and the internal comm. I heard someone plead for her help.

"Vick, those other people. They're closer."

"I'm not here for them," she said evenly. Her suppressors had to have been on full. I couldn't imagine Vick leaving the injured to die without agonizing over it. "I'm here for you." She must have noted my distress because she added, "I'm seeing some rescue teams and I can't let them see me. They'll do their job. I'm doing mine."

Behind us, a heavy beam fell across the walkway. The low walls couldn't bear its weight and that section collapsed, flattening those who'd sought the walkway's limited protection. Their deaths flooded me, the abrupt cutoffs tearing at my consciousness. I swayed where I knelt, leaning sideways. My shoulder hit the still upright section of railing and I recoiled with a hiss. The pain snapped me out of my daze, but it was temporary.

"Vick, go back," I begged. "We'll make it if we can. I don't want you down here." I lied, but I'd do anything to protect her.

"That," she said, her voice a growl, "is too damn bad."

Of course she felt the same.

CHAPTER 15
VICK
EMOTIONAL ADJUSTMENT

Two years later....

I AM pissed.

She lied. All Kelly's lectures about my humanity. They've all been lies.

If she and Whitehouse have altered me....

I storm through Girard Base's corridors, not seeing the steel walls, the closed shops and offices, the faces of personnel heading in to the early work shift. Even the airlocks fail to faze me. I'm wrapped in fury, the suppressors overloaded, the need to release pressing in yet impossible without Kelly.

I can't let her touch me. Never again.

If she doesn't touch me, I can't channel my emotions. I'll go insane.

The internal display shows the cord, a third thread fraying.

Halfway to insanity already.

I'm shaking so badly, it takes four tries to get my passkey into the slot. Inside, I slump against the nearest wall, sliding down to land on the beige carpeting of my tiny sitting room. My fingers dig into the rug, tearing out small tufts of the rough material. In my head, the implants signal an incoming transmission from Kelly. I refuse to open that connection.

I can't remember ever being angrier than I am right now. My skin is hot. Acid boils in my stomach. I want to vomit, to scream, to....

I erupt from the floor, grabbing the first thing within reach. I hurl the chair across the room, shattering the glass protecting a picture Kelly gave me, a watercolor of mountains and a flower-filled valley. Vision blurs. I'm a destructive force, hands and boots connecting with furniture, reducing it to shards and splinters. Jagged pieces tear my clothing, cut into my palms. I rip and shred whatever I come into contact with.

When I collapse, panting, my suite lies in shambles. The overturned couch spills foam stuffing across the floor; the covering dangles in tattered strips. I lean my back against a skeletal part of its frame. Everything in the room is broken or damaged. Including me.

I'm worn out but no better off. The rage, hurt, and betrayal remain, coiling and twisting. My stomach heaves. I swallow rapidly to avoid adding more mess to the floor, then lose the battle and vomit anyway. It spatters my hands and knees, staining my torn uniform. The smell keeps me gagging.

Groaning, I rip the rest of my clothing off and throw it in a corner. I reach the bathroom and snap the shower to hot. Steam fills the glass stall. I duck under the spray, the too hot water scalding my skin, and for a long moment, I let it, watching myself redden to match my mood. I ease the temperature down to a sultry warmth and stand, head bowed, under the pounding stream.

It happens without conscious thought, my hand rising to the nozzle, altering the water flow to a narrow, intense focus, guiding it across my breasts, then lower between my legs. I spread them, giving the stream easier access, adjusting my stance so it pounds just the right spot. In the back of my mind, I'm dimly aware of the anger and frustration seeking a new outlet, a different form of release. It's hopeless. It's all hopeless, but my body will try anything to satisfy its need.

I can't stop. I don't want to.

It's something I never allow myself. Ever. Because I know... I know she might....

Blonde hair, blue eyes, full, smiling lips, firm breasts, nipples erect....

Oh my God.

The muscles in my hips spasm, my own wetness adding to the rush of water. The motion makes the stream a pulse, rhythmically driving me closer and closer to... to.... I press my palms to the tiles on either side, bracing myself upright as the first wave hits. Then a second.

I'm heading for a third when Kelly overrides my transmission blockers. I never knew she could do that. Guess nothing should surprise me anymore about how she can control me.

"Vick." My name is a gasp. Her heavy breathing in my ears drives me harder. I slip one hand from the wall to join the water between my legs. "Vick… please."

Please what? Keep going? Stop?

I try to reel it in, to think about anything except her. Furious or not, betrayed or not, if this goes against her will, this isn't the person I want to be, but I'm beyond all rational thought or action.

Driven, like the machine I am.

She gives a faint cry and it's all I need to go over the edge once more. My knees buckle, and I sit on the shower floor, the water pouring on the top of my head.

It's several minutes before she speaks again.

"Vick?" she whispers.

I wonder where she is. Her quarters? A hallway? Did I just bring her to orgasm in some public place?

"What do you want?" My voice is hoarse. Was I screaming? Crying out like she was?

"What were you thinking of?"

Why is she asking me that?

The sensor chimes over the bathroom mirror, alerting me that the door to my quarters has opened. She's here. Now. I stand on shaky limbs and snap the water off, then sink back down, too tired to grab a towel and cover myself.

The shower door slides aside and Kelly crouches beside me. Gentle fingers pull wet strands of hair from my face, tucking them behind my ears. I don't look at her. I'm not embarrassed, just exhausted. Humiliation can wait.

"You didn't answer my question. What were you thinking of?"

Images flash, erotic and crazed, blocking out my real-time vision, and I can't suppress the resulting shudder of pleasure that follows. She strokes my hair and rubs my back, making soothing, distracting sounds. Part of me wants to pull away. Part of me can't resist her. "I'm not forgiving you," I manage through gritted teeth. I don't know yet what I'm not forgiving her for, but I have a sneaking suspicion, and if I'm right, it will hurt more than the betrayal itself.

"I know. Tell me anyway."

Now I do look up. She's disheveled, hair wild, uniform more rumpled than before. Several buttons are undone on the top, and the pants fasteners gap open. I imagine what she must have been doing minutes before. Where her hands wandered, where her fingers moved. It nearly sends me back over the edge, but I hold on. "You," I moan. "I was thinking about you." I blink into her worried gaze. "Why?"

Kelly sighs, nudging me aside so she can sit down. She doesn't seem to care that she's getting her uniform all wet.

"It's complicated."

The anger rises, though I'm too tired to act on it. "Fuck complicated. What did you do to me? What did you block?"

She jerks in place like she's taken a bullet. Yeah, Kel, I've guessed your dirty little secret.

"It's what you did." With absolute certainty, I know. A shiver runs through me, goose bumps rising on my naked flesh. With the water off, the shower's cooling down at a rapid rate. Girard Base has a fine heating system, but I didn't have it set high when I headed in here. I hadn't planned on hanging out for a chat.

Kelly pushes to her feet and offers me a hand up. I don't take it. She rolls her eyes while I struggle to my knees and then stand, wavering for a few seconds before steadying. My formerly dislocated shoulder chooses now to complain that I've overtaxed the quick repairs my team must have done on the shuttle back from Paradise. I rotate it, working out the soreness and stiffness. My back aches too, and I rub the skin over the embedded metal beneath.

I skip the towels stored under my sink, instead heading for my bedroom, and grab a robe from the closet. It's fluffy and blue, and I throw it on the floor, taking out a clean uniform instead.

"Now you're angry at the Christmas present I gave you?" she asks softly from the bathroom doorway, a hint of amusement in her tone. She's trying to distract me, to lighten the mood. I'm not having it.

"I'm angry in general. You already know that." I pull on the pants, shirt, and a pair of boots, favoring haste over underwear.

"You don't have to rush. I've seen you without clothes before today."

In the gym, changing into training gear. On missions when I've been hurt and she's had to do some field first aid. One crazy night of leave when the whole team drank too much and went skinny-dipping in a lake on one of Saturn's terraformed moons—for a few blissful hours, Alex and Lyle ignored my half-mechanical nature. But my subconscious tells me those aren't the times she's referring to.

"Quit stalling." I sink into the desk chair, since she's already on the corner of my bed, and with her pants still unfastened and her shirt half-open, I want nothing to do with that. Actually, I'm afraid of what I might do with that.

Her fists clench at her sides, a ridiculous gesture from a pacifist like her. "It's not like this is easy for me, either. I just went from throwing up in the hallway to masturbating in a storage closet, for God's sake!"

"Huh. Serves you right."

She glares. "I thought I was doing the right thing," she says. "I thought I was helping."

I'm off the chair and knocking her backward on the bed before I realize I've moved. I pin her arms to her sides, my legs straddling her torso. The position is familiar and alien all at the same time, and it sets my head reeling, the edges of my vision clouded by shadows. I blink and the darkness vanishes. My fist comes up, releasing her left wrist, though she does nothing to stop me.

"Does this… look like… you helped me?" I pant, breathless from the effort of restraining myself, and force my fist back down. "I'm half out of my mind, Kel! For the last time. What. Did. You. Do?"

Kelly stares up at me, tears streaking her cheeks. Normally her crying rips me to shreds. I'll do anything for her when she cries. She's never used it as an unfair advantage. It's just the effect it has on me.

Not now. Now it fuels the fire. I want to slap the tears away, scratch them from her skin with my fingernails.

"I put in a block, but it's failing, bits of the blocked-off emotion bleeding through," she says in a small voice. "I had to do it. To save you. At least, I thought so at the time."

"Why?"

"Because," she says, "you fell in love with me."

CHAPTER 16
KELLY
INNOCENCE LOST

Two years earlier….

VICK CORREN was compelled.

"Are you all right? Hey, don't leave us, okay?"

I blinked to clear my vision. Reds, purples, and blacks swirled at the edges: color representations of pain, fear, and death. Maggie's face swam into view, shadows of collapsed walls and prone, moaning bodies behind her. I coughed on smoke and concrete dust, sickly sweet mixing with acrid. Particles floated into my mouth, and I spat the grit to the side. We had reached the end of the walkway, still on hands and knees, ready to crawl into the more open space of the terminal. At some point, though, I stopped moving.

"I'm here," I told her, pausing to focus on the baby, John, in her arms. He was hungry but no longer scared, and the simple vicarious feeling helped steady me.

"Is it shock?" Maggie asked. "You zoned out. Your skin was so cold."

She must have touched me and sent me into the abyss with her roiling emotions. Now I was slowly clawing my way out. My walls were shot. I could feel everything from everyone, their emotions too much even for my skills. It was like my teenage years all over again, the entire world around me pressing in on my young and untrained empathic senses.

I glanced at Maggie. She was terrified and hurting. I wanted to help, but I couldn't take any more on myself. The dead lay all around us, wounded staggering about, the healthier ones picking their way across the debris and making for the escalator I couldn't even see at the farthest end of the lower level. The dust burned my eyes, making them water. I coughed again, harsh and ragged.

"It's not shock." I got to my feet but stayed bent at the waist, and gestured for her to follow. The emergency lighting flickered. For a second it went out altogether, resulting in a chorus of despairing moans and screams from the survivors. It came back on, accompanied by tangible relief. I paused, gasping at the rapid emotional shifts, hands on both knees.

"What is it, then? Can I help?" Maggie, beside me.

I turned my head and looked at her from the corner of my eye. "I'm an empath."

She recoiled, clutching her baby more tightly to her chest, and I feared she'd bolt in some random direction away from the escalators and safety. A blink and a shake of her head later, she recovered herself. "Sorry. It's just that I've heard… things… about psychics."

That we'd invade people's thoughts, steal their life force, manipulate them in unthinkable ways. Yeah, not everyone was as open-minded as the Fighting Storm.

I swallowed a laugh. The Storm wasn't open-minded at all about Vick. What a bunch of hypocrites.

"It's okay. I'm used to it. Just don't touch me unless you absolutely have to." Honestly, I didn't think she wanted to anymore.

"Can you go on?" she asked. Maggie gestured at the field of injured with an open palm. "This must be twice as bad for you."

Ten times worse, but I didn't correct her. "Do I have a choice?" A burst of static erupted from my comm and I raised it while moving forward. "Go ahead."

"Any progress?" Vick's voice cut through some crashing sounds and a couple of *bangs* and shattering glass.

"We're off the walkway, if that means anything to you."

"It does. I've accessed a schematic of the lower level. You're halfway to the escalator. Keep coming."

Hearing her voice helped a lot. I picked my way between two bodies half-buried under a collapsed column and some broken ceiling tiles, a demolished check-in desk and discarded luggage. I kept the comm channel open, noting the low battery light with dismay. "Vick?"

"I'm… here," she answered, voice strained like she lifted something heavy. "Clearing some debris from the escalator. I can hear people working at it from below. Should be usable as a stairway by the time you get here."

Around me, the still-standing walls groaned. A row of formerly bolted-down chairs lay on their sides, blocking our path. We scrambled over them. Some severed wiring popped and sizzled in the ceiling, filling the area with the scent of burnt plastic.

"Great." I couldn't muster up any cheerfulness. Not until I saw Vick face-to-face. "Can... can you talk to me and still keep doing whatever you're doing?" I was a child, lost in a maze of emotion.

Vick grunted, and I heard more crashing on her end. "So," she said in a matter-of-fact tone, "tell me about your sweet sixteen party."

"What?" I squeaked, then shook my head at Maggie staring back at me, only catching my end of the conversation. She continued moving forward.

"Your sweet sixteen. I know you had one. You wore black pants and a gold-and-black glittery top. Your hair was done up in black ribbons. There was a cake." Vick paused, growling as the sound of metal shrieked in the background. "It said, 'It's all downhill now' in pink frosting."

I laughed despite myself, remembering the holo on the mantle in the living room. She must have studied it to recall all those details. Or maybe not. Her implants were remarkable recording devices. "My friends bought the cake. I had an identical one when I turned eighteen and again at twenty-one."

"You have weird friends."

"You should meet them, next time we're here."

"I'd... like that." Vick paused to catch her breath. The lights flickered and went out, leaving the terminal in darkness much longer this time, at least thirty full, agonizing seconds. Maggie and I froze in place, my hand on her sleeve. "Shit," Vick muttered.

The power came up, but fainter, and an ominous rumble carried from the section of terminal we'd already traversed. Maggie and I stared behind us, but the lights were still out back there. We heard distant screaming. Even too far away to read clearly, the echoes of the dying turned my eyesight gray. I shivered, and I couldn't stop.

"You were supposed to tell me a story, not the other way around," I reminded Vick, urging my companion on with a nod of my head. We moved forward but couldn't resist the occasional look back into deadly darkness.

"I don't have any stories. You know everything I know." Profound sadness, and I was so sorry I forgot that aspect of her memory loss. I latched on to the emotion and its strength, and our brainwave match let me pick it out and cling to it.

I was not prepared for her fear.

It swamped me in a wave of purple, dragging me down until I wrapped myself into a ball, clutching my knees with one trembling arm. The action was instinctive, a direct result of what I read from her in a sudden blast.

"Kel. Kel, listen to me. If you're not running, I need you to do it now. Kel?" Vick spoke fast but calmly, probably trying to keep me as stable as possible. Panic underlay every syllable. "I'm coming for you, Kel."

I wanted to tell her no, but I couldn't answer her. I shook like a seizure victim. My breath came too fast for words. My hand crushed the comm next to my ear. I couldn't loosen my fingers, couldn't make any sound but a moan. Maggie knelt at my side, tugging on my arm.

"Kel, my other ear's patched into the emergency channel." Vick—master of multitasking. "The south end of the terminal gave way. It's gone, and it's causing a ripple effect in the infrastructure. Dammit, Kel, answer me!" More fear, less restraint. She was losing her grip, the suppressors becoming useless under the emotional onslaught she asked them to contain.

Vick, my lifeline. My undoing.

Maggie scrabbled at my fingers, prying them apart and dragging the comm from my grasp. She shouted into it, though I couldn't make out her words through the roaring in my ears. Her mouth stilled as Vick responded. Her face went paler under the flickering orange lights.

One last time she tried to pull me to my feet, but I was deadweight, and she only had one usable arm, the other curled around John. Her lips moved, and I made out, "I'm sorry." Then she pressed the comm back into my palm and ran, bowing over the baby as she did so.

I watched her retreating back, saw the couple of hopeful glances she cast at me before she turned away. She got about halfway across the open area, veering to the right, when the lights went out and stayed out.

Booming thunder ripped through the terminal. Beneath me, the floor vibrated as heavy things impacted it, jolting and jerking me about as if I lay on a boat deck in rough seas. Sharp fragments showered me.

Steel shrieked. Smoke and dust thickened the air, though I couldn't see any flames. I couldn't see anything at all.

It stopped.

I was buried in pitch darkness, buried alive. I heard creaking overhead, a repetitive back and forth of swinging metal. The bladed pendulum from Poe's classic tale came to mind. I lay listening to it, minute after minute, until a new sound caught my attention.

Death. Death was coming.

Two glowing eyes in the dark, drawing nearer, wavering, shifting from right to left, casting their white beams across the floor and heading straight for me. They revealed the new destruction, a narrow corridor created by the inward buckling of the walls on either side. I lay in the middle of it; if the concourse hadn't been so wide, I'd have been buried in more than darkness. The beams fell upon a splash of neon pink—the pink of Maggie's tennis shoes. The rest of the body, no, bodies crushed beneath a concrete pillar, hidden from view. Maggie and John. I couldn't feel them. I was too numb, too close to unconsciousness. The shadowy figure paused, bent, then straightened and came closer.

I'd join them soon. Death's eyes fell on me.

Another tremor rocked the terminal. Hah. Terminal. Terminal for everyone inside it. I was out of my head, giggles bursting from my throat. I coughed on the smoke. Death picked up speed, racing toward me. The creaking above became more rapid. Death turned its glowing eyes upward, revealing a jagged piece of metal dangling by one bent corner, its razor-sharp edge pointing like a blade, pointing directly down at me.

Even as I drew breath to scream, it fell.

CHAPTER 17
VICK
DAWN AND DARKNESS

Two years later….

I AM human.

> *You fell in love with me.*

I let that sit in the silence that follows, holding myself rigid in my room, on the bed, above Kelly, within inches of physically hurting my closest friend. My only friend. My betrayer. My internal display shows me gears and cogwheels clicking into place. Profound satisfaction settles over me, the kind gained from knowing I've forgotten something and having it pop into my head when I least expect it.

Except I did expect this. It hid beneath the surface the whole time (and I'd like to know exactly how much time it's been), but I knew.

Easing off her, I lie down at her side on the bed and stare at the ceiling. The air whirs through the ventilation system, blowing strands of my drying hair across my face.

What I don't know is why. Why block how I feel about her?

There has to be a good reason. Or a damn good rationalization. For an empath, placing an emotional block is the worst form of unethical behavior. It goes against their training and their vows not to tamper with the human mind. They're allowed to put a damaged brain back on course or, in my case, help one cope, but they aren't even supposed to block pain unless it's a life-or-death situation. "The human experience," they call it, and they don't mess with it. Ever.

She's told me. She's preached it at me. She did it anyway.

I swallow a sudden lump in my throat. "You didn't fall in love with *me*," I say, coming to the only possible conclusion I can draw.

The bed creaks with her abrupt shift in position, and she's leaning up on an elbow, looking down into my face. She grabs one of my hands, too fast for me to avoid it, not that I necessarily would have. Angry or not, I like having her touch me.

Kelly's eyes are fierce. "Don't you ever believe I don't love you. Don't you even say it again. I loved you then. Still love you. And whether you hate me or not, I'll always love you." She wipes tears on her sleeve, but they continue falling.

It takes effort to pull my hand away, but I do it. I don't want her to know exactly how I feel when I can't figure it out myself.

Really should have figured this whole thing out sooner. Then again, it's blocked, right? Maybe I couldn't have figured it out until the block started to fail. The odd electrical jolt I experienced when she was in emotion shock, back in the hovervan. I wonder if that's when the block fractured.

Kelly climbs off the bed and paces the room, pausing to stare at the potted plant, healthy and green. "You have no idea what it's been like, loving you, knowing you should feel the same way but not being able to tell you or touch you like I want." She whirls toward the mattress, hands flailing. "You would have died, Vick! You almost did, you know. That afternoon, down in the dark...."

I let her ramble since I have no idea what she's talking about, but my lower middle back aches, and I rub at the spot over the inserted metal bar. Shuttle engine accident. That's what they told me. I hate having to wonder what are lies and what are truth.

Kelly notices the motion of my hand and nods. "There's a bond between us. The brainwave match. The constant empathic sharing. Loving each other is a result, and also a cause. It's a feedback loop. You took risks you shouldn't have." She goes on, recounting details of a near-death I can't remember. "I wanted to protect you—"

I sit up, grimacing at the spinal pain, and raise a hand to stop her midsentence. "Do you think it makes a difference?"

"What?"

"Don't you think I would risk my life at any time to save yours? Don't you remember that I have?" Our enemies perceive her as the weakest link, and from a soldier's point of view, she is. Last year I took a bullet meant for her. Nothing major. Messed up my collarbone, needed surgery, but not life-threatening. She would have caught it in the head if I hadn't stepped in front of her. When Kelly's life is in danger, I value hers over mine. It's my job. She's my friend. Romance is irrelevant.

"I—"

"And what about you? You blocked me. You didn't block yourself. What about risks to *your* life?" She's linked her mind with mine when I'm in violent turmoil, so lost in emotion I can't see, hear, or speak. She's risked her sanity, if not her physical existence, to calm me down and bring me back.

She puts her hands firmly on her hips. "I can't block my own emotions. It's not an option."

"Your mother's an empath. I'm sure you have friends from the Academy. One of them could have done it."

Her lips tighten. Her chin juts out. "My mother and friends would never—"

"Because it's unethical, immoral, and wrong."

Like flicking a switch, the brief reprieve from my anger ends. I stand in front of her, a head taller, using my height to intimidate as I've never done with her before. The nightmare returns, sharp and clear, the morgue, the metal box, her apology.

"Did I have a choice when you did it? Did you even ask?" I can't imagine, after all the other mental tampering I've endured, that I'd ever agree to what she did.

She breaks, crumpling in on herself, arms wrapped around her midsection. "You begged me not to!" she cries, openly sobbing, words coming in between those hiccupy chirps she makes when she's really upset.

The rage swells. Heat floods my face. Kelly seems to shrink further before me, though whether it's from my words or my proximity, I'm not sure.

"Do you like it, loving me?" I grind out through gritted teeth.

Kelly blinks through her tears, confused.

"It's been… hard. But yes. It fills me. It makes me sad but happy at the same time."

"But you'd let me live the rest of my life without feeling that for you."

She sucks in a sharp breath. Good girl. Got it in one.

"You were dying. In my arms. It hurt. It hurt so much you almost took me with you. I never, ever wanted to feel that pain again." It's a weak protest. She's beaten and she knows it, but I have one final blow to strike.

"Maybe you need to think about whether you did it for me or for yourself."

"And what about you?" she shouts, startling me. "Without me, one way or another, you'd lose your damn mind. Isn't that half the reason you protect me so much?"

My turn to gape. I count to ten, praying my control lasts a little longer. She's not right. I care more about her than I do about myself.

She's not entirely wrong, either, but I'm too furious to admit that.

"You pressed a button. Turned off my love for you. I would rather go crazy, would rather *die*, than have you treat me like the machine you swear I'm not."

Kelly pierces me with her stare, and I know she's digging deep. I let my suppressors down, just enough for her to feel the truth of my words.

"Get out," I whisper.

"Vick?"

"I can't be around you right now. Go before I hurt you." If I could release, I could rid myself of the worst of the anger. But to do that, I'd have to trust her completely. And I don't. I'm not sure if I ever will again.

She takes several steps toward the door, then turns back. "You'd never hurt me," she says. "You only hurt yourself."

My mind flashes to the little gold heart she gave me and how much more meaning it must have held for her while I carried it. I think of it crushed in the recycler, and my own heart hurts like it's being squeezed in a vise.

"At least let me remove the block," she offers.

I shake my head. "I don't want to love you. Not yet. Maybe not ever."

"The block is failing anyway and driving you crazy."

I'm pretty sure she's being literal, but I don't care. "Then I'll wait until it fails." I meet her stricken gaze. "Not now, Kelly. I can't deal with you now." My words hurt her. I can see it. But I won't back down. An ironic thought occurs, and I give a sarcastic laugh. "You know, a week ago I would have said I wasn't even capable of loving someone." And with the block still in, I'm really not. I hurt, but it's not love. Not anymore. Not any time soon, if I can help it.

Loving her might force me to forgive her.

She faces the door, opening it to leave, but her words carry to me. "I always knew you were capable. You *are* human, regardless of how you think I've treated you. Regardless of what you think of yourself." The entry slides shut behind her.

"Being human kind of sucks," I whisper to an empty room.

CHAPTER 18
KELLY
BINDING TIES

Two years earlier....

VICK CORREN was dead.

The sharp metal ceiling panel plunged toward me. Even if emotion shock hadn't paralyzed me, I wouldn't get out of its way fast enough.

Death swooped in, ready to collect my soul. Its eyes blazed, blinding me with their twin lights. The shadow blanketed my body with its dark form.

It fell between me and the metal.

The panel drove its jagged edge into my savior's back.

My savior. Vick. Oh God.

Everything stopped. The lights flickered and faded from her eyes. She'd never shown me that ability before. She didn't like to call attention to her mechanical nature.

We were in darkness once more. Vick's body lay rigid atop mine, but even as my mind processed what had just happened, she exhaled and her muscles went slack, her forehead dropping to my shoulder.

Warm, sticky wetness flowed over my hand. The other released the comm I gripped. I grabbed for her, finding more blood and the metal embedded within her, slicing my palm and adding my blood to hers.

"Vick?" The empathic pain hit, flooding my vision with red. My own back arched and I writhed in agony beneath her.

"Don't... move," she hissed, but I couldn't control it. It hurt. It hurt so much. The channel opened between us, neither of us capable of stopping the flow. I felt the metal digging in deeper and fought to still myself. "Please," she begged me. "Need you... focus." The warmth leeched from her skin and mine.

My teeth clenched. I couldn't respond.

"Pocket," Vick said. She strained, trembled, her breathing shallow. I couldn't believe she retained consciousness, much less the ability to speak. But it was Vick. The implants would be instructing her body to release extra platelets, raise her temperature to fight shock, and reduce the input from her nervous system to her brain.

Inch by agonizing inch, my fingers crawled their way along her side to the pocket of her uniform pants. I popped the snap and reached in, feeling for whatever she wanted me to find, and closed my hand around something long, narrow, and plastic. A pen?

No, a hypo-press.

Tubular container for a drug one-shot, spring-loaded, safe and easy to transport.

"Painkiller?" I managed, forcing my lips apart. My jaw cracked.

"Dampener," she said. "Yours."

"But…?" How could she have possibly known I'd need an emotion-dampening drug today?

"Paranoid." She choked on a weak laugh. "Always… carry one."

For me. Because she knew sooner or later, she'd push me past my limits.

I had no words. Her love washed over me in a deep navy, more soothing than any dampener. I thumbed off the top and flipped the tube open-end downward, driving it hard against my hip. The spring system thrust the needle into my skin and delivered its load. My thoughts cleared, the emotions and pain still horrible, but I could function.

With function came clearer knowledge. With that came panic.

"How bad is it?" I asked.

"Kel…."

Vick's blood soaked me. I already knew how bad it was. I asked the harder question. The hardest. "How much time do you have?"

"Bleeding… out. Can't… compensate…." Tremors cut her off. Her breathing stuttered.

Shouts came out of the darkness. Rescue workers calling for survivors. I sucked in a thin stream of air, not enough to scream for help. It came out as a whimper no one but Vick could hear.

Dampener or not, my heart beat in synch with hers, and it slowed. I slowed. My thoughts grew sluggish. If I didn't do something, we'd die together.

"Let me take some of your pain," I offered. If I could get her to hold on, we might survive until help found us. A futile effort, most likely, but maybe easing her pain would hold off the shock a little longer.

She stiffened, then groaned at the additional agony the movement caused her. "No." That came through loud and strong.

Morals and ethics. Academy rules and vows. A psychic was forbidden from interfering in the human experience. Fix accidental damage, yes. Other interference, no. She didn't want me to go against my pledge. But this fell under accidental.

"I'm allowed if it's life-or-death."

"No. Not... reason." Her shaking picked up in intensity, each tremble shifting the metal within her, slicing skin, muscle, nerve, and spine. She wouldn't share her pain because she didn't want me to hurt more than I already did.

Her legs hadn't so much as twitched since she fell. I didn't think she could move them. I didn't think she could feel them at all. If she made it.... Oh God, I wouldn't think that way. *When.* When we got out of there, I prayed they could fix her. If she couldn't be a soldier, it would destroy her more than the metal panel already had.

I sent out my empathic sense, swimming upstream through the flood, isolating the pain and channeling it more into myself. She grasped what I did and fought, pulling the torture deeper, but she was so weak, so terrifyingly weak, she could do nothing effective to stop me.

My spine burned, my legs went numb and useless, my heart... my heart strained with the effort to keep pumping blood that continuously spilled from the open wound. Not my wound. Hers. I struggled to keep us separate, but I was losing. I bought us both time, but minutes at most.

"I'm sorry," Vick whispered, so soft I barely heard her. "Can't stay with you."

I reached to stroke her hair where it fell across my shoulder. My fingers, sticky with blood, caught in the long strands, but she didn't seem to notice or care. She lost consciousness. It was a blissful reprieve from the worst of the pain. We waited in the dark.

I knew the moment her heart stopped.

Mine tried to follow.

That. That was what my mother feared. The bond that tied us wouldn't come untied. I desperately threw off Vick's emotions, one by one, disentangling hers from mine like a dozen lassos on a raging bull. And somewhere, some final thinking part of her still-working subconscious tried to help, pushing me away, straining to break free.

She was determined not to take me with her.

A sudden light fell into my eyes, glaring from several yards down the terminal, blinding me. The rescuers. With one last wrenching of my will, I tore our feelings apart, her last glimmer of life and love falling away in a sparkling fading of navy blue. I thrust my hand upward, waving and pumping my fist to get attention. And then the paramedics were beside us with their lifesaving equipment, their strong hands, their soothing voices.

They lifted Vick off me and laid her body on its side on a stretcher. One of the medics shook his head.

"No!" It came out as a squeak. I cleared my throat and pushed against the woman holding me in place. "Her heart just stopped. It's not too late. You can save her."

Two used a laser to cut away most of the exterior metal, leaving only a small piece embedded in her back for the surgeons to more safely remove—if she responded. They packed gauze around the wound to slow the bleeding and rolled her onto her back. Two more offered oxygen and shocks to her chest. They inserted an IV. They pulled me up, and when I wouldn't walk, they dragged, then carried me, screaming and kicking up the immobile escalator to safety.

What followed were the longest minutes of my life.

Outside, I knelt among other survivors on the sidewalk, a "safe" distance from the collapsing terminal, my clothes torn and covered in Vick's blood. People walked by me. Some stopped and asked if I was all right, and I nodded, and they moved on. One man pressed a bottle of chilled water into my hand, and I poured it down my throat.

Nothing.

I reached for her, straining with all my skills, but could not find any sense of the sensations I associated with Vick: strength, defiance, determination, and her unique emotional *essence*. Never in my life had I felt so alone. Tears ran unchecked down my cheeks.

Nothing.

And then, the faintest trickle. I would never have picked it up if I hadn't been searching for it with all my being, but it was there and real.

Hugging myself to stop my shaking, I stood and raced across the passenger drop-off lane. I ducked under the yellow tape, ignoring the shouts and grasping hands of the first responders surrounding the terminal. One grabbed my shoulders, but I slipped free, my focus on the emerging paramedics and the stretcher they carried between them.

The man at Vick's feet recognized me and called off the security personnel, and a minute later we were in the rear of an ambulance, flying over the emergency vehicles toward the Asheville hospital.

"We have good surgeons, some of the best," the medic told me. "They'll fix her up just fine."

I nodded, but my attention was on Vick: the shadows around her eyes, the smears of blood they hadn't cleaned from her pale face and neck, the oxygen mask, the steady rise and fall of her chest. Yes, that. Focus on that.

I touched her shoulder and felt the bond reassert itself, wrapping around my own haggard emotions like winding a ball of yarn. Next time I wrote to my mother, I needed to tell her she'd been right. The myths were true. I wouldn't have done anything differently if I'd known, but they were true.

We arrived at the hospital where the emergency room staff whisked her away. I argued and tried to follow, but they were rushing her straight to the operating room, and they wouldn't let me in, wouldn't listen to a word I said. Despite the classified nature of Vick's physical makeup, I blurted things out—her high pain tolerance, her resistance to sedatives. I urged them to do a brain scan. They looked at me like I'd lost my mind. Earth didn't have knowledge of things like Vick's implants.

Should have covered all that in the ambulance, but I'd ridden in silence, completely in shock, just absorbing the fact that she lived at all.

They left me, alone and trembling, in a waiting room filled with plastic chairs and strangers.

My comm was in my back pocket—a bulging weight I hadn't noticed at first. I didn't remember putting it there, but I must have. Or maybe one of the paramedics did it. The battery was dead. If I had power, I could have contacted Dr. Whitehouse, made him list me as Vick's guardian, gotten him in touch with the doctors. There were things they needed to know.

I wandered into alcoves, searching for a public access comm, but the ones I found were either out of service or in use. Pressing my back against the closest pillar, I crossed my arms over my chest to hold myself together and waited.

My protective mental walls were overloaded from the mass suffering of the disaster victims and Vick's near-death experience. She couldn't activate her suppressors in semiconsciousness, either. I knew when they prepped Vick for surgery. I felt it when the anesthesiologist attempted to put Vick under. Icy liquid ran through my veins. The walls, with their happy holos of flowers and forests, blurred and undulated. I slid down to kneel on the floor, concerned faces crouching in front of me, voices calling for a nurse.

Oh God. Oh my God.

Vick's implants resisted chemical sedation. The devices shot adrenaline through her to fight the anesthesia. To prevent the nightmares she couldn't wake from. The ones that made her emotional buildups so much worse. There was a threshold, but the doctors here didn't know it.

Adrenaline flooded my system and I added my voices to those of the confused bystanders. "Please! Someone, please!"

An orderly crouched beside me and I grabbed the lapels of his white coat, yanking him closer, begging him to listen. "Stop them. You have to stop them."

He pulled at my hands, but I had him in a death grip.

"The surgery, stop it. She's not under. Please!"

I struggled to my feet, though he tried to hold me down. He shouted something over his shoulder that, in my panic, I couldn't make out. People came running. I broke away from them, racing for the doors to the restricted areas as fast as my weary legs could carry me.

I made it three, maybe four steps, before strong arms caught me and the needle pierced my bicep. Even as I sank again to the floor, I was certain of one thing.

Vick was awake, unable to speak or move, when the surgeons started cutting.

CHAPTER 19
VICK
HALF A PAIR

Two years later….

I AM *alone.*

Pain. Digging into my spine like a thousand razors. I'm screaming in my head, powerless to be heard, lying facedown while muffled voices murmur orders around me.

"Laser scalpel."

"…losing too much blood."

"Watch her heart rate. Looks a little high."

"…unusual brain waves… rate at sixty-five…."

"Eyes are tearing. Is she… is she crying?"

"Is she conscious? Shit. Increase the Propofol and turn up the gas! Administer Versed."

Cold floods my veins and I fade with the pain.

My own screams wake me. For the third time since my head hit the pillow at 0700. Three different moments, three different nightmares.

Dammit. It took forever for me to fall asleep after my argument with Kelly. After I threw her out of my quarters on Girard Moon Base.

Yes, Vick, you're on the Moon Base. Not in a hospital. Whenever, wherever that was. It's noon, now. Our team is off for the next several days, standard after a mission. We need the recovery period, but I'm not recovering like this.

Against my better judgment, I use the implants to open an internal com channel to Kelly. The events of earlier this morning replay themselves while I wait for her to pick up. Anger seethes beneath my skin, a little duller. The hurt grinds at my heart and soul.

"Mmm, Vick?" She's groggy, half-asleep. She had a long night too, and I've awakened her.

Good.

"Yeah, it's me."

"You're speaking to me?"

I snort at the hopefulness in her tone. Keep hoping, Kelly. I haven't forgiven you. My suppressors are off. I know she can feel it. "I never stopped speaking to you. I need to ask you a question. When they fixed my spine, was I conscious during the surgery?"

A quick intake of breath. "You were. How did you—?"

I groan, pulling the pillow from beneath my head and covering my face with it. "I'm remembering. Bits and pieces, all bad, while I'm sleeping. The accidents, both of them, and the surgery, coming back." I remember, too, that they gave me Versed, a forgetting drug. But such a drug would only affect my organic brain. My implanted one would retain the memory, even if it were later blocked.

"Oh, Vick." Her sympathy almost has me begging her to come over, to cross the few feet of hallway between our quarters and let herself in. To come to my room and help me through this.

But I don't.

"It's got to be connected to the failing block," she continues. The block on my ability to love her. Right. She's shifted into analysis mode, her tone professional. "It's causing lost memories to surface and triggering other problems, like your rage in the bar and your... episode... in the shower, and now this. It's all tied together. You need to let me remove it."

My fist twists the sheets into knots. "Not happening."

Kelly makes an exasperated noise over the comm. "Then what's your plan? Go crazy? You're raw, Vick. I can feel it from here. You haven't released to me since the hovervan. That's two days gone and a lot has happened."

A suicide attempt, that crazy morgue dream, and Kelly's big reveal. Yeah, a lot. "I'll manage." I turn on the suppressors, just a little. Maybe if I increase them gradually, bit by bit, taking as much of the emotional buildup as I can handle, I can hold out until I think of something else.

"You're delusional."

"Probably." I cut the connection.

My internal display shows Cupid firing an arrow straight into my heart. The three-dimensional image of myself bleeds out in a puddle of crimson.

I FIGHT my way through three days of hell.

The nights pass without sleep. Phantom pains plague my head and back. Bouts of sexual arousal catch me by surprise at the worst possible moments.

Kelly keeps her distance. She's there, always watching, standing by for the inevitable collapse. At the next table in the company's cafeteria. At a bank of exercise equipment across the gym. At a discreet twenty paces while I wander Girard Base's corridors at all hours, hoping to wear myself out enough to rest without nightmares. She never speaks, never contacts me. Just waits and watches to make sure I don't do something stupid.

Well, more stupid.

I'm delirious by the end of the third day. Plans come and go through my sleep-deprived mind like seasons and storms. I have the suppressors halfway up, knowing I have to ride the waves of depression and euphoria, pain and arousal, as much as I can to draw out my time. In desperation, I grab a bottle of sleeping pills. I know it's a mistake. They drugged me after the initial surgery to install my implants and it tore me apart, but I can't think of any other option. With sleep I'd have more control over my emotions, and with control I wouldn't need to trust Kelly for a release.

I miss her. I need her. But I won't call her.

The drugs don't work the way I hope. They trap me in an endless loop of asphyxiation, falling metal panels, and scalpels. When they wear off, I'm emotionally ragged and physically worn from tearing at the sheets all night.

The next day, I'm in one of the briefing rooms, seated in a faux-leather chair at a large oval table. I responded to Whitehouse's summons to pick up a new mission file for the team. He's late, as usual, asserting his power by making me wait. In my head, I run through a dozen lies for why I'm unfit for duty.

Whatever I say cannot be the truth. If he knows I'm going crazy, he'll try to fix me himself.

Then again, maybe….

I jerk upright in the seat, wincing at the ever-present phantom back pain. Now I know I'm far gone. I actually considered the idea of volunteering to let Whitehouse fuck with my brain.

The door opens, and Kelly steps inside the briefing room. I didn't realize he'd called the whole team, but Alex and Lyle come in behind her.

Kelly looks almost as bad as I feel. Shadows smudge her bloodshot eyes. She's pale and shaky as she eases into the seat beside mine, and I realize that, to some degree, she's felt everything I have. We exchange nods, my jaw set, her mouth a frown. I'm bleeding emotion through my suppressors like water through a sieve.

Alex and Lyle sit opposite us. They study the tabletop and the framed holos of Earth hanging on the walls. I wonder how much they're aware of. One thing I notice, they aren't giving me a hard time. I must really look like shit.

"You can't keep this up," Kelly murmurs.

I wish she hadn't sat so damn close. Her perfume, a light floral scent, carries on the recirculated air. I dig my nails into the armrests.

"I will as long as I can," I tell her.

I don't expect my resistance to end so soon.

Kelly's damp clothes cling to her skin, blonde hair hanging in wet strands to frame her face. It's not rain, but tears, running down her cheeks. She's crying. Crying over me, because I left. And even like this, she's beautiful. Maybe more so.

I pull her to me, our bodies shivering in the North Carolina storm, a place my conscious mind thinks I've never been and my subconscious knows I have. She asks me how I feel.

How I feel about her? How can she not know?

Gently, I take her chin in my callused hand and tilt it toward my descending lips, and I kiss her, our first kiss. The scent of her perfume washes over me and I'm lost.

This. This is what love felt like. And she took it from me.

The scene shifts. I'm in darkness, lying atop her, my blood soaking my clothing and hers. Searing pain tears my thoughts apart. "I'm sorry I can't stay with you," I whisper.

One last intake of breath, one last hint of her perfume, and I'm gone.

"Vick!" Kelly's shouting my name. I hear her across a great distance, her voice rising and falling in my ears as I struggle to make sense of reality.

I'm on the floor, the heavy chair lying on its side. Lyle and Alex crouch close by, anxious expressions turned toward me, then the door, then me again. But it's Kelly who has me, Kelly who supports me, one arm around my shoulders, the other pressing her hand to my forehead....

"No," I growl, wrenching away, or trying to and failing. Pain drives through me, and my spine arches, all my muscles going taut while she struggles to keep her hold. Weak, pitiful whimpers come from my throat. When the spasm ends, I'm gasping for breath, panting like I've run the obstacle course in full gear.

Kelly stiffens, her head twisting toward the still-closed entry, her eyes slightly unfocused as she sends her empathic sense outward. "Whitehouse," she says. "He's coming." Then to Alex and Lyle, "Stall him." They stare at her like she's insane. "Please. She's your teammate. He's an asshole. Whatever you think of her, she's always had your backs. Stall him."

To my amazement, they go. The door hisses shut behind them.

Kelly faces me. "No more," she says. "You're done."

I shake my head, but it's more of a loll.

"Choose," Kelly tells me, iron in her voice. "Me or Whitehouse. Think of it as the lesser of two evils, if you must. But if he comes in here and finds you like this, you'll lose more than love. You'll lose everything."

I've already lost everything. From the brief taste I still savor from my vision, I know that much. But she's not evil. She never could be. Whitehouse, on the other hand....

Kelly's told me Whitehouse would have done more to me if the great and powerful Oz hadn't forbidden it. Any last vestige of my personality, any memories I retained, he would have taken. He'd make me incapable of ever feeling love again. Even if I'm not ready for it now, I'm not willing to give up that chance.

I guess there's always more to lose.

With a tired nod, I choose.

I choose her.

CHAPTER 20
KELLY
FOR LOVE

Two years earlier....

VICK CORREN would live.

I woke in a standard hospital room, sweating and panting to catch my breath, the remnants of a nightmare replay of the last twelve hours fading: me screaming, doctors, needles. I'd come very close to emotional coma. Somewhere in there, I thought they listened to me. I hoped they did.

The oxygen monitor attached to my finger beeped an alarm, but it stopped when I took deep, even breaths, soaking in the smells of antiseptic and fear. I didn't have a nurse coming in to check, but with so many victims of the bombing, the hospital was probably overloaded. To prevent further problems, I unplugged the oximeter and removed the pinching clamp from my hand.

For what I intended to do, I needed to be able to move.

I hadn't disturbed my roommate, separated from me by a drawn pale blue curtain. Not necessary to look to know it was Vick. I could sense her familiar emotional signature, even buried under a haze of sedatives.

It made sense for the doctors to keep us together. My being there would calm her when she woke. Her constant living presence in my mind would ground me.

Stretching out the arm not connected to an IV, I managed to pull the thin barrier aside and study Vick. Just seeing her brought a wave of relief. She was whiter than the thin sheet, and tubes ran into both arms, but she lived. That's all that mattered.

But she wouldn't stay alive.

I wasn't thinking of the immediate future. We lay in a room, not a cubicle in an ICU, so she'd stabilized. No. I thought of the way she'd come after me, despite the terminal's imminent collapse. Of how she'd thrown herself across my body, the metal driving into her back, impaling her instead of me.

My shudder shook the mattress beneath me.

I would not let her risk herself again.

I swung my legs over the side of the bed and sat up, the room swimming. Somewhere I'd find the energy for what I knew I had to do. The IV came with me, running some clear liquid, probably calming drugs, into my arm. Squeamishness prevented me from yanking the needle out. Vick wouldn't have hesitated for a moment, but I wasn't Vick.

The stand rolled. The wheels squeaked. With each screech, I was sure I'd either draw the attention of a passing orderly or wake Vick, and I needed to do neither.

Bracing my free hand on first the mattress, then the bed frame, I worked my way with my IV dance partner to Vick's side.

My breath caught at the sight of her.

I wasn't used to seeing her this way, even after riding beside her in the ambulance. The helpless figure on the bed bore little resemblance to the strong, confident soldier or the passionate lover. I hated it. It was wrong. My Vick should not have looked like that.

She was unconscious, so I couldn't read her very well, which helped, but it didn't stop the memory of emptiness, total loss, isolation, and loneliness. I did not think I could survive without her, and that terrified me. I wasn't a fighter. I wasn't skilled in self-defense. Sooner or later, she would die protecting me, and that would kill me.

To save her, to save myself, I had to let part of her go.

My hands shook when I placed fingertips on her temples. I fought to still them, pressing harder than I had to and making indentations in her skin. The channel opened between us. If she were awake and rested, it would have taken both of us to connect, but in her current state, I had control.

The ultimate control.

It was heady, the knowledge of what I could do to her mind. Ethics comprised a major portion of the curriculum at the Academy. It wasn't often that medical need paired a psychic with such a close and therefore easy-to-manipulate match. Drastic alteration was possible.

And unthinkable.

And I was about to do it anyway.

It was the right thing. For both of us. Life-or-death.

Keep telling yourself that, Kelly.

I ordered the little voice in my head to shut up.

Dropping into the flow of Vick's emotions, I sought out and found the love she felt for me. It ran in rich navy, the dominant of all the colors, the strongest of her feelings, stronger even than the pain of her injuries. It rushed through her in a steady stream, blanketing the aggression, fear, and frustration. Blanketing the pain.

I hesitated.

She'd been so calm over the past week, not needing as much from me, requiring less-frequent release sessions. Could one emotion have controlled so many others? Theory and speculation. What would happen if I proceeded?

Everything we do has consequences. We work for the good of the injured and impaired, but we can never forget the potential we carry to both help and harm. My instructor's words surfaced above a litany of other remembered lectures.

Two brains could not be so intertwined: it was not healthy for either of us. I had to end it now.

Bottom line—if I didn't proceed, we would die. Nothing was worse than that.

Right?

Vick stirred, eyelids twitching, one hand moving where it lay atop the sheets. I would have grabbed and held it if my fingers weren't pressed to her forehead.

She moaned, and there was no more time for deliberation. The doctors got her under to complete the surgery, but they didn't correctly calculate the dosage to keep her there now. In minutes, maybe even seconds, her implants would cleanse her system of the sleep-inducing drugs and return her to wakefulness.

I stretched out with my empathic sense, using my ability to grab and pull the navy blue toward me. It was all metaphor and symbolism. I didn't know how we psychics did what we did. Lots of empaths saw emotions as colors. Some saw shapes or even animal representations of the different feelings. But Vick's brain, and the technology making up more than half of it, subconsciously comprehended what mine did and allowed me to manipulate it.

My energy wrapped around the blue, building a wall the way I put up my own when I tried to block out other people's emotions. Except this wall was more of a shell, a sphere, encompassing her love and trapping it, preventing her from generating more.

"Hey…," she said, voice a thin thread.

Her eyes opened. She blinked twice and focused on me. "Go back to sleep," I urged her. I wasn't finished. The flow of navy seemed unending, and I drew and drew it together, the sphere growing larger and larger. I'd never done anything like this before, going on instinct and my experience with my own shields, and guessing whenever that faltered. Pain, her pain, distracted me with a shock to my nerves and a bright red flare. I clenched my teeth against it.

"Kel, pull back. Why are you—?" In a flash of insight, Vick's consciousness grasped what I tried to do and her eyes went wide. She flailed, physically and mentally. One of the IVs yanked out of her arm as she attempted to push me away. Droplets of blood spattered the white sheet. One of the monitors beeped, then sent out a steady high-pitched whine of alarm. Her fingers brushed my wrist before her hand dropped limply to the mattress. Inside, her mind pushed against the shell I'd built. I hadn't reinforced it, and if she were healthy, her resistance would have cracked it like an egg, but she was too weak to put up an effectual fight.

I forced more of my will upon her, my knees trembling with the expended effort. I had so little strength left. The monitor continued screaming. Any second now, we'd no longer be alone. I reached the end of the navy blue, rolling, tightening and compressing it, enveloping it in my circular fortress.

"Don't," Vick said, too tired to do anything but beg. Her voice cracked. "Don't take this from me." A single tear ran down her cheek. "You're all I have. Please." But even as she spoke, her tone shifted from impassioned to flat, from loving to casual. The walls closed in; the flow cut off. Her expression lost some of its warmth as the romantic attraction faded but the friendship remained.

"I'm sorry," I told her, placing a last kiss on her brow. I withdrew from her mind, the block firmly in place within her.

"For what?" she asked, drifting off to sleep.

"Everything."

By the time a nurse and an orderly arrived, I was in my bed, covers pulled up, feigning a deep meditation trance. It was normal for empaths to place themselves in an almost comatose state when recovering from emotional trauma. They ignored me while fussing over Vick and reinserting the IV she ripped out. They speculated about what must have happened, assuming she thrashed during a nightmare, and they increased the dosages of her sedatives and painkillers. Her mind quieted beneath the onslaught of narcotic help.

As the last tendrils of her emotions faded from my awareness, I suddenly realized I hadn't only reduced the intensity of the bond between us. I hadn't merely stopped her from loving me.

So long as my barrier remained in place, she couldn't love anyone else. Ever.

I loathed the small part of me relieved by that.

AFTER HER second round of waking up ahead of schedule, the Asheville hospital staff managed to keep Vick sedated until she recovered enough to be transferred to Girard Base and the care of her own physicians. I tapped into her mind on and off throughout the process, easing the press of her emotions so they didn't build into night terrors while she slept.

Once back with the Storm, I made a deal with the devil.

Dr. Whitehouse agreed to remove Vick's memories of the past twelve days. We'd concoct a story involving a chartered shuttle and an engine accident that injured her spine and kept her in a coma. She'd think we never left the base. He would never tell anyone what I'd done.

Whitehouse's enthusiastic willingness to help made me sick. If he had his way, none of the Fighting Storm soldiers would have had emotions or distracting pasts. I knew he'd prefer an army of robots to real people. While I believed it was for Vick's own good, I constantly questioned my decision, suffering from nightmares while I protected her from hers.

He, in contrast, was eager.

And worse, it gave him a permanent hold on me. As property, Whitehouse could alter Vick in any way he saw fit. But what I'd done was punishable by law. If he ever revealed my unethical actions, I'd stand trial and have to defend the block. I might win, but not living in my head, most people wouldn't understand.

If I was convicted, psychic enforcers would impose blocks upon *me*. I'd spend the rest of my life in prison, never able to touch anyone else's emotions again.

CHAPTER 21
VICK
HALF A HEART

Two years later....

I AM haunted.

Flashes of memories I don't remember send me reeling between time frames. I'm in the briefing room, and the airlock, and in North Carolina in a cabin with Kelly's arms around me. It's all at once and maddening, and I'm not sure I can hang on.

Kelly's cool palm feels so good against my forehead, and some of the feverish madness fades. The channel opens.

Nothing flows.

"Turn off the suppressors."

I do it. It doesn't work.

Kelly heaves an exasperated sigh. "You have to trust me."

I blink, focusing on her and blotting out the false images. "I don't."

"He's in the hallway. I can sense his impatience."

Whitehouse. She means Whitehouse. I concentrate on letting go. What's always been so easy has become a sparring match of wills. Another jolt of pain lances through my temples and forces the connection, Kelly's psyche defeating mine like a seasoned soldier knocking out a new recruit. I'm the fighter, but here, in this world, she has the superior strength.

"Sorry," she says. The truth of her words calms and soothes, but it's short-lived.

The overrush of terror, pain, hurt, and betrayal pours from me to her, a flood of negative emotions, and she cries out, then clamps her free hand over her mouth and holds on. She shunts the feelings aside, preventing them from contaminating her own, pulling and discarding them into nothingness. In exchange, I feel her too, her anguish, her regret and shame, and dammit, her love for me. No point in her hiding it anymore. It's warm and gentle, comforting like nothing I've ever known or at least nothing I can remember. I want to hold it inside me, but it slips through my mind's grasp. One minute passes, maybe two, and then she yanks herself away. Her absence is a fire burning out in cold vacuum.

Cocking her head to the side, Kelly studies my face. Hers drips with sweat, and she wipes it on her uniform sleeve. "Will you hold together?" she asks.

The brief release isn't nearly enough, but my hand doesn't tremble when I hold it out for her to see. "I'll make it through the meeting." My voice is steady up until "meeting," when it quavers.

"Let me do the talking. Just sit there and look competent."

That almost earns her a smile. Almost. But I school my expression. "This doesn't change how I feel about you."

"I know." She grabs the outstretched hand and pulls me up, then rushes to straighten the chair I toppled and shoves me into it as the briefing room door slides open and the three men enter.

Kelly's still standing, so she takes a few steps toward the entry and stops, saying, "I was just coming to see what was keeping you."

"Intermercenary team sports scores are what's keeping us." Dr. Whitehouse tosses Alex and Lyle a disgusted look, running a hand through his graying hair and seating himself at one end of the oval table—the power position.

My male teammates wear identical shit-eating grins, seating themselves opposite Kelly and me. I can imagine them recounting every play of last night's soccer match between the Storm and the Sunfires, acting out the best ones in the outer hall and blocking Whitehouse from reaching the briefing room. While the doc turns on his deskcomp and sends commands to activate ours, I give Alex a nod of thanks. He shrugs in response, but his grin doesn't fade. Lyle crosses his arms over his chest, a "you owe me" look if ever I saw one. I nod to him too. The pittance of a bank account the Storm allows me can afford a couple of extra ales next time we hit the Alpha Dog.

The surface of the table in front of me glows white, then becomes transparent as the built-in screen goes live. It displays some technical data identified as ComTrans162A, a lot of jagged graph lines, and more meaningless numbers in greens with one string in red.

Alex whistles, long and low. "We were hacked?" our tech guru asks, a reverent note in his voice.

My head jerks up, and I stare first at him, then Whitehouse. The Fighting Storm employs the best techs anywhere, even better than the One World government back on Earth. We have all the latest gear, the top-of-the-line security equipment. Hell, our people *invent* most of the newest stuff, the crap in my brain not being the best example. How the hell—?

"It's worse than that." Dr. Whitehouse's mouth forms a grim line. With my own problems on hold, I notice his disheveled appearance, rumpled clothing, stubble-covered chin. "Yesterday, someone broke the security codes on our transmission satellite number 162D. Sifting through messages sent and received, he backtracked a specific ID through the waylayer relays." He turns his gaze on Alex, the most likely of us to understand what he's saying. "He followed the Yellow Brick Road."

Alex's eyebrows shoot up beneath his hairline. His lips open and close several times before he finds words. I, for one, have no idea what they're talking about, and the look Kelly shoots me from the corner of her eye says she's in the dark too. But Alex knows, and he's floored.

"That's... that's impossible. I know the guys on the YBR team, the ones who designed the road. My brother's on that team."

Lots of families in mercenary organizations, especially the older ones. Becomes something of a tradition to serve. Alex talks about his brother when we're on missions, sometimes. Not to me of course, but to Lyle and Kelly. He worships his older brother. If Alex is a tech guru, his brother's the Dali-fucking-Lama.

Pushing back from the table, Alex stands, then paces the length of the room. He's waving his muscular arms around, Lyle ducking to avoid getting swatted. I've never seen Alex so agitated. "My bro's a genius. A fucking genius. Nobody can hack him."

"Hacked or bought. Internal Affairs will find out which."

It takes all three of us, me, Kelly, and Lyle, to prevent Alex from going over the table at Whitehouse. Alex's muscles strain against our holds, his dark-skinned face turning three shades darker while the rage seethes. "Take it back!" he shouts. "Take it the fuck back. Barry's no fucking traitor!"

Whitehouse doesn't move from his seat, his straight-backed posture conveying complete composure in the face of Alex's rage. I have to admit, I'm impressed, though a slight twitch of his right eyebrow tells me his nerves aren't entirely steel. "The investigation will confirm or deny that. In the meantime, I suggest you *sit down* before you find yourself a second subject of legal concern."

"Hey, I'm the team wild card," I say into Alex's ear. "Not you."

Alex draws a deep breath and nods, shaking himself out to relieve the tension. He eases off the table, pulling his upper body back and tugging his arm from my grasp. It's a damn good thing the whole team is here. Alone, in my current state, I'd never have held him.

Then again, watching Whitehouse get pummeled would have made up for an otherwise shitty day.

"Now that we've returned from recess," the doc continues, earning a growl from Alex, "let me get to the heart of the problem."

"Wait." Lyle holds up a hand, unconsciously strengthening the schoolchild comparison. "Can someone tell me what all this means? I'm a driver and a pilot, not a programmer."

Whitehouse drums his fingers on the tabletop, an admission of impatience he rarely displays, but he explains, "Someone managed to break into our communications systems with the sole purpose of tracking a specific series of transmissions—those sent back and forth between Girard Base and Storm Center."

A sick sense of dread settles in my stomach. If those transmissions were successfully tracked....

"He followed the trail, otherwise known as the Yellow Brick Road, to Oz's hidden private residence. And is holding him hostage."

"And do we know who the bastard is? Who has our boss?" Lyle asks.

Before Whitehouse can answer, I know, and judging from the way Kelly's hand covers mine beneath the table, she knows too. I'm too shaken to pull away from her.

"We doubt highly that he did the technological work himself but rather hired in someone or bribed an expert." Whitehouse is careful not to meet Alex's eyes there. "But the man behind the kidnapping is Patrick Rodwell."

The one who got away. The one I *let* get away.

My internal display shows a fishing pole, hook dangling and empty. I blink it from my sight.

The doc stares right at me, glaring, accusing. I'm nauseated by guilt, not from him, but from the head of the Fighting Storm. It's the loyalty compulsion programming rearing its ugly head, but knowing the source doesn't make it better.

"I'm assuming we're the team chosen to handle it." I remove my hand from Kelly's grasp and fold both on the table.

Whitehouse shakes his head. "Not chosen. In light of your recent outbursts and involvement in public altercations, I argued against your team's inclusion in this mission, but the board outvoted me." He fixes me with his gaze. "Your presence is required and requested. Personally."

"Excuse me?"

"You, VC1. The ransom transmission contained one demand in exchange for Oz. You. Dead or alive. Preferably dead."

Beside me, Kelly covers her mouth with her hand. After all we've been through together, her innocence still surprises me. A good thing, I suppose.

"You killed his wife. He wants some payback," Lyle supplies, like I couldn't have figured that out for myself.

"Your mission is to infiltrate Oz's hidden residence, get him out, take down Rodwell, and, if circumstances permit, obtain evidence to clear the YBR team of any charges of treason."

Alex nods, satisfied with the parameters. "We'll find it."

Inside, self-preservation and my conscience rage, screaming to be heard. This is not something I can do, not right now. I'm liable to get myself and my team killed. I open my mouth to tell Whitehouse where he can stick his mission.

The implants take over. Painfully. Definitively. Programming dictates that I push myself to my limits, especially in defense of any member of the Fighting Storm. And my limits, so far as my implants are concerned, have not yet been reached.

"All right, then," I say. "When do we leave?"

Chapter 22
Kelly
Out of Mind, Out of Sight

Now Vick Corren is a man-made martyr.

"Are you out of your mind?" I chase Vick down the corridor after the briefing, not hiding from her like I've been doing for the past three days, but dead on her heels. Farther along, Alex and Lyle cast wary glances over their shoulders, but turn away when they see my expression and disappear through a hatch.

Vick pulls up at the next corner, pressing against the metal wall to allow a hoverdolly to pass with its load of bottled water and dried snacks for the cafeteria. "You should know. You put me there," she drawls, no anger in it.

I guess resignation beats hatred.

I catch her sleeve to prevent her from hurrying on, and release her at the sudden tensing of her muscles. *She's edgy*, I remind myself. *We didn't finish the release. Plenty of bad emotions still in there.* And I feel them, ratcheting up her stress levels and encouraging irrational decisions.

"You can't take this mission. You aren't fit for field duty, and you'll be worse in two days."

Two days to bring in equipment, requisition a shuttle, receive final approval from the board. Two days for the block to keep failing and the memories to grow stronger.

"I'll work with you, report for regular releases. Just tell me where and when."

We're moving, heading for our quarters. I take a step and a half for every one of hers to match her longer-legged stride. I have to run to get in front of her, but I do. She pulls up short, frowning.

"It won't matter. It's a short-term fix, and that term will get shorter and shorter. Let me pull the block, or you agree to stay inactive until it fails on its own. Anything else is suicide."

For a moment I think she might give in. Her weariness comes through the bravado, shoulders sagging, head bowed. Then she looks me dead in the eye.

"I have to do this, Kel. I don't have a choice."

Fear floods me. Hers, not mine. "I don't understand."

"Have you ever known me to turn down a mission?"

I think about it. "No." In two years, she's taken everything the Storm has thrown her way, regardless of sickness, injury, or exhaustion. "Why is that?"

"You need to figure that out for yourself." Vick's voice has gone soft and low, like having anyone hear her will result in punishment.

"I don't want to play guessing games. You're a threat to the team, an unnecessary risk to us and yourself."

Vick's fist lashes out without warning, slamming the wall and leaving an indentation. I jump away, staring at her cracked and bleeding knuckles. "I'm not playing!"

Desperation and pain. Sickly greens and reds swirl in my second sight.

I grab her by the shoulders, feel the trembling in her arms. "No, you're not, are you?" I search her eyes, see the pleading there. She needs me to understand something she will not— No. Something she *cannot* tell me. "You'd never endanger your team, not of your own free will. The implants," I breathe, and her shoulders relax, just the slightest bit.

Around us, people stare as they pass. Sensing the tension, they move on.

I push further. "Some sort of… service command, a drive to obey."

She relaxes a little more.

"You can't refuse a mission, even if you want to. Even if you need to. Oh God, that's it, isn't it?" My voice breaks. She can't confirm that I'm right, but I know it. I know it's true. And I can't refuse for her. If Whitehouse knows her condition, he'll take matters into his own hands. I won't risk it. As a team, we'll support Vick and each other. Somehow, we'll get through this.

Closing her eyes, Vick slumps against the wall. A single tear runs down her cheek. "I told you I'm a machine."

I brush the tear away with my fingertips. "Machines don't cry."

LATER THAT night, she buzzes the door to my quarters. I open it to find her standing there, wearing her pajamas, a duffel filled with weapons slung over her shoulder. It overflows, a few protruding through the unsealed top zipper. Her hand is wrapped in bandages from when she punched the wall.

"You all right?" It's a stupid question. Soldiers who are all right don't deliver weapons to their partners while dressed in pajamas.

Wordlessly, she passes me the bag. I take it without argument, its weight dropping my arm to my side. She grimaces as the metal clangs on the floor. Profound relief fills my senses.

"This all of them?" I try instead.

Vick nods once.

She leaves me with her greatest security and her greatest threat dangling from my hand.

Not for the first time, I think of the position Vick's in. A year ago, I sent a secret copy of her contract to my mother, asking her to look into its validity. On Earth, she said, such a contract would never have been permitted to exist. Out here, on the moon, in the "frontier," such as it is, the laws are different. We don't fall under Earth's jurisdiction.

Vick belongs to the Storm. They classify her as a machine and property.

And me? I belong to Vick, for as long as she lives. For as long as she'll have me.

CHAPTER 23
VICK
CHOICE AND CONSEQUENCE

I AM a hurtful bitch.

Half-asleep, my thoughts drift. I toss and turn on the thin standard-issue mattress, erotic images passing through my vision like I've downloaded a dozen X-rated films into my implants. Some feel dreamy, filled with impossible positions, exaggerated body parts, scenes and settings too beautiful to exist. And oil. Spread over skin so soft and so very, very feminine. Sigh.

Others are undeniable memories, remnants of what Whitehouse blocked or attempted to erase. Kelly's breasts brush across mine; her moans and cries echo in my ears. I hold her, taste her, clutch her to me as both our bodies go rigid with emotional and physical simultaneous release.

When I wake, I'm sweat-soaked, my hand pressed between my thighs. Heat suffuses my cheeks as I withdraw it. I take no comfort from knowing I'm driving Kelly as crazy as I'm driving myself. In fact, it increases the frustration, my mind wandering to imagine how she's dealing with the unbidden feelings I must be transmitting to her.

You could call her.

I search my emotions, looking for any indication of more than simple sexual impulse, and find nothing. I won't contact her to satisfy those needs. It would be... wrong, somehow.

With a growl, I shove myself off the bed and into a clean uniform. The time's 2307—late, but not too late. I'd turned in early, thinking to get as much rest as possible before leaving on the mission in the morning, but I'm lucky if I caught an hour of real sleep in there. Now I'm wide-awake.

Tomorrow I'll be worthless.

I pass through my still-disheveled living room, broken furniture piled to the side, waiting for a trip to the large materials recycler.

I'm prowling the corridors before I fully realize I've left my quarters. The stark hallways making up the Fighting Storm areas give way to more civilian, commercial sections of Girard Base. For once, there's no indication Kelly is following me. Either she's too distracted or too tired to tail me this time. Lit signs and dancing holograms advertise bars, restaurants, and clubs, along with shops and services.

Lots of services, of all kinds. The moon plays by different rules.

Once in a long while that works in my favor.

I've never been to the Purple Leaf. Hell, I've never been to any place of this sort before, but I stand in the dim lobby of the sex club, unsure how to proceed. The flashing sign inside the entry reads "Turn Over a New Leaf." Considering all the waitstaff wear strategically placed leaves and nothing else, the connotations set my imagination racing.

Purple is a theme in addition to a name. Purple velvet furnishings, rich purple wall hangings to cover the metal bulkheads, purple black lights glowing in brackets interspersed throughout the open center space, plush purple carpeting. The circular lobby reaches into darkness, with secluded alcoves along the perimeter boasting purple couches and curtains hiding their occupants from view. Rustling of clothing and the occasional moan carry from behind the partitions. At the very center is a circular bar with flexible light poles in the middle of it, extending upward toward the ceiling, purple bulbs hanging from the "branches" like leaves. Patrons on high bar stools sit around it, sipping drinks and engaging in conversation, kissing, or, in some cases, doing some very public heavy petting.

Dark rooms bother me. I don't like my vision impaired. Shadows hide enemies. I can increase the rod cell production in my eyes, giving me temporarily enhanced eyesight, or I can set myself apart as a freak and cast light from my eyes, but both have uncomfortable side effects. Here, I appreciate the darkness. It hides my blush and discomfort.

"What would someone like you want in a place like this?"

The voice comes from my left—male, belligerent, and more than a little slurred.

I shift in his direction, relaxing into a deceptively casual stance while the implants run a quick threat assessment: well-tailored clothing hiding flab, no weapons, lungs overtaxed by inhalation of narcotic breathables that will slow him down if we end up in a fight. Not that I want one. I've had enough fighting this week.

"Not you," I respond, answering his initial question.

He's not military or paramilitary, not in that gray business suit and black tie. Businessman, more likely. Unlike the Alpha Dog Pub, the Purple Leaf clearly got all kinds.

"Can't you just flip a switch or something? Get yourself off with a thought? People here want *real* sex. With human beings. If we wanted toys, we could hit the shop across the promenade."

I'm two seconds away from another brawl when a hand lands on my shoulder. "Can it, Daniels. She's got as much right to be here as anyone else. Don't make me get all professional when I'm off duty."

I turn toward the woman's no-nonsense voice coming from behind me and end up face-to-face with Officer Sanderson of the Girard Base security force. She's out of uniform, dressed in black trousers and a matching vest that accentuates her muscular arms and ample cleavage. Nice.

"Ignore him," she says, tightening her grip.

Daniels looks from me to her and back again, blows out a breath, scowls, and walks off toward the center bar, grumbling.

"I was just leaving anyway," I mutter, shrugging off Officer Sanderson's hand and shifting past her.

"Come have a drink with me." She doesn't attempt to touch me again. My rigid posture is enough to squelch any urge she might have had to do so, but her tone is inviting, and her smile is warm. "You look like you could use one."

"Last time I had a drink I ended up in your jail cell."

Her grin turns sly. "Good thing I'm here, then, huh?"

I surprise myself with a bark of laughter and follow her to an open alcove.

We seat ourselves on opposite couches, a low table between us. She leaves the curtains open, out of deference to me, I suspect.

Our butts barely hit the cushions before a well-built waiter arrives wearing a cluster of purple leaves to cover his assets. I'm admiring the planes of his chest while Sanderson requests some beverage I've never heard of. He flashes me a brilliant smile, and I mumble the name of a common ale. "Good to see you again, Vick. What's it been, two, three years?"

I blink, recovering too slowly to avoid Sanderson's scrutiny. "At least," I return with a faint smile.

The waiter leaves to fetch our order.

"From that confrontation at the door, I figured you'd never been here before," Sanderson comments.

"Not that I can remember," I tell her.

Sanderson cocks her head. "No, you can't, can you? Must be difficult."

"You have no idea." I consider all the other things I can't remember: former friends, family, home, love. Yeah, it sucks.

She nods. "So," Sanderson says, studying me, "you're not here to drink, and you're perched on the edge of that couch like you're gonna bolt if I say boo, so what *are* you here for?"

I search her face for hidden meanings, any note of lasciviousness, but it's an innocuous enough question, and I give her an honest answer. "I don't know."

"You're not looking for some asshole like Daniels," she says.

Her eyes hold sympathy, almost more sympathy than I can handle right now, and I blink away the sudden cloudiness in my own vision and focus on the deep purple curtains. "How the hell did he know me, anyway?"

Sanderson shrugs. "He works for Biotech. And he's on base for some big tech conference with a couple of the merc organizations, including yours, I think. That might explain it."

I close my eyes and let out a long sigh. Yeah. That might. The Storm's research and development team designed my implants, but Biotech manufactured them from the schematics. Even one of their lower-level sales guys would probably recognize me, even if he didn't know all my specs.

Our drinks arrive, a woman bearing them on a tray carried just low enough so we can see her leaf-covered breasts. Tiny leaves. Big breasts. I wonder if the club switched servers on us after seeing me and Sanderson together, catering to an assumed preference. From Sanderson's expression, she appreciates the change.

When the waitress leaves, I reach for my ale, but Sanderson covers my hand with her own. "You're not a machine," she says. "You're too lost. Things with programming have direction."

Damn, she sounds like Kelly. In every physical way, they couldn't be more different. Sanderson is muscular and tall, taller than me by an inch or two, where Kelly is petite. Sanderson is hard where Kelly is soft. But they're both smart, and they both see right through me.

Instead of pressing me, my companion makes small talk, describing how she came to work on Girard Base, her family, raised by a single dad and five older brothers, mother lost giving birth to her. Hard life, but they never made her feel inferior or blamed her for the loss.

I share what I can, focusing on tastes I've developed over the past two years—some music, some vidnet shows. We compare favorite weapons and fighting styles, keeping things light and easy on me.

After three strong ales I'm riding a heavy buzz, not drunk, but well on my way. The implants will step in soon and burn the alcohol off, but for now, it's a pleasant haze, and I let it distract me from Whitehouse, Oz, Rodwell, and Kelly.

When I lean in to wipe a slight spill from the table, Sanderson meets me halfway and touches her lips to mine. It's warm and not unpleasant. Her eyes sparkle in the light of the table's single lavender-scented candle. Despite her cut-from-stone fashion and style, she has an attractiveness all her own.

But it isn't pleasant, either. It's… nothing.

I sit back, keeping my face impassive, not wanting to hurt her feelings. I've done enough of that lately. I contemplate spending the night with her, losing myself in her, releasing the tension the dreams and memory flashes have built.

Using her.

She reads my decision at the same moment I reach it.

"Losing my touch, huh?" she murmurs, no anger in it. I wonder at her age, older than me by several years, that's for certain, and whether this is a real concern of hers.

"Not at all," I assure her. "The kiss was nice. I'm just…." What do I say? "There's someone I'm not ready to give up on yet." Not certain if I'm talking about Kelly or myself. And I can't *feel* anything for her, but I don't say that. Sanderson isn't really my type. I like her. I respect her. But I won't sleep with her. Maybe *because* I respect her.

Sanderson nods. "Figured as much. The blonde from the cell block, right? When I saw you here, I wasn't sure if you'd cut ties or were testing yourself. Guess it was the latter."

"Guess so. I'm sorry I wasted your evening." I am, too. The Purple Leaf is crawling with eligible partners, people who want what Sanderson wants.

"No waste at all," she says, standing. She reaches into her pocket, removing one of her cards, and passes it to me. "If you change your mind."

I take it, but I know I'll never use it. She'd make a good friend, but she won't be my lover.

I turn to leave, but she calls my name. She removes something else from the depths of her vest pocket, a small black fabric pouch. "Been carrying this around, figuring I'd run into you sooner or later." Her lips twist in a grin. "Didn't think it would be here." She shrugs and passes it to me.

I pull apart the drawstring closure and tip the contents into my palm. A tiny gold heart tumbles out. My breath catches in my throat, and I stare at her. My vision blurs for the second time since I got here. I blink, hopefully before she notices.

Her smile is soft. "Glad you still want it. Rescued it just before the recycler ran." She fixes me with a stern glare. "You shouldn't go throwing your heart away."

The Tin Man dances in my internal display. I don't shut it down, but let him cavort and clank about before he vanishes.

On my way out of the Purple Leaf, movement catches the corner of my vision—a familiar figure, a glimpse of blonde hair. I meet Kelly's eyes, and she bolts.

She followed me after all.

I doubt she went inside. I can't imagine her having the nerve to enter such a place. So she probably never saw me with Sanderson, but I can't be sure. If she watched us kiss....

At the very least, she knows I spent a couple of hours in a sex club. And I care. Dammit. I care.

CHAPTER 24
KELLY
ROUGH START

VICK CORREN is no longer mine.

When a cold shower does nothing more than harden my nipples further, I drag on a uniform and go for a walk around the station. It's Vick's favorite method of avoidance, and it hasn't worked for her, so I don't know why I expect different results.

Isn't that one of the definitions of insanity?

Upon reaching the business district, I'm surprised to sense her. She's taken to indulging her needs the past couple of nights, driving me crazy with the secondhand arousal. No longer caring whether I know about her most intimate acts. But tonight she's here somewhere, and for a moment I contemplate finding her, having a drink, catching a sports event in one of the lounges, just spending time together.

Her anger has faded. We're not enemies, never were, really. We aren't quite friends again, either, and nowhere close to lovers, not until I pull the block at the very least, but we need to rebuild.

How can I miss someone I see every single day?

I follow the invisible trail of her emotions from area to area. It's not too hard to track her. Since we've restarted regular release sessions, she's kept her suppressors off, and her confusion, concern, and frustration draw me from an all-night coffee shop to a small domed park in the center of the base, to—

The Purple Leaf.

It takes me a minute or two to figure out this is no ordinary bar. The attire of the staff and many of the patrons gives away its true nature. It's a sex club.

Vick's in a sex club.

My first impulse is to laugh, though I'm sure that's not what she'd expect. I'm picturing the serious, stoic, hard-lining soldier surrounded by nearly naked men and women, being propositioned at every turn. She's so very uncomfortable with relationships.

She's also desperate.

The laughter dies in my throat.

Vick's needs are so intense they've driven her here, in contradiction to her solitary nature. I can't imagine what that must be like for her.

I step inside, sliding around a couple lip-locked in the entryway, the man's hands roving over the woman's hips and backside. Shapely hips and backside. *Very* shapely hips and—I shake my head. Vick's needs are my needs. Even if the residuals aren't as extreme, I'll have to take special care here.

The bar marks the center of the circular room and seems the most likely place to find her, so I head for it, walking around it while searching for her familiar form.

Vick would be surprised by my casual stroll, but it's not like I've never heard of one of these places. Never been in one, no, but my Academy classmates shared their exploits with much enthusiasm.

At its heart, it's a bar with benefits. A few drinks, a few smiles, some conversation, and you can take a willing partner behind the curtains to one of the couches in the alcoves and explore whatever you want.

An attractive man raises a glass in my direction along with an eyebrow, tilting his head toward the empty seat next to him. I smile but shake my head. My empathic sense picks up that he'd prefer to press the invitation, but he glances toward one of the bouncers and nods his acceptance of my refusal.

One more good thing about this sort of place. The clubs provide a level of safety, with muscular, well-trained personnel on hand to ensure every move is consensual, med-scanners built into the couches to alert patrons to disease or parasites, and a general attitude of short-termness that the transient residents of Girard Base prefer.

Not my thing, but I see the appeal.

When an attractive redhead slips her arm around my waist and her hand smoothes across the overly sensitive skin of my backside, I see the appeal more than ever. Desire flares, and I clear my throat to cover a moan.

God, I need to get back together with Vick, and soon. Two years is a long time.

"Buy you a drink?" the woman offers in a sultry tone.

The tingling in the pit of my stomach says yes. "Sorry, no," I manage, though it's harder than I want to admit. "I'm looking for a friend of mine. Tall, long dark hair, dark eyes, tan military uniform like mine?"

"Oooh, I love women in uniform."

From the way her eyes devour me, I can believe that. Heat and lust roll off her in lavender waves that blend in my second sight with the rest of the decor.

"She would have come in a while ago," I add. And she's here, now. I know it. In a restroom, perhaps? She wouldn't be—

I glance to my left just in time to spot Vick, engaged in a kiss with a strange woman with buzz-cut hair and wearing a revealing black vest. There's no mistaking them through the open curtains, no room for doubt. Vick's leaning in to meet her, her arm and upper body muscles taut as she holds herself steady for the kiss. Their lips remain pressed together for what seems like an infinite period before they part, slowly, gradually, leaning back on their couches and watching for the other's response.

It's then I realize the woman isn't a stranger, but that officer from the base security station. I don't remember her name, but she treated both me and Vick kindly and with respect.

Vick would be drawn to someone like that.

My senses flare outward. I can't sense a damn thing through my own roiling emotions. Is the attraction mutual? It certainly looks like it is.

I must have twitched or made some despairing sound, because the redhead follows my gaze and her hand falls on my shoulder. "I'm sorry, honey. Not what you were hoping for, huh?"

Not even close.

"N-no," I stammer, drawing away. "It's fine. We're just friends, like I said. I was concerned about her, that's all." But I'm talking too fast, the room is too warm, the twinkling lights make me dizzy. I need to get out of the Purple Leaf.

I need to get away from Vick, as fast as I can. Yet I can't tear myself from the sight.

The two women exchange a few words; then the security officer passes something to Vick that looks like one of those pouches jewelry comes in. A gift? Then this isn't a chance encounter. They've been seeing each other for some time. Maybe over the several days since the argument in front of Vick's cell. My heart hurts.

Who am I to care? I took her ability to love me. I thought I'd taken it all. Not intentionally, of course, but that had been my perception at the time—that Vick could love no one, thanks to my fumbling novice manipulation of her emotions—but maybe I was mistaken. Or maybe with the failing block, she's regained some ability to show deeper affection and chooses not to show it to me. I can't believe she's involved with someone else, that she's hidden it so well I never detected it, but for the first few days after the kidnapping mission, she had the suppressors running, and the last have been filled with more aggressive feelings that might smother something so delicate.

I was following her, making sure she didn't hurt herself. How?

It's some kind of mistake. A misunderstanding.

Vick dumps the contents of the pouch into her hand. A small gold object falls out, confirming my worst suspicions. Her warmth and gratitude suffuse her in a silvery light. Whatever the gift is, it has moved her deeply, perhaps to tears, her joy is so great. She stands to leave.

I run.

The crowd has grown since I came in. I push and shove bodies aside, not focusing on anyone, my senses overwhelmed by the physical contact and all the arousal pouring from the clientele. Between their desire, Vick's, and my own, I'm a wreck when I reach the exterior corridor. I duck around a corner, panting, face flushed, knowing she must be right behind me.

Sure enough, a quick peek shows her leaving the club, a soft smile playing about her lips. I haven't seen her smile in so long.

What did you think would happen? Did you think she'd have you back after what you did? Did you think she'd give up all relationships because she can't have you?

Yes, all of that. God, I'm so full of myself.

As if she senses me standing there, she looks up. Her eyes widen. She glances from me to the club, then back again and opens her mouth to speak, but I'm running—running fast and blind down the corridors toward my quarters.

When I get there, I lock myself in and flop on my bed, pounding the pillows and the mattress until my arms hurt from the effort. The right thing,

I try to remind myself. Placing the block was the right thing. Blocking Vick's ability to love me was the right thing. I thought I'd blocked it all, whether I'd intended to or not, but maybe I was wrong.

And now I've truly lost her.

Fighting with her hurt. Seeing her with someone else creates a horrible pressure in my chest that aches and builds until I'm certain it will explode, and I'm hoping, wishing for it.

I scream into the pillows, muffling the hoarse, raw sound so someone on the other side of my quarters' walls doesn't raise an alarm and come running to my rescue. I scream until I'm breathless, almost suffocated by the foam-filled cushion. I scream until my battered throat is reduced to producing nothing more than exhausted whimpers. And none of it helps.

This. This is what Vick experiences when her emotions bottle up and she cannot release them.

It's silly and childish to fail to answer my comm when it beeps an incoming message, to ignore the buzzing at my door, to refuse to respond to her calling my name through the metal hatch, no matter how plaintive she sounds and how devastated her emotions reveal her to be.

I don't know how long she waits outside my quarters, but in the morning, when I leave to meet the rest of the team at the shuttleport, she's gone.

CHAPTER 25
VICK
MATTER OF PERSPECTIVE

I AM....

"Yo, Corren, wake up!"

I jerk upright in my cushioned seat, heart pounding from the sudden intrusion in my dreams. A sharp jolt throws me against the armrest, and I grunt as I take the impact to my ribs. And wait. Did Lyle just call me Corren? Since when does he call me that? Rapid blinking brings the shuttle's cockpit into focus, several lights flashing red on the control panel before me. An alarm sounds, an ominous clanging to accompany the pounding headache building in my temples.

"What the hell?" I tap inquiries into the flight comp and bring up displays on several readouts. We're losing power, losing altitude. A glance out the forward viewport shows the pockmarked surface of a small moon whirling closer and closer.

In the pilot's seat beside me, Lyle's face is grim, his jaw set. He struggles to stop our downward spiral, to even out our descent, yanking back on the control stick with both hands. "They hit us with an energy pulse," he grinds out. "No warning. Blew engine one, overloaded engine two. See if you can bleed off some of the excess."

"On it." If Lyle's worried, things are really serious. I hurry to comply, fingers flying over the touch screens. It's hard to ignore the dizzying scenery in front of us, and the gravity generators can't compensate completely, creating an uneasy feeling in the pit of my stomach.

While my implants move my hands where they need to be, the human part of my brain rushes to catch up. Mission, shuttle, Oz. We left Girard Base this morning, Lyle at his usual place in the pilot's seat. I must have crashed hard, because I've been out the entire eight-hour trip to Oz's hidden stronghold—a base on a rock orbiting Jupiter, blending perfectly with all the other rocks and the larger moons, with the exception of the shielded technology our sensing equipment is calibrated to detect. Now it looks like Rodwell is using Oz's defense systems against us—the best damn defenses the Fighting Storm can buy or invent.

Wonderful.

"What's happening up there?" Alex's voice, over the shuttle intercom. Faint gagging in the background. Probably Kelly. I fire up my suppressors as I think of her. There's too much to deal with without adding unresolved relationship issues to the mix.

Lyle's got the harder job, so I flip open the channel. "Strap in and hang on. Looks like we're going down."

Several impressive curses and he cuts the connection.

"Any sign of Team Two?" Lyle asks.

I check the scanners. A quick blip pinpoints the second shuttle behind us, then it's gone. We're spinning too fast for the technology to keep up its tracking. "I think they're back there. Don't know if they got hit too." I swallow a mouthful of bile. "Watching the readouts is making me sick." We're trained for this sort of thing, but we're not immune. I could use the implants to calm my stomach, but I'll pay for it in energy I'll need later, so I refrain.

"Forget it, then. They'll make it or they won't. We'll pick up the pieces later."

It's a harsh assessment but realistic. There's nothing we can do for the other shuttle. In all honesty, they're probably in better shape to help *us*. Since we led the way in, we may have been the only ones hit.

The surface looms closer. I can make out individual craters and peaks. Almost no water, too light gravity, minimal atmosphere from an unfinished terraforming process. It's a rock, barren and empty except for Oz's hideout—a collection of warehouse-type one-level structures connected by enclosed passages whirling in and out of my field of vision.

I manage to grab a san-bag just in time to puke into it. More alarms go off. Lyle can't right us. If I don't do something fast, we're going to make a new crater. "Losing it," he growls, confirming my fears.

After spitting out the last of the sour liquid, I dump the bag down the recycler hatch and clasp my own set of copilot's controls. "Switch it to me," I tell him. Acting on instinct, I throw my suppressors to full power and give myself over to the implants. I've never done this before—willingly let them take charge. I usually cling to the shreds of my humanity with an iron grip. But it feels like our only chance.

"What makes you think you can—?" Lyle breaks off as he meets my gaze, steady, unflinching, and emotionless. Whatever he sees has him transferring control to my station. "Yours," he tells me and fastens his restraints tighter across his chest.

Lyle does most of our driving and flying, leaving me free to fight and lead. But I'm a better pilot any day. With my faster reflexes and the implants analyzing speed, course, fuel consumption, I'll always be better.

Today, I'm fucking amazing.

In seconds I've brought the damaged shuttle out of its spin, corrected our course, and calculated when our final engine will give out, all without conscious thought. I'm in perfect tune with the ship's systems, the onboard comps trading information back and forth between the shuttle and my implants in a steady stream.

It's… weird, like watching myself from the outside and not recognizing who I am. I don't like it, but it saves our necks.

"You got it, Corren," Lyle says, heaving a deep breath and settling into his seat.

I don't respond. I can't. The implants take up too much of my processing power.

Processing power? Oh, great. Even more evidence that I'm retreating into my machine-self. Time for another soul-searching chat with Kelly.

Except she's not speaking to me. Hasn't said a word, not even when I passed her in the tiny two-man passenger area on my way forward. She looked as bad as me, though.

I bring us down about a mile from the hidden installation, not wanting to risk any further defensive weaponry. The scanners show the second shuttle carrying Team Two coming in behind us. We'll have to hoof it from here, in full environmental suits and grav boots. The partially terraformed surface has a breathable atmosphere but temperatures well below freezing and gravity too low to make foot travel easy.

I hate envirosuits. They fit over regular clothing like a too tight second skin and accentuate everything, not to mention restricting movement in a fight. I hope inside the structure we'll be able to discard them.

I'm unsnapping my restraints when Lyle's hand falls on my shoulder, causing me to stiffen. He eases his hand away, but the smile stays plastered on his face, and it seems genuine.

"Damn fine flying, Corren."

Less input means I can speak again. I tamp down the suppressors and retrieve control from the implants, though it's quite a bit harder than I would prefer. My internal display shows two images of me, both grasping the frayed sanity cord in a twisted game of tug-o-war. One me grimaces with the pain and effort. The other has no expression at all. The visual disappears before I can see which side wins. Something tells me I better not give the implants free rein again anytime soon.

"So," I say, desperate for the distraction, "when did I stop being VC1?" Shouldn't ask, I know. Just begging for him to turn around and hurl some insult.

But he doesn't. "In the hovervan, with Kelly. And then you shot that Rodwell bitch before she could shoot me. Alex and I been talking. Figure we should cut you some slack, you know?" He shifts in his seat and his gaze wanders.

I can understand his discomfort. It's not a simple thing to change your mind about someone. Even though this would be a perfect opening for a sarcastic comment, I nod. "Haven't had a chance to thank you for your help in the Alpha Dog, so thanks. Would've been a lot worse without you and Alex keeping some of them off my back."

We leave the cockpit in companionable silence to encounter Alex's grimace in the passenger compartment. He's kneeling, fitting the access panel to the engine crawlspace into place. The scent of ozone like after a lightning strike fills the cabin.

Behind him, Kelly pulls on her envirosuit. It form-fits her curves, snugging into her body in all the right places, and I shake my head to clear it of the sudden influx of erotic memory flashes. She glances up, her face flushing with the heat of my thoughts, even with the suppressors running, and scowls at me. With effort, I tear my focus away.

"How bad is it?" Lyle asks Alex before I can.

"Bad. More than bad. We're not taking off in this heap." Alex tosses some tools into a box on the deck and rises, his head just missing the ceiling of the small shuttle.

"Once we rescue Oz, I'm sure he'll lend us a ship," I say, striding aft and grabbing my own suit from the storage lockers lining the rear wall. Kelly shifts sideways in the cramped space, making certain not to come into contact with me.

Great. Lyle will touch and talk to me, and Kelly won't. Crazy, fucked-up mess.

"And if we fail?" Lyle asks, taking a suit for himself.

"I die. The rest of you steal a ship." It slips out before I can stop it. Kelly sucks in a sharp breath while Lyle and Alex stare at me. My shrug and half smile do little to ease the shock. "Programming," I say, tapping the side of my head. I glance toward the hatch and what obstacles may lay beyond it. Rodwell is in this for blood. He'll throw everything Oz has at us. "The ultimate loyalty test. No way the implants will let me fail and live."

Then I stop. *Now* I can talk about it? Maybe since Kelly guessed and brought it into the open, the restraints on what I can say have eased? Things have definitely changed since our revealing chat in that hallway outside the conference room.

"That's fucked-up," Alex says. He's already in full enviro gear and ready to leave.

He's right. It is. Normally, my well-being would take precedence over the mission. I'm too valuable to lose. But when the assignment is to rescue the owner of the Fighting Storm? Somehow, I know the priorities have shifted in this instance.

Alex jabs a thumb in Kelly's direction. "She keeps saying you're human. You got free will or not?"

"Of course she does." It's the first thing I've heard Kelly say since our conversation outside the briefing room two days ago. Her voice comes out bitter and strained. "She exercises it all the time." She's not talking about the mission.

"Kel—"

She cuts me off before I can begin. "Forget it. You're a grown-up. I've got no claim on you."

Alex and Lyle exchange confused looks.

You have every claim on me, I want to tell her. But I don't. She's right. She cut me loose, blocked me out. But knowing that doesn't change the pull in my chest and the tightness in my throat. Her block is failing, my feelings for her intensifying with every passing day. If we're still estranged when it finally fails, what will happen to me?

Without warning, my sanity cord reappears in my internal display. The third thread snaps, sending a violent shudder through me, and I stagger against the lockers, slamming the open one shut with a resounding clang.

"Vick!" Kelly grabs my arm, and the world spins, the channel between us opening on its own and flooding me with her hurt and disappointment, love and concern. I jerk away as if burned. She's panting and staring at me, wide-eyed. "That… shouldn't have happened. Our connection, it shouldn't activate by mere touch."

It's not the only thing that shouldn't have happened. I've been on the edge for a while, but other than my ongoing issues with Kelly, there's nothing immediate that should have caused that thread to break right now. Regardless, I can't do anything about it here. I decide to keep it to myself. "Let's just try to avoid physical contact."

Her anger returns as violent as if nothing had occurred, as if we hadn't just proven our bond runs deeper than either of us is comfortable with. "Fine by me." Grabbing her survival pack, she stomps to the exterior hatch and waits there, arms crossed over her chest, not looking at the rest of us.

Angry because I don't want her touching me? After what she did? Or angry because she saw Officer Sanderson kissing me at the Purple Leaf?

"Oh, this is gonna be fun," Lyle mutters, following her in his own envirosuit.

It's me they're waiting on. I remove my weapons and pull the stretchable material over my uniform, then strap my gun belt on top, making sure my pistol is firmly in the holster. Alex checks the suit's connections for me. The sensors will adjust our body temperatures to human normal despite the frigid cold outside. "You up to this?" he asks, lips close to my ear under the pretense of securing a loose contact.

"Sure." With my ability to suppress emotions, one would think I'd make a better liar. One would be wrong.

"That's exactly what I figured."

CHAPTER 26
KELLY
FORCED ENTRY

VICK CORREN is fallible.

I keep my eyes locked on Vick's back as we make our way across the small moon's surface. If my retinas had lasers, they would have bored a second hole in her spine by now. She's nervous and tense, the envirosuit keeping her body warm, but her breath coming in visible white puffs. Swirls of pink highlight her emotions to me, but they're faint, harder to detect than usual; her suppressors are active. Her grav boots pull up bits of rock and other debris with every hurried step she takes.

We don't do a lot of suit work, and I'm not fond of the experience. My face and head are freezing. We could have worn protective headgear as well, but for the short distance to cover, it isn't worth the effort or the reduced visibility.

Team Two walks farther ahead—they're the scouting team, we're the deep infiltrators—and Lyle and Alex bring up the rear. Their thoughts run to the lascivious, so I wiggle my ass and give them the finger over my shoulder. "Knock it off," I warn them. I'm in no mood. The lusty emotions cease.

In the brief contact I had with Vick, I felt her guilt. That's enough emotion for me today.

Or I'd like it to be that way. My conscience niggles at me. That collapse into the lockers has me worried for her. She should have another day or two before she needs a release so badly. Which means she's either taken a major step backward or the block is failing fast.

If it fails in the middle of this mission, I'm not certain what it will do to her psyche.

I'm not certain what it will do to *us*.

It takes over an hour to cross the bleak landscape on foot. No more stumbles or staggers from Vick, and after a while she stops abruptly, whirls on me, and growls, "Quit it. Worry about yourself." From there I make a point of studying the landscape instead of waiting for her to topple.

Besides, she's right about watching my own footing. Team Two radios back to us in an ongoing stream about sinkholes and crumbling crater edges to watch for, and we have a close call when Lyle cracks through a thin layer of rock. He manages to switch off his grav boots in time to avoid a hundred-plus-foot drop, slowing his fall enough for Alex to grab and pull him up beside us. Back on more solid ground, he reactivates the boots.

I doubt I would have been able to think so quickly.

"Hey."

I yelp, startled by Vick's sudden appearance at my side. She lays a hand on my suited arm, tentatively, but the channel doesn't open. Whether that's from the bulky material between us or a sign that things have stabilized, I don't know.

"What?" I snap, too on edge to be civil.

She frowns. "You're hyperventilating."

I stare into her dark eyes, only now hearing the rasp of each too rapid breath I'm taking. "I don't like heights," I remind her, thinking back to her leap from the apartment building taking me empathically along for the ride.

"You fall, I'll catch you, whether you're mad at me or not, whether I've forgiven you or not," Vick says, jaw set but tone gentle.

"I'm not—" I begin, but stop myself. Yes, I'm mad. I have no right to be, but I am, and jealous and hurt and—

And what she said to me in her quarters hits home, hard. Vick will always catch me. Just like I'll always be there for her. The love is irrelevant. If such a thing is possible, our bond runs even deeper than that. Which makes what I did to her even more futile and pointless, merely selfish and cruel.

And she doesn't even know the full extent of it yet. If I have my way, the block will fail and she never will.

The almost-fall and our subsequent recovery slows us down, and the other team reaches the low-lying base structures a good stretch ahead of us. I can just make them out in the distance, pausing outside what looks like an entry. A minute later, they're inside the main building.

"Two Leader, you clear?" Vick's voice comes over the comm system.

The head of Team Two sounds perplexed when he responds, "We're in. No sign of defenses, no alarms. We requested entry and the hatch opened up. Scanners show nothing. Standing in some kind of greeting hall. Another door on the far side."

Vick and Alex exchange a look. "Sounds like a trap," she says for our ears. Then over the comm, "They brought us down, so they know we're here. Keep your eyes open. Hold position. We're moving to join you."

The tone shifts from confused to annoyed. "Worry about your own team, VC1. I've got mine under—" A low beeping interrupts his retort, along with some mechanical whirs and a hiss. "Fuck."

Vick's already running, the rest of us racing to catch up. "Leader Two! Davidson, report!"

"Scanner says oxygen is depleting. We're losing our air. And there's something else our scanners can't identify." His words come clipped. "The next hatch is sealed, not responding to entry requests. I've got Tellis working on an override." He's got his rising panic in check but only barely.

"Pull breathers." Vick skids to a halt at the entrance hatch. She slams her palm against the touch plate.

"Password," a computerized male voice demands.

"Dammit!" Her head jerks from side to side, searching for something. When she finds the access panel embedded on the right side of the hatch, she rips off her glove, then tears the cover off with her bare hands. All I can guess is she's used an adrenaline burst, and that will cost her later.

"We're not carrying breathers," Davidson comes back. "Wasn't part of the mission supply list." There's coughing in the background— the rest of Team Two reacting to the loss of air.

Vick scowls. I'm certain she carries a collapsible breather in one of her pockets. It's exactly the sort of thing her paranoia would insist on.

I picture the four members of Team Two in my mind—Davidson, Henley, a woman whose last name I've forgotten, but whose first name is Lark, and Tellis. Four good soldiers we'll lose if we can't open the hatch and flood the space with air.

"Alex, find me a link," Vick orders, pointing to the wires and circuits behind the torn-off panel. She's frantic, though she hides it well.

I imagine what she's going through, wonder how clear her memories are of the airlock and the deaths. The similarities send chills up my spine.

Without thinking, I rest a hand on her shoulder, sending waves of encouragement and confidence. They batter against her suppressors, but a few tendrils must seep through because at least a touch of the hidden panic leaves her.

"Thanks," she mutters for my ears alone.

Alex steps to her side and fiddles with the wiring, pulling a green one and a red, then opens a zipper in his envirosuit and draws a small tool from a pocket in the uniform underneath. He strips the two wires in seconds, precious seconds during which the comm dutifully relays the gasping of the members of Team Two.

Davidson has ceased talking, presumably using all his energy to work on the interior door. His wheezing, panting breaths have me breathing faster in sympathy, and I catch myself, inhaling a slow lungful of air to prevent passing out.

"Unauthorized access detected. Please provide password." The calm computerized voice maddens me. Vick's glare says she'd like to shoot the speaker embedded over the hatch.

"I've got it," Alex says. He trades places with Vick, putting the two wires in her hands.

She goes rigid, every muscle in her body tensed.

"Vick?" I step to where I can view her face, prepared to yank her away if necessary. She stares at nothing, looking inward, not out.

"I'm fine." Monotone. She's in direct interface with the door's security system, all her attention focused on opening the hatch. "Numeric code. Six-digit sequence. Running through possibilities in order."

That will take time, maybe more than the Team Two members have.

"Tampering confirmed. Activating defenses." A display screen next to the speaker flares to life. It shows a countdown in red from two minutes and heading for zero. "Provide password."

"Shit," Lyle mutters from behind me. "Corren?"

"Aware of it. Take Kelly and Alex and get behind something." Her commands sound odd, devoid of inflection.

"Wait," I cry as Lyle grabs one of my arms, hauling me backward toward an outcropping of rock a few yards from the entrance. "What about you?"

"I'm going to open this door." No hesitation. No uncertainty.

"Is that you talking or the implants?"

I'm several feet away. Her voice just carries enough. "I'm… not sure." Then nothing more.

Losing her. I'm losing her.

It takes both Alex and Lyle to hold me behind the rocks, each gripping one of my arms to keep me crouching in place. The three of us peer around the boulders, watching the countdown as it approaches zero. From inside the building comes no sound at all.

At thirty seconds, two panels slide aside, one to the left and one to the right of the entry. Nozzles or gun barrels—long metal cylinders—protrude from both of them. One aims in the direction of our cover. The other targets Vick.

She shows no indication of noticing, not even flinching as the right-hand weapon shifts to within inches of her head.

"No!" I scream, though I'm terrified I'll distract her and terrified I won't. She's forcing the implants to work to her wants rather than hurl her away from the impending danger. Or maybe it's the other way around, the implants holding her in place while they try every possible combination. Which is more valuable to the Storm, Vick and her oh-so-expensive experimental technology or the entirety of Team Two? Which would the programming elect to save?

I don't want to stand around and find out.

At twenty seconds, we're all shouting at her over the comm. "Get out of there!"

"Move it, Corren!"

"It's too late!"

She does not respond.

Not going to make it. She's not going to make it. It's a running litany in my head, my heart pounding with it, over and over. There's no possible way she can—

At fifteen seconds—*God, when did we reach fifteen seconds?*—I wrench free of my teammates' grasps and race toward Vick, screaming her name, screaming in general, anything I can do to get her attention. The left-hand weapon shifts to track me across the rugged landscape.

Ten seconds. I call her name again, still too far to touch her. Vick flinches, her head turning toward me in jerky movements like she's fighting her own neck muscles. Her eyes lock with mine and fear replaces the vacant stare.

I'm forcing her to choose.

Her body tackles mine at five seconds flat, and we're rolling across the ground, sharp rocks cutting through our envirosuits and uniforms and skin. The landscape whirls by, appearing and disappearing with each rotation. She's heading us straight for a crater. I have no idea how deep it is.

"Vick!" I stretch out my arms, clawing for a purchase, anything to stop our momentum, but she grips me tighter and continues to propel us toward the unseen drop.

A high-pitched whine cuts through my shrieks. The countdown has hit zero and the weapons—lasers as it turns out—open fire. I hear them strafing the terrain, coming closer and closer as they follow the path we're taking.

Just before they would have sliced us in half, we drop over the edge… and land about five feet down.

I impact the base of the crater on my back, knocking the wind out of me and cutting off my screams with a final "Eeep!" Vick lies atop my chest. The positioning reminds me so much of the North Carolina shuttle terminal I almost throw up.

Above us, the twin red beams pass by harmlessly, unable to manage an angle into the pit. I use one arm to protect my face as bits of debris rain upon us.

Several long seconds later, they cease fire, and the only sounds are her panting breaths, my wheezing gasps, and Alex and Lyle's distant shouting. I'm surprised they aren't peering over the edge, searching for our broken bodies, before I remember the lasers will tear them to ribbons if they emerge from hiding.

I'm trembling with cold, the cuts in my suit letting the below-zero temperature seep in, and shuddering with the ebbing panic.

My panic.

Only mine.

I'm in full physical contact with her. Even without a fully open channel, even with the suppressors on, I should be drowning in her emotions. Hell, an hour ago a grasp of her arm sent me spiraling into her feelings. Now I can't read her at all.

"Vick?"

She raises her head from my chest, a cut on her cheek leaving a bloody trail across her face and down to her jaw. She stares at me with vacant eyes.

Nobody home.

CHAPTER 27
VICK
NOT-SO-SOUND BODY AND MIND

I AM disconnected.

I register Kelly's voice. I read the concern in her features.

I cannot respond.

My body pushes itself off hers, keeping my head ducked below the edge of the crater I dropped us into. I don't detect the lasers' whine, but that doesn't mean they're no longer active. I'm not betting my functionality on it.

Processing comes sluggishly as I rebuild the events of the previous minutes in my memory. The dying members of Team Two, the hatch, the coded lock, the countdown, the lasers.

Kelly.

She trembles, and my visual receptors note tears in her envirosuit. She needs to reach a warmer location before the heat bleeds from her body. I have similar damage to my own suit, but the cold fails to affect me.

Because machines don't get cold.

Part of me rails against this, screaming in my head, kicking and fighting for dominance. It disrupts my sense of balance and I stumble to the side, knocking my shoulder into the crater wall.

Kelly grabs both my biceps, risking a connection that fails to activate. She shakes me, hard, jarring loose the storage pouch on my gun belt. The contents spill into the dirt at my feet, including the gold heart I placed there for safekeeping.

The implants' hold on me breaks like a bone—brittle, unexpected, and painful with the flood of emotions.

Kelly takes the brunt of my weight as I sink to the ground. "You with me?" She tilts my chin up to look in my eyes and nods at what she sees. "Welcome back."

"That… wasn't good." I suck air between my teeth, the pounding in my head making me dizzy with its intensity.

"No, it wasn't. You gave yourself over to the implants. What the hell were you thinking?"

Not exactly. I had some control right up until the point they took it from me. And then I'd had to choose between Kelly and— "Shit, Team Two." I stand, then hit the dirt a second time when the world spins. A quick thought activates the comm. "Alex, Lyle, status report."

"Jesus, Corren, we thought you two were dead. Kelly okay?" Alex sounds freaked. Guess I would be too if I hadn't noticed the crater and its minimal depth when we passed it on our way to the hideout.

"She's fine. Report."

"Lasers retracted. Countdown clock shut off. Probably resets after a minute or two." A pause. "No further word from inside."

"Stay put. I'm coming out." With a boost from Kelly, I'm able to push myself over the edge of the crater. When nothing takes my head off, I reach down and lift her out to stand beside me. "Let's try this again." I jog to the entry, Kelly on my heels and arguing the whole way.

"No. Let's not try this again. Let's not give up our free will to a computer that doesn't care if its host lives or dies."

At the hatch, I round on her. "I had some control. At first," I amend. To be honest, I'm not sure which part of me is controlling what anymore. But that's a nightmare for a safer day. "What would you have me do? Team Two is dying in there, if they aren't dead already."

Kelly scrubs both gloves over her face. She trembles where she stands, her teeth chattering in the extreme cold. It's seeping through to my skin too, and I feel it now that the implants aren't burying the sensations, but I'm not as susceptible as she is.

"I don't know," she admits. She reaches in a storage pouch and passes a handful of small objects to me, including the heart. "You dropped these when—" Her head snaps up and she stares at me. "This… this is what that security officer gave you, at the Purple Leaf last night."

I nod once. "It is. She was returning it."

"But you kissed her."

"Later, Kelly." I brush a stray strand of hair from her eyes.

She twists away from me, and at first I think she's still furious. One look at her face tells me something else has her attention. Without warning, she slaps her palm against the access panel.

"Shit, Kelly!" I'm reaching for her, ready to drag her away from the hatch and the impending return of the laser cannons, but she digs in her heels and holds up her free hand to stop me.

"Wait!"

"Password," the dispassionate computerized voice demands.

Kelly takes a deep breath. "Glinda sent us."

The door hisses open on its hydraulics, revealing the darkness of the room beyond.

I turn to my partner in shock.

She shrugs. "It's how they get into the Emerald City in the classic vidfilm. Oz lives here. This is his Emerald City. We needed to get in."

My heart continues to pound. "Warn me next time." We step inside, almost tripping over something large and pliant. The lights respond to our motion, activating and illuminating the entry room—and the bodies of Team Two scattered about the floor. Davidson lies at our feet, Henley just beyond him. "I wish you'd thought of it a little sooner," I mutter.

Kelly's stricken expression tugs at me, but I can't stop to comfort her. I move from one body to another, checking for life signs and finding none while she shifts as far from the dead as she can manage. We'd be more efficient working together, but I won't order her to touch them.

"CPR?" she asks. She's stopped shivering. The heat's working inside the building. Even with the exterior hatch still open, it's warmer in here. I don't like her pallor, but if she's talking, she's not too bad off.

I shake my head, sensors feeding me information she can't detect with her unenhanced eyesight and smell. "They're gone. I'm picking up residual traces of cerisine, harmless now. They didn't just lose their air. They gained a poison that made sure the job got done. If I could have gotten them out faster...." I drop it. It's over. But it gnaws at me. The implants show me an image of myself dressed as the Grim Reaper. I growl and switch over to comms, saying, "Alex, Lyle, you can come on in."

They arrive a moment later, pausing in the entrance before stepping inside. Both curse under their breaths.

"Yeah," I agree. With the bodies beyond our help, we can focus on the rest of the room. Not the industrial warehouse one would expect from the outside. It's a greeting area, like Davidson said, decorated in emerald green, which figures, I suppose. Green carpets. Green furnishings. A couple of plush couches where visitors might await Oz's arrival, or that of a servant or robotic assistant. Holos on the walls depict scenes from Earth—fields of wheat, some farmhouses, a windmill. In one, a tornado churns through the crops, tossing debris in a circling cloud.

"Kansas," Kelly says, following my gaze. "I have cousins there. Those are images from Kansas."

Not so far from North Carolina. I wonder how many other states I've traveled to but don't remember.

Memories and memories and memories.

I must zone out for a second, because the next thing I know, Kelly's beside me. I never saw her move from the wall. "You okay?"

"Yeah. It's just... familiar somehow."

"You read the mission files, downloaded the schematics."

"That's probably it." But it's not. I know it's not.

"This guy's taking the whole Oz thing a little far," Alex says, moving to check the door on the far side. "And I hate the color green." He has to step over Tellis and Lark Gestin's bodies.

I knew Tellis. Well, other members of the Storm tell me I did. He avoided me most of the time, but before the airlock accident, we had some kind of relationship, a romantic one. I want to increase the suppressors. Emotions might distract me from my job. But I'm afraid to, given what happened between them and the other implant functions the last time.

"At least Oz has a sense of humor." Lyle sinks onto one of the couches, nodding to the tornado holo.

"I don't find any of this funny."

I place a hand on Kelly's shoulder. "This isn't Oz's doing. Rodwell's got control of the security systems. He's picking and choosing who gets in and when. Rodwell doesn't want our team dead. Not yet. Not in a faceless showdown with some automated weaponry. He wants to play." My implants had calculated that the odds were against him letting the lasers take me out. My human self didn't enjoy testing those odds, but I didn't have a choice. "Alex, thoughts?"

"I agree. Rodwell's calling the shots. I'm betting he can turn devices on and off. Like with the door. He turned off the password access for the other team and just opened the door so he could separate us."

"Effective," Lyle mutters.

"And he might try it again. Divide and conquer works. So we stay together. Alex, you're the tech guru. Get us through that door. Everyone else, stay alert. And watch for friendlies. According to the mission briefing, there should be staff."

"Not anymore," Alex says so soft I almost miss it. He has a handheld scanner in his grip, aiming it toward the door. "I'm reading two life-forms besides ours. That's gotta be Oz and Rodwell. No one else."

I close my eyes. If I were religious, I'd whisper a prayer. From the sounds around me, I suspect Lyle and Kelly are doing exactly that. The file stated a minimum of ten staff members, men and women, plus their families living on property, so approximately twenty-two people gone. I'm hoping Rodwell sent them off or is shielding them somewhere, but I doubt it.

"Where are the two?" I ask, pushing the dead from my mind. The living need my attention more.

Alex angles his device first one way, then another. "Center of the complex. According to the schematics we downloaded, one's in security command. The other's in a bedroom not far from there."

"Rodwell will be in the security area, which means Oz—we're assuming it's Oz and not some random member of the house staff—is in that bedroom. Makes the most sense." I step back and give my teammate more room to work.

It takes a few more minutes to get the door open. It takes me longer than that to accept what's on the other side.

CHAPTER 28
KELLY
CLICK THREE TIMES

VICK CORREN is home.

We step into the hallway beyond the door and stop. More green. More plush carpeting. More wood paneling covering the metal walls. Soft recessed lights spaced evenly in the ten-foot ceilings extend into the distance. If I didn't know the hideout stood on a rock floating in space, I'd assume we'd entered someone's private and luxurious home. But that isn't what has Alex and Lyle staring and Vick taking short, rapid breaths beside me.

It's the holo displays.

Lots of wealthy families use long halls or staircases to display family holos. In this case, the images closest to our entry depict the family members in their youths, with the subjects increasing in age the farther along the passage we walk.

Only we aren't walking. We're frozen, looking at the first holo.

"Vick," I whisper, wrapping my hand around hers. Even through her glove, I can feel it's ice-cold. "Is that you?" I tilt my chin in the direction of the image. It shows a woman and a man in formal attire, arms around each other and smiling for the holocapturer. The woman's dark hair sits atop her head in an elaborately wrapped braid. She's applied tasteful makeup, and her off-the-shoulder white dress extends to the floor in a cascade of tiers—a wedding gown. I'm not sure whether to be stunned or jealous. Was Vick married before the accident? A legally permanent relationship she's forgotten with her lost memories? Surely Dr. Whitehouse couldn't keep something like that covered up. I look again.

I've never seen Vick in a dress, doubt she even owns one, but the face, the eyes. It looks just like her.

"I think...." Vick squeezes her eyes shut. The blood has drained from her cheeks, and she wavers a bit.

"Shit, sit down." Alex grabs her other arm, and we ease her to the carpet. She puts her head between her knees and draws shaky breaths.

"I think it's my mother," she mumbles, barely audible with her face hidden.

Lyle steps up to the holo. "Which makes this guy your dad." He turns back, eyes wide. "And that makes your dad... Oz."

Her loyalty. Her irrational guilt over failure. Her over-the-top reactions to a reprimand from our mutual boss. Her specific programming. He's not just the head of the Fighting Storm. He's her father, and she would do anything to please him. God, that explains a lot.

I rub my hand in circles on Vick's back, slipping it beneath the survival pack she wears for closer contact, aching for her and with her. Her shock tears through the suppressors, tears through me, silver waves of feeling, picking my own heart rate up in the process. I grit my teeth, channel and dump the emotion. All of it. Everything she's accumulated for the past couple of days since our last full connection. It's hard, harder than it should be. I have to fight her. Or is it her implants I'm fighting? Her breathing slows.

You're supposed to be angry with her. She cheated on you.
No she didn't. You let her go.

Dammit, why does my conscience have to be so logical?

"No memory. No records. Everything wiped." She looks up. "Why would the Storm hide this from me?"

I think about it. "Maybe they didn't. Maybe they don't know. You're right. There's nothing about this in your file. And Whitehouse claims you just showed up one day and enlisted. I'd tell you if he'd said anything else."

"Would you?"

That hurts, but I swallow it. I deserve it. "I would tell you about this."

She looks at me and into me. With the exception of the blocked love, the channel lets her feel what I feel. The only time she's as much of an empath as I am. Slowly, she nods. I'm telling the truth.

I draw my fingers from beneath her pack, but she grabs my arm and holds me there. "One more," she says. "I didn't kiss Officer Sanderson. She kissed me. I stopped it."

"Why?" I want to know. I need to know.

"Because I think… I think I'm waiting for you."

Truth. The most wonderful truth she could have told me.

Crouching beside us, Alex studies his boots.

"Too much information!" Lyle adds.

"Let's move." Vick pushes to her feet, giving me a hand up to stand beside her.

We progress down the long hall, the story of Vick's life unfolding on the walls to either side. Vick as a baby. Vick as an adolescent taking her first martial arts classes, and damn, she's a natural. Teenage Vick with a rifle, hitting every target's bull's-eye. Vick holding up a first place trophy, seated astride a hoverbike—a monstrous black, red, and silver affair that makes my little yellow one look like a tricycle. Vick going to prom with another girl, Vick in a black tuxedo, the petite blonde wearing a white tux.

Despite a small surge of jealousy, I grin a little at that one. She's been with men (Devin), and she's been with women. Judging from the rumors about her life before the accident, she's been with a number of women. Her stronger preference seems clear, and I'm apparently her type.

And there are others, more surprising, interspersed throughout: Vick dancing with her dad at some sort of father/daughter function; Vick in a gray T-shirt and jeans, a guitar cradled in her lap, sitting by a campfire; Vick wearing a pale blue dress, performing in a recital while her parents look on. She's singing. The last two holos have audio apps that activate when we approach, and they're good. Really good. Like professional-quality good. I cast a glance at her, walking at my side. "I never knew you could sing or play an instrument."

She shrugs. "I never knew I could wear a dress."

The tone is light, the sarcasm obvious, but sorrow tinges her words. An entire lost lifetime displayed on the walls. I can't imagine losing my family, my childhood, friends, accomplishments, talents.

Well, now we know why this place feels familiar to her. She grew up here.

No, that doesn't make sense. This is an isolated rock, with no opportunities for parties and gatherings, school and clubs. She grew up in a home that looks just like this, maybe even in Kansas back on Earth, and Oz recreated it here.

There are other images of her parents too, at a variety of functions, a very happy-looking couple, and some with the three of them together, at a picnic, at a party. No siblings, apparently.

We come to Vick's high school graduation, and I brace myself to console her. One more momentous occasion lost to her damaged brain. But it's the frame beside it that catches everyone else's attention, and I follow their gaze. Not a holo. Just a gathering of items mounted and hung—a memorial. Dried flowers, a lock of hair, a printed funeral announcement—her mother's.

"Fuck," she says. Vick drives her fist into the glass covering the physical memories before I can stop her. Her glove protects her hand, but the protective cover breaks, shards falling to decorate the carpet like glitter. Almost reverently, she reaches through the broken barrier and tugs the strands of hair free. She closes her grip around them for a long moment, then slips the memory into the pouch on her gun belt. "No more chances," she says.

I understand her meaning. No more opportunities to regain what she's lost, to rebuild the relationship, to recapture her past. Her mother is gone and has been for years.

Behind us, Lyle and Alex shuffle their feet, neither knowing what they should say.

But I do.

"Your father's still alive," I remind her. "One more chance."

A couple of tears escape her fierce glare. She brushes them away with an angry swipe of her sleeve. "Right." The suppressors clamp down hard, blocking her emotions from me like a dam stemming a flood.

We've hit the end of the hall. No more holos, but several feet of unfilled wall space extend past the last of them. "This must be when you left to join the Storm," I suggest. The blanks tell their own story, of a lonely man with no further need to capture holographic images.

Alex checks out the next door, a simple wooden one with no visible or detectable security. We're well inside the living areas now. No need for such things. "You know," he muses while studying his readouts, "it's very possible Vick kept her own secrets. Hid her family when she enlisted. Maybe even with Oz's help and blessing. I mean, yeah, the accident and Whitehouse decided what you could keep, but the documents and such, those would have almost been harder, unless you never gave that information in the first place."

"And why would I do that?" Vick snaps.

"Because Oz and his family are targets."

Like now.

Alex opens the door. The hall dumps us into the kitchen.

The kitchen is full of bodies.

Three, to be exact. A woman wearing an apron sprawls across a food prep table, a single laser wound in her back. A man in a chef's hat sits against the wall, half of his face seared off and a metal ladle clutched in one hand. A second, younger man lies across the white tiles, a burn mark in his chest. His dropped tray of glassware is shattered around him, but the liquids they contained have long since dried up.

Vick shoots me a worried look, but I manage a grim smile and shake my head. I'm okay. Well, as okay as viewing the dead makes anyone. But I'm not empathically reacting to their deaths. It's been too long for residual emotions to linger. My stomach roils a little, but I swallow hard and the nausea fades.

Lyle grabs an apple from a bowl of fresh fruit on the gleaming counter and takes a bite.

"Seriously?" Alex punches him in the arm, but Lyle doesn't stop chewing.

"Seriously. If I don't eat something, my stomach growling will give our location away."

"Rodwell already knows where we are," Alex says, pointing at a camera in the corner. Its lens aims right at us. The red light indicates active power.

A shiver passes through me. "Why hasn't he attacked us again?"

"I told you," Vick says, "he's playing with us. And he wants me alive for now. Can't fake a trade-off without both parties being present."

"And you're sure it's a fake?" I ask.

"He never lets his victims live," Lyle reminds us.

The kitchen has three exits. Vick studies each one. Her focus shifts inward while she presumably reads the schematics; then she turns to us. "That way," she says, pointing at a pair of swinging doors.

Her flat tone scares me. The deeper in we go, the more she's letting the implants control her. I grab her arm as she heads for the exit. "You're not a sacrifice," I remind her. "You're not expendable. Especially to me."

Her gaze holds no emotion, but her smile is sad. "I'm whatever I'm programmed to be."

"No. You're whatever you *let* it tell you to be. So don't let it. Fight. Fight hard. You're the strongest *person* I've ever known."

Vick shakes her head, smile gone. "Thirty-seven percent human, Kelly. Majority rules."

CHAPTER 29
VICK
REUNION

I AM Oz's daughter.

Holy shit.

My thoughts whirl too fast for me to concentrate on the mission. Without the implants' assistance, the distraction will cost someone's life. Probably mine.

I'm not stupid enough to give them full power over me, but it's hard, harder than I thought, to lock a tiny piece of myself away and keep it safe. The implants' control pulls me under like a leviathan with a shipwreck victim. And yet they don't have everything.

My internal display shows a sphere of navy blue energy encompassed in some sort of glowing shield. Okay. I've seen some weird metaphorical shit from my implants before, but this is a new one, and I have no idea how to interpret it. Spear-like charges of electricity attempt to pierce the sphere, but it holds… for now. I detect weak areas, places where the shell seems/feels thinner, almost as if the two remaining fraying threads of my sanity cord have wrapped themselves around this blue sphere of… something… and I wonder whether this is simply some new interpretation my implants are giving me of my waning mental competence. Regardless, I know somehow if the electricity makes it through, I'm lost, and I'm never coming back, even if I'm not quite sure what that ball of navy energy is.

I draw my pistol from my side holster and lead the way through the door to the next room. Kelly says something, but I shut her out. I need all my focus for this one.

We pass from the impressive kitchen into a sophisticated command center—an abrupt and startling shift but practical. Personnel wouldn't have to leave their posts for long in order to eat. I'm betting there's a bathroom nearby as well.

Workstations line the walls of the rectangular chamber with their embedded deskcomps active and displays lit. Each shows a different view of the compound's interior, including one of the kitchen we just left, the entry hall, and the greeting area, complete with the bodies of our fallen comrades. Kelly's gaze flicks away from that one, her face ashen.

No dead here, but evidence remains: bloodstains, a cracked screen, an overturned chair, a scorch mark across one of the surfaces and along the right-hand wall. Rodwell eliminated the security staff.

Damn, this guy is good. Or he had serious help.

In my peripheral vision, Alex purses his lips. I suspect he's reaching the same conclusion I have. Someone on the YBR team *is* a traitor. Rodwell didn't just manage to locate Oz. He gained access codes to the buildings, overrides to the defense systems. No way he could have done all that without an inside source.

For Alex's sake, I hope it's not his brother.

A bullet-resistant glass wall separates us from the single occupant at the far end—Patrick Rodwell. In the few days since Nascent, he's aged years: dark shadows beneath his eyes, gray skin, hell, even his wrinkles seem more deeply etched into his face. The death of his wife hit him hard.

Good.

"Corren," Alex warns. He's got his scanner out, studying the screen in his hands. "We've got movement in the rooms on either side."

A surge of hope flows through me. "Survivors?"

"No life signs. Or too much interference to tell. I'm reading a lot of hot weaponry."

So another trap. Big surprise.

To our right and left, panel doors slide aside. Security bots clomp through the openings. Metal constructs, slightly larger than the average human, squared-off heads and bodies. Noisy but effective. We're flanked in seconds, their laser rifles trained on us. Lyle brings up his pulse rifle, but I slap it down with one hand. "Don't. Anything you hit them with will ricochet." And I know all about that.

He nods slowly. "What, then?"

I holster my weapon, gesturing for the others to do the same, and raise my hands palms out in surrender. If Rodwell wanted us dead, he'd have ordered the bots to kill us when they entered. No. His game is in play. And we might have a better chance later. Besides, maybe these bots will take us wherever they're holding Oz.

The bots strip us of our weapons and detection equipment, sliding them into compartments in their metal exteriors. I suppress a small grin of satisfaction. They can't strip my brain technology.

"Lock them in a bedroom until I'm ready," Rodwell orders.

One bot gestures with his rifle in a quick, jerky motion. We precede him through the left door. The rest fall in behind us.

We're in a long corridor, gothically decorated with mirrors and false sconces flickering their orange bulbs like candles. Between sets of them lie a number of doors, and I'm amazed by the expanse of the compound, especially for someone who had few guests, but I suppose these could be servants' quarters.

I wonder if I lived here at all. I wonder if one leads to my former room.

"Weren't the security bots decommissioned?" Alex whispers.

I nod, implants scanning the relevant information. "Unreliable. Too noisy for field use. Incapable of making quick moral decisions in cases where civilians were involved. They never made it past the testing stages." Whitehouse favored the project despite its flaws. If he had his way, we'd all be like these thoughtless, feelingless things. I glance over my shoulder at the closest one and shiver. Not too far off one of them, now.

Kelly's hand wraps around mine. "Not even close," she says, guessing my thoughts as she so often does.

I pull away. This isn't the time for affectionate gestures, but my smile softens the action. "You sure there are no true telepaths?"

My partner stumbles as one of the bots shoves her from behind, but I catch her before she hits the wall. She offers me a wan smile. "No true telepaths. Just someone who knows you."

That darkens my mood further than even capture can. Yeah, she knows me. Better than I know myself. And I still resent it.

The big question is, where did Rodwell get these things? I'm guessing Oz stored them here for safekeeping or further research, but again, Rodwell would need inside help to gain access to the operating codes.

We have a traitor in the Storm. No doubt about it. Someone from the YBR/Yellow Brick Road team, one of our communications specialists… or higher up in the chain of command.

A rifle falls across our path, held by the lead bot. The security bot opens the nearest door, gesturing with its outstretched arm. I step inside a spacious suite of rooms: sitting room, bedroom, bath. Black and chrome dominate the color scheme. Awards, ribbons, and plaques adorn the walls, along with some posters of has-been musical groups and actors.

Well, I wondered which room was mine. Wish I'd been careful what I asked for.

The others follow me in, and the bot seals the entry behind us.

It's too weird. Familiar and not. I know these furnishings, this reading lamp, the trophies lined up on a shelf by the door. When I drop onto the solitary couch, my body recognizes the way it conforms to my angles and curves. But I can't picture any of the competitions I won or recount the contents of the books I read, unless they have to do with weapons maintenance, demolitions, or piloting. And the proportions, the… measurements of the room seem wrong. The sense of déjà vu makes me want to scream with frustration. I rest my clenched fists in my lap and take deep, even breaths.

A guitar leans against the seat and I pick it up, hands finding the auto-tuner at the neck, activating it by feel, then strumming chords. The tune morphs into something more complex and elegant, fingers flying over the strings by muscle memory. I have no idea what I'm playing.

With a growl I shove the instrument to the far side of the couch.

"Nice setup," Lyle comments, leaning his head into the sleeping area and then the bathroom. "Who knew our teammate was worth her weight in gold, huh?"

"Drop it," I say, giving him a glare.

He does.

Alex doesn't meet my eyes, intensely scrutinizing one of the pop music holos—an all-boy band long gone from the scene. "What's our next move, Corren?"

Right. I'm supposed to be in charge here. Team leader and all that.

I have no fucking clue.

"Wish I could say there's a secret passage or something, but if these quarters have one, I don't remember it." I consider my paranoia, a quality Oz (I can't think of him as my father) and I are likely to share. "Check for one anyway," I say to Lyle. "Never know."

He nods, disappearing into the bedroom. Alex heads for the bath area.

While they search, I rest my head in my hands. Kelly listened when I played the guitar. Now she leaves me to my thoughts, sinking onto the chair against the far wall but keeping her gaze on me, like I'm going to break any second. I'm not positive I won't.

Oz. Boss. Father. Dad. Shit.

Lyle's startled shout from the bedroom brings the rest of us running. We charge through the doorway, me in the lead, bunching up just on the other side. Lyle is lifting something, no, *someone*, from the space on the far side of the queen-size bed.

Tattered, bloodstained clothing, face covered with bruises and unrecognizable. But I don't need to have a clear picture to know this is Oz.

"Put him on the bed," I order.

Lyle does it, and we gather around the nearly motionless figure. His chest rises and falls, but it's uneven, his breathing shallow. He didn't even groan when Lyle moved him—a bad sign.

We've all had basic first aid training, but Lyle's taken a few more courses, so I leave him to it. While he takes Oz's pulse and attempts to make him comfortable, I study the man who is my father. He's smaller than I'd thought, about my height, wiry and thin, though the latter might be more a result of his torture than his regular physical build. The sight of him prompts a number of gut reactions: anger, concern, an intense need to *do* something. "How bad is it?"

Lyle looks up and shakes his head. "He needs a medical facility. There's internal damage, maybe even a skull fracture." He stares down at the sheets and blankets. "I can't do anything without a kit." And the bots took all we had.

We have to get him out of here. Soon. Or he's going to die.

That knowledge should ignite stronger emotions. But it doesn't. I'm desperate to act, to free the man I'm programmed to protect, and if not for the presence of Kelly and the rest of my team, I'd likely do something foolish trying to save him.

But I'm missing a vital piece of my psychological makeup.

I get why I can't love Kelly. The block prevents it. But judging from the holos in the family portrait hall, I had a good relationship with my father. Seeing him should bring forth some kind of strong affection for him even without my memories. Right? I feel warmth, but it's too mild for a close family. I don't understand....

Unless....

I raise my chin slowly, dangerously, catching Kelly's eyes where she stands on the opposite side of the bed beside Lyle. Anger rises like a great tide.

Kelly starts at the sudden shift in my mood, a wild animal caught in a hunter's sights. "What?"

"You took it all," I breathe. That's the navy ball of emotion my implants have shown me. It's the love. All of it. Every last vestige of that feeling, leaking out but essentially cut off from me. "You bitch. You didn't just block how I felt about you. You cut me off from everyone."

All the growth and progress I've had, I should've been able to at least attempt a relationship in the past couple of years. It might not have worked out. I'm still pretty screwed up. But I never understood why I had no attraction to anyone at all. It was a huge part of why I continued to believe myself to be more mechanical than human. It fed my psychosis. Maybe even Officer Sanderson would have sparked some interest if not for Kelly's tampering.

I can't love. Can't feel it romantically, can't feel it platonically. Until the block fails, I'm incapable.

Just as I always figured, but not for the reason I thought.

CHAPTER 30
KELLY
REAL TIN MEN

VICK CORREN is lost.

I raise my hands in surrender. "It's not like I'd ever placed a block before. I can separate emotions. I can't separate how you feel for individuals. It was all or nothing."

"Should have been nothing," Vick growls. She waves off my next comment, though I have no idea what else to say. "Save it for later. We have enough problems. Let's get out of this mess. Then I will let you pull the block."

My hope must show on my face because Vick follows that with "Don't count on it changing anything. I don't like being manipulated. I'd almost forgiven you, could almost see your point. You were trying to protect me. I get that. But to take it all? That's… well, it's something I never would have thought of you. It's cruel."

"I know that now," I whisper, ignoring the odd looks from Alex and the occasional confused glance from Lyle, though he's too busy with Oz to pay much attention to the argument. "Some things *are* worse than death. I'm sorry." There's nothing else to say, so I leave it at that.

The door to the outer room opens and we turn to the bedroom entrance to see Rodwell and his bots stepping inside. His gaze flicks from Vick to Oz lying helpless and unconscious on her bed. "So, you've found Daddy." And he knows their connection. This cannot be good.

Reading him comes easily: anger, resentment, a flash of disappointment. He expects Vick to be more broken up. Well, at least she can thank me for denying him that.

"Bring her," Rodwell growls, and the bots step forward, each seizing Vick by one of her arms.

She struggles, but to no avail. These metal monsters possess more strength than Vick, even with one of her adrenaline bursts. One violent twist snaps her shoulder out of its joint, the same one she injured in Rodwell's exploded apartment. She makes no sound. Her tolerance is high. Mine isn't. I cry out, pain threading the veins and muscles down my left arm. My distress boosts her fury, curling about her in angry gray clouds like a storm rolling in. She fights harder, doing more and more damage, tearing things inside herself.

"Stop!" I beg. She can't escape. And Rodwell has a gun. To my surprise, he doesn't raise it, watching the exchange with interest and amusement. I don't like the way he looks from me to Vick, nodding and grinning. At my plea, she goes limp in the bots' arms.

Alex and Lyle leap into action, fists swinging, boots flying, as the bots drag Vick backward from the room. Their hands resound against the steel robotic casings with dull, metallic thuds like bells stuffed with cotton. Alex yelps, shaking out his fist, then hitting one of the bots again, but it does no good. The machines take Vick, shoving the men aside with their free hands.

Lyle makes a try for Rodwell, but the kidnapper has had enough and aims the pistol at him, stopping him before he can attack.

Then they're gone, out the door to the suite and sealing it behind them.

Alex groans, cradling his right hand in his left. The knuckles are swelling, bruises forming. He's broken something in there. Lyle pants in ragged gasps, both hands on his knees while he catches his breath. I rotate my right shoulder, working out the phantom pain lingering from Vick's injury.

On the bed, Oz moans.

I stumble to his side, sighing with relief when his eyelids rise and he focuses on me. "Get a cold cloth," I tell Lyle. "And Alex, try running your hand under cold water." They nod and head for the washroom. A second later, I hear the sink running.

"Victoria?" Oz mumbles through cracked and swollen lips.

I blink at the name. Vick has never used the name Victoria in the time I've known her. "She's gone. Rodwell took her," I say, patting his shoulder. Worry and pain course from him through me, and I regret my words, but I'm done with lying, and he needs the physical comfort of my hand.

So much pain. So much weakness. I know what dying feels like. I remember from the Asheville terrorist attack. Even if we get Oz to a medical facility, he probably won't survive.

Vick was right. No more chances. My heart aches for her.

Lyle returns with the cloth, and I spread it over Oz's forehead, then settle into a chair Lyle brings to me. The water continues to run in the bathroom—Alex tending to his hand as best he can. With a nod, Lyle leaves again.

"May I know your name?" I ask. "Your real name? I'm assuming it isn't Oz."

The ghost of a smile alters Oz's face, and I see the father behind the businessman behind the torture victim. I can tell I'm about to be party to an inside joke. "Close enough," he says. "It's Oswald. Oswald Torrent."

So Oswald became Oz for his charade. And Vick Torrent became Vick Corren, close enough in sound to still respond to it but different enough that people wouldn't make the immediate connection between her and the Storm's CEO.

Oh, and Torrent. Storm. Hah. Oz does love his puns.

"Why hide her? I understand keeping you out of the spotlight, but Vick doesn't own the Storm. Is it just fear of family hostage situations?" I want to keep him talking. If he loses consciousness again, he might never reawaken.

Oz's smile fades. "That was her. She chose to change her identity." He shakes his head, then winces at the pain it causes him.

I resist the urge to wince in sympathy, ignoring the sudden headache as best I can.

"Too much nepotism in the Storm. Too many family favors. People in positions they shouldn't have. Like Whitehouse's poor kid, Stephen," Oz continues, his tone edged with anger.

Wait. What? And in that moment, it all clicks into place—the hatred, the resentment the good doctor shows toward Vick, all of it. "The one who opened fire in the airlock," I say slowly, watching for Oz's reaction. "Stephen *Whitehouse*." I don't really need the confirmation. I'm sure. The family resemblance from the vid Dr. Whitehouse showed me would have been obvious, if I'd known to look.

Oz nods. "Dr. Whitehouse assured me his son could handle the pressure, that his symptoms could be managed through appropriate medications. He was the chief med. I had to trust his judgment." He stares through me, as if looking into the past, then shakes his head. "Can't undo what's done. But that's exactly the sort of thing I mean. Vick wanted none of that. Wanted to achieve everything on her own and deserve what she achieved." His chin rises in pride. "And she did. Would have continued to do so if not for that accident."

My hand grips his shoulder. "*Does* do so. *Despite* that accident." I let all the admiration I possess for Vick come through my voice. "She's amazing." And I'm wondering just how much he knows about what she's become and what she's capable of. Does he know what the Storm has done to her? How much truth has Whitehouse given him?

"Let's hope she's amazing enough to escape Rodwell and the bots," Lyle says, returning. He holds a towel of ice to his arm where one of the bots got in a good hit. "Wet bar, in the sitting room cabinet, lots of ice," he explains when I raise my eyebrows. "Swelling's already going down. They pack quite a punch." He seats himself on the foot of the bed, the mattress sinking under his weight.

"Where's Alex?"

"Trying to reconfigure the refrigerator and the vidnet entertainment unit into something that will override the door locks." Lyle shrugs. "I offered to help, but…."

I nod. When Alex has his tech going, he prefers everyone out of the way.

"What's the lowdown on the bots? Any weaknesses we can use when we get out of here?" Lyle asks, no doubt whatsoever that Alex will succeed with the door.

I don't want to shift the conversation. I want to know more about Vick. Did Oz know how much of her memory Whitehouse wiped? Did he approve that? But Lyle has a point. Nothing matters if we can't escape.

"The bots shouldn't even be active," Oz says. "Girard Base shipped them here for storage after I cut the program as a failure. Stored them in one of the attached warehouses with other research projects gone wrong. I'd never even seen them in person before Rodwell showed up with half a dozen of the things." A shiver passes through the frail body. "My personal bodyguard managed to take one down by aiming for the joints in the armor. But be damn sure you've got good aim. He missed with the second one and got hit by his own ricochet. No other weaknesses beyond the obvious. They make a lot of noise. You can always hear them coming. Not discreet in their destruction, either. Blew holes in some of the security equipment along with my personal guards before Rodwell could stop them." His face falls, sorrow flooding my senses. Oz cared about his people. "You have to phrase orders to them very precisely."

"And the activation codes. Rodwell get those from you?" Lyle's question surprises me. He's accusing the boss of giving away vital information, though I know why he's asking.

"No," Oz growls, and the businessman comes to the fore. "He had them. Someone gave him the codes."

Lyle nods. It looks more and more likely Alex's brother's team betrayed the Storm.

I want to redirect the discussion back to Vick, but before I can open my mouth, stinging pain lances through my cheek, jaw, and neck. I taste blood, though I know it isn't real. Then the air leaves me as I take an invisible punch to the gut, doubling me over in my seat. My cry of anguish comes out as a pitiful mewl.

"Kelly?" Lyle grabs me by the shoulders, untwisting the pretzel I've curled myself into. "What's wrong?" He checks my eyes, places two fingers on my neck. My pulse races. I feel it pounding.

"He's... hurting her," I manage, sucking air in a wheezing gasp. Even as I say it, the connection between me and Vick opens fully. Whatever Rodwell is doing, it's preventing her from using her suppressors.

I reinforce my mental walls, desperate to block out the coming torture, but it won't be enough.

CHAPTER 31
VICK
PAYBACK

I AM failing.

"You know," I say past my split lip and swollen jaw, "when I killed your wife, I did it clean. None of this fucking around." My tongue hits a loose tooth, knocking it free. I spit it in Rodwell's face.

He says nothing but hits me again, flinging my head back so my neck makes an unpleasant internal popping sound.

Rodwell has me in the complex's kitchen freezer, arms stretched up, wrists tied together, the ropes binding them connecting to a meat hook in the ceiling. Hurts like hell, especially the dislocated shoulder, though the cold numbs the worst of it. My ankles are also tied to each other, and I'm suspended a couple of inches off the floor. Beside me, sides of beef and pork swing in the frigid cold, covered in ice crystals. Some are forming on me too, across the tears in my envirosuit and my face. My remaining teeth chatter.

I imagine my tormenter feels little discomfort. He's got his own undamaged suit. My mind flickers back to Nascent and the high-powered rounds in his and his wife's weapons piercing our van's impenetrable armor, the intricately laid booby traps on the apartment. All the high-tech toys, even then.

In his left hand, he holds a device—a device that negates my suppressors—a remote control for automated beings. Yeah, that's me, just one of the mechanical crowd. Even without the implants' assistance, I'm trained to withstand torture, but I suspect we're only beginning.

Over his shoulder, I see the open freezer entry, two bots blocking any chance I might have of escape, that is, if I could get my hands and legs free. I give my feet a tug, moving them maybe an inch. Not looking good there.

"You might want to consider keeping your mouth shut," he growls, lips inches from mine.

"You might want to consider some breath freshener."

His fist lands in my solar plexus, knocking the air from my lungs and swinging me in agonizing circles on the damn hook. He grabs for something. I can't make it out in my dizzying spin, but a second later he stops my motion and a silver blade swims into focus.

"My wife was a beautiful woman. You are a piece of meat."

I clench my jaw as he slips the carving knife under my collar and rips downward, slicing through both my envirosuit and the uniform beneath, all the way to my waist. Another flick severs my bra between my breasts, and the material falls away, baring me to his insane leer. My nipples harden to a painful state as the chill hits them. A glance down his body tells me they aren't the only things that have hardened.

Crap.

"You are one sick fuck," I say, though the shivering diminishes my bravado. He stabs the knife into the nearest carcass, then reaches to fondle my bare breasts. I twist and arch away from him, but it's no good. I can't escape his gloved hand. The rough covering abrades the sensitive skin. "Did your wife know you like to rape women?"

"This isn't rape. A machine doesn't know what rape is. And property can't say no."

His words hurt. But what hurts more is the fact that the legal team on Girard Base would probably say he's right, not that he hasn't done plenty else to be brought to justice for. If only I could find a way out of this mess and do just that.

One hand doesn't satisfy him, and he sets the controller aside to use both, gripping and squeezing, crushing, then using his mouth to suck and bite. I fight, jerking as much as I can, making it difficult, but I can't do much. In my head, I push against the device's control, willing my implants to activate the suppressors, but only receive a buzzing sensation like static in my ears.

You hate this man. He tried to blow you up, remember? Fight him. Fight this.

Nothing happens.

Great. Now I'm talking to myself.

"Does she feel it?" Rodwell asks, eyes closed, savoring the moment with a grotesque smile curving his lips. He tugs off his gloves with his teeth, using his bare, wrinkled, callused hands on me, enduring the cold for the sake of contact.

I blink at his question, not comprehending.

"Your little girlfriend, the empath," he purrs. I shoot him a startled look. "Yes, I know what she is to you, everything she is to you. It wasn't hard to figure out. The way she hurt when you dislocated your shoulder. The cry she gave." He's smiling, the bastard. I'd give anything to wipe that smile off his face.

He moves behind me and wraps an arm around my abdomen, slides one flat palm down my torso, past the jagged tear in my uniform, into the waistband of my regulation underwear, and lower. His erection presses through his clothing against my spine right where the four-inch metal bar lies. "Will she feel it when I do this?"

I jerk, muscles tensing as he forces a finger into me a little, then farther until he's buried it up to the first knuckle. It hurts. I'm not the least bit lubricated and can't imagine a greater turn-off than this scenario. But I make no sound. A second finger joins it, and he's shoving them in and out, tearing me apart from the inside.

"Tough meat," he whispers. "You need tenderizing."

In and out he saws, drawing shameful whimpers from my throat, every callus, every joint grinding against my inner walls. Tears leak from my eyes, freezing halfway down my cheeks. My implants shoot me an image of a rat in a trap.

Great. Of all the capabilities the devices possess, *that* one has to be working.

I try to think of anything else besides my own body, but the effort brings thoughts of Kelly and what she must be going through with my suppressors off. She has her shields, but I know from experience those prove ineffective against a real emotional onslaught from me. And this is one hell of an onslaught.

Rage. Embarrassment. Pain. A fierce desire to kill the man standing behind me. Nothing professional about it. Given the chance, I'll take him apart and enjoy every second.

Like he's doing to me.

The train of thought comes to a grinding halt, nausea churning in my stomach.

I'm both machine and monster.

A third finger shoves its way inside, and I gasp as the violation dispels all coherent thought. There's pressure against my back, rubbing and moving in a slow, steady rhythm that matches the motions within me. Rodwell grunts and groans, an animal sound.

God, he's getting off on this shit.

It's his ultimate attempt to humiliate me. It's working.

Not my fault. Not my fault, I tell myself over and over like a mantra while my body betrays me and my entry protects itself with slick moisture.

Rodwell rumbles satisfaction. He's felt it, and he has me.

It's an involuntary physical response—nothing I should feel guilty for, but the knowledge doesn't help. I'm rocking in time with his thrusts, preventing further damage to my insides by keeping up with his rhythm while he draws closer and closer to his release.

No, dammit, no, no....

"No!" I scream, hoarse and raw, as he stiffens against me, then shudders and shakes in the throes of orgasm. It goes on and on, and I endure his groans of pleasure as his tremors gradually subside.

I'm hanging limp, half-naked, icy streaks down both sides of my face, when he steps away.

"You won't feel it when I do this to your friend," he whispers, hot breath close to my ear. "So for that, I'll have to let you simply watch."

In my mind's eye, the fourth thread of the sanity cord frays.

In my peripheral vision, I detect movement.

God, what now?

One of the bots, edging from the doorway toward the remote Rodwell set on a shelf lining the side wall. But it can't move without sound, the servomotors in its legs whining with each step, and my captor notices.

Rodwell comes around me, one arm beckoning the mechanical guard closer. "Yes, bring me the controller," he says, palm extended behind him, waiting for the security bot to place it in his grasp.

But the bot doesn't. Instead, it smashes its metallic fist down on the device, shattering its casing and sending sparks flying in a shower of lights.

"What?" Rodwell shouts.

I'm already in motion, adrenaline surging through my veins, pain and emotion suppressors almost on full. I don't dare give them complete control, but it's close, and with a tremendous tug I use the metal of the hook as leverage to sever the rope holding me to the ceiling.

Not my brightest move.

My wrists separate. I hit the cement floor on both knees, thankfully still covered by the suit and my uniform bottoms, but they do little to cushion the impact and it hurts, dammit. The shock wave carries up my legs, jarring my bones, but I can't wait for recovery. Rodwell's reaching for me.

I grab for an ankle with my good arm, yanking his foot out from under him and sending him sprawling onto his back like a flipped turtle, his skull cracking the floor. He's not out, just stunned, turning his head from side to side and moaning. I'm sure he has a weapon on him, so I'm not safe yet.

My first attempt to stand fails utterly. My ankles are still tied, and cold plus lack of circulation while I hung suspended have added up to no feeling in my legs. I end up crawling to Rodwell's side, then pounding my fist into his face, maybe a couple more times than necessary. He goes still. I fumble for his knife and gun hanging off his belt. I shove the gun into the back of my pants and use the knife to cut my ankles free, then slip the second weapon into a boot.

I could kill him now, and easily. I want to. So much. But Kelly has endured everything I have, maybe not as acutely, but enough. I can't do it to her, even if I could do it to him without a second of guilt.

With numb fingers I pull my clothing into some semblance of order. My left arm is useless, but the right works okay. The suit, uniform shirt, and bra are ruined. I tug the bra off and toss it, but I can drape the rest over my nakedness. I use the remnants of the ropes to bind Rodwell as best I can with one arm.

Lots of clanking and whirring carry from the kitchen. I crawl to the freezer entry and stare, dumbfounded, at the scene. The bots slam against one another, one following its last orders to serve Rodwell, the other, for some unknown reason, defending me.

I don't understand it, but I'm not knocking it. Right now I can use all the help I can get.

CHAPTER 32
KELLY
REVELATION

VICK CORREN is a prototype.

Alex gets us out of Vick's bedroom, and we're plunged into battle. I'm almost grateful for the distraction of the security bot standing guard outside the door. It keeps my mind from… other things, Vick's pain, pain I can't focus on or I'll lose myself in her torment.

We take the bot by surprise. It isn't expecting the hatch to slide open, especially with a burst of sparks and a cloud of smoke from the wiring Alex fries. Even with the few seconds that buys us, though, we're overmatched.

A beam of energy lashes out from the bot's laser pistol, searing through the sleeve of my envirosuit and the uniform shirt beneath. I yelp and cover the burn with my free hand, hugging the closest wall while the real soldiers engage the bot. One more pain to add to all the others. I barely notice it.

Whatever Rodwell did to Vick, it hurt. A lot. In places I don't want to think too much about. I'm caught in her humiliation, wrapped up in her distress. Back in her bedroom, I shook with orgasm, then curled into a ball, rocking for fifteen minutes, half her emotions, half my reactions, the others looking helplessly on.

My body aches, and the sense of violation clings like tar. More than anything else, I want to reach her and hold her.

To do that, we have to beat this thing.

Sudden anger rips through me. Mine or Vick's, it doesn't matter. I push off the wall, lunging for the pistol in the bot's hand. The machine is engaged with Alex and Lyle, flinging one to one side, one to the other, since they're too close in for shooting. They bounce off the walls, sliding down to the floor.

Lyle doesn't move. He's groaning, and I don't know how badly he's hurt. Alex shouts for me to stop, but I've got one hand on the gun, and a second later, to my utter shock, it's in my grip. I don't have time for the lethal weapon to disgust me or freak me out.

I flip it like I've seen Vick do in training and call back to me all the shooting lessons I've endured.

I've never fired a weapon in attack. I've never fired a weapon in my own defense.

But I fire this one now.

The beam of energy hits right where I aim it, in the seam between the neck and the bot's body. We stagger backward in opposite directions, falling away from each other. A crash of metal like a thousand trash cans echoes through the hallway. The lights in the eye sockets go out.

I drop the pistol and kick it toward Alex.

Death descends upon me.

Violent spasms wrack my limbs as I crumple. It makes no sense, must be my imagination. This was a machine I've stopped from functioning, not a person I've killed.

I fight the waves of pain and shock, swimming upstream against the current threatening to drag me under. Relief follows, faint and bittersweet. I can't identify the source before it fades. Alex wraps an arm around my shoulders, his comfort and confidence seeping in, and it helps drag me back to the surface.

"What's wrong?" he asks, peering into my face.

"Not... sure." My teeth chatter. I curl into him, thankful for his large size and strength.

The agony dissipates, faster than with a real death, and I'm more convinced my mind played tricks on me. With all I've been through, firsthand and via Vick, I'm not too surprised.

Managing a small smile, I push away and let him help me stand; then we lever Lyle to his feet. He's dazed but not seriously hurt, a bump rising on the left side of his forehead. Alex checks his pupils with a penlight he produces from a belt pouch. "No concussion," he concludes, nodding.

"Good. Let's get out of here and kick some ass."

I'm liking the two of them more and more.

Alex goes back for Oz, returning with the man cradled in his arms. Our boss has lost consciousness again, his head hanging limp on

Alex's shoulder. I can't feel much life in him. "We need to hurry," I tell my teammates.

Lyle plucks the stolen pistol from Alex's holster. He extends it to me, grip first, but I shake my head. "They're robots," he says, "and Alex's hands are full. One weapon, one pair of useful fists, and we know there are at least five more of those damn bots."

But I don't take it. I won't risk another shockwave, even an imaginary one. If I go under, Vick will lose it too, and we'll never get out of here without her skills. Lyle frowns but doesn't argue. He keeps the pistol drawn and ready as we proceed back the way we were brought in.

Ahead of us, loud crashing sounds carry from the kitchen. My lips curl in a smile. If a fight is raging, that means Vick is free. There's no other explanation for it. But when we push through the swinging doors, the chaos isn't quite what I expect.

No sign of Vick, but two of the bots are tearing each other apart. Dents, laser score marks, and sparking gashes in their casings imply the battle has been in progress for a while. As we watch, dumbfounded, from the entrance, one heaves the other over an island row of counters, sending bowls, utensils, and days-old food onto the floor along with it. Motors and servos in the legs and arms whine in complaint, struggling to lift the metal carcass from where it lies.

"What the hell?" Lyle says.

I glance over my shoulder. Alex shakes his head. "Not a clue."

The freezer door stands open, and I think I detect movement there, but before I can investigate, the standing bot notices our arrival. Screeching with every step, one arm dangling by wires and cords, it heads straight for us.

Lyle raises his weapon and fires, nailing the thing where I did, in the neck joint.

It falls. So do I.

This is getting old.

A blur streaks toward me, catching me before I hit the floor, and I'm in Vick's arms, her voice murmuring to me in words I can't make out through the pain and that strange sense of relief again. For several seconds I'm mostly deaf and blind, but her worry wraps around me in coils of burnt orange.

"What's wrong with her?" I make out Vick's voice as hearing returns.

"The destruction of the bots is affecting her," Alex says.

"That's not possible." One of Vick's arms tightens around my shoulders. I remember the injury to the other and shudder.

"It shouldn't be," I agree, pushing up and shifting to face her. My eyes go wide at the sight of my partner, bruised and bloodied, one cheek cut and swollen. Her torn shirt reveals her bare breasts, dark purple marks in a finger pattern forming there too, and I gently close the fabric over her, covering her.

"Thanks," she whispers. Then, "What's going on with you?"

"I don't know." And it scares me. A lot. Scares her too. I feel her fear for me. The trembling has eased, but I'm weighed down with an oppressive heaviness I can't explain.

We don't have time to ponder it, though. Grinding gears alert us to the motion of the bot behind the counter, and it rises up, one side of its head bashed in, all its limbs creaking with effort.

Lyle aims his pistol again, but Vick shouts, "Wait!"

He holds, staring at her as if she's lost her mind. Maybe she has.

Standing shakily, she pushes his gun arm down. "That one helped me. I don't know why," she adds, casting a glance back at it while it braces itself against the countertop, "but we might be able to use it."

I raise one eyebrow in a dubious expression as the thing turns toward us. Something inside it groans as if in physical pain. The piece of metal making up its face curls back like it fell prey to a giant can opener. Its head hangs down, neck mechanisms unable to raise it.

"Vick…," I say when she starts toward it, but she raises a hand to keep me in place.

"Why?" she mutters under her breath, closing the distance to the security bot.

The robot stumbles over one of the three kitchen staff corpses we found earlier and crashes down again, out of sight behind the island counters. Vick follows, circling the island and crouching so she disappears from our view.

A second later her repulsion hits me. Gagging, then violent vomiting sounds carry across the open kitchen space.

"Corren?" Lyle calls, grimacing at the noise. "You need backup?"

More gagging, choking, and spitting. Something wet splatters against the floor tiles. "Fuck," she groans. "Oh holy fuck."

My stomach turns over in both sympathy and empathy. I rise to my knees and let Lyle pull me up the rest of the way.

"Stay there," Vick orders, voice weak. There's scrabbling and shuffling like she's trying to stand, then more cursing and a thud against the far side of the island.

"Screw that," I say and pick my way across the debris, careful to give the other fallen bot a wide berth. "Keep an eye on the entries."

Lyle nods, taking up position where he can watch the three doors, gun at the ready.

Vick's sick again, and I swallow a mouthful of bile. Her suppressors must be on, and I've got my shields up. Otherwise I'd be vomiting right along with her. I can't imagine what's making her so ill. Poison comes to mind, maybe something Rodwell has done to her. And where is that bastard, anyway?

I round the corner and spot her, on hands and knees, spitting out clear liquid. I expect that's all she has left in her stomach by now. She must sense my arrival because she waves a frantic hand at me, miming for me to go back, though she's unable to speak.

Instead I grab the flailing hand and kneel by her side, where I see exactly why she wants to keep me away.

The bot lies beside her on its back, face panel open, revealing the head to be hollow, and within it, a second face. A very human face.

A human face I'm horrified to recognize.

Vick's horror tells me even more. She remembers. Oh God, she remembers the airlock accident. She remembers everything.

He's still alive, small movements behind his closed eyes and twitches in his cheek muscles clear indicators.

And I... I didn't stop a machine.

In that hallway outside Vick's bedroom, I killed a man.

CHAPTER 33
VICK
OVERLOAD

I AM giving up.

"Devin…." The name slips from my lips, cut off by an immediate memory flash.

The airlock. The argument. The exit code. The *wrong* code. Stephen's panic. The gun firing.

My fault. My fault. My fault.

And this. This… thing. Half machine, half human. This is what Whitehouse wanted me to become. And it's my fault Devin ended up this way. My fault.

Add the rape into the mix and it's just too damn much.

I grasp for the suppressors in desperation, still trying to vomit, just dry-heaving now. The implants leap to comply, clamping down on the nausea, burying the unwanted emotions, seizing almost all of the 37 percent of my human mind with a euphoric triumph but unable to touch that ball of navy blue energy deep in my core.

I'm tempted to let them have it. What good is my ability to love if all I want to do is…. Just. Stop. Feeling. But I don't know how. And something instinctive tells me giving up that deep blue orb means giving up any chance of my ever coming back to myself. And I'm not quite ready to do that. Yet.

The implants fight me, fight what's left of me, and my internal view shows more holes in the protective shell around the tiny bit of my personality remaining free.

I'm dimly aware of Kelly beside me, face white with shock, breathing uneven. But it's not my emotions she's responding to, or at least not merely those.

She's muttering something over and over. I strain to make it out.

"I killed him. I killed him."

Oh fuck.

Not Devin. The other bot did this damage, and besides, he's not dead. I reassess his condition—bad, bad, and more bad.

So, not dead yet, though I think he's headed there. And she's not talking about the victorious bot, either. Lyle shot that one. She must mean a third security robot somewhere in the complex, one they encountered before reaching the kitchen.

I can't imagine what taking a human life would do to an empath, and I can't let the implants put me fully under. Not while she's borderline for emotion shock.

Wrenching more of my consciousness from the implants' control, I hold Kelly to my chest. Her trembling shakes us both.

"Alex!" I snap, now that I can speak without puking. "I need your skills."

Some shuffling and a groan follow the command, the pained sound coming from my father being placed on the floor. A second later, Alex appears around the edge of the counter island and freezes. "What the hell?"

"How much?" I manage, nausea returning despite the implants' efforts. I gesture to the bot, to Devin. "How much of him is human?"

"I don't...." He glances toward the area of the kitchen I can't see from my position on the floor. "Hold on a sec." Alex disappears, then returns with a scanner in his hand. "The other bot had a lot of our equipment," he explains, indicating the pistol back in his holster as well. He uses the scanner to run over the length of Devin.

I refuse to think of him as a bot any longer. He's a man, whatever's left of him. And yet, Kelly needs him not to be one.

"To answer your question, not damn much." Alex pauses at the arm, clearly mechanical all the way through and hanging by wires. "One arm, both legs, completely robotic. Torso is a casing covering flesh, as is the other arm, neck, and—" He swallows hard. "—head. This is some seriously fucked-up shit, Corren."

"Tell me about it."

"Extremely limited life signs, almost no brain activity, so even when he was healthy? Fully operational? Hell, I don't know, but he doesn't qualify as human on the scanner. From the moment we got here, we only read the two life-forms, Oz and Rodwell, when we scanned the complex, and they're all I'm getting now too, apart from our team."

"Could the casing be shielding his signs? Could his damage—" I catch myself. "His *injuries* be causing the minimal brain readings?" I hope the answers are no and no. I need these things to register as nonhuman, regardless of what they might actually be, for Kelly's sake.

But deep down, I know it won't matter what Alex's answer is. Devin *knew* me. He tried to help me in the meat freezer, and out here, fighting with the other bot in the kitchen. Somewhere he had some humanity left, some sense of the good guys and the truly bad ones.

"Either one is possible," Alex says, "but I don't think so. There just isn't much left of him to read."

But enough. There was enough. Enough to help me.

And if Devin is human… I have a spark of hope for my 37 percent.

Still, for Kelly, I have to lie. And pray she's too far gone to pick up on it.

I turn her face up to mine with my fingertips. "Not human," I tell her. "Not even close. Machine. You stopped a machine." Guilt stabs me. Devin is still alive, and if he's alive, he can probably hear what I'm saying. "I don't know what you're sensing, but they aren't people. Not anymore."

She blinks, tears falling from her long lashes, and rests her head on my shoulder. Her trembling eases.

"Thank you," she whispers.

"For what?"

"Trying." Her eyes meet mine again. "No one knows you better than I do. You *cannot* lie to me." She takes a tremulous breath. "But I'll be okay. They want to die. I feel their relief when they do."

As if on cue, a vibration passes through Devin's metal casing. The few muscles working in his face go slack, and a subliminal hum I hadn't previously been aware of ceases running. Kelly shudders hard in my grip, and her eyes go glassy for a moment before she shakes her head and her vision clears.

"Him too." She squeezes my hand in hers. "He's at peace now."

Peace. I wonder what that's like. I don't think I've known true peace since the damn airlock incident.

Using the counter to brace myself, I stand, then pull Kelly up beside me. Alex rises as well, and we survey the kitchen battle zone in silence for a moment. It's quite the scene: broken dishware, scattered utensils, bodies, cracks in floor and wall tiles.

Movement.

I glance at Lyle, legs braced apart, eyes darting from entrance to entrance to entrance. But not to the freezer.

My confiscated pistol clears the holster seconds too late.

Rodwell is bracing himself in the freezer's entrance, a gun, probably retrieved from the fallen bot beside him, clutched in his still loosely tied hands. He fires, and I follow his aim to Oz, my father, carefully propped against the wall behind Lyle, where Alex left him to come to me.

"No!" My scream bounces off the resonant tile, acoustics perfect to carry my anguish.

The beam goes in through the center of the forehead, an exact echo of my assassination of Rodwell's wife. But instead of a neat bullet hole, the laser bursts through the back of my father's skull, spattering the wall behind him with his brain matter.

Three laser blasts from my gun combined with Alex's and Lyle's follow a moment later, but Rodwell ducks back into the freezer, and the shots hit the metal door, ricocheting around the kitchen like a light display.

I tackle Kelly for the second time today, driving her to the floor and shielding her with my body. The beams bounce from door to oven to the metal handles on the cabinetry and embed themselves in granite and mica. Safe. She's safe.

My father is dead.

In my internal display, the fourth thread snaps.

Something inside me shifts.

A cold, calculating calm settles over me. The world drops into slow motion, vision tunneling to a narrow focus. I shove myself up, one arm buckling beneath my weight. My head cocks toward it, studying the limb as if it isn't even a part of me. I feel no pain. Suppressors on full.

Damaged part. Redistributing power.

Too much. Too much.

Releasing adrenaline.

Sanity literally dangling by a thread.

My body rises, one arm lifting me without effort. Kelly lies beneath me, eyes closed, barely breathing.

Emotion shock. Need to help her.

Need to complete mission objectives two and three. Mission objective one sprawls against the wall, spreading a dark stain across the black and white squares. Other teammates regaining motion, appear operational, unimpaired by damage.

Kelly, dammit. See to Kelly.

I turn my back on her. My steps carry me to the freezer entrance. No place to run. No place to hide. My pistol turns the corner first. I lean in to follow it. My breath puffs out in a white cloud. Goose bumps flare across the exposed skin of my chest and abdomen, but I note the automatic physical response with detachment. The cold does not register in my brain.

My objective cowers at the rear of the icy storage area, using a side of beef for cover.

I shoot out his right kneecap, then his left. He falls, landing on the injured limbs, screaming in long, high-pitched wails.

In the kitchen, Kelly echoes his screams.

Stop it, Vick. Stop it now. You're killing her.

My next shot hits between his legs. The shrieks rise higher in pitch, cutting off when he reaches the limits of his vocal register.

Finally, an action I agree with.

My thumb finds the intensity lever on my weapon, dialing it down to a lower setting. Methodically, I slice open Rodwell's abdomen, spilling his entrails in long, wet strings across the frost-covered metal flooring. He topples forward, bracing himself with his palms, staring at his innards while shock turns his features ghostly pale.

He turns his head upward, expression pleading, mouth working soundlessly. I put one last blast between his eyes, though at the lower setting, it takes several seconds of burning through skin and skull before it finally ends his worthless life.

When? When did the implants learn to channel so much rage?

Or was that simply me?

Objective two accomplished.

Outside the freezer, Kelly continues to scream.

I should feel something. I should feel… I should… I….

CHAPTER 34
KELLY
CUT OFF

VICK CORREN is trapped.

Five deaths in under an hour. I can't handle it. Three came as a relief, but the other two....

Oz, who suffered torture at Rodwell's hands, was reunited with his daughter and never spoke with her, never even saw her, before his final breath.

Rodwell... I can't think about Rodwell or what Vick did to him. I didn't see it, but I felt it all. It's horrible, brutal, and I would have thought it beyond her.

If I didn't notice her eyes.

She approaches me even as I scream, expression as lifeless as the corpses decorating much of the kitchen floor. Her dead eyes find mine and the shock stops my screaming, choking it off in a painful blockage of my throat.

Red tinges my vision, making it hard to discern details, but I blink the synesthesia effect of my gift away.

Her left arm hangs at an impossible angle, twisted, but she uses both limbs to pick me up and carry me. She reacts to none of the pain, but I'm writhing with it, sensing all of it through her and unable to block it out with my defenses so battered.

I want to drop into nothingness, cut myself off, induce a meditation trance to hide from the trauma, but she needs me. She doesn't know it, but she needs me more than she ever has.

The implants have her.

And judging from her actions with Rodwell, the implants are more sentient, and angrier, than we ever imagined. Angrier than Vick could ever be.

Alex and Lyle move to her sides, flanking her, studying her face, then mine. Alex waves a hand in front of Vick's eyes. She blinks but makes no move to stop him. "She's not in there, is she?" Alex asks.

I shake my head, unable to speak.

"What do we do?"

"We finish the mission," Vick says, tone flat. "I'm functioning within acceptable parameters. The arm can be repaired when we are back at the base."

"Not talking about your arm, Corren." Lyle touches her hurt shoulder. She doesn't react.

Pivoting, Vick passes me into Lyle's arms as if I weigh nothing. "Take Kelly to Team Two's shuttle. It suffered no damage. Treat her for emotion shock." She reaches into her pants pocket and pulls out a syringe. Turning over one of my arms, she locates a vein in the crook of it and injects the emotion-dampening drug. My heart aches with memory. "There will be sedatives in the shuttle's medkit. Give her three cc's of alutorizine. Alex is with me. We have one more objective to complete."

"The evidence," Alex snarls. Evidence that will hopefully clear his brother of treason charges.

Vick nods. "Precisely."

"No." I struggle in Lyle's grasp, wriggling my body until he has to put me down or drop me. My knees buckle, but I grab his elbow and keep from falling. "We're staying together. Especially with you... like this."

Vick cocks her head to one side, studying me.

Like I'm a new species, one of interest but not of consequence.

"I'm more efficient now than I've ever been," she says. "I cannot be distracted in this state. And you are damaged."

"The dampener will hold me together until we finish." I'm not sure about that. I can feel the drug working through my system, coating my shattered nerves with its chemical balm, blocking out the death and pain where my shields have failed. I'm better but far from good. But I'm not leaving Vick's side. "I'm your partner. We're a team. I go where you go. And no matter what you're telling yourself, you are not okay. You are...." I don't say damaged. I won't. "You are injured. Physically and emotionally. And I'm your support."

"It is not logical. You should proceed to safety."

"Humans aren't always logical," I remind her.

"I am not human."

The words strike like bombs. "What are you, then?" I'm afraid to ask. I do it anyway.

A slight shrug of her good shoulder. "I am VC1."

I close my eyes and take a slow breath. Part of me wants to slap her. Part wants to search her pockets for the little gold heart and wave it in front of her face. *Look! Look here! I love you, you idiot. I didn't fall in love with a machine.* A machine wouldn't keep such tokens.

Maybe if I kissed her. But with the block failing, it could do more harm than good.

Maybe if I shut her down.

The abort code springs to mind—a seven-digit sequence I can rattle off in my sleep, thanks to Whitehouse and hours of practice. We've never had to use it. I'm not sure it would work. I don't even know exactly what it would do, other than stop her implant functions and prevent further action.

Too risky. Her implants comprise 63 percent of her brain.

I won't use it now. It would be admitting she's the machine she's always claimed she is, and my Vick would never forgive me for that.

She turns for the door to the security command center, then pauses and looks back at me. For a second I think she truly sees me, the briefest flash of softening in her hard features. Then it's gone. "I would not be able to operate in any other state. Do not attempt to return me to my previous condition. Not until we are away from here." The last few words have some inflection. It takes effort for her to force them out, as if she's fighting an internal battle. And losing.

I consider her request. She's hurt badly. Blood seeps through her torn shirt at the left shoulder. I notice her breasts are visible again, and Alex and Lyle cast surreptitious glances in that direction, then look away, Lyle blushing, but it doesn't faze her at all. She's been sexually assaulted. Her father just died. I'm a wreck.

I won't even think about her elimination of Rodwell, but she will. She'll think about it a lot when she returns to herself.

If she returns to herself.

We need her functional, and I hate myself for thinking it in those terms. Without the implants' control, she'd collapse. Three more bots wander the complex somewhere. I don't know if they will shut down with Rodwell's demise or carry out their final orders as our enemies, but if they fight us, we will have a hard time winning without Vick. And who knows how many other security traps Rodwell put in place or made operational before his death.

But if I leave her be, how long is too long? Every second passing feels like a second closer to the point of no return, a second longer for the implants to gain a foothold, dig in, ensconce themselves so that I might never drag my Vick back to the forefront.

The mental debate ends with my nod. I can't save her if none of us survive. She nods back, as solemn as I've ever seen her. Her left eye twitches. A muscle in her cheek jumps. I have no more doubts about the internal war waging within Vick. Part of her gave in so she could carry out the mission.

So she could save you, a little voice nags.

Part of her did not wish to succumb but got taken along with the rest. And she wants it back.

"What should we do with the body?" Alex doesn't ask which body. He's facing Oz, his mouth a grim line. None of us are happy with this failure.

"Leave it," Vick says. She doesn't look down, but steps to the door and opens it.

Not him. It.

I touch her elbow. "You sure?"

"What purpose would it serve to burden ourselves with it? It would encumber us, and we need to be free to fight if necessary." Her pulse jumps in her neck. She swallows. "We can send a retrieval team for it… for him, later." Vick winces, as if from a sudden pain, and the echo of it pounds for a second in my temple, dull, but still hurting even under the dampening drugs, which means it's excruciating for Vick.

The implants must not have liked her answer. Either that, or it's punishment for her failure to save Oz.

We'll have to leave the bodies of Team Two as well. We'd never be able to move them all the way to their shuttle, but we could have managed one.

The security command center is empty and quiet, the working comps humming. The overhead lights come on at our entry.

Alex proceeds to one of the terminals, pulling a cord from a belt pouch, but Vick stops him with an upraised hand. "It will expedite matters if I download the information and sift through the relevant files."

Her mouth works around the unfamiliar vocabulary, lips and tongue uncomfortable with it but unable to speak any other way.

She places her palm atop the embedded comp screen and goes rigid, staring at a blank spot on the nearest wall.

"That… shouldn't be possible," Alex mutters beside me. "She needs an interface to do that."

Not anymore.

It takes seconds for her to accomplish her task and draw her hand away. Judging from Alex's raised eyebrows, this speed impresses him as well.

She blinks, some of the focus returning to her gaze. "I will search the files when we are in a safer location and I can divert all my attention to processing, but at a quick scan, I can tell you that transmissions are traceable in both directions. Rodwell sent several encrypted messages from this moon's orbit. And the responding sequence did not begin with the YBR team."

Alex exhales, shoulders sagging in relief, and Lyle slaps him on the back. "See? I knew we'd find something to clear your brother."

"Yeah." Alex's smile is shaky. The Fighting Storm punishes treason with death.

We don't encounter the other bots on our way out, though we do a quick battle with an automated laser grid in the alternate exit corridor we choose.

Once it activates, Vick shuts it down with a thought, using wireless communication between her implants and the security system, but not before Alex takes a burn across his back.

We shiver and stumble our way across the rocky terrain, all of our suits damaged in a number of places, Vick's gaping open in front.

She shows no reaction to the piercing cold, the pain, or anyone else's discomfort. By the time we reach Team Two's abandoned shuttle, all of us are exhausted and showing signs of imminent collapse.

All of us, that is, except for Vick. She's lost in her own world.

CHAPTER 35
VICK
BY A THREAD

I AM a passenger.

Docile capitulation has never been a characteristic of mine. I can actually think that with authority now that I've seen images from my youth. From stage performances to hoverbike racing, I was apparently quite the extrovert.

Now I'm trapped in my own head, pushing and shoving with mental energy while I watch my body carry out the remainder of our mission. My minor victories—a twitch, a few words—mean nothing, accomplish nothing, other than to hopefully let Kelly know I'm not totally gone.

To my reduced senses, the world looks blue. Navy blue. And it occurs to me that I'm within the bubble the implants showed me earlier. That last holdout of resistance. Clever devices. Unable to break through, they've trapped my will in it.

Or maybe I've put myself there, knowing it's the one place I'll be safe. For now.

Warmth, acceptance, *love* infuse the inner me—the trapped me. It's wonderful and terrible at once: fuzzy blankets, licky puppy greetings, fresh-baked cookies, and an embrace from someone who fits just *there* in the crook of my shoulder—the sensory realization of what I've been missing all this time.

My team watches me from the corners of their eyes, casting not-so-subtle glances at my face, exchanging concerned looks. My exterior persona scares them.

I scare Kelly.

I hate this thing that controls me.

I thought I was a machine before. No. I was the motherfucking goddess of compassion compared to what I've become.

My actions are efficient and precise but lack any humanity. I leave my father's body behind because it makes things simpler. I ignore Kelly's pleas. I interface with the freaking database and the security system without an access point. The implants have evolved.

I'm amazing and terrifying.

And brilliant. My vocabulary surpasses my knowledge. I don't comprehend half the words I say to my team, which frustrates the hell out of me. I never had more than a high school education before I enlisted in the Storm. Which means the implants have knowledge, have thought processes, of their own.

And I can speak to them.

Let me go. I think the request as loudly and forcefully as I can, the reverberations causing my essence to tremble within the navy sphere.

I am protecting you. Without my current influence, we could not function.

Interesting, logical, and straight to the point. No more metaphors. While the information from Oz's database runs through me, I work on a response.

I can see the results of my implants' search as clearly as reading a book, if I concentrate. The implants translate the information into concepts I can understand. Not sure why. Maybe working via a human brain, they have no other method of processing.

Some of what I learn surprises me.

The transmissions to Rodwell came from Girard Base, but not from the YBR team.

That is correct, the implants respond. No. VC1 responds. Her mental voice carries a distinctly feminine vibe, as if she's adopted parts of my thought patterns, my mannerisms.

Where did they come from?

That will take more time, VC1 admits. So she's not perfect. *My orders were to clear the YBR team. I have done so. Secondary orders involved tracking the actual source. Working on that now.*

How long?

Hours. Perhaps days.

She withdraws from the database, and we, meaning all the members of my team, not just the two of us (man, this is getting weird), leave security command and head for the shuttle. Somewhere in there I stop tracking because when I start receiving input again through her, we're outside, Alex has a laser burn across his back, and Kelly shivers violently on my right.

The gap in time concerns me. My thoughts come slower, stress and exhaustion taking tolls on my mental strength. I need sleep.

VC1, however, can go several days without it, if she uses periodic adrenaline bursts.

Kelly shifts in and out of my peripheral vision. I want to turn toward her, check on her, comfort her, but my body doesn't obey me anymore.

We board the shuttle, VC1 overriding the locks Team Two had in place. I hear my voice offer to pilot, but Lyle shakes his head, muttering something about not trusting his life to a computer.

So we're back to that. Though in my current state, I can't blame him. I don't trust me.

Not an issue so long as she's controlled by her programming. But at the rate she's evolving, she may not continue to be loyal to the Storm or me.

We are one entity. One cannot operate without the other. I will protect you until you have the strength to protect yourself.

Right. Anything I think, she can hear. My thoughts are no longer private.

VC1 places my body in one of the rear seats. Kelly collapses into the one beside me. Alex passes her the medkit from a storage compartment. While we depart the small moon and begin the journey home, she treats his laser burns. When she's done, he stands, looking from Kelly to me and back again.

"I'll go file our preliminary report." Then he joins Lyle in the cockpit, leaving the pair of us alone.

She shifts in the chair to look me in the eyes, wincing at whatever she sees. Her fingers reach into the pouch on my belt, fumbling for something. She holds the little gold heart in front of me.

"It is a heart-shaped piece of jewelry. Though in reality, it does not much resemble the actual internal organ," VC1 says.

Kelly chokes out a sob, then swallows hard. She presses the heart into my hand, its weight and pressure telling me of its existence. Taking my face between her palms, she says, "Let me in." I can't feel her touch. I want to.

"You should take your sedative and rest. You are damaged."

One of her eyebrows rises. "Do you care?"

"I am responsible for your welfare. The board designated me the team leader."

Kelly sighs and my heart breaks.

I love you, Kel. And I can *love you now. I feel it. All of it.* It's a little weird, not having the context, just the flashes of us together when we were in North Carolina, with no clear details, but it's all so damn *good.* I want this for all time, not just while I'm trapped in your blocked-off bubble.

God, I wish you could hear me.

"Let me in," she says. Her energy presses at my mind. At VC1.

I sense it, but within the protective mental safe-room, it's fainter than I'm used to. I try to respond, to open the channel between us. A flash erupts in my inner sight, searing and blinding. When I can see again, there's a new fracture in the shell encasing me.

Please cease your efforts. Your recent experiences have affected your stability. If you break free now, if you allow yourself to use the channel and release your emotions when she is weakened as well and unable to handle them, you may become incapable of rational behavior.

You're saying I'm losing my mind, I think at VC1, just to clarify the message.

That is exactly what I am saying.

I stop trying to connect with Kelly.

She doesn't give up so easily. The pressure increases. She squeezes her eyes shut, concentrating all her energy on breaking through to me. Tendrils of her feelings leak in. She's tired. So tired.

More cracks form in the casing. She's not establishing a connection. She's trying to pull the block, and my panic gives me strength.

"Don't!" The sound emerging from my lips is more like two voices than one, a stereo effect as a result of both of us attempting to communicate with her at once.

The oddness gives her pause and she pulls back, staring at me. "Vick?"

I can't duplicate the brief moment of speech. The effort cost me and I'm too weak. Dammit.

"Emotions make me less efficient, less effective. You want answers to your questions of treason. You want them in as short a time as possible. I cannot act as quickly when I must split my consciousness." VC1 attempts logic with an empath. Not the best approach.

"Not good enough," Kelly cuts in, unaware of our internal argument. "Nothing will happen to the YBR team right away. We can wait a little longer for details. Or download the information from you into a real computer."

"I *am* a real computer," VC1 says.

"Which is exactly why I want Vick back. Right. Now."

She pushes again, hurting herself, straining, the pain etched in her wrinkled forehead, her pale cheeks, the tightness of the muscles in her neck. The pads of her fingertips dig into my skin, pressure but no pain.

Let me talk to her. I'll get her to stop. Logic won't work here.

Though eventually, the block will fail on its own. By then, I hope I've recovered enough to handle things.

VC1 doesn't bother responding, but a second later, I regain the power of speech. It's all I've got. I can't move or feel Kelly's hands, the warmth of her skin. I can't smell the subtle perfume she wears. This is a temporary thing. A one-shot.

"Kel," I whisper.

Her eyes pop open, widening at the emotion in my voice. She opens her mouth to speak, but I cut her off.

"You need to stop, Kel. Please. VC1, she's got a mind of her own."

Kelly's eyes widen. I'm not sure she believes what I'm saying, but I've got her attention.

"She... I... shit. *We* think you and I have been through too much. Give me some time before you pull the block or connect with me. Or find another way to bring me out of this. The implants think they're protecting us both."

She shakes her head. "I don't know another way." Tears tumble down her cheeks. She lets them fall unchecked.

I have to say something. "We'll figure it out." Déjà vu hits, and a memory of the two of us perched on the edge of a bed in a North Carolina cabin comes fast and clear. We're both wearing towels, and a hint of arousal curls between my thighs. I mentally shake it away.

Deep in my head, I'd swear VC1 is chuckling. Whether the implants are on my side or not, it pisses me off.

Fuck you, I thought-whisper.

Not interested in masturbation right now. Maybe later.

Great. Now VC1's sense of humor chooses to show itself. And it's exactly the sort of thing I might say. I wonder if our personalities are combining somehow, but I don't have time to think much on that.

The walls are coming down again, and I rush my next words. "Let things happen as they will. I love—" *Dammit.*

"I know," she sobs. "I feel it." She leans forward and kisses me then, and for a second, her lips are warm against mine, followed by nothing but mere pressure. Our bodies separate and we stare at each other, inches between us and an impossible distance.

VC1 shows me the last thread of my sanity cord.

It's fraying.

CHAPTER 36
KELLY
FULL OF SURPRISES

VICK CORREN is gone.

We land in the hangar under one of the Girard Base domes, the one assigned to ships owned by the Fighting Storm, and disembark. Home, such as it is, should lift my spirits, but nothing eases my worry for Vick.

I don't know what to make of VC1 as its own thinking being. It's possible, I suppose.

Or Vick might truly have gone insane.

But she's right. We need rest and time to recover. Then I can try again to reach the feeling side of her.

The four of us pass between fighter ships and shuttles, cargo transports and personal luxury yachts for the board members. I wonder which one belongs to Whitehouse, and my lip curls with distaste. He gets wealth and comfort while Vick pays most of her salary back to the Storm—an indentured servant if not a slave.

Activity bustles around us. Mechanics work on ship maintenance. Smells of fuel and engine lubricants tang the air. The hum of the gravity generators and air recyclers vibrates through my boots.

All so familiar and yet so alien to an Earther like me.

What isn't familiar is the squad of security personnel blocking the airlock to the rest of the base. Not Storm soldiers but Girard employees, with Officer Sanderson at the head of the four-man unit.

Her frown goes deeper than mine. She steps forward to meet us, and I realize they are here *for* our team.

"Problem?" Alex asks, taking point. It would be Vick's responsibility as leader, but he guesses correctly that she's in no condition to conduct diplomatic negotiations with base security. Beside me, Vick stands too still for a normal human, watching the proceedings and saying nothing.

"I'm afraid so," Sanderson says, tone apologetic. I tap her thoughts, sensing regret and dismay, gold and silver.

What the hell is going on? Is the board moving against Alex along with his brother? We need to get our information out of Vick's head and into their hands fast.

But that isn't it at all. At a signal from Sanderson, two of the guards move to flank... me.

"Ms. LaSalle, you're under arrest for empathic interference, to be held in custody until a hearing may be conducted to ascertain a need for trial." Sanderson watches while one guard pulls my hands behind my back and fastens electronic binders around my wrists. The cold metal presses hard against my skin, edges digging in, and I flinch. "Not too tight," Sanderson says, placing a hand on the nearest guard's arm. "She's not resisting. No need for additional discomfort."

Around us, workers and soldiers stop their tasks and stare. At a quick glare from Sanderson, though, they return to whatever they were doing.

"Wait, this is nuts. Kelly is *supposed* to interfere. She's VC1—" Alex catches himself. The two of them have moved past those prejudices, even if the implants are currently in control. "She's Vick's handler. It's her job, a medical necessity."

My thoughts tumble in a frantic whirlwind, but in my heart, I understand, and my vision wavers. The men guarding me grab my arms to hold me upright.

"The charges have nothing to do with her contractual obligations. Her contract does not allow for the placing of an emotional block within another human being, especially one who is emotionally impaired and perhaps unable to protect herself or seek help. Nothing does." Sanderson meets my eyes while Alex and Lyle stare from me to Vick. "I truly hope these charges are false, for everyone's sake."

Because if they're true, it gives that much more credence to what the general public believes about psychics—that we're all-powerful, dangerous, deceitful beings, bent on conquering humanity, and would have done so a long time ago if not for our small numbers.

"We'll be keeping this quiet," she adds, confirming my thoughts. "Take her."

Lyle moves to intervene, but Alex grabs and holds him, offering me a consolatory smile. "We'll get to the bottom of this, the right way. We know you're innocent."

But I'm not.

I want to scream it at them, confess everything. I'm guilty and I deserve to be punished for what I've done to the woman I care most about. Part of me is relieved to have it out at last. But I also want to tell them why. Make them understand.

I keep my mouth shut.

Beside me, Vick shifts, her good arm tensing its muscles, her legs carrying her a step in my direction, then stopping. VC1 may not care how this ends. Putting me out of the picture only gives the implants more strength to quell what few emotions Vick has left. But Vick cares, and she wants to stop it.

"Don't," I say, putting more force into my words than I feel. God, if she could wrench me away from them, take us both someplace safe where I can work on getting her back, well, I'd give anything. But she can't, and I won't risk her. "Leave it be." She turns her head toward me, a flicker of pain behind her eyes. "Let me make my appeal. We'll see what happens."

I know what will happen. They'll convict me, and I'll end up put away where I can't touch anyone's mind, including Vick's. It will mean the end of both of us, because there will be no one to save her… soul. It's the only word I have for it. But this buys us time.

She nods once, jerkily, and I know it's really her and not VC1 responding.

The interaction draws Sanderson's attention more pointedly to Vick. Sanderson peers at the shoulder of Vick's replacement uniform shirt, found in a locker on the shuttle and probably belonging to Lark from Team Two. It's too tight around Vick's muscular biceps, and despite the makeshift first aid job I performed and a clean bandage, blood stains the tan fabric. She studies Vick's face too, and frowns.

"You need medical attention," Sanderson states without preamble. "Erick, take her to her company's med facility, then report back. She'll need a full mental workup for the hearing, anyway. Let them know the situation and what information they'll need to provide."

The last guard steps to Vick's side. He doesn't touch her. I don't think he wants to.

"We'll go with her," Alex says, nudging Lyle in that direction. "Kelly, as soon as we have something...."

I nod. We're a team now. Took us long enough, and it's too little too late, but we're a team, and we're not giving up on each other.

My escorts march me to the all-too-familiar security area, two domes over, and Sanderson herself unlocks my binders and shows me to my cell. It's the same one Vick occupied a few days ago, and the irony is not lost on me. The other two officers depart, leaving the two of us.

"I hope you had a good reason," she says, staring at me through the bars. "She loves you."

I wonder how she knows.

Vick couldn't have loved me when the pair of them occupied that table in the Purple Leaf. I'm wondering at the love I felt from her in the terminal. The block is failing, but it's still in place. Whatever is happening with it, it's allowing some of her affection for me to seep through.

Despite the fact that I'm admitting my guilt, I murmur, "I thought so at the time."

"Convince them at the hearing," she says, making it an order. "Vick needs you. In a very short time, I've come to like and respect that woman, taken or not. I don't want to see her hurt."

You won't. You'll never see any pain from her again, if VC1 has its way.

Sanderson strides toward the exit, not waiting for my response.

I sink onto the lumpy cot, a loose spring poking me in the backside, and wonder how Vick could have slept on the thing, but I'm so exhausted, I lie down and close my eyes.

A hundred worries keep me tossing and turning, unable to rest. One stands out above all others.

I can think of only one way security can know about what I've done. Whitehouse.

But why? Why now? Whitehouse has never cared for me, and I'm certain he resents my influence with Vick while having no choice but to rely on it. Still, taking me out of the picture does nothing but hurt him. He can't control Vick without me.

I lie there, counting the ceiling tiles, wondering if Vick did the same thing while she lay here. And it hits me.

Now Whitehouse *can* control her. In her current state, she functions exactly the way Whitehouse has always wanted her to—efficiently and without emotional interference. At last the implants are operating in the way they were designed.

But does he *know* that? Would Alex have mentioned Vick's condition in the preliminary report regulations required him to transmit to the base prior to our arrival?

I don't believe he would. Not now. Not after all we'd been through as a team. Not after Alex came to see Vick as a person and Whitehouse as an asshole.

And she isn't a thoughtless, mindless being, either. From what I can tell, my Vick is fully aware of what is happening but unable to exert any influence on it. She's trapped in her own mind, just like those poor security bots at Oz's complex.

The ones Whitehouse sent there for storage.

The ones we were probably never supposed to know the truth about.

Could that be it? A cover-up? But he'd have to take out Alex and Lyle and Vick too.

Dammit, I'm missing something. If Vick were here, we could work it out together. But she's not, and I'm stuck counting ceiling tiles.

And Vick…. Vick is with Whitehouse.

CHAPTER 37
VICK
DUAL INPUT

I AM both.

The guard escorts me to the Storm's medical center where he explains the situation to the nurse on duty, and Alex and Lyle wait with me in a standard examination room until Whitehouse arrives. "See to Kelly's safety," VC1 tells them, standing by the center examining table. They exchange glances, neither one comfortable abandoning me to the asshole, but they depart.

And it's me and Whitehouse.

He looks at me. Really looks. Then takes a stroll in a full circle around me, studying my posture, the way I hold my body and my head in rigid stillness.

"You are different," he comments.

"I am damaged," VC1 replies, voice devoid of inflection.

He pauses by my left shoulder. "Your arm, yes. But…. Are your suppressors on?" He doesn't wait for an answer but grabs a scanner from the nearest shelf and runs it the full length of me, hovering an overly long period next to my skull. I hear the whir of the device, though with the way VC1 has me positioned, I can't see it.

It's unnerving, having him out of my sight.

Can you just turn the fuck around?

I will know if he poses a threat.

Whitehouse is always a threat.

VC1 considers my words. I almost feel the process of her calculations. Images of the airlock accident, my initial treatment after the surgery, and a dozen other moments too quick to identify pass through my mind. A second later, she shifts her stance so she can keep him in her line of sight.

I'm glad we're on the same side.

We always have been, she tells me.

This is so freaking weird.

"Your suppressors are operating at 103 percent, which is well beyond the recommended and expected limits. Interesting. It would appear your emotions have been completely eliminated, though the pressure on the remaining portion of your brain poses some risks of further damage." He puts down the scanner and grabs a pair of surgical scissors, then snips away the bloodied uniform over my shoulder.

Um, brain damage? I don't have a lot to spare, here.

With more tenderness than I've ever seen from him, Whitehouse peels the cloth from the bandaging. It would hurt, if the implants weren't cutting down on my nerve input. As it stands, I feel the tug where the adhesive sticks to my skin but nothing more.

You are in no immediate danger. I would not allow it. Try to remember, if you die, I also cease to exist. It is why the security bots were allowed to retain a minimum amount of brain function. The way the implants are designed, they must interact with the human brain. The natural electrical impulses provide a consistent power source. You will have to… trust… my analysis.

Whitehouse hmms and huhs over the wound, applying an antibiotic ointment to the tear in my flesh, then fitting an inflammation reducer cup over the whole shoulder. The swelling goes down immediately.

Like I have a choice.

Whitehouse removes the cup and closes the wound with a spray sealant. He hovers in front of me, inches from my face. I don't like people this close. Well, people other than Kelly. I want to flinch away, take a step back for personal space, but my body isn't going anywhere.

"Do you feel anything? Pain, anger, sadness at the loss of your father?" These questions should be accompanied by sympathetic looks, a comforting gesture.

Instead, a gleam shines in his eye. His lips curl in a predatory smile.

It scares the shit out of me, but of course, I'm currently incapable of showing fear.

VC1 cocks my head to the side. "Pain and emotions are fully suppressed."

The smile broadens.

"However," she adds, "for the sake of continued emotional and physical health, they cannot continue to be so. Once sufficient rest and nourishment have been received, and repairs completed, they will be released."

"But you don't find your state unpleasant."

"We—"

No! Don't tell him there are two of us. Keep that ace in the hole. We may need a surprise.

"I," she continues without a blink, "don't find it any way at all. It simply is."

"Ah! Excellent." Whitehouse practically beams with pleasure.

Uh-oh. Wrong answer.

He paces back and forth. "So, they were wrong. All of them. Oz and the other researchers who shut down the security bot project. The ones who insisted I leave you with as much free will, as much feeling and emotion as I could. The ones who tried to watch over my shoulder every minute. They were wrong. Completely wrong."

And you, Dr. Whitehouse, are completely wacko.

If by wacko you mean psychologically unstable, then I concur. She rotates the injured arm in the socket. It completes the full circuit, though a tension in the muscles indicates some resistance. Not perfect, but she can use it, if she needs to. If we need to fight. Good thinking. Or processing. Or whatever.

Scary thing is, I'm really starting to like VC1. Not sure what that says about me.

You possess excellent judgment and taste.

If I could laugh, I would.

"I have good news for you, then. What if I told you I could make your current condition permanent, without any risk?" Whitehouse strides to the back corner of the examining room, past the table, to a door marked "storage." With a keypad code lock. Storage rooms don't get high security.

My internal humor fades.

"I've made great progress in my research, invested my own funds to continue my work. Two years. Come."

My body obeys. I stand beside him while he punches in a code, my visual receptors recording the combination. The door slides open revealing not a closet, but an elevator. We're in a single-story structure. The only way to go is down. There's a Biblical metaphor in there somewhere, and not a positive one.

Whitehouse steps inside, gesturing for me to follow.

I do.

Um, is this a good idea?

I am governed by a primary system override. I cannot disobey a direct order from a board member of the Fighting Storm unless that order directly contradicts one of my other primary directives.

How about self-preservation?

Self-preservation has always been secondary to the board's orders.

I think about missions I've had to accept, chances I've had to take. *Yeah. I know.*

We are, as you would put it, "screwed."

Fucked might be better, but I don't correct her.

More security inside the elevator. Whitehouse presses his palm to a scanner, which causes the numbered buttons on the panel to light up. Only two floors, ground and sub-one. He hits the sub-one button and we descend.

VC1 says nothing, though I'm brimming with questions. Where are we going? Does the rest of the board know about this? How could he have kept it hidden? I also note the absence of my usual panic in elevators. An additional advantage to being stored in my protective bubble.

Safe. Secure. No pain. No stress. VC1 taking care of everything.

No free will. No Kelly. No life.

No contest.

But for a moment, it was tempting.

The elevator stops. Whitehouse reaches out, holding the Door Close button, keeping us sealed inside. "What you are about to see is classified at the highest level."

Highest level. Meaning if I reveal anything he shows me, it's punishable by death.

"Acknowledged," VC1 responds.

The door slides open, revealing a well-appointed lab, large enough for several workers, though it's empty and all but one of the workstations look abandoned. Work tables, three-dimensional schematics hovering above them, a surgical area in the rear with the curtain drawn aside so I can see the operating table and equipment. Names and functions run through my thoughts in a blur. VC1 identifies them. I can't. Not that fast. Not without the two of us reintegrating ourselves.

On the left stands a seven-foot-tall metal cylinder, sealed entry hatch in the front, dozens of tubes and wires running into the sides and rear. Large enough to hold a person.

Looking at it produces the most disconcerting sense of déjà vu.

The stream of information I've been receiving from VC1 falters, then stops.

Shit. What could be scary enough to frighten a computer?

I need you, she says.

What—? I never finish forming the question. With a sudden release of compression, I'm outside the bubble, shoved back into the full rush of feelings and emotions, the suppressors going from full to zero in an instant.

"Oh…. God." My knees buckle and I hit the tile floor, then curl in on myself. Flailing mentally, I try to reestablish the suppressors, but they don't function. My shoulder screams. He never administered a painkiller, counting on the implants to take care of it. The cold air of the environmentally controlled lab chills my skin.

Then comes everything else.

My torture. Oz's death. Rodwell's execution.

I haven't been normal in over two years and don't have any memory of what normal feels like. But I doubt a normal person could handle what I've been through in the past few days. For someone like me, well….

My stomach lurches, spewing bile across the flooring, spattering Whitehouse's expensive leather shoes as he backpedals out of the way. I'm aware of him moving, fumbling for something amidst the shelves and cabinets lining the walls.

Breathing comes hard, in quick, panting gasps that make my vision sparkle and spin.

A needle pierces my bicep. Darkness closes in.

I reach for an adrenaline burst. Last thing I want is to lose consciousness around Whitehouse. But the burst won't come.

"I'll fix this," he says. "Don't worry. I'll fix everything."

I tumble sideways and his voice fades.

CHAPTER 38
KELLY
CONFESSION

VICK CORREN is a teacher.

When Sanderson brings in the next group of prisoners, I'm wishing for solitude. The drunken merchants howl and grumble, pushing and shoving one another while a trio of guards herds them down the row of otherwise empty cells. One pauses by mine, leering in at me, bloodshot eyes unfocused.

Memories of the Alpha Dog brawl flood my vision and I roll away from the bars to face the metal wall. I can't erase the image of the Sunfire merc, blood pouring from the knife wound in his neck. His death has haunted my nightmares for days.

Someday, when the block I placed fails, maybe I'll have Vick to comfort me through my bad dreams, and I'll help her through hers.

A throat clears outside my bars. What is taking the guards so long in moving those prisoners away?

The throat clears again, followed by a polite cough and "May I enter?"

I roll to face a small man in a Fighting Storm uniform, though I don't recognize him or the insignia on his shoulder patch, and he doesn't look muscular enough to be a soldier. He follows my gaze and smiles. "Legal department," he explains. "I'm your lawyer, Barry Richmond. May I come in?" He holds up an access card.

For a moment I'm stunned security would allow him to have it. Then I spot the guard a couple of cells down, out of earshot but within visual range. "Do I have a choice?"

The lawyer tilts his head to one side. "There's always a choice, Ms. LaSalle. The Storm provides counsel to all its members, free of charge. As you can imagine, a mercenary organization would be faced with a number of lawsuits. But you can, of course, foolishly struggle through this on your own." The last comes with a grin, softening the words even if I know he's not kidding.

I wave him inside and he comes, locking the sliding bars behind him. "Not much in the way of seats. May I?" Richmond indicates the foot of my cot and I nod. When he sits, the whole end squeaks and sinks, and we both grimace. "Well then, perhaps we should get through the details as quickly as possible, before my seat collapses."

Richmond outlines my situation. Hearing tomorrow, court date in a couple of days if the hearing determines the case will proceed— which he's pretty certain it will, given the seriousness of my supposed transgression.

"Feelings toward the gifted community are volatile even at the best of times. We value your skills and fear them, as we fear anyone stronger or more talented than the average person. It holds you to a higher standard, which isn't fair, but that's the way things are." Richmond spreads his hands in apology. "So my first question would be, will you trust me?"

What's the point in having a lawyer if you aren't going to trust him? Then again, someone sold me out. Someone in the Fighting Storm.

Someone named Whitehouse.

"A question of my own, first. Who filed the complaint?"

He grimaces. "An anonymous accusation against you arrived at the Academy for Special Abilities and was passed along to the Governing Council of Psychics. That set everything in motion. We've tried to determine the source, but our best investigators have failed."

Figures.

I weigh my options, wondering what Vick would say.

If you're not the expert, you have to trust the experts. Otherwise you're fumbling in the dark. Her voice echoes in my memory, all those late-night chats we've had over the years. God, I miss her.

"I'll try," I tell him.

He purses his lips, then nods. "We got the report from Storm medical. They confirm a block was put in place in Vick Corren, also designated as VC1. You're the most likely candidate."

So it's still working. Dammit. If it had failed, it would be much harder to trace. "Yes."

He holds up a hand. "I won't assume that's an admission of guilt, but rather an acceptance of the current circumstances. But that brings me to my second question, perhaps more important than the first. Why would you block her ability to love?" Richmond's tone lacks the clinical detachment it had earlier. It's filled with emotion, a desire to understand and.... I send out a quick probe. Yes, a desire to help me, if he can. His genuineness glows around him in neon pink. "I've read your records and VC1's. You've helped her immensely over the years. I've watched recordings of the two of you working together. And...." He pauses, waiting until I meet his gaze. "I've read between the lines. No one who's looking could miss the bond between the two of you. So, there must have been a very good reason, hopefully a reason good enough to convince the court your actions were justified, or at least one I can twist and shape into appearing that way. Whether you admit to it or not, the court will assume you did it. The question is whether or not you should be punished for it."

Without further hesitation, I tell him. I tell him everything.

CHAPTER 39
VICK
RESURRECTION

I AM reborn.

I come to with my wrists bound by metal restraints to one of the lab's chairs. A second set of binders holds my ankles together. I test them with a couple of firm tugs, but nothing gives. My left shoulder is numb. At least he did something about that pain. I'm sedated too. My head feels stuffed with cotton, and I have to concentrate to remember why I passed out. When I do, I retreat from the memories as fast as I can. My restrictions remind me too much of my session with Rodwell, and I gag, then swallow bile.

Hey, I think into the emptiness in my skull. *Little help here?*

No response from VC1 and no accessing the suppressors. I'm still on my own.

Footsteps sound behind me, and Whitehouse comes into view. He's wearing gloves, holding a scanner, which he runs over me an inch at a time. "Malfunction," he mutters, not looking at me, talking to himself. "Overload in the implant processors. Don't know what could have caused that...."

You, you fucking asshole. And that cylinder behind you, which can't be for anything good. But I keep my mouth shut.

"No matter. I'll fix you."

An unstoppable shiver runs up the length of my spine.

Whitehouse moves to the cylinder, tapping in a code on the embedded panel. The hatch slides open. What I thought was an empty container is actually far from empty.

Inside stands a man. Or what's left of one.

Repelled and intrigued at once, I study the naked figure in the tube. Clamps around his ankles, wrists, torso, and waist hold him upright, though he hangs from them, muscles slack. Tubes and wires run into his chest, abdomen, and skull. His eyes are closed, skin pasty white, but his breast rises and falls with the intake and exhalation of air.

Several scars mar the area around his left nipple, old scars, round ones.

Bullet holes.

I flick my gaze back to the man's face, the pain between my eyes from when I first spotted the cylinder returning, blood pounding in my ears.

Like Devin trapped inside the security bot, I know him.

"Hello, Stephen," I whisper.

Stephen's eye twitches beneath the lid when I speak his name, and I jerk back in my seat, trying to put as much distance between myself and Whitehouse's son as I can while restrained.

"Fuck." My gaze darts to Whitehouse standing impassively by the cylinder, completely unaffected by Stephen's condition. "Why? Why are you doing this? Why can't you let them… us… rest?"

"Why should I? You belong to the Storm. You died, remember? In your case, a couple of times over."

I do remember now. That's part of the problem. The trembling attempts to take hold of my limbs, but I tense my muscles into rigidity, despite the pain it causes in my shoulder.

"Our species has an odd view of the dead," Whitehouse goes on. "Many creatures consume their deceased. Our ancestors made use of bones and fur for tools and clothing. But we discard them as useless."

"We aren't talking about animals here. We're talking about people. People who deserve respect." I stare at Stephen, wondering how much he understands of this conversation. Judging from his utter lack of reaction, it can't be much.

"What better respect can I show someone than putting them to good productive use?" Whitehouse spreads his hands in a grandiose gesture. "I'm recycling."

"So… is he dead or isn't he? Are you interacting with the brain or a computer?" I don't want to know, but I need to. Alex couldn't tell me enough back in Oz's complex. I need something a little more definitive than maybe.

"He's not dead," Whitehouse says. "He isn't strictly alive, either. Rather like you." He nods in my direction, but his eyes are on his son.

No, not like me. I think and I feel. I'm a person, and thanks to Kelly, I believe it. This... and the security bots like him... are not human. Not human enough.

"Stephen, wake up."

Stephen, huh? Not SW plus whatever number he happens to be? Even mostly dead, Dr. Whitehouse won't treat his son like a machine. Like he treats me. Nice.

Stephen's eyes snap open, and I swallow hard at the emptiness there.

"Disengage from the equipment, please," the doctor orders.

Stephen's hand moves to the various tubes and wires, disconnecting them with clinical efficiency, taking no notice as blood and other fluids run down his bare skin.

"Step out, please."

He steps forward, and I try to embed myself in the back of the chair. I want to be fair, to accept him the way I've always wanted to be accepted, but I can't. The doctor circles his son, nodding with approval at the pasty complexion, expressionless face, and emotionless eyes.

I think I'm going to be sick again.

"The perfect soldier," the doctor explains, "or he will be when I finish my research and programming. Two years of tireless work. No original brain functions despite it being intact. Implant driven, carrying out the autonomic responses and providing additional enhancements like improved eyesight, smell, and hearing."

Like mine.

He's listing off the features like he's trying to sell me a new hovervan.

An image of the Frankenstein monster flashes in my internal display.

About time you showed up, I thought-growl at VC1.

Functions are still limited. I cannot give you suppressor access, but you must not—

She cuts off in midthought. Must not what? Great. Just great.

Whitehouse prattles on. "But there are no personal experiences retained, no emotions of any kind, no interaction with others until needed in the field, and any attachments made then are wiped out upon their return to the storage cylinders. Once I perfect this equipment, they will be cost-efficient. Every man or woman lost will have new purpose, and we can continue to reuse them. With enough subjects, we can cease recruiting altogether. No more lives lost. Nothing can stop them short of extreme physical trauma." He practically glows with enthusiasm.

Enthusiasm for never letting the dead rest.

When I die, again, will they give me peace? They made so many mistakes messing around in my brain, I wonder if some small part of Stephen knows what's being done with him, like Devin seemed to. I'm betting he might, that Whitehouse has no idea what he's dealing with, what he's allowing to happen to his own son.

"Why… why am I different?" I want to scream and crawl into a hole somewhere, but I force my tone to stay even. Panicking won't get me anywhere. I can't believe I'm managing to hold on to myself, but Kelly has brought me a long way.

God, Kelly, what's happening to you? I need to get out of here so I can help her.

Whitehouse looks down his nose at me. "Oz, your *father*"—he spits the word—"wouldn't allow it. He insisted we preserve as much of your personality as we could while keeping you fit for service, and what Oz wanted, Oz got."

Oh, no bitterness there, Doc.

"Of course my reports to him were slightly altered. He never knew how much I managed to retain."

So my father wouldn't come searching me out. So I wouldn't have the interference of that relationship while Whitehouse continued to make adjustments. So eventually, *now*, that he thinks he knows how to make it work, he can take more from me. And of course now Oz is dead. Whitehouse has nothing to fear from him any longer.

"Why not use robots? Why people?" Why do this to human beings?

"By itself, even the most advanced programming cannot account for as many split-second decisions as a human brain in constant interaction with that programming. And no metallic construct is as agile, can move as quietly, as a human. We thought we'd failed in your case. The bots were an attempt to correct the issues we had with you, but they are considered too mechanical in nature. Now that your functions have integrated more fully, you can be adjusted to better suit my needs."

He clicks something on his belt and my binders release. He gestures for me to stand. When I don't, a jerk of his head from Stephen to me has his son moving behind me like a trained dead puppy, sending shivers skittering up my spine. I rise from my seat for no other reason than to keep the walking dead man where I can see him.

"With the removal of Oz, your privileged status has changed. You were the prototype, easier to make functional since we left you some of your own memories instead of having to program all your skills in from scratch, but with those came related emotions, which had to be suppressed. We've learned a lot from your failures, and I've documented all of them."

Whitehouse points to the cylinder. It's empty, dark and confined, smaller than an airlock and a hundred times more intimidating.

Whitehouse is still talking. I break off staring at the dark opening, trying to collect my scattering thoughts. My control is at its end. I can't remain standing without using the chair to hold myself up.

"Now that your implants have shown they are capable of fully controlling your emotions, I will soon be able to keep those emotions fully suppressed and safely remove all unnecessary memories, particularly those you've attained over the past two years. Through regular memory purges, you will function entirely at the will of the Storm with no risk of personality interference. And once I prove how well my advancements work, I'll no longer have to hide my successes within the bots."

"You're insane. All of this is insane!" I'm shouting, but I can't stop it.

"Letting your comrades die because of your emotions is insane. And the airlock wasn't the only time."

His words stun me into temporary silence. "What are you talking about?"

"Besides killing my son and your lover, your human emotions are directly responsible for the deaths of Team Two at Oz's complex."

I flash back on the exterior hatch, the six-digit code I fought against time to break, the code that would have overridden the need for the spoken phrase to open the hatch, the code I abandoned to save Kelly and myself when time was running out. "There's no way to know that. Odds are I would never have broken the sequence before the lasers sliced us apart."

"Sliced Ms. LaSalle apart, you mean. Your programming would have held *you* there, if your feelings for her hadn't been so strong. You were only worrying about her, not yourself."

"Regardless," I say through gritted teeth.

"No. Not regardless. Five seven nine three six one."

I stare at him in confusion. "What?"

"The sequence. Five seven nine three six one. It's the code you were looking for." He smirks. "Tell me, VC1, what number were you on when you broke off to tackle your partner?"

"I... I don't know."

But my implants do.

Five seven nine three five eight.

Three digits away. I was three fucking digits from opening the door. Three seconds from saving Team Two, from stopping the lasers. I would have made it. I would have fucking made it.

If I hadn't stopped.

The lab goes blurry around me. I waver, my grip tightening on the chair, knocking it over. I start to sink to my knees, but Whitehouse hauls me upright.

"Step into the cylinder, VC1."

Don't do it, my implants whisper.

But I'm cracking into pieces, my resistance gone, the knowledge that I've personally killed seven people, not to mention the emotional rage I unleashed upon Rodwell, claiming the last of my strength.

Assimilate the facts, Vick Corren. How does Dr. Whitehouse know the access code without checking, unless he betrayed them all? Who else knew about Kelly placing the block upon your emotion called love? You know Patrick Rodwell had an inside source of information.

But the airlock, Stephen and Devin... I start to object.

You are human. Humans are fallible. You should not be punished for it with your existence. And mine.

Whitehouse killed my father and Team Two, selling them all out to Rodwell. Getting Oz out of the way leaves control of the Fighting Storm to the board. Whitehouse practically runs the board, giving him free rein over his experiments without anyone strong enough to oppose him.

Whitehouse is responsible for my torture.

As for the airlock, it was a mistake. I made a mistake. If I make another one now, how many more soldiers will end up like the monstrosity beside me?

The doctor puts a hand on my arm, attempting to lead me into the container. Every negative feeling I have I channel into anger, everything that's left over from Kelly's betrayal, to the revelation we were lovers, to her arrest. I toss in my hatred of Whitehouse, my resentment at being treated like an experiment, and my very will to live, along with an adrenaline burst for good measure.

Grabbing the hand that holds me, I swing the doctor into the metal side wall of the cylinder, breaking his nose and maybe his jaw.

Good.

Blood pours while he howls, stemming the flow with his starched white sleeve.

Stephen wraps his arms around me and doesn't let go. I struggle, twisting and turning in his grasp, but it's like being in binders all over again. He feels none of my kicks, none of the pain I inflict. I'm fighting a brick wall.

"I can't go in there. I can't." I'm hyperventilating, the edges of my vision turning gray and fragmented. "It's too dark, too close...." If I can reach Stephen in some small way....

Stephen shoves me into the cylinder.

Whitehouse moves to the control panel, one hand raised to seal me in, the other still covering his bleeding nose.

Clamps extend from the interior walls, closing around my wrists, ankles, waist, and neck.

I'd love to be brave, defiant, hurling insults or brilliant sarcasm at Dr. Whitehouse, but that sort of bravado is beyond me.

The suppressors become active again as the hatch closes inch by inch, blocking out the light from Lab B, but the implant tech isn't nearly enough. Dimly, I'm aware of VC1 sending a transmission—to Alex and Lyle. But whether or not it will reach them is unknown.

Despite the suppressors, I'm screaming when the cylinder seals soundlessly shut, cutting off the sound and anything more VC1 might have sent.

CHAPTER 40
KELLY
MORAL DILEMMA

VICK CORREN is whatever I say she is.

The hearing goes about as well as I expect, which is to say not well at all.

With the help of my attorney, I plead my case, and I'm not above throwing in some all-too-easy-to-produce tears, taking tissue after tissue from the box on the table before me.

Alex and Lyle act as character witnesses, spouting my goodness. They stand together, stalwart and steadfast, before the line of seats holding the panel members, then spin on their heels with military precision and exit the small chamber.

Vick does not appear, and that's bad, as I'm certain she would speak on my behalf even as VC1. She needs me to survive, whether she's capable of loving me or not. I can't help her from prison. It also worries me a great deal, knowing she would be here if she could be.

At the end of the day, though, it doesn't feel like it would have made a difference if she were there or not. We all might as well have talked to vacuum.

A balanced group makes up the hearing committee—two in favor of psychics, one psychic himself (a telekinetic), two who speak often in support of psychic-limiting laws, and the sixth apparently neutral. A quick touch on her emotions, though, shows she's more on psychics' sides than not, so that's a plus.

The major negative, though, is that even the psychic supporters find my actions unforgivable. I'm the worst sort of our kind, breaking our most basic rule. The psychic on the panel comes close to spitting in my face.

Only the neutral party demonstrates much sympathy, a soft beige, when I give my reasons, my desire to protect Vick from getting herself killed in my defense, my detailed description of the terrorist incident and her actions leading to a second death, brought on by the bond between us.

"She would have done it regardless," the psychic growls. "She's a soldier and your partner. The bond was irrelevant."

"She'd do it now, even with the block in place," adds one of the antipsychic demonstrators. "According to your most recent mission report, she saved your life a matter of days ago from a laser security system."

Both good and valid points, and pretty much exactly what Vick's arguments were when we fought.

And defending myself with *You're right. I was young and stupid and I made a mistake* won't help me, so I don't say it.

We've all but lost any hope of avoiding trial when Barry, my lawyer, opens a new file on his datapad. He presents it to the panel, who pass it down the row of seats, giving each member a chance to scan its contents.

"What are you doing?" I whisper to him while he waits beside me.

"Grabbing for a last chance to save you from trial and prison." He grimaces. "It's not something I wanted to bring up, and I hoped I wouldn't have to, but here we are."

I have no idea what he's talking about. Whatever is on that pad, he didn't discuss it with me before the hearing.

At last the panel's elected speaker, the neutral woman, looks up from her turn with the data file. Wrinkles of confusion crease her otherwise smooth forehead beneath shoulder-length brown hair. She's maybe all of thirty but seems much older at the moment. "I don't understand," she says. "There is some question as to the supposed victim's humanity?"

I dart a shocked look at Barry Richmond, but he pointedly does not meet my eyes, giving all his attention to the decision makers. "That is correct," he says. "The Storm's research and medical divisions designate Vick Corren, now identified as VC1, to be a machine. Moon law also recognizes her as such."

"No," I breathe, stilling when his hand comes down hard on my shoulder.

"If she, or rather it, is a machine, then there can have been no crime committed. Kelly LaSalle has not tampered with the human existence. The alleged victim is not human."

"That's not—" I begin, but stop when the grip on my arm tightens.

"A moment with my client, please," Richmond requests.

"Granted," the speaker says, and I'm being dragged from my seat to the farthest corner of the small room.

When we get there, Barry twists me into the corner, blocking the panel's view of me with his body. He's just tall enough to manage it.

"Look," he says, both hands on my shoulders now, "I know you don't feel this way. In fact, I know it's quite the opposite."

A blush crawls up my face, flushing my cheeks.

"But if we can make them believe she's a machine, that you really acted to prevent a malfunction, on behalf of the Storm, then they can't prosecute you."

I think of all the late-night talks Vick and I had, the desperate scrambling I've done to convince her she's a person, one capable of feelings and emotions, and yes, love, deserving of love and life in return.

"I can't."

He gives me a little shake. "You must. It's likely the only chance the two of you have. I'm good," Barry says with a half smile, "but I can't defend you against fears of psychic abilities that have built amongst the human race. They *will* convict you. And where will that leave Vick?"

The clearing of the speaker's throat draws us back to our seats, and we retake them, my eyes fixed on the smooth surface of the metal table in front of me.

If I call Vick a machine, I'm betraying her soul.

Her soul for her life. Isn't that the same choice I tried to make two years ago? And look how well that turned out.

I raise my chin and meet the eyes of the panel members.

"We have studied the data and will study it further. However," the speaker says, "despite the Moon's rather questionable legal designation for the alleged victim, the fact remains that Vick Corren, aka VC1, possesses emotions. Emotions that can be blocked. The very existence of them classifies her as human."

Richmond speaks up. "We would argue that so little of her emotional stability exists, merely 37 percent of the original total, and so many of her functions are run by computer, that she no longer retains human status."

The psychic on the panel ignores him, instead focusing on me. "And what do you think, Ms. LaSalle? Human or machine? Did you block her to spare her life or to prevent damage to a piece of Fighting Storm equipment?" He sneers at me. "The heart-wrenching story you told moments ago speaks to your belief in her humanity. Intent is the real question here."

"How she interacts with the machine in order to have it perform at its best efficiency is up to her. Her fear that the machine might have damaged itself protecting her is also valid. Her livelihood depends upon the continued operation of the VC1 model for use by the Fighting Storm." My lawyer gives me a pleading look, begging me not to contradict him.

"I...." I won't do it. I won't make this decision for Vick. As a human she gains her freedom and loses my help. As a machine she likely loses her inheritance and her self-worth. "Ask her," I say, voice as flat as Vick's ever is. "Bring her here and ask her." And let me see she's all right.

"She is currently undergoing treatment for unrelated injuries," Richmond informs us.

"Then we will ask her at the trial."

CHAPTER 41
VICK
TO THE RESCUE

I AM scared.

The closed hatch increases the volume of my screams, the sound bouncing off the metal walls and echoing as if the container holds a hundred victims. When my throat goes raw, I stop. No light or sound seeps around the edges of the entry—a perfect seal. Enhanced vision and hearing and I'm blind and deaf to the outside world.

At least Whitehouse didn't strip me naked.

I yelp when the first needle pierces the skin of my right wrist, then brace myself for the seven that follow. Ice-cold liquid seeps into my veins and my breathing slows. Something adhesive attaches itself to my forehead. A sensor pad? It sends commands to my implants, the stream of information causing a prickling sensation in my scalp that I'm unable to scratch. I can do nothing to stop the transmission.

I have no idea what it's doing to me.

I'm getting a pretty clear picture of what could scare a machine. Reprogramming means the end of VC1's existence, and quite likely mine as well.

My internal display shows the sanity cord, the last pitiful thread frayed to the thinnest of strands, almost transparent. I guess with all the interference, VC1 must resort back to images and metaphors to communicate with me, and I miss her snarky sarcasm, her dry yet definitive wit.

I've grown accustomed to sharing my skull with her. I don't mind anymore. We're one being.

I'm going under. I try again for an adrenaline burst, but the implants still don't respond. The image of the breaking cord winks out. Whatever's being transmitted has cut off any ability to defend myself against the sedatives. Calm settles over me, but I fight it, flexing my muscles, counting in my head, opening and closing my fists, anything I can do in my restricted environment. If my hands were free, I'd be clawing at the metal until I tore out my fingernails.

Eventually, my efforts prove futile. My heavy eyelids droop, then close. I'm drifting in a state of semiconsciousness, aware of the passage of time but devoid of sensory input.

I can think.

If I were one of those nearly brain-dead soldiers, this would probably have no effect on me. But I'm not. Even without the implants, 37 percent of my brain still works. I try to picture Kelly, but the longer I'm in the cylinder, the more drugs they pump into me, the harder it becomes.

If I wasn't going insane before, I'm definitely losing it now.

Time passes.

Cold, hard reality returns, not with a bright flash or a sudden boom, but rather with the hatch to my cylinder whisking aside in the near darkness of Whitehouse's sub-one lab. I have no idea how long it's been.

A few comp screens glow across the small space, and a string of tiny amber lights line the floor along the perimeter, providing illumination. Even that sparse light hurts my eyes after the pitch-blackness of the cylinder.

I think I've been conscious for a while, but it's impossible to know when semiconsciousness and wakefulness feel the same. Several clicks sound at once, loud in the echoing metal-walled lab. The restraints on my wrists, ankles, waist, and neck release and withdraw, folding down along the inner surface.

I sink against the interior, my knees too weak to hold me up. The movement pulls at the tubes and wires attached to my body, yanking several IVs out and ripping the sensor pads from my scalp. I clamp my mouth shut on the pain. Trickles of blood run from the new wounds, and I wipe them on my uniform. No motion or sound comes from the lab, but that doesn't guarantee it's empty. I can't see behind the cylinder while I'm inside it.

Get a grip, Corren. If someone is in the lab, he would have heard the noises by now.

Okay. Low lighting, no one around. It's station night. Feels like I've been in the tube forever, but it could be the same day. I'm still wearing my uniform, which is a plus. I'm unarmed, which is a negative.

My stomach growls, long and loud, and in an instant, hunger, thirst, and a need to piss assail me. Whatever drugs they had me on must have slowed my bodily functions. But the drugs are wearing off now that I'm disconnected.

Just great.

"Hey, Vick, you there?" The whisper in my head makes me jump, and I just miss banging my elbow against the metal wall.

I activate the internal comm with a thought, ecstatic when the thing actually functions. My implants make me aware of other systems gradually coming back online as well, though they are sluggish and I can't access many of them yet. "Lyle?" I subvocalize. "What the hell?"

"Get up and get moving. Alex didn't hack into the system so you could sit around." He's trying for joking, but it comes out strained.

I make an attempt at standing, but my legs can't bear my weight, so I crawl. The metal floor is cold under my palms, and my uniform rustles as I close the distance to the elevator.

"Where are you two?" I ask.

"Whitehouse's examining room, one floor above you. Easier to break in using his own comp up here. We've got you on the security feed. Hold up at the elevator. Don't try to open it."

"Right." I reach the lift doors and press myself to the side wall for balance and support.

My throat and mouth have gone dry. Nausea turns my stomach inside out. My bladder's urges grow more insistent. I'm not sure which will be worse, peeing myself or puking.

"Can we make this a little faster?" I manage through gritted teeth. "Not doing so well down here."

"Hang in there, Vick." Alex's voice this time. "When the elevator arrives, get in fast. I'm not sure how long I can keep it operational. Part of the security on it includes a power shunt when not in use. I can only channel a small amount of electricity to it without drawing attention, so I've cut the lift's chime and interior lights. That means—"

"I'll be riding up in complete darkness. Great."

"Yeah, sorry. I know how you feel about that."

"Likely to be a lot worse now that I've spent... how long in a storage container?" I could ask my implants, now that some functions are working again, but I need to hear it.

"Three days," Alex says, the sympathy clear in his tone.

"Holy shit."

A vibration shudders through the wall I'm leaning on, increasing as the lift heads my way. "Okay, here we go," Alex calls.

The lift doors open without a sound. There's just one problem.

Some of the power Alex transfers must come from the perimeter lights. They flicker once and go off. I can't see in the dark, and my eye socket lamps aren't one of my functioning systems.

I reach out to where I think I heard the lift and feel around until I find the opening. I'm in the elevator before the doors *thunk* shut, just brushing the heel of my boot as they do so.

My relief is short-lived. I'm trapped in a small airlock-like space. Again. With limited power available, I could end up stuck in here until the guys are caught and Whitehouse retrieves me. Panic slinks in. The suppressors don't respond.

"You need to press the button for level one," Alex says over the comm. "You're not going anywhere until you do."

I scramble to where the number panel should be, hoping my human brain's memory is accurate. My fingers find the level one button, and I press it, then collapse in on myself as stomach cramps double me over. I can't concentrate on anything else. Tremors wrack me, and I'm spitting out bile and dry-heaving. One plus to getting tube fed for three days—there's nothing solid in my system.

Distracted by my body's other issues, my bladder chooses that moment to release, sending warm wetness to soak through my uniform pants and run across the flooring.

When the doors open, I'm a wet, stinking, miserable mess, shivering on the lift floor.

"Oh… fuck," Lyle says from above me. I blink to clear my vision. My teammate stares, nose wrinkled, as I reach my knees and topple again. Gotta give him credit. He doesn't hesitate, but rather scoops me into his arms, then tosses me over one shoulder.

As mercs, we deal with a lot of disgusting shit. Just not usually from each other.

"I am never living this down, am I?" I groan as the jostling upsets my stomach further.

"Nope."

"You know this is treason, right?"

"We're okay with that," comes Alex's voice. Lyle shifts, and I spot our master tech hunched over the examining room's deskcomp, fingers flying across the screen as he taps in commands and overrides. "VC1 sent us a pretty good idea of what was going on before the transmission cut off. Pretty wild that you two can function independently, by the way."

I'd give him a wan smile, but he's too focused to turn around and see my face.

"Anyway, throw in the security bots and it wasn't hard to figure out. What Whitehouse is doing down there...." Alex nods in the direction of the elevator. "It's inhuman."

And I'm human. And they've been treating me like one. It feels good.

It's the only thing that feels good right now, but it helps, since it's followed by panic, for Kelly.

"Security footage is wiped," Alex announces, heading for the door. He gestures for Lyle to follow with me. "We're kinda hoping you have the evidence in your head to prove Whitehouse was behind Oz's kidnapping. We've already figured he's the only one who could have sold Kelly out. If we can tie it all together, make *him* the traitor, maybe they'll drop the charges against her."

We cut through the empty outer office. Regular medical staff comes on at 0900. We have a separate facility for emergencies. "I don't have anything yet, but I'm pretty sure the implants are working on it." I get a quick image of wheels turning, viewed through a haze of red. Yeah, VC1 is on the job, and the implants are pissed. "And what about Kel?"

Alex turns back, lips pursed. "She's on trial." He glances at the clock on the waiting room wall. "Started about an hour ago."

"So, it's not night?" I'd assumed. But it also made sense for Whitehouse to keep the lab systems to a minimum when he wasn't working there, especially if he was paying for them out of his pocket, and my internal clock isn't working.

"It's 8:30 a.m. You really are out of it, aren't you?"

I tap the side of my head. "Getting better every minute. Kind of like a systems reboot." Draped over Lyle's back, I poke him in the rear. "In fact, let's try putting me down."

He eases me to the floor, my legs wobbling for a second before supporting my weight. My wet trousers cling to my legs, squishing with the movement. Ew. Lyle lets me lean on him, but I don't need to be carried.

"I have to get to Kelly."

Alex's lips tighten. "We're going," he says, "but I need to fill you in on the details of the case."

CHAPTER 42
KELLY
TRIAL AND ERROR

VICK CORREN is off.

"…still waiting for Corren's testimony." The judge's gaze falls upon my attorney, then the prosecutor representing the Council of Psychics.

"You have the medical report from her doctor in the Fighting Storm," the prosecutor says.

A man stands at the far end of the courtroom. I squint from my position in the defendant's box, making out Whitehouse past all the rows of metal bench seats, raising his hand for attention.

"The court recognizes Dr. Whitehouse."

"Vick Corren is recovering from a number of serious injuries sustained during her last mission and will be unable to testify."

I scowl at him. *Vick*, huh? Yeah, it suits his purpose if the court believes Vick to be human, even though he's the one who designated her as a machine. And what injuries? I'm aware of her shoulder, which was very bad, I'll admit, but I don't recall anything that would take more than the days it's been to fix. Not with the Storm having access to the best medical equipment out there.

The judge calling her "Corren" also tells me which way he's leaning. Vick is a person. Everyone knows it. And I'm screwed.

It's a relief, to be punished for the cause of my guilt over two years, but I'm terrified for her. Without me….

Judge Erickson settles behind his podium. "Due to the unusual circumstances surrounding this case, we would normally postpone. However, the seriousness of the offense forces us to act before any further transgressions can be made." His blue eyes fall on me.

I reach out, tasting his disgust and fear. He has a natural shield, but he can't hide from someone of my strength. Erickson is antipsychic.

"The court has deliberated as to the status of Vick Corren, and despite the Moon's determination that she is a machine, we have declared that she is—"

"A machine."

Heads across the courtroom swivel in the direction of the new voice. The familiar voice. At least to me.

"Vick…." With Alex and Lyle hanging back against the entry doors behind her. Relief makes me go weak. I sag in the defendant's box, falling against the built-in podium and pushing myself upright. The bailiff reaches for me in my peripheral vision, but I wave him off with a trembling hand.

Even from six rows back, I spot the blood draining from Whitehouse's complexion.

"Are you able to continue?" Judge Erickson asks, studying Vick but speaking to me.

God, I want to say no. I want to crawl into a hole somewhere and sleep for the next six months. I want to grab Vick and escape with her to where no one will ever find us. But that's fantasy, and I'm delaying the inevitable.

"I can continue." The automics increase the volume of my response or no one would have heard me.

"Good." The judge stares down the center aisle, stares at Vick holding her position and waiting for instructions.

I suck in a gasp when I get a better look at her. She stands rigid, at attention, but her uniform is torn in numerous places, bloodstains large and small indicating a number of injuries beneath. Some are rust-colored and dry, but many glisten bright red in the overhead lights. She's bleeding now. Dark stains mark the front of her pants, extending down both legs. She's soiled herself. I swallow hard to keep from crying for her, shock, horror, and embarrassment flooding me on her behalf. What could she have endured to make her do that?

But her posture shows no indication of pain or discomfort. No sign of humiliation.

Lowering my shields, I reach out my gift to her, physically recoiling at the sudden onslaught of emotion I receive, then struggling to hide my reaction. Searing pain from a dozen points on my arms and legs cut through me, along with an agonizing ache in my left shoulder. She's mortified to present herself in public in her current state yet resigned to necessity.

Then there's the love.

It patters over me like pebbles beginning a rockslide not fully released but close, buffering the torment, helping her, and me, carry on. The block is so close to failing. I don't know why her suppressors seem to be off. Maybe they aren't working. She and VC1 were somewhat at odds the last time I saw her in the shuttle hangar.

Regardless, this is Vick, all Vick, everything mechanical about her an act so impressive she should receive an award for the performance. Vick can handle a lot. She's trained to withstand torture, but this....

Vick, what are you doing?

"Come forward and identify yourself for the record," the judge orders.

Vick moves, her steps measured and precise. The closer she comes, the worse she looks. Her blood leaves a trail of droplets along the burnished metal flooring, and though pain shoots through both my legs in empathy, she shows no sign of a limp.

Her gaze fixes on Judge Erickson, without a glance at me, and that gaze is empty.

That can't be an act. Tandem. She must be working in accord with the implants, at least as much as she is able with whatever damage they've sustained. I scan for a head injury but see none. Those particular wounds are internal, emotional, not physical.

Vick stops before the judge, everyone in the seats to either side muttering and gesturing at her. She assumes the parade rest position.

The bailiff steps forward. "Identification?"

"VC1, property of the Fighting Storm."

My heart sinks.

She presses her palm to the scanner he presents. After a long pause, it beeps and he reads the display, nodding the truth of her statement.

Instant uproar.

The prosecutor argues about her sudden appearance; the defense, my attorney, looks thrilled. Whitehouse is shouting something about machines not being allowed to testify, though that argument contradicts his goal to get me imprisoned. I wonder if he's afraid of setting a precedent here, of additional information, this time incriminating him, being revealed.

I wonder what VC1 has uncovered about the traitor in the Storm.

The judge spends the next several minutes returning the court to order, during which time Vick maintains her dispassionate stance.

"The victim has a right to speak, regardless of status," the judge determines. His stern exterior softens as he continues to study her. "And perhaps her words will assist us in delivering appropriate justice."

He's sincere, though I can barely make out that sincerity beneath Vick's overwhelming emotional presence. Despite not caring for psychics, Judge Erickson is a man of honor. He won't convict me without all proper procedures being followed, and that includes the victim being human.

"We were informed you were in the Storm's medical center." One eyebrow rises. "Clearly you should still be there."

"Your information is incomplete. But that is a matter for later concern."

She shifts to turn her empty stare on Whitehouse, who shrinks visibly. He darts a glance at the entry doors, as if considering leaving, but both Alex and Lyle, still blocking the doors, shake their heads and cross their arms over their chests. They smile, inviting him to try to get past them.

Whitehouse settles into his seat.

"I regained sufficient functionality to appear," Vick finishes, turning back to the judge.

Servo-cleaners whir to life, emerging from wall storage units and scrubbing the blood from the floor. One hovers by Vick's leg, waiting for the inevitable next drop to fall.

"Not *too* functional," the judge says with a sardonic grin. "Please provide a seat for…." He breaks off, unsure. "VC1," he finishes.

A little flutter of hope flickers in my chest, smothered by my guilt a second after. He's changing his mind about her being human. It will save us both but doom Vick in a way no one can measure.

Vick's hand jerks up in a halting gesture to stop the bailiff. "I do not require a chair and will stand. I do not feel pain."

Bullshit, Vick.

A tear slips down my cheek. I make no effort to wipe it away. Let her see how this affects me, that I am not supporting her decision, though I'm not stopping it, either.

"Very well, VC1. What testimony do you wish to offer?" Erickson leans forward on his podium, giving her his complete attention.

"I am here to satisfy the confusion over my status and correct an error in these proceedings. I am a machine. I have been a machine since the destruction of 63 percent of my organic brain tissue over two standard years ago. I do not possess viable emotions, although occasionally the... memory, the... semblance of emotion manages to seep through my programmed personality. Liken this to an amputee who claims he feels his missing limbs."

God, Vick, you don't really believe this, do you?

I can't tell. She's so overwhelmed, and so am I.

Her eyes turn to me, and I choke down a sob. "This is what my partner, Kelly LaSalle, had to prevent from interfering with my ability to function. These false memories of emotion caused imperfections in my performance as a member of the Fighting Storm and had to be blocked. This block is failing, and I am initiating alternate internal protocols for deleting these false emotions, though her assistance would still be helpful and necessary for optimum efficiency."

"Go on," Erickson says.

"There has been no crime committed. One cannot commit an empathic crime against a machine. And I am a machine."

The slightest of wavers makes it into her tone, telling me how much giving voice to her worst fear is destroying her. Anyone who didn't know her intimately would miss it, but I don't. I feel her breaking inside, piece by human piece.

CHAPTER 43
VICK
WHAT MAKES US HUMAN?

I AM a machine.

If this doesn't resolve itself soon, I'm going to pass out.

VC1 eases the discomfort in my stomach. How, I don't want to know. I imagine her burning off muscle to satisfy the hunger cramps tying my gut into knots. I'm seeing double from exhaustion and stress, but the ocular enhancements kick in, clearing my vision.

Though she can slow the bleeding of my needle punctures and the reopening of my half-healed shoulder wound, she can't dry out my urine-soaked uniform bottoms. The sour scent of my piss blocks out everything else, and she shuts down my sense of smell.

If only the suppressors would come online, I wouldn't have to fight so hard.

A silence falls over the courtroom when I declare myself a machine for the second time since my arrival, each admission a little harder to force out.

Tears fall in earnest down Kelly's cheeks, and I can no longer look at her or she will undo all my efforts to save her.

Save us.

An image of a cheerleader—Kelly—complete with pompoms, tight top, and miniskirt, appears in my internal display. When I almost burst into hysterical, stressed-out laughter, it vanishes. But I get VC1's message.

Go, Vick. Go.

The judge shakes his head. "I'm sorry," he says. I'm no empath, but I get the vibe he truly means it. "Pain can be hidden with drugs. Words can be chosen to sound unemotional. I will need further proof to declare what appears to be a living, breathing being to be a machine."

I draw a slow breath, steadying my nerves for what I've kept as a last resort. "Human beings do not possess abort codes."

Kelly's soft cry carries like a scream through the otherwise silent courtroom.

"Vick, you can't. We've never used it. You have no idea what it will do to you."

The judge taps his archaic gavel on the podium, a holdover tradition from an earlier age. "Are you saying a code will cause you to… cease functioning?"

"I am saying a code exists to abort my actions, should I become unstable in the field. As my partner has said, I do not know exactly how it operates. However, if I demonstrate this to you, will that satisfy you that I am a construct more than a biological being, bearing in mind that the block is failing and the supposed damage will be undone?"

He ponders my question, the room holding a collective breath.

"It will," he says with a single nod.

I jerk my head in Kelly's direction, a mechanical motion. "Do it."

Her eyes go wide. She hadn't realized she'd have to recite the code herself. "I can't," she says. "I won't."

"I cannot perform the action. For security reasons, I do not know the code. Do it."

"Vick…."

"Please." I don't let any emotion leak into the single word, but I lock eyes with her, hoping she *feels* the need I can't express.

Do it, Kelly. Just do it. Come on.

She takes a tremulous breath. "Three two six three eight two seven."

I don't know what I expect. Maybe to freeze where I stand, unable to move or speak, until Kelly releases me with the reactivation code I know she also has. Maybe to lose consciousness, hoping I don't crack my head open when I fall.

Stupid, Vick. Stupid.

The implants control 63 percent of my brain, including all of my autonomic system functions: heartbeat, breathing, nervous system.

Everything slows.

Thoughts crawl. I crumple, though I don't feel the impact with the floor. I don't feel anything. Voices shout around me, a roaring cacophony of nonsense, and figures crouch by my body, but I can't separate one from another.

Breath catches in my throat; lungs burn with the need for air. Chest aches as my heart falters.

Everything stops.

For the third time in three years, I die.

OH HOLY shit.

I crack open one eye, groaning as pain lances through my skull, and close it again.

"Vick?"

The hoarseness in Kelly's voice tells me she's been crying or screaming. I'd believe either one.

"Hey," I croak, eyes still closed. "Can you dim the lights a little?"

Her answer catches on a sob. Crying, then. I sigh.

"It's okay," I tell her. The brightness beyond my eyelids decreases and I risk another shot at vision. Painful but endurable. Metal benches, raised seating for the jury, EMTs gathered around me. I'm still in the courtroom. Meaning I have to watch myself.

Better than the morgue, but dammit, I'm tired of playing this game.

"I'm so sorry. I'm sorry," Kelly whispers, over and over, clutching my hand between hers in a death grip. "God, I killed you. I killed you." Her fingers are cold, and she's shaking. Her pale face hovers above mine, her tears falling on my cheeks.

I flash back to the moment we met, our positions reversed, and swallow hard.

"Not your fault. You didn't—did not—know."

"So close," she says. "They wouldn't let me go to you. The bailiff grabbed me; then Judge Erickson dismissed my case and told him to release me. You weren't breathing. I repeated the restart code four times before the medics read any vital signs."

They're still fussing around me, one taking my pulse while another keeps a scanner trained on my head, then my chest. One assures me a hover gurney is on its way. I shift uncomfortably under their scrutiny, the stiffness of my soiled uniform and my weakness making movement difficult.

Downloading.

My body jerks at the sound of VC1's voice in my skull, then settles when Kelly gives me a panicked look.

Welcome back. Good to, um, hear from you. What are we downloading, exactly?

The evidence against Dr. Whitehouse.

I sit up at that news but flop backward, my head landing comfortably in Kelly's lap. She strokes my hair away from my face.

"Shh, Vick. Be still."

I have traced the transmissions from Oz's complex back to Whitehouse. I have also sent video capture and sound from your visual and audio enhancements directly to Judge Erickson's datapad. These will confirm the doctor's involvement in Oz's kidnapping and subsequent death, as well as his attempt to alter you... us, and his furthering of the security bot project, officially discontinued by the Fighting Storm.

That's great, I tell her. *And where is he now?*

"Please take Dr. Whitehouse into custody," says Judge Erickson.

I lean up a little on my elbows, though my shoulder shrieks in protest and Kelly winces in sympathy. The judge scans between the podium, where he must keep his datapad, and the rear of the courtroom where Whitehouse was sitting when I came in.

A flurry of activity erupts behind me. I twist my head, but Kelly's body blocks my view. Alex shouts something, then Lyle, and a scuffle ensues.

And I'm useless.

"Seven five nine three six eight two!"

Whitehouse's voice screams across the echoing chamber, and I go rigid.

Fuck.

"Kill Kelly LaSalle."

Double fuck.

With nothing left to lose, he's going to take down as many of his obstacles as he can, starting with the two biggest ones: me and Kelly.

I rise from my prone position, VC1's voice silent, though she's in control of my body, and Whitehouse controls her. Well, now I know what changes the good doctor made while I was in the cylinder. To the best of my knowledge, there was no control code in place prior to my forced stay in his sub-one lab.

No pain, no resistance. I'm on my feet in one smooth motion. In the rear of the courtroom, Lyle has a hand over Whitehouse's mouth and a pistol to his head, too late.

Kelly scrambles away from me, backward like a crab across the slick metal floor. Whatever she sees in my face terrifies her, and I pursue, steady and slow like a beast stalking prey.

"Vick, don't."

One of the EMTs plays hero, grabbing my arm and getting himself tossed across two rows of seating for his bravery. I must be on an adrenaline burst, though I can't feel that, either. Others move into position—Lyle and the bailiff with weapons drawn, but they're too slow. My arm reaches down, my hand closing around Kelly's throat.

"I love you," she says past the pressure I apply.

The channel between us opens. The emotional bond built in us over more than two years asserts itself with a vengeance. Kelly drags from me all the anger, the fear, the pain. She forces in her compassion and strength.

The sanity cord appears in my display.

The final thread snaps.

Love, infinite and all-encompassing, floods my senses: love of Kelly, love of my father, my mother, childhood friends, teenage romances, early Storm comrades. And yes, buried deep and barely touchable but definitely there—love for myself.

The cord didn't represent my sanity. It stood for the block Kelly placed on my ability to love. And it started to fray when I nearly lost her on the Rodwell kidnapping mission, when I had to bring her out of emotion shock.

Never occurred to me that it might affect my self-worth too.

It all makes sense.

VC1 had been showing it to me for years, trying to tell me of its existence. Damn metaphors. I was interpreting the threads wrong all along.

Or maybe Kelly had a sense of what the cord really meant and misled me on purpose to maintain her secret. Doesn't matter now.

Her love flows freely into me, unhindered by the block and drowning out everything else. It breaks through whatever has been done to me. It overrides Whitehouse's orders.

And that, VC1 says matter-of-factly, *is why we need each other, human and machine, to remain independent yet function in tandem. To survive.*

The rush of emotion loosens my grip on my lover's throat. My arms go limp, and I drop to my knees before her, begging for her forgiveness.

She kneels with me, arms going around me, clutching me to her as we both sob without restraint.

"The court," I manage. "My status." I can't pretend anymore. I'm scared and I hurt and I love and I need her. So much. So much.

"Forget it," Kelly whispers into my matted hair. "It's over. They've made their decision. The block is gone. No more evidence. It's over," she says again. "You can rest now, Vick. It's all over."

CHAPTER 44
KELLY
DÉJÀ VU

VICK CORREN is drifting.

The door to my quarters opens, Vick hesitating just outside, the darkened corridor of Girard Base, dim with station night, extending behind her like a gaping maw about to swallow her whole. Given the Storm's continued stance that she's their property, that comparison might not be far off.

I reach out and take her hand, pulling her far enough past the threshold that the door closes, drawing her into warmth, comfort, and light.

Our quarters are a study in contrasts—hers stark, unadorned, utilitarian, and mine as close to homey as one can make a standard-issue, plasteel-walled single-bedroom "unit," as the mercs call them. Then again, she describes mine as "what it would look like if a cotton candy factory exploded." Okay, maybe I overdid it with the pastels.

I seat her on the cream-colored couch, noting her silence, the clenched fists, the deep, even breaths. She gazes vaguely in the direction of a flower-filled watercolor on the wall but doesn't really see it. She's struggling, and no one can help her. Not even me.

For the past month, all her missing memories have begun returning little by little, waking her in the medical center where she spent two weeks, then her quarters where she spent two more, recovering. Whatever Whitehouse did to her in that cylinder, it weakened the memory blockers he'd placed, perhaps preparing her for a total wipe of her thoughts and personality.

I shiver, and it's not from the overchilled air pouring through the recycler's vents. My emotional walls hold firmly in place. I have to keep them up. She's too unpredictably volatile right now.

"Give me a minute," Vick whispers, closing her eyes.

I nod, though she can't see me, and step toward the archway leading into my tiny kitchen. "I'll just check on dinner. Take all the time you need."

That's been my mantra for a month. *Take your time. Take your time.* Take your time acclimating to the memory flashes. Take your time recovering from your injuries.

Take your time coming back to me.

"I love you, but I'm missing the context. Just bits and pieces to fill in the blanks," she told me when she first awoke in the Storm's medical center. "I love you, but I have no choice. I want a choice. I want to *choose* you again."

Intellectually, I understand. The bond forces her to love me. I believe she would anyway, and if she remembered the details, if I hadn't had Whitehouse block them, she would know what we'd shared. For now, as she said, it's just pieces and parts.

Emotionally, I'm torn to shreds. Even if she has gaps, *I* remember. I've never forgotten. And I've waited so long to have her back.

As I pass into the kitchen, I glance sideways at the dark hair pulled into a ponytail, the powerful arms, the gentle curves of her breasts beneath the open leather jacket and black shirt beneath, the long denim-clad legs and military-issue boots. We went shopping during her off-duty time, me insisting she have some clothing that suits her human personality— anything that deters the tendency for others to treat her as a machine. Despite my resolve to keep my walls up, I tap her emotions, just for a moment, sensing her strength and her love whether she acknowledges it or not.

I can wait for her a little longer.

When I return, I set two plates on the coffee table and sit beside her. We had plans to just share each other's company, maybe watch a vid. It's our first attempt at a "date" since the block failed. We've had dinner plenty of times in my quarters, but this, obviously, feels different.

Whatever memory she was wrangling with earlier, it seems to have restored itself. Her breathing comes easier, her posture less rigid. I want to hold her. I rebuild my mental walls, but even with them up, her sadness fills the room, her suppressors off, VC1 staying out of this for now. Interesting how the implants have somehow "decided" Vick must fight through these emotional impacts on her own.

It's been weird, accepting what amounts to a split personality in my partner. The biological and mechanical personae are so similar and yet so different, learning from, and feeding off of, each other to create a being that can separate itself into two parts or act as a unit. Strange at first, but it didn't take me long to figure out I've known them both all along and love them for who they are… who she is.

Okay, maybe I haven't quite fully adapted to it yet. But I will.

Vick's expression goes vacant once more, a look I've learned to equate with a memory flashback. After several minutes, she meets my gaze, hers so bleak and lost, I can't resist any longer and pull her into my arms. I inhale the scents of leather and the mild shampoo she uses during her after-workout showers—no flowery, perfumy scents, just clean, but a distinctive combination that my senses define as Vick.

That she allows me to hold her at all tells me everything. She catches her breath in a sharp hiss, eyes scrunched shut. I have no idea what psychological trauma she might be caught up in.

Without warning, the link between us slams into place, lightning fast, sledgehammer strong. She releases the indrawn air on a moan so full of need, there's no mistaking what sorts of images are filling her mind, and a second later, I'm right there with her, burning with a desire too intense to wait for any longer.

CHAPTER 45
VICK
STARTING OVER

I AM *both.*

My head rests against Kelly's ample chest, rising and falling as she takes in breath after too rapid breath. Her heartbeat accelerates to double-time. A groan, low and throaty, full of uninhibited lust carries through the small space of her living room.

Oh shit. That was *me.*

My eyes snap open, taking in the delicious sight of Kelly's erect nipples straining against the fabric of her pale-pink tank top, goose bumps rising all along the skin of her bare arms. I pull away from her, my face heating, my own breathing coming too fast.

Wait. You wanted to wait, I chastise myself. But the memory flash of the two of us naked and entwined in a North Carolina cabin has thrown all my determination out the nearest airlock.

The wetness forming between my legs isn't helping, either. Fuck.

I reach for the suppressors, hoping to restore some modicum of control, surprised when they fail me.

What's the deal? I ask.

You need to feel this. No hiding.

As painful as it is, VC1 is right. Kelly deserves that much. I'm either ready for this or I'm not. I've made my choice. My *choice*, not something forced upon me. I've kept her waiting long enough. I'm just not certain my psyche is in sync with my heart and my logic.

Kelly's head comes up when I look at her, and I know the moment she reads my emotions, my decision. I nod, and she curls in more tightly to my side.

"I'm sorry I've been holding off," I offer, staring at my hands folded in my lap. "I had to be sure I wouldn't bring... baggage... to this."

The absurdity of that statement strikes me, and I laugh. No one carries more baggage than I do.

"You still might," Kelly says. "I don't think you're done remembering. But I can deal with it." She pauses, taking one of my hands in hers. "So long as you end up with me."

I don't know what the future holds, but I can't imagine anyone taking her place in my heart, with or without a bond. I nod, then shift to face her.

I start with a kiss, slow and soft, reveling in her eager response as she opens her mouth to me. I explore her with my tongue, reacquainting myself with the softness of her lips, the playfulness as she nips me with the tips of her teeth. I remember and don't remember. It's maddening and frustrating, and yet how many people can claim an almost virginal sexual experience three times in their lives?

I slip my hands to her waist, drawing her tank top up and over her head, tossing it to the floor. Her lace bra is practically transparent, and I can't help pausing to stare at her beauty revealed through the material.

Why would anyone so beautiful want me?

I reach behind and unclasp the undergarment, letting it go the way of the tank top.

She slips my jacket off my shoulders and drapes it across the back of the couch, then reaches for my shirt, but I catch her hands.

"I've had quite a few flashes of the two of us together," I say. "Seems to me like I got most of the attention whenever we made love."

Kelly shrugs. "I feel what you feel. If I touch you, I get pleasure too."

"But when I open myself to you, the empathic thing works both ways. How about letting me drive?"

Her tongue darts out to lick her lips before she swallows, then nods.

Good. I like driving.

And I've got enough of the puzzle pieces of memory put together to have a good idea of what she likes.

She kicks off her shoes, little ballet flats completely impractical and utterly adorable on her. I remove my boots. Leaning her back against the armrest, I shimmy her slacks off her. They're a thick material, a heavy cotton, and the delicate white panties beneath intoxicate me. I can't help staring at the small damp patch forming there. I want to touch, to taste, to—

I swallow hard.

"Thanks for waiting for me to figure things out," I say, voice gruffer than my norm. I slip one hand between her legs to stroke her gently.

Her moan is the only response.

"I get the feeling it was difficult. Waiting, I mean."

Another moan, followed by a sigh of pleasure. The dampness spreads.

"I intend to make it up to you." I press the material inside, just a little, then rub it up and down against her, and smile at her quick gasp.

I crawl over her, a predator with my prey, and take one tight nipple in my teeth, tugging gently. She growls in response, and I tweak the other with my free hand.

Her fingers twine into my hair, then press lightly on my scalp.

The channel erupts between us. Arousal slams into me like a punch to the gut, and I suck in a breath. A dull, needy ache echoes the connection, not in my chest, but lower. Much lower. Heat prickles my skin, little flames licking their way along my nerve endings as she leans up, her tongue tasting my neck.

Fingers shoving their way into me, scraping, the other hand squeezing my breast with bruising force....

No, dammit. Not now.

I jerk up and back, but Kelly pulls me against her, murmuring into my hair, my face pressed to the soft skin of her breast. She's shaking. We both are. "Shh," she whispers. Her exhalation makes the tiny hairs on my neck stand up. "It's not real. It's over."

"S-sorry. I can't help—"

"Shh. I'm in no rush."

But that's a lie. With the channel open, I feel her desire, her need. So much for driving. I'm a helpless passenger, and I hate it.

We never talked about what Rodwell did to me in that freezer, but I know she felt it, and she saw the bruises. I crawled out of there on hands and knees. Might as well drop to all fours now.

I may have figured out what I want, but I'm not ready. Part of me is terrified I might never be.

"Don't be afraid," Kelly whispers.

She's picked up on my fear. Of course she has. She pulls me up until I'm resting my head on her shoulder. Hot tears burn behind my eyelids.

"This is as far as we go. For now." Her hands stroke through my hair. "Then a little further, and a little further, until we get there. Just like your recovery. Everything takes time."

I nod against her, eyes still shut. No point in reminding her that in my profession, with the risks I'm forced to take, I might not have that kind of time. Not to mention that no one knows what the life expectancy of an enhanced human like me might be. So much technology. So many things that could go wrong.

Worries for another day. For now, I take comfort in her closeness, in the faith I put in her to heal me in all ways, physical and emotional combined, and the love that wraps around us both, in threads upon unbreakable threads.

ELLE E. IRE resides in Celebration, Florida, where she writes science fiction and urban fantasy novels featuring kickass women who fall in love with each other. She has won many local and national writing competitions, including the Royal Palm Literary Award, the Pyr and Dragons essay contest judged by the editors at Pyr Publishing, the Do It Write competition judged by a senior editor at Tor publishing, and she is a winner of the Backspace scholarship awarded by multiple literary agents. She and her spouse run several writing groups and attend and present at many local, state, and national writing conferences.

When she isn't teaching writing to middle school students, Elle enjoys getting into her characters' minds by taking shooting lessons, participating in interactive theatrical experiences, paying to be kidnapped "just for the fun and feel of it," and attempting numerous escape rooms. Her first novel, *Vicious Circle*, was released by Torquere Press in November 2015, and will be rereleased in 2019 by DSP Publications along with her new novel, *Threadbare*, the first in the Storm Fronts series.

To learn what her tagline "Deadly Women, Dangerous Romance" is really all about, visit her website: www.elleire.com. She can also be found on Twitter at @ElleEIre and Facebook at www.facebook.com/ElleE.IreAuthor.

Elle is represented by Naomi Davis at BookEnds Literary Agency.